EMBRACING
THE MOON

What Reviewers Say
About Jeannie Levig's Work

A Wish Upon a Star

"Jeannie Levig has been putting out lesbian romances for a few years and is going from strength to strength with each book. ...*A Wish Upon a Star* is a perfect book if you're looking for something a little different from the usual romance fare. While there's plenty of chemistry between Leslie and Erica, there are no meet-cutes or perfect people to be found in it. Instead, Levig takes us on a journey of finding love that's familial as well as romantic. If you haven't read her before this would be an excellent place to start and fans of this author are sure to be pleased too."—*Lambda Literary Review*

"This is another fantastic book by Ms. Levig. It is not only a romance but also a story about maternal love, friendship, and loyalty. Kudos to the author for featuring an older couple both in their early fifties but so full of life. Alongside them, there is Siena, Erica's daughter who has 'Autism Spectrum Disorder.' She is portrayed with incredible authenticity as both a child and a person with special needs. It seems that the author did her research well not only in Siena's personality but also in her relationship with others." *LezReviewBooks*

"[B]e prepared to be taken on an emotional rollercoaster ride because these endearing characters will latch on to your heart and they won't let go!"—*Lesbian Review*

"*A Wish Upon a Star* by Jeannie Levig is a fabulous read. This book has those little moments that pull at your heartstrings. A slow burn romance that uses tension in the most glorious way. ...I cannot say how impressive these characters are. They are three dimensional and are 100% relatable."—*Romantic Reader Blog*

"This lovely romance features a couple of mature women who begin as friends with undeniable attraction towards one another. Each has faced challenges in their lives and each are wary of changing their personal status quo. In the end I found myself thinking this is what love is all about, overcoming challenges and weathering the storms life throws at you and making a home filled with love. A memorable and sweet read."
—*Late Night Lesbian Reads*

Threads of the Heart

"What a beautiful and moving story about five women learning invaluable lessons about love, self-awareness, cause and effect, consequences, betrayal, trust, truth, relationships, friendships, family...and life."
—*2015 Rainbow Awards*

"[The main characters'] individual stories were interesting on their own but the interaction between the characters really makes this novel great. ...The steamy scenes were so well written and extremely hot—in fact the best I've read in a long time. They were very varied and inventive. I thoroughly enjoyed the book and was so sad to finish it. I wanted it to go on and on!"—*Inked Rainbow Reads*

"The first thing that struck me about this book is how skillfully Levig handles switching between five different points of view. ...Each of the characters has a distinct voice that reflects her joys and struggles. The story is structured in such a way that there was never any confusion as to whose perspective I was inhabiting."—*Lesbian Review*

Embracing the Dawn

"*Embracing the Dawn* by Jeannie Levig has to be considered one of the best books of 2016 and one of the best audiobooks of 2017. We also see a lot of the relationships with secondary characters, and how important those friendships are to the growth and happiness of our main characters. Levig handles all of these relationships with a deftness that is truly a joy to read, and reread. The story is well plotted, the characters have depth, and the story sucks you in and keeps you turning pages."
—*Lesbian Review*

"*Embracing the Dawn* was written beautifully and it has slipped straight into my Favorite and Must Read Again shelves. It was so raw and honest. The story was very believable and I think that's what has stood out from most books I've read recently. Bold Strokes Books has really upped the ante recently with their authors. This was a fantastic novel. I was gripped from the beginning."—*Les Rêveur*

"Seldom have I read such a passionate and insightful love story as this. Ms Levig's novel flows like a magnificent river, sometimes roaring other times meandering but always effortlessly and impressively moving gracefully on."—*Inked Rainbow Reads*

"This is a fantastic lesbian romance audiobook that has many ingredients for its success: romance, family drama, personal struggles, and great sex scenes. Both main characters are very well written with wonderful depth, very distinctive personalities and a background story that makes them very credible.Their chemistry is a bonus as Ms. Levig builds it from literally the first page and the reader/listener sees it progress into something more meaningful but perpetually sizzling."—*LezReviewBooks*

Into Thin Air

"Two things are apparent to me after reading Jeannie Levig's three novels. 1. She is an absolutely fantastic writer. 2. She is anything but formulaic. Every single one of her books has been good, but all so different. This writer knows how to draw emotion from her readers. …Levig challenges you with this book. This story is like a pendulum of emotions, so well crafted that you can't stop. This is a really fantastic book, you haven't read anything like this one, I promise."—*Romantic Reader Blog*

"Jeannie Levig created such a poignant story that drew so many intense emotions out of me. Each of her characters were so realistic with their flaws and unique personalities traits and I felt so close to each of them. …This story surprised me on so many levels because it is one of the few books that I have ever read that threw all of my expectations out of the window. I have cycled between delight, outrage and sorrow throughout this story and I loved every word of this book because it sends several messages and it is so worth the read."—*Lesbian Review*

A Heart to Call Home

"Can we please all pause and celebrate the fact that both of these women are in their mid to late 40s? Because there are so few in lesfic and it's refreshing to see! *A Heart to Call Home* is beautifully written. It has so much angst and tension that works well alongside the chemistry and pull between Jessie and Dakota. Even though I knew it's a romance and that they would have a happily ever after, their crisis still brought tears to my eyes."—*Lesbian Review*

"What a fantastic novel! Jeannie Levig continues to blow me away with her beautiful story telling. Jeannie Levig writes conflict between protagonists better than many authors. You can feel the tension coming off the page that added another element to this wonderful novel."
—*Les Rêveur*

"Jeannie Levig knows how to develop a character. She weaves her story around her protagonists and draws you right into the amazingness of her stories. I'm never sure where I am going to go, what I'll read and I can never predict the ending. Levig keeps me guessing throughout the whole book and I love her for it. …Levig definitely doesn't play by the rules and loves to add a curveball here and there. Levig does it again with bringing you an amazing story that grips you to the last page."—*Romantic Reader*

"The main characters embark on a soul searching journey which is moving, poignant and sometimes heart-breaking. The reader joins this emotional rollercoaster suffering and enjoying along with the characters. It is one hell of a ride."—*Lez Review Books*

Visit us at www.boldstrokesbooks.com

By the Author

Threads of the Heart

Into Thin Air

A Heart to Call Home

A Wish Upon a Star

Embracing the Dawn Romances

Embracing the Dawn

Embracing the Moon

EMBRACING THE MOON

by

Jeannie Levig

2022

EMBRACING THE MOON

ISBN 13: 978-1-63555-462-5

This Trade Paperback Original Is Published By
Bold Strokes Books, Inc.
P.O. Box 249
Valley Falls, NY 12185

First Edition: June 2022

CREDITS
EDITORS: VICTORIA VILLASEÑOR AND CINDY CRESAP
PRODUCTION DESIGN: SUSAN RAMUNDO
COVER DESIGN BY JEANINE HENNING

Acknowledgments

This book has taken a long journey to get here, with many starts and stops, life issues, and a pandemic in its midst. Given that, I want to begin these acknowledgements with a huge thank you to my readers for your patience and support over the past several years since my last book. Some of you have reached out to me during that time to check in on my next release and offered patience and support as I struggled to get this story onto the page. Some of you have shown your support through continued mentions and recommendations of my backlist titles and brought new readers to my readership. And some of you have found my writing and stories during this time offering new reviews and ratings that keep the energy flow moving around my work. ALL of you have made such a huge difference for me during this long haul and kept my writer spirit nurtured and nourished. I thank you all for your support, encouragement, and faith. I love you all and truly hope you enjoy Gwen and Taylor's story.

As always, I want to acknowledge my best friend and First Reader, Jamie Patterson, for being with me through every word I write. I know in the depths of my soul that without your love, friendship, support, and belief in me this book would not have come to fruition. Thank you so very much.

A huge acknowledgment and thank you to my content experts, Julie, Suzie, and Kim, for your answers to my questions on certain medical aspects of this story, to Lisa for all the information and photos of the Sacramento area, and to my beta readers, Carolyn and Geoff for your input and suggestions. All of your contributions made this a better book.

Thank you to my family and my spiritual circle for loving me no matter what and for not looking at me *too* oddly when I space out because I'm concentrating more on fixing a plot flaw than on our conversation.

And always, always, always, my deepest acknowledgment and gratitude to all of the amazing folks at Bold Strokes Books who are so deeply committed to excellence in publishing. To Radclyffe for creating this supportive space in the world where creativity is so richly nurtured and writers are encouraged and assisted in their growth. To Sandy—always, but especially on this book—for your gentle patience and understanding and always for being there with answers and ideas whenever needed. To my incredible editors, Victoria Villasenor and Cindy Cresap, for your time and knowledge that you give every scene, every line, and every word in my books. Vic, you might never fully grasp the enormity of the role you played in keeping me writing on this project and, subsequently, any future ones. Your check-ins when I'd vanish off social media, the group Zoom calls you set up during the pandemic and now continue, and always being there with encouragement when I needed it most made such a difference. Thank you for it all.

And now, to the reader about to start this story, thank you for your interest, your time, and for choosing to share this experience with Gwen, Taylor, and me. Peace, and love, and happy reading.

Dedication

To Jamie

Like the friendship in this book,
ours has been the constant that has always been
and will always be.
Thank you.

CHAPTER ONE

Gwen Jamison pulled into her best friend's driveway and turned off the engine of her brand new, pearl red, crossover SUV. With four-wheel drive for hard-to-get-to campsites and trailheads and a ski rack for the upcoming winter weekends in Mammoth, it was the car of her dreams. She smiled with joy, lovingly stroking the steering wheel. She'd driven it home from the lot the previous night, then here this morning. She couldn't wait to show Taylor, then get it out on the freeway for their trip south to EJ and Jinx's.

She slid her gaze to the car parked next to her, one she didn't recognize, and fought back a frown. Nope. Nothing was going to spoil her excitement today. She grabbed her travel mug of peppermint tea, then climbed out. Not even Taylor running late because she was still in bed with last night's pickup.

At the top of the steps, she rang the doorbell. Then again. With an exasperated sigh, she finally unlocked the door and let herself in.

She stopped and listened.

Not a sound.

She moved across the tiled entryway, the squeak of her Nikes going silent when she reached the plush carpet of the living room, then returning with her first step up into the kitchen. With long-standing familiarity, she started a pot of coffee since Taylor would need some, then she began sorting the pile of mail that covered the bar. Sometimes she wondered if Taylor deliberately left it there until Gwen's next visit.

Gwen couldn't help herself. She was a neat freak. She made a tidy stack of the mortgage and two credit card statements; the cell phone bill; a jury summons, the dates for which she hoped Taylor hadn't already missed; and a postcard from someone in Venice, Italy. Who still sent postcards instead of pics on social media? Then she set a $2 off coupon from Taylor's favorite pizza place and a Bed Bath & Beyond flyer beside the pile. Taylor had a thing for new sheets and towels and kitchen gadgets she never used. She might find something on sale she couldn't live without.

The morning felt like the beginning of a workday. Open EJ's office. Check. Start the coffee. Check. Sort the mail and anticipate EJ's needs. Check. Check. The similarities stopped there, though. Gwen couldn't recall a single time she'd had to roust EJ from bed to get her moving, whereas Taylor...This wasn't the first time, and surely wouldn't be the last. She scanned the grocery ads while she waited for the coffee to brew.

The sound of an upstairs shower turning on drew her attention to the double doors of the master suite halfway down the railed walkway that overlooked the living room. *No, no, no.* A shower meant more sex, and more sex meant more waiting. Their departure would already be later than they'd agreed on. A mischievous thought sparked to life, bringing with it a devious grin.

She scooped up the junk mail and dumped it in the recycle bin, then retrieved two mugs from the cupboard. She filled both with steaming black coffee, the only way Taylor liked it, and made her way up the spiral staircase by the front door to the second level of the condo. She let herself into the master suite and ignoring the rumpled covers of the unmade bed, crossed to the archway of the en suite. She paused and took in the scene through the clear glass of the huge shower.

Taylor had a slender redhead pressed against the wet tile, her lips to the back of her neck and her hand slowly working between her thighs.

The redhead's moans were audible over the hiss of the spray.

Gwen allowed herself a pleasurable moment to take in the two naked women, but mostly, she admired Taylor. When they'd been introduced on Gwen's third day as EJ's administrative assistant at Bad Dog Athletic Apparel over a decade ago, she'd been mesmerized by Taylor. EJ had waved her hand in front of Gwen's face to recall her attention. Gwen had blushed so deeply, she'd had to excuse herself to perform some imaginary duty until her color returned to normal. Taylor had grinned, and that was the beginning of her merciless flirting with Gwen.

In her mid-forties at the time, Taylor had been stunning, her sleek, dark hair, long and lush; her body, lean and toned; and her eyes—those captivating eyes. Heavily lashed with a warm amber hue from her mother's Brazilian heritage, their seductive smolder reached into a woman's soul when Taylor turned up the heat. And not much had changed since then. Now fifty-five, Taylor carried some extra weight, and there was a bit of a droop to her round buttocks, some extra lines at the corners of her eyes, and some silver threads through her hair, but she was still sexy as hell.

Gwen had seen the numerous women who succumbed to her allure and flirtations, observed from the second Taylor set her sights on one to the moment they walked arm in arm out the door, even noted her own reactions when Taylor turned her charms on her. And she'd come to the conclusion that *sexy* came from the inside. She was certain Taylor would be bedding any woman she wanted well into her eighties, regardless of what age might do to her appearance.

Any woman but Gwen.

Early in their acquaintance, Gwen had considered sleeping with Taylor because…Well, frankly, it'd be incredible. There was something about Taylor, though, even before Gwen knew what it was, that set off warning bells in her. Loud ones. While Taylor would certainly give her a good time in bed, Gwen caught glimpses of something more to her, deeper than that cavalier, superficial, only-out-for-fun facade she projected, something that tempted Gwen's heart and made Taylor the absolute worst woman for her to have a fling with.

She allowed herself one more moment of enjoyment at the image of two beautiful, naked women in front of her, then set the coffee mugs on the bathroom counter. "So you're ready to go, I see," she said over the stream of the shower and the murmur of moans.

The redhead turned sharply and screamed at the sight of Gwen.

Taylor paused briefly, then straightened and slipped her fingers from between the redhead's legs. She gave Gwen a playful grin. "Almost. I was just coming downstairs to see if you were here." She cocked her head. "Unless you'd like to join us, honey."

The redhead, huddled in the corner with one arm across her breasts, her other hand covering her mound, looked from Gwen to Taylor, her eyes wide. "Honey? Are you—" She cut her gaze back to Gwen. "Are you her wife? I swear, I didn't…She never—"

"No, no," Gwen said, crossing the bathroom. "I'd never be her wife." She pulled a bath sheet from the towel bar beside the shower. "But

I do need to get her going. We're running late, so you need to leave." She opened the glass door and motioned the redhead out.

"I really didn't..." The redhead met Gwen's gaze.

"It's okay," Gwen said. "You didn't do anything wrong." She held the bath sheet open, and amazingly, the woman stepped into it.

Gwen wrapped it around her and gave her a gentle pat on the shoulder.

"It'd only take a minute to finish," Taylor said. "It seems mean to send her off unsatisfied."

Gwen and the redhead both glared at her.

Taylor spread her arms. "How did I end up the villain here?"

Gwen ushered the redhead to the counter and handed her a cup of coffee. "I'm really sorry, but trust me. I'm saving you from a whole barrage of her brush-off lines later." She watched as the redhead moved into the bedroom and began finding her clothes, then turned back to Taylor. "Have you packed *anything* yet?"

"Well...I kind of..." Taylor turned into the shower spray. "Okay, no."

"Fine. I'll pack for you." Gwen turned to leave the room. "And you'll just have to make do with what I give you."

"Be nice," Taylor called after her.

Gwen chuckled as she made her way to Taylor's closet. The redhead was gone. She must have dressed on her dash to the front door. Or maybe she was in the other bathroom. Gwen felt a little guilty that someone else had gotten caught in her and Taylor's typical crossfire, but she'd meant what she'd told her. Gwen had heard many a replay of Taylor's morning-afters. Better to rip off the Band-Aid.

Taylor had no idea how she came off when she was hitting on a woman. She didn't seem to understand the impact she had—her looks, her confidence, her eyes and the way she devoured a woman with them. Gwen had seen it so many times, particularly in the early years when she'd go to lesbian social events with Taylor and EJ, mostly as the designated driver, but a little also because Taylor and EJ were trying to figure her out. Their gaydar was intact and spot-on. They both picked up on that vibe in Gwen, but then there were the guys she dated, and Gwen never mentioned her past. Why would she? They were barely more than acquaintances at the time, and later as they truly became friends, it felt awkward because she hadn't been transparent before. Besides, with the way Taylor flirted with her, if she knew Gwen was into women, she would have been all over her, and Gwen hadn't been strong enough at the time to fend her off. She would have caved. And she'd never wanted to be just another one of Taylor's tarts, as Gwen had dubbed them.

For many of the women Taylor bedded, one night with her seemed to be all it took for them to start imagining all kinds of futures with her. And Gwen could see why. Taylor's initial approach reeked of sincerity, and to give Taylor her due, she *was* sincere about what she was offering, just not about spending her life with someone. When she was focused on a woman, *that* woman was all she saw and all that was on her mind. Gwen could understand how that could be interpreted as something else, something more. She'd even tried to explain it to Taylor, to no avail.

Gwen retrieved a suitcase from the back of Taylor's walk-in closet and grabbed a few blouses and several pairs of designer jeans from their hangers. She pulled a couple of sweaters from the shelves in case Taylor needed something warmer for the fall evenings, then took everything to the bed and started packing. By the time Taylor came into the bedroom, she'd neatly folded two shirts Taylor hated on top of the rest of the items filling the suitcase just to make a point.

Taylor eyed them but made no comment.

Gwen smiled sweetly. "I laid out something for you to wear today." She motioned to Taylor's favorite jeans and a soft, worn Melissa Etheridge T-shirt.

"Awww, you *are* being nice." Taylor rewarded her with a tender smile, then took a sip of the coffee Gwen had left for her. "And thanks for this." She lifted the mug. "I needed it."

"You're welcome, but don't dawdle with it. You can take some with you." Gwen returned to the closet and grabbed a handful of Taylor's underwear from one of the built-in drawers, then tossed a pair to Taylor on her way back to the suitcase. "We were supposed to be on the road fifteen minutes ago."

"What's your rush? We have all day, don't we?"

"I'm excited." Gwen's voice squeaked. "EJ and Jinx are getting *married*. That's a big thing."

"Not until Saturday." Taylor took another swig of coffee, picking up her pace.

"But I want to get there. I want to spend these next couple of days with them, getting ready, helping with all the last-minute details." Gwen's enthusiasm grew as she spoke.

"You didn't get enough of all that while you were planning the entire wedding for EJ?" Taylor scoffed.

"You know I love that kind of thing," Gwen called as she made a final pass through the closet, collecting Taylor's garment bag and the bridesmaid's dress that hung alone on a separate rod. It was identical to her own, but she still took a moment to admire it.

Made of coral-colored chiffon, with a snug V-necked bodice and layered, scalloped skirt, it complemented both Gwen and Taylor as well as Jinx's friend Sparkle and EJ's daughter, Mandy, and her daughter-in-law, Tiffany. Jinx's friend Reggie had opted for the same brown tux and coral cummerbund as EJ's son, Jacob. And the brides…They'd both be all in white, Jinx in a silk tuxedo and EJ in the most beautiful dress of Italian lace Gwen had ever seen. She and EJ had found it in a tiny boutique, the last stop of a very long shopping day after they'd all but given up and were thinking about where to grab dinner. It was all going to be beautiful. Gwen could hardly wait.

Normally, weddings didn't do much for her. She'd never been all that romantic. Maybe it was that her practical nature overrode everything else. Or maybe she'd just never been with anyone who made her feel that way. Regardless, most of the time, the concept was lost on her. But *this* wedding…EJ and Jinx. They'd become her romantic myth couple, her inspiration that had ignited a hope in her soul that maybe—just maybe—there might be someone out there waiting for her. She paused on the thought. Perhaps she was more of a romantic than she'd realized.

"Oh, my God!" Taylor screamed from the bedroom. "Oh, my God, no!"

Gwen raced to the doorway. "What's the matter?" She frantically scanned the room, then found Taylor, naked in front of the full-length mirror. "What's wrong?" Her heart pounded.

"I have a gray hair!" Taylor said, sounding panicked.

"What?" Gwen patted her chest, trying to calm herself. "So what? You have quite a few. You've had them for years."

"Not on my head." Taylor's gaze remained riveted on her reflection. "On my…in my…" Her hands went to her pubic hair, and she started pawing through it. "Down here."

Gwen sighed with exasperation. "For God's sake, Taylor. You scared me." She returned to where she'd dropped the dress and the garment bag and picked them up. "I thought something happened."

"Something *has* happened," Taylor yelled. "I can't believe I'm going gray in my…you know. Down there."

"*I* can't believe with all the time you spend focused on that part of your and every other woman's anatomy, you can't say the words." Gwen strode to the bed, spread open the garment bag, and began putting the dress and a couple of pairs of slacks and silk blouses into it. "You have a gray hair in your mound…your bush…your pussy. It's not the end of the world."

"Easy for *you* to say, little Miss *Thirty-something*," Taylor muttered. She combed her fingers through the dark triangle at the apex of her thighs, as though looking for the intruder again. "And I can say those words when it counts."

"I certainly hope so." Gwen unzipped the compartment at the bottom of the garment bag and slipped several pairs of shoes inside. "It'd blow my entire image of you to envision you saying, 'Oh, baby, I want to taste your *down there.*'"

Taylor shot her a glance. "You have an image of me doing and saying things like that?" Her lips quirked, and she arched an eyebrow. "We haven't talked about it in quite a while, but if you'd like—"

"You're packed." Gwen jerked the zipper on the garment bag closed, then the suitcase. "I'm leaving, with or without you, in ten minutes." She rounded the end of the bed and snatched up Taylor's half-drunk coffee just as Taylor reached for it, and headed toward the door. "If you'd like to make the drive by yourself, that's fine. You just won't get to ride in my new car."

"You got a new car?" Taylor's tone was that of a ten-year old learning a trip to Disneyland was imminent. "When?"

"I'll tell you all about it if you make it downstairs in time," Gwen said sweetly. "Ten minutes."

In the kitchen, she rinsed out the cup, along with the one she'd given to the redhead, and placed them both in the dishwasher. She poured the remainder of the coffee in the carafe into a travel mug for Taylor, then waited.

She wouldn't leave her, and Taylor knew it. The threat *would* move her along, though. It always did. It was one of the games they played, along with Taylor's flirting with Gwen and making suggestive remarks, like the one about Gwen joining her and the redhead in the shower. She sometimes wondered what Taylor would do if she ever accepted one of her invitations into something sexual. She even played the *what-if* game with herself occasionally, then tucked the idea away again, keeping it buried down deep like a secret treasure.

She frowned. Or more like a hidden vice.

❖

Taylor woke to the opening lyrics of Pink's "Just Give Me a Reason" and the shifting of the car as it took a gentle curve.

Gwen was softly singing.

Taylor let her eyelids flutter open. Angled in the reclining passenger's seat, her back against the door, she had a perfect view of Gwen's profile. Her shoulder-length, blond hair was pulled back into a short ponytail to reveal the creamy white skin of her cheek and the slender column of her neck. Her lips and jaw moved subtly as she quietly shaped the words of the song. She kept her gaze fixed on the road, the deep blue of her eyes darker with focus and her small, delicate hands relaxed in their grip on the steering wheel. Then the corner of her mouth twitched, and she stopped singing. "Are you going to lie there and stare at me all day?" she asked with a smirk. "Or are you finally going to sit up and keep me company?"

Taylor smiled lazily, then shifted onto her back and stretched her arms over her head. She *could* lie there and stare at Gwen all day—easily. At one time, she'd thought she could do more, but EJ had threatened her with wrath, banishment, and maybe a little pain if she went anywhere near Gwen in that way. Besides, Gwen had been so young when they'd first met. Not usually a deterrent. But she was straight. Again, not normally a factor. But…she was Gwen. Even Taylor felt protective where Gwen was concerned. It was nuts, though. Over the years, she'd learned that Gwen could take care of herself, along with everyone else.

They'd become close friends—best friends—their connection even deeper since EJ had relocated to live with Jinx and was now in Sacramento only two or three days a week, leaving Taylor and Gwen with much more one-on-one time. It'd been the three of them for so long, until three years ago. And in those three years, there'd been ample opportunity for lines to be crossed. Taylor had even felt it from Gwen more than once. She couldn't *just* sleep with Gwen, though. There was already more than just that between them, and if they opened that door, they could easily lose everything else. And Taylor needed the everything else. More than that, if Taylor crossed that line with Gwen, she'd be lost. "You're the one who told me to take a nap," Taylor said, shaking the thought.

"That's because you looked bedraggled." Gwen glanced in the rearview mirror, then tapped the directional signal. "You can't show up exhausted. We have to be ready for anything EJ needs."

Taylor reset her seat into an upright position. "Like what? Climbing Mount Everest?"

"Anything." Gwen leveled her gaze on Taylor. "Last-minute details, shopping, late-night talks, reassurance…"

"Reassurance?" Taylor laughed. "She's marrying Jinx. I've never seen her more sure of anything."

Gwen grinned and eased the car onto the off-ramp. "I know." The words were almost a squeal.

Taylor yawned and looked around. "Where are we?"

"Selma."

"And we need gas already?" Taylor flipped down the sun visor and checked her reflection in the vanity mirror. *Damn.* Her mild hangover was still evident around her eyes. "What kind of mileage does this thing get?" She knew not to pick on Gwen's new pride and joy too much, but she had to poke at her a little. Otherwise, Gwen would think something was wrong.

Gwen shot her a glare. "It gets great mileage. A whole lot better than that gas hog you drive."

"Say what you want about the mileage," Taylor said, finger-combing her hair into place, "but my little Z4 is a babe magnet." She cut Gwen a sideways glance in time to catch the eye roll. She loved Gwen's eye roll. It was so cute.

"Like *you* need a special car to get women." Gwen pulled into the gas station and stopped beside the pumps.

"So why are we getting gas if we don't need it?" Taylor asked.

"I want to stretch and get a snack." Gwen shifted her full focus to Taylor and gave her the customary once-over she always gave her and EJ before she let them go to meetings or out in the world—an occupational habit of being an efficient and trustworthy admin assistant.

Taylor waited to see if she passed inspection.

"And I haven't gotten to put any gas in the tank yet," Gwen said, lightly fluffing Taylor's hair. "So I'll just top it off while we're here." She adjusted Taylor's earring, then cocked her head, a satisfied glint in her eyes. "Beautiful."

Taylor smiled, warming slightly, as she always did, under Gwen's attention. "You take good care of me."

"Yes, I do." Gwen opened the door and climbed out. "So go get me a snack, please."

"You got it." Taylor slammed her own door. "What do you want?"

"Surprise me," Gwen called to her, swiping her card through the slot in the gas pump.

Inside the mini-mart, as Taylor scanned all the choices she knew Gwen wouldn't allow in her new car—nachos, ice cream, a barrel of big, juicy, drippy dill pickles—her gaze fell on Gwen through the plate glass front window of the store. She couldn't help but stare, as she did many times when Gwen was preoccupied.

Gwen always looked so put together in every way. She wore jeans, like Taylor, but hers were black, not faded denim, and were the exact shade of her Nikes. How did she do that? Her black-and-white striped top was casual and yet still classy, dressed up by the collection of silver bangle bracelets decorating one wrist and the twisty, silver hoops at her ears. Her body was small and compact, but her movements displayed the strength and confidence at her core.

The guy filling the car in front of her said something, and Gwen smiled, her eyes flashing in that genuine way they did. She answered with a wave toward the bright blue sky.

Taylor sized him up and wondered, far from the first time, why Gwen had never settled down with anyone or had even dated the same man for any length of time. It certainly wasn't from lack of opportunity. She'd been with Richard the longest, but even that relationship had been less than two years. Anytime Taylor brought up the subject, Gwen would sidestep it with a joke, or a distraction, or just some vague, trite response about never meeting the right person.

"Excuse me." A teenage boy reached behind Taylor to the candy shelf.

She stepped aside, pulling her attention from Gwen with annoyance. Then from the corner of her eye, she spotted the Abba-Zabas—the perfect snack for Gwen. The taffy candy bars with peanut butter centers were Gwen's all-time favorite. She pinched one, testing for freshness— because they had to be fresh—then another, then grabbed a package of

Hostess Snoballs for herself and a couple of Smart Waters. She handed the clerk a twenty and added a magazine from the rack beside the register. As she waited for her change, she turned her attention back to Gwen and ogled her backside, the way those black jeans hugged her ass. She actually felt the slap of EJ's hand on her arm.

That's Gwen, EJ would say. *Knock it off.*

Taylor retrieved her change and the bag of goodies and headed out the door.

Gwen finished cleaning the windshield and dropped the squeegee back into its home in the water as Taylor approached. She smiled when she saw Taylor. "What'd you get me?"

Taylor couldn't help but grin. "You're going to love me."

Gwen arched an eyebrow. "That good?"

"*That* good." Taylor pulled the candy bars from the bag and held them up like two playing cards.

Gwen's eyes widened, and she gasped. "Abba-Zabas!" She reached for them.

"No-no." Taylor held them over her head. "You have to say it first." The few inches she had over Gwen's five foot three enabled her to keep the candy out of her reach as she grabbed for it. "Say you love me."

Gwen scoffed. "Don't be ridiculous. Give them to me." She made another attempt, this time with a little hop.

Taylor shifted to the side. "Nope. Say you love me, or no Abba-Zabas for you. And they're so fresh and chewy, too."

"Argh. Taylor!" Gwen ran around her, but Taylor spun. Gwen laughed. "All right," she said begrudgingly. "I love you."

Taylor drew in a breath in feigned astonishment. "You have to say it nicer than that."

Gwen sighed. She softened her expression and gave Taylor a coy smile. "I love you."

Taylor eyed her skeptically, still holding the candy above her head. "You have to say it all."

Gwen gave her that cute eye roll, then batted her lashes. "I love you, and you're the queen of everything."

"Okay. Was that so terrible?" Taylor handed over the Abba-Zabas with a smile.

Gwen snatched them and tore one open. "Just for that, you have to drive the rest of the way. I'm going to be savoring my snack."

As Taylor sped down the on-ramp and onto the freeway, Gwen opened the bag. "What's this?" She pulled out the magazine. "Oooooh." She began to laugh. "A gossip rag? We haven't done this in a long time."

Taylor chuckled. "I thought it'd be a fun way to kill the last couple of hours."

"And Snoballs?" Gwen asked in evident exasperation. "Really, Taylor? Marshmallow, chocolate cake, and cream in my brand new car? You're going to get the steering wheel all sticky."

"No, I won't. I'll be careful," Taylor said, thinking she maybe should have gone with some cookies or chips or something less gooey. "I got some napkins."

"Napkins don't help with sticky unless they're wet." Gwen tore open the package. "Here, I'll do it."

"You'll do what?" Taylor asked. "Eat my Snoballs?"

"No. They're disgusting. No real food is bright pink." She pinched off a small chunk. "I'll feed it to you. I can do it without getting anything on you, me, or the car." She held the bite to Taylor's lips.

And she could. Gwen could eat a caramel apple without getting a drop of sticky on her. She once painted her entire living room without a single strip of painter's tape around the windows or along the trim that she did in a contrasting color. It was amazing. *She* was amazing. Taylor took the bite and savored it. Both she and Gwen only indulged in junk food like Snoballs and Abba-Zabas on a road trip. It was part of the fun of taking one.

Gwen set the Hostess package on her thigh and took a bite of her first candy bar. She moaned as she chewed. "Maybe you are the queen of everything."

Taylor smiled. "Of course, I am."

Gwen started leafing through the magazine.

Taylor couldn't remember how they'd begun the practice of amusing themselves with all the crazy stories. It drove EJ nuts when she had to participate, but it could entertain the two of them for hours.

"Uh-oh," Gwen said, her forehead creased. She tweaked off another piece of Snoball and fed it to Taylor. "There's another pregnancy by aliens. This time a senator." She raised an eyebrow.

"Do you think they actually had sex, or does it happen through some other means?" Taylor chewed.

Gwen scanned the page. "It doesn't say. Ooooh, Derek Dunkirk has famous, but secret, gay lovers," she said in a conspiratorial tone.

Taylor gasped in feigned outrage. "The Masked Raider? No way. Read something else, before your new car gets struck by lightning."

Gwen laughed. "Well, we're all doomed anyway, because the Halloween death comet is on its way to collide with Earth. See?" She held up a blurred picture of a chunk of rock that looked marginally like a skull and crossbones.

"Oh, yes," Taylor said, settling deeper into the driver's seat for the rest of the trip. "That one I have to hear."

They spent the next hour and a half entertaining themselves with the ridiculous stories in the gossip magazine and making plans for their last days on Earth.

Gwen stuffed the pages back into the bag with the crumpled snack wrappers and empty water bottles just as Taylor reached the exit. "Hey, we're here," Gwen said excitedly.

"And with time to spare." Taylor flashed her a wicked grin. "See, you could have joined me and Stephanie...Melanie?" She tried to remember. Last night seemed so long ago. *Tiffany?* "Anyway, we would have had plenty of time."

"Why would I want to join you and anyone?" Gwen retrieved some gloss from her purse and touched up the frosted pink of her lips. "Call me demanding, but I require *all* of my lover's attention."

"Even if you could have *all* of *two* lovers' attention?" Taylor asked off-handedly. She loved this flirtatious game they played, even though the suggestions it conjured in her mind could drive her to distraction sometimes. She turned onto EJ and Jinx's street.

"Are you saying you couldn't satisfy me on your own?"

"Oh, baby," Taylor said with a lurid lilt. "I could and *would*. I'm just offering you the chance to do something you've never done before. You know, expand your horizons." She maneuvered the car into the half-circle drive in front of EJ and Jinx's ranch-style home and turned off the engine. "But now that I think about it, maybe we should start with you sleeping with just one woman before we set you up with two."

"Thoughtful of you." Gwen smirked.

The front door of the house flew open and EJ hurried toward the car.

Gwen smiled and waved at her. "But I don't believe I've said that I've never slept with a woman." She pulled on the door handle and leaped out into EJ's arms.

Taylor stared after her, stunned. *Never said... What?* What did that mean? Had she? Taylor's mind flooded with images. Everything, every thought, every feeling she'd ever had for and about Gwen came crashing through the door that had just been kicked in. She watched as Gwen and EJ pulled from their embrace.

Gwen jumped up and down a couple of times, then they hugged again. "You're getting married!" Her pitch was high.

That's right. EJ was getting married. The wedding. That's what they were there for. Taylor tried to focus. But Gwen with a woman? Shit!

CHAPTER TWO

Gwen set the tray of cheese and cold cuts in the center of the table, while EJ arranged the condiments around it.

Taylor stepped into the kitchen. "All right, our bags are upstairs," she said, rubbing her hands together. "Now what?"

"There's a pitcher of iced tea in the fridge," EJ said. "Will you get it?" Her emerald green eyes sparkled with her smile, and her cheeks glowed a rosy pink.

"You look so happy," Gwen said, brushing a few strands of blond hair from EJ's forehead.

EJ's smile widened. "I am. I can't believe we're getting married. When we set the date, it seemed so far away, and now, here it is."

Taylor retrieved the tea and filled the four glasses at the place settings. "Where's Jinx?"

"She should be down in a few minutes," EJ said, pulling out a chair and settling into it. "She went for a bike ride and needed a shower."

As though on cue, a thunder of footsteps came from the other room, and EJ and Jinx's large, brown and gold mixed lab charged in and hurled himself into Gwen's lap—at least the half of him that would fit.

Jinx raced in behind him.

"Pete!" Gwen squealed, then hugged the big dog's neck and buried her face in his fur. "How are you?"

"Pete," Jinx said, echoing Gwen, but her tone was far less happy. "Behave."

EJ laughed. "You know he can't where Gwen's concerned. He loves her." She reached over and scratched his ear, while he snuggled more deeply into Gwen.

Jinx chuckled. "I guess we all have our weaknesses." She leaned down and kissed EJ.

"Yes." EJ looped her arms around Jinx's neck and curled her fingers into the dark chestnut hair at her collar. "We do." She kissed her softly.

Emotion swelled in Gwen's heart at the evident love they shared. "Awwww." Tears pricked her eyes.

"You can't start crying already," Taylor said, sliding a napkin her way. "The wedding isn't till day after tomorrow."

"I know. It's just all so sweet and romantic." Gwen recalled how different EJ had been before she'd met Jinx, so compartmentalized and controlled. And she'd been almost as emotionally unavailable as Taylor— *almost* because Jinx had managed to melt her heart, whereas Gwen had never seen any woman come close to melting Taylor's.

Pete wriggled against Gwen, reclaiming her attention.

"He sure is happy to see you." Taylor laughed.

"I know the feeling," EJ said, still holding Jinx close to her. "He and I both have been waiting for you guys all morning. Where have you been?"

"What do you mean?" Taylor's tone was defensive. "We were right on time."

EJ arched an eyebrow at her.

"Don't pay any attention to her," Gwen said to EJ. "She just feels guilty because she was still on last night's date when she should have been packed and ready to go. Not to mention finding a gray hair in her bush and acting like Armageddon was at hand. That took some time. Yes, it did," she added in baby talk as she leaned into Pete's face.

He licked her cheek.

"Okay," Jinx said, drawing out the word. She gave EJ another kiss, then straightened, a blush creeping up her neck. "I think it's time for me to go." She turned to Gwen and Taylor. "I love you both dearly, but some things need to be kept between the three of you."

"Sweetie, you're leaving?" EJ asked, taking Jinx's hand.

"Yeah. Sparkle called." Jinx interlaced her fingers with EJ's. "Mike's back is giving him trouble today, so I need to go with Reggie to pick up the tables and chairs for the reception."

EJ narrowed her eyes. "Is that true? Or is it another way for her to keep us apart?"

Jinx grinned. "Probably the latter."

"Why would she want to do that?" Taylor asked as she started making herself a sandwich.

"She believes it's bad luck for us to see each other before the wedding." Jinx's gaze remained on EJ, and she stroked the back of her knuckles with her thumb.

Gwen had seen her do that before to calm EJ.

"Isn't that just the day of?" Taylor asked.

"Exactly." EJ pinned Taylor with a glare, as though she were the one at fault. "She's insisting Jinx stay at her and Reggie's tonight, too."

"Maybe she just wants a last little bit of time with *her Jinxie.*" Gwen used Jinx's dearest friend's nickname for her to help make her point. "Before she's formally married. You know, for the same reason it was so important to you for me and Taylor to be here with you a couple of days early."

EJ cut a glance to Gwen, and her expression softened.

Jinx smiled. "I've always liked Gwen."

"When you put it that way, I sound like a bitch." EJ frowned. "Sparkle could have just said that you know." She shifted in her seat, then rose. "I'll walk you out," she said to Jinx.

Jinx chuckled. "You coming, Pete?" she asked as they strolled toward the door.

Pete swiveled his head to look at Jinx, his ears pricked, then looked back at Gwen.

"Go ahead," Gwen said. "I know you go where she goes."

He scurried off her lap and after them.

"If you're not back in five minutes," Taylor called, "we're going to come interrupt whatever you're doing."

"No, *you're* going to interrupt them." Gwen forked some sliced turkey and cheese onto her plate. "I had my show for the day this morning in your bathroom."

"At least I warned them. Your entrance was a complete surprise." Taylor took a swallow of her tea. "And what about that other surprise you dropped just as you got out of the car?"

Gwen winced. Yeah, what about that? No one could have been more surprised than Gwen at that revelation slipping past her lips. What the hell? "Not now. We can talk about that later." Or never, if she could swing it. "This is EJ's special time. It should be all about her."

"Come on, you can't drop a bomb like that and expect nothing to come of it." Taylor leaned forward and took a bite of her sandwich, coming across as nonchalant as a cat stretching in the sunshine, but Gwen knew better. Taylor was dying to hear a story. "After all the time we've known each other and all the women-with-women conversations you've been a part of with me and EJ—you've even been to women's events with us—and you've never said anything?"

Gwen sighed. She had to get out of this. She had no idea why she'd alluded to being with a woman. Just got caught up in the banter, maybe? "It was forever ago. I was a teenager. It was that experimentation that everyone does. It was nothing." Half was true. It *was* forever ago, and she had been a teenager. The rest, not so much. Not at all. But it was long since over and done with. She'd made her peace with it, made her decision from what she'd learned, and that was that.

Taylor eyed her in that way she did when she was trying to work out a way around someone's defenses.

An evil idea came to Gwen. "How about this? I'll tell you a little piece of it every time you get a new gray hair. You know…" She shifted her gaze to Taylor's lap. "Down there," she whispered. That should make her way less eager to bring it up.

Taylor glared.

"All right. What are you two talking about?" EJ asked brightly as she strolled through the doorway.

Gwen met her with a smile. "Oh, just—"

"Nothing," Taylor said pointedly. She turned to EJ, obviously ready for a change in subject.

And that should be that. At least for now. Gwen relaxed into her chair, pleased with herself.

"So what are we doing today?" Taylor asked EJ. "Gwen says we're here for you, at your beck and call, to meet your every need and satisfy your every whim."

EJ took her seat again and reached for the bread. "Oh! I like that." She laughed. "Seriously, though, I'm so glad you guys are here. And it *will* be nice to have tonight with you. But this afternoon, we have appointments at the spa. Mani-pedis, facials, massages. All the fun girl stuff. Mandy and Tiffany are meeting us there."

"You were going to drag Jinx through all that?" Taylor asked with a scoff.

EJ frowned. "Of course not. But she was going to have lunch with us and be here for the evening. *And* I should have been able to sleep with her tonight."

"What about the slumber party you promised we'd have?" Gwen deliberately egged EJ on. She knew EJ well enough to understand that her biggest objection was that Jinx's absence had been Sparkle's idea. EJ and Sparkle had become friends, but they could still rub each other the wrong way at times.

EJ gave Gwen a rueful smile and raised her glass. "Well, now we'll have it."

As they ate and talked, Gwen watched and listened to the two people in the world she loved the most, the people most important to her. On the surface, it could have been any other meal they'd shared over the years, but underneath, everything felt different. For so long, they'd been three single women, none of whom had seemed to have any interest in love, partnership, or marriage. Then EJ had met Jinx, and that had changed.

As much as EJ had fought it, as much as she'd tried to stay away, she'd fallen in love. And somehow, *that* had changed everything else. And not just for EJ, but for Gwen, too, and maybe even Taylor. That was when it'd started becoming increasingly difficult to deny her attraction to Taylor, to keep it buried so that even when it did make itself known, it was only a flicker, easily snuffed out with a diversionary tactic or a change in subject.

The three of them had always been together, or if Gwen was alone with one of them, it was almost always EJ. Once EJ had moved to live with Jinx, though, and was in the same city with Gwen and Taylor usually less than half the week, that was a game-changer. Gwen and Taylor ate out, had drinks, spent time at each other's places on the weekends, even jogged and worked out together, when Gwen could guilt her into it. And through it all, Taylor was as annoying as she'd always been. Always late. On the prowl for hookups even when in mid-conversation with Gwen. Needing someone to pick up after her and keep her organized. Okay, the latter didn't bother Gwen. That's what she did, but still, something about doing it for Taylor felt different.

"So you're sure about all this marriage stuff?" Taylor asked EJ. "We could hit Bella's tonight if you want to test your resolve."

Gwen gasped. "Taylor!"

EJ only glared.

Taylor burst into laughter. "I'm just kidding. You two are so easy." She reached across the table and took EJ's hand. "Jinx is great. I can see how happy she makes you, and I'm glad you found each other."

The words seemed sincere, but Gwen wondered if Taylor had trouble saying them. She knew how afraid of falling in love Taylor was, and why. And she remembered how closely Taylor had watched EJ at the beginning of her and Jinx's relationship when EJ had changed her approach to women—to Jinx—so drastically. Until then, EJ had dated women the same way Taylor did, casually, with one-night stands being the primary component. But as soon as she'd met Jinx, all that had changed. EJ couldn't stay away from her, no matter how hard she'd tried. She'd done things she'd never done before, and that was Taylor's biggest fear, losing herself in love and doing something stupid—again. For EJ, it'd all worked out wonderfully, but the whole idea still terrified Taylor. Would she ever let herself love anyone?

Taylor shifted her gaze to Gwen. "Something wrong?"

Gwen's neck and face heated. How long had she been staring at Taylor? She'd been so lost in thought. "No. Nothing's wrong," she said way too quickly.

"Are you sure, honey?" EJ rested her hand on Gwen's forearm. "You look a little flustered. And you're *never* flustered."

"I'm not flustered." Gwen straightened in her chair and collected herself. "I was just thinking we should probably get going." She glanced at her watch, as though she had a clue when they needed to be at the spa. "What time are our appointments?"

"And there she is," Taylor said, grinning. "Organized and in charge, as always."

"You're probably right," EJ said. "We should get this cleaned up and head out."

Gwen released an inner sigh of relief. She didn't want to explain what she'd been thinking. But why not? She'd only been remembering aspects of her, EJ, and Taylor's friendship over the years. What was wrong with that? EJ had been right, though. She had felt flustered—the perfect word for it—when she'd suddenly found herself staring into Taylor's eyes. She tried to recall what she'd been pondering at that precise moment. Taylor's fear of falling in love? If Taylor would ever let herself fall again? What was wrong with that? Shouldn't a friend care about a friend's happiness? The next thought that had been about to make itself known once again edged around the borders of her consciousness. Gwen pushed it away. No time. They had to get going.

❖

Gwen arranged a couple of pillows behind her, then leaned back against EJ's headboard. "I'm stuffed." She moaned. It felt good to be out of the unforgiving fit of her jeans and into the elastic waistband of some Bad Dog boxers and the loose drape of her old and tattered favorite men's pajama top. "I ate way too much eggplant parmesan. Why didn't you two stop me?"

Taylor flopped down across the king-sized bed, adjusted a cushion against Gwen's bare legs and rested her head on it. "That massage did me in way before the food. I'm still so relaxed, I feel like an over-boiled noodle. I could barely stay upright during dinner." She turned onto her side and cuddled into the comforter beneath her, then slid her hand under the back of Gwen's knee. "This feels so good."

EJ settled across from Gwen and reclined into her own pile of pillows. She draped her legs over Taylor's. "It was a nice day, though. Wasn't it?" She gave them each a tender look. "Thank you for coming early, before everything gets busy and crazy tomorrow."

"We had to," Taylor said lazily. "It's our last night with our friend as we've known her. Even tomorrow night, you'll already be rehearsing being an old married woman."

Gwen couldn't help but laugh at EJ's indignant expression.

"Speaking of old, are you going to show me your new gray hair?" EJ flicked up the hem of Taylor's red satin nightshirt with her bare foot and nudged the leg band of Taylor's bikini briefs with her toe.

Taylor jerked her hips away and slapped at EJ's foot. "No. I am not."

"Why not? Gwen got to see it."

"No, she didn't." Taylor pulled her shirt back down over the tops of her thighs.

EJ glanced at Gwen, obviously for confirmation.

Gwen shook her head. "I didn't. She just screamed about it. Like a little girl." She smirked at Taylor. "I thought she set herself on fire or something."

Taylor sniffed. "I don't expect either of you to get it. You're both blond, and you"—she shot Gwen a dismissive glance—"you're barely thirty."

Gwen rolled her eyes.

Taylor grinned.

"I'm thirty-seven." Gwen bounced her knees, causing Taylor's head to bobble. "And you'd better be nice, or I won't come visit you in the nursing home in a few years."

EJ laughed. "I don't want this to change. I want times like this with the three of us no matter who's married, or dating, or even if we have to do it in a nursing home."

"What are you talking about?" Taylor rose onto her elbow and stared at EJ. "We do this all the time. You're still in Sacramento half the week."

"I know," EJ said, her voice catching. "I just—"

"Ignore her." Gwen took EJ's hand and squeezed it. "I know what you mean. Things are changing, and you want to make sure we all keep our friendship a priority."

"Yes, thank you." EJ leaned over and rested her head on Gwen's shoulder. "That's exactly it."

Taylor sighed and flopped back down. "Why didn't you just say that, instead of getting all weepy?"

Gwen bounced Taylor's head harder.

"Ow!" Taylor made a face.

"I have something I want to give to you both," EJ said as she regained her composure. She opened the drawer of the nightstand beside her. "I'm supposed to pass out the bridesmaids' presents tomorrow night at the rehearsal dinner, but I want to give you yours now." She handed each of them a small silver gift bag, then held a little white box in her lap.

Gwen eyed her questioningly.

"Go on," EJ said. "Open it."

Inside, wrapped in sparkly tissue paper was a heart pendant of blown glass with flowing striations of shades of blue. It was framed in white gold and hung on a delicate matching chain. Gwen drew in a breath in admiration. "Oh, EJ. It's beautiful. Thank you."

"Let me see it," EJ said eagerly, taking the necklace from Gwen. She held it up to Gwen's cheek. "Perfect. I tried to make sure this strand"— she pointed to the widest one across the middle of the heart—"matched your eyes."

Gwen smiled. "I want to wear it." She gathered her hair and held it up while EJ fastened the chain around her neck.

"Wow, this is gorgeous." Taylor sat up and folded her legs beneath her. She gazed at her own pendant, then undid the clasp and attempted to put it on. With her hair loose around her shoulders, she got her fingers tangled in it.

"I'll do it." EJ scooted over to her and took the necklace.

Taylor rose to her knees and looked at herself in the mirror of the vanity across the room. "Wow."

EJ smiled, meeting Taylor's eyes in the reflection. "I had yours made a little sturdier, since you're hard on jewelry."

Gwen's heart swelled and tears blurred the image at the affection in EJ and Taylor's shared gaze, at the love she felt for them both, at EJ's happiness, at the deeper friendship she and Taylor had found. Her throat tightened with emotion. To maintain her composure, she looked to the heart-shaped pendant of amber—enhancing the warmth of Taylor's eyes—browns, burnt orange, and the slightest hint of yellow. It hung on a slightly thicker chain of yellow gold and lay nestled against Taylor's smooth, bronze skin in the low-cut open collar of her satin nightshirt, just above the swell of her full breasts.

Gwen's pulse quickened with the desire to trace the heart with her fingertips, then run them down into Taylor's cleavage. She'd grown used to such responses and to controlling them, but the emotion that accompanied this one caught her by surprise. What was wrong with her? She swallowed hard to stave it off. When she tore her gaze from Taylor's chest, she found Taylor watching her in the mirror.

Taylor smiled, but it wasn't the usual seductive look she gave Gwen in moments like this. There was no lewd quirk to her lips, no suggestive arch to her eyebrow. Her gaze was soft, her mouth gently curved. Her expression held a hint of something that stole Gwen's breath.

Gwen looked away, her face heating as a blush overtook her. She searched for something to focus on and found the box EJ had been holding lying beside her on the bed. "What's in here?" she asked before anyone else could say anything.

"That one's mine," EJ said, stretching out between Gwen and Taylor.

Gwen wondered if Taylor was still watching her but couldn't make herself check. What was that? And why had it affected her so strongly?

There'd been times when their attraction to each other had flared in the same moment and they'd had to step back, but this had been different. It'd made her blush. And Gwen rarely blushed.

EJ held up a third heart necklace, the blown glass of this one in greens. "I got these for us to represent our love and friendship for each other." Her cheeks pinkened. She met Taylor's eyes. "I know, corny."

"Not at all," Taylor said, her expression tender. "I love it. And I love you."

The emotion Gwen had been fighting back crested and broke at Taylor's uncustomary response. Where was the snarky remark, the sarcasm? She burst into tears.

Taylor sighed. She turned to Gwen. "Are you going to tell us what's wrong with you?"

"I don't know what's wrong." She waved her hands in front of her face. "It's all just so…I don't know."

EJ laughed and scooted over to her. She slipped her arm around Gwen's shoulders. "It's okay. You don't have to explain yourself. It's probably just the wedding vibe. Weddings make everyone a blubbering mess. Remember me after Jacob and Tiffany's? I was a wreck."

"Yeah," Taylor said with a scoff, "but we found out later—*a lot* later for being your best friends—that was because you'd gone all wonky over Jinx." She eased alongside Gwen and ran her hand over Gwen's knee. "So who have you gone all wonky over?" Her usual flippancy was back. She slid her fingers beneath the hem of Gwen's boxers and tickled her inner thigh.

It was exactly what Gwen needed to jolt her back to her senses. She shot Taylor a glare.

Taylor chuckled and withdrew her hand. "Just checking in. We haven't talked about it for a long time."

"There's a reason for that," EJ said as she swung her legs over the edge of the bed and rose. "Gwen's way too smart for your antics."

"Hey!" Taylor flipped over. "Are you saying the women I date are stupid?"

"No," EJ said innocently. "They just don't know you. Gwen knows way too much about you to ever go there. You should give it up."

The two went on as though Gwen wasn't in the room. It was fine with her, though. She could use another minute to finish pulling herself together. Taylor's return to her usual flirty demeanor had recalled Gwen's thoughts and emotions, but Taylor's light caress still lingered on the sensitive flesh of Gwen's thigh. She considered EJ's words about Gwen knowing Taylor too well to ever *go there* and wondered what EJ would think if she ever did. Would she think less of her?

Gwen glanced at her two best friends, who'd moved into EJ's walk-in closet and were looking at an outfit on a hanger. EJ loved Taylor. She might question Gwen's sanity—hell, Gwen would question her own sanity—but wouldn't she trust that if Gwen did *go there*, she'd know what she was doing?

Taylor laughed and wrapped her arm around EJ's shoulders.

EJ buried her face in Taylor's thick, dark hair, as though hiding in embarrassment.

Why was Gwen even thinking these things? Maybe EJ was right. Maybe it was all merely this wedding crap. She'd been so happy about the wedding, so excited. She rolled off the bed in irritation and started for the door. "I think I'm calling it a night," she said as casually as she could manage.

They turned and looked at her with shocked expressions.

"What about the movie?" EJ asked.

Damn! The movie. "Oh, yeah," Gwen said hesitantly. "I forgot about the movie."

"Remember? That's why we came in here?" Taylor smirked.

"I do now," Gwen said in annoyance. She had to try not to take her sudden bad mood out on Taylor, even though it somehow felt like it was Taylor's fault.

EJ hung the pantsuit they'd been looking at back on the rod. "We should start it so we're not up too late." She crossed to the bed and picked up a remote, then turned on the big screen TV. "Tomorrow's going to be a long day. We'll need some sleep."

As they settled again, Gwen noticed Taylor eyeing her but ignored it.

EJ climbed between them and adjusted her pillows.

As the music rose and a house appeared on the screen, Gwen relaxed, snuggling into her own spot once again. She was grateful Taylor was on the other side of the bed. She couldn't pinpoint why, but she couldn't imagine—or maybe didn't want to imagine—lying close to Taylor for the next two hours. She twined her fingers with EJ's. This felt a lot safer.

EJ smiled down at her and pulled her hand into her lap.

Gwen sighed in relief at the comfort it brought her. She'd have to figure out what was going on with her. Or maybe it'd be gone by morning. For now, though, she could just enjoy this time with her two best friends.

CHAPTER THREE

Taylor stood at the window of the master bedroom of the remodeled farmhouse that Sparkle and Reggie used to live in. It was one of the original buildings on the property that comprised the Canine Complete compound. The all-in-one dog grooming, boarding, training, and emergency veterinary hospital was their livelihood and heart's fulfillment, and on this beautiful fall afternoon, it was the venue for EJ and Jinx's wedding. The grounds were gorgeous—lush green fields, trees dressed in full autumn colors, pristine white railed fences dividing the landscape into designated areas and matching the seemingly always fresh paint on the buildings.

From Taylor's vantage point on the second floor, she could see over the tops of the privacy screens that had been set up to keep from view the brides' approaches when it was time and into the rows of seating filling up rapidly. It wasn't a large wedding, maybe eighty-ish people at the most, and that included the wedding party. It would be a celebratory one, though. The day's vibe was one of pure happiness and love.

Joy for her longest-standing friend fluttered in Taylor's heart. She and EJ had been through a lot together: starting at Bad Dog at the same time and seeing each other through training and the probationary period; becoming close outside of work when EJ went through a rough patch with her son when he was in his teens; coming out to one another, Taylor early on and EJ not until toward the end of her marriage; then the years of clubbing and serving as each other's wingwoman. She couldn't imagine her life without EJ in it. She turned and took in the scene behind her.

EJ sat in front of the vanity mirror, Gwen entwining a wreath of coral-colored flowers that matched the bouquets into EJ's hair.

Mandy, EJ's daughter, perched on the edge of the bed, tapping a tube of mascara against her thigh. "I'll finish your makeup last because once I do, you can't get all weepy anymore."

EJ laughed. "Do you really think I'm going to make it all the way through the ceremony without tearing up?"

"We can only do our best," Mandy said with a wave of her hand.

A phone on the vanity chirped with an incoming text.

Gwen picked it up and tapped the screen. She drew in a deep breath. "Okay. It's time."

EJ tensed and gripped the edges of the stool she sat on. "All right. Mandy, finish my eyes. Hurry."

Mandy leaped up, then leaned close with the mascara brush.

Taylor and Gwen shared an amused look. It wasn't as though EJ couldn't do her own makeup. Mandy was so much like EJ, though, in that she had to be either doing something or, at least, have something to think about doing, lest she pace and fidget.

"Okay," Mandy said, straightening. "You're all set."

EJ stood and turned to Gwen, then Taylor. "Well, how do I look?" She held out her arms.

The Italian lace dress was exquisite, and it draped her every curve perfectly. The rich hue of the blossoms in her hair deepened the color in her cheeks.

"You look amazing," Taylor said softly. "Jinx is a very lucky woman."

EJ brought her hands to her mouth, and her eyes brimmed with tears.

"Mom, no!" Mandy keened. "Taylor! Don't make her cry!"

"I didn't do anything," Taylor said. "Besides, isn't it waterproof?"

"Yes, but it can still smudge." Mandy yanked a tissue from the box on the vanity and moved to EJ. "And her eyes are getting all red for the pictures."

Taylor stepped to EJ and slipped her arm around her. She pulled her to her side as she took the Kleenex from Mandy and dabbed beneath EJ's eyes. "Knock it off," she said in mock reprimand. "You're getting me in trouble."

EJ and Gwen laughed.

"I'm sorry." EJ snatched the tissue from Taylor and gently pressed it to the moisture on her cheek. "I'll be fine. Just…" She opened her arms. "All of you, come here."

They eased into a group hug, then stepped back.

"Okay," EJ said. "I'm ready. Let's go before I'm late for my own wedding."

Downstairs, Jacob and Mandy's husband, Russ, met them in the foyer. Jacob's expression went soft when he saw EJ. "Mom, you look—"

"Stop!" Mandy pressed her palm to his mouth. "You're going to make her cry."

"Sorry." He held out his arm for EJ to take. "But you do," he whispered as she slipped her hand through the crook of his elbow and nestled in close.

Their group was met behind the privacy screens by Tiffany.

Jinx's sister, Andrea, waited to be ushered to her seat to signal the start of the ceremony. She smiled at EJ and kissed her cheek. "Are you ready?"

EJ beamed and nodded.

As Jacob walked Andrea down the center aisle, Taylor peeked around the edge of the screen and scanned the area.

Gwen stepped up beside her and rested her head on Taylor's shoulder, while she took in the scene as well.

Taylor pressed her hand to the small of Gwen's back and rubbed it soothingly.

Gwen had been such a contradiction in her demeanor over the past couple of days, something so outside of her nature, it made Taylor wonder about the existence of pod people. One minute, Gwen was her usual—the epitome of composure, efficiency, and quick repartee—the next, she was emotional, scattered, and at a loss for words, the latter mostly in response to Taylor's customary teasing.

Taylor had no clue what to make of it. She'd even looked up a few times to find Gwen watching her with an expression she couldn't read. And what was that look they'd shared in the mirror their first night in EJ's room? Taylor knew what *she'd* been thinking, but Gwen blushed. What was that about? Hopefully, they could talk about it on the way home. It was starting to concern Taylor.

She followed Gwen's gaze across the way to where Jinx stood with Reggie and Sparkle in her white tux, looking for all the world like a teenager going to her first prom.

Sparkle adjusted Jinx's collar, then brushed something from the back of her jacket.

Jinx stared at Taylor and Gwen, anxiety evident in the set of her features.

Taylor smiled and sent her a reassuring thumbs-up. What the hell did she have to be nervous about? Was she afraid EJ would run? *Yeah, right.*

Jinx visibly relaxed and looked embarrassed, as though reading Taylor's thoughts.

Gwen stiffened, then straightened, making one of her sudden shifts. She turned quickly. "Okay, everyone get lined up."

The group moved into position just as Jacob returned and took his place beside Tiffany. The soft orchestral music that had been playing turned to the opening piano notes of Debussy's "Clair de Lune," a piece that was somewhat difficult to walk in time to, but Jinx had insisted. Something about it always made her think of EJ.

Taylor and Gwen moved into place, and when they started down the aisle, Taylor couldn't hold back a grin at the sight on the platform at the front. Stacey, the wedding officiant, a friend of Jinx's she'd served time with nicknamed Namastacey, stood in the center with Jinx. Jinx's best people—Sparkle, Reggie, and Tiffany—fanned out to the right, and Mandy, Russ, and Jacob to the left, leaving a space for Gwen beside where EJ would stand. Taylor would take a spot on Jinx's side for symmetry since it didn't matter who went with whom. EJ and Jinx's love had made them all a family.

As they reached the end, the heat of Gwen's body so close to hers drew Taylor's attention, and a strangely ethereal sense of rightness settled within her. She'd teased Gwen about marrying her before, and this would be great fodder for jokes about them walking down the aisle together, but she wouldn't use it. This feeling was too perfect to ruin it that way. Then it vanished when they parted to take their places, and Taylor shivered at the loss.

Finally, Pete, with a pillow strapped to his back and the wedding rings stitched to the fabric, trotted up the aisle to stand beside Jinx.

The "Wedding March" began, and everyone stood to watch EJ make her way to the woman she loved.

Jinx was fixated, her gaze riveted to EJ, her face split wide with a huge grin.

Taylor swallowed hard, fighting back her emotion.

When EJ reached Jinx, Jinx took her hand, and they turned to face Stacey.

"Thank you, everyone," she began, "for coming together today in witness and celebration of this union between Echo Jenay Bastien and Jinx Michelle Tanner, as they commit to one another in marriage."

A tear slipped from the corner of EJ's eye and trickled down her cheek.

There went the makeup. Taylor blinked back her own tears so as not to ruin hers.

"Jinx and EJ," Stacey said, continuing with the ceremony. "It's written that the greatest of all things, the most wonderful experience we can share, is love. And into your lives has entered a deep and nurturing love, and you've asked this gathering of your friends and loved ones to help you celebrate that love."

As Stacey went on, Taylor considered her surroundings and exactly what was happening. Her best friend, who'd once been so much like her, was getting married, and everything that entailed. What must that feel like? Would *she*, could she, ever commit herself to loving and spending her life with one woman? At one time, she'd never even questioned it. The answer would always have been a resounding *no*. It was the very thing she'd avoided above all else. She couldn't risk losing herself in love. The last time she had, it'd cost her four years of her life. She'd never even been tempted until…Her attention drifted to Gwen.

Gwen was transfixed on the proceedings, a wistful smile ghosting her lips and a sheen of moisture misting her eyes.

She'd make a beautiful bride. Taylor trembled slightly. She caught herself. *What a stupid thought.* It wasn't like she'd never had it before, though. Not that exact thought, maybe. Not marriage per se, but others like it—spending her days and nights with Gwen, living with her. Loving Gwen and letting Gwen love her. *Christ!* What was she thinking? She forced her gaze back to EJ and Jinx. This wedding had everyone drowning in the romantic myth.

"And now, Jinx and EJ will exchange their vows," Stacey said. "Jinx?"

Jinx glanced at her and cleared her throat. "EJ…" She took EJ's hands in hers, then brought them to her mouth and kissed them.

EJ took in a breath and blinked rapidly.

"Baby, I never even dared to dream of someone like you coming into my life, and especially of someone like you ever loving me. You took my breath with that first look, stole my heart the minute you stepped into my arms for that first slow dance. I started loving you right then, and I'll never, ever stop. I promise to love you always, no matter how we change or what form that love takes. I promise to kiss you thoroughly every single day, the way a woman who is deeply loved deserves to be kissed. I promise to stand by your side through good times and challenges, through certainty and questions, through anything and everything that comes our way. I promise my heart to you, EJ. I love you *so* much."

Stacey smiled, then turned to EJ and inclined her head.

EJ sniffled. "Jinx." Her voice broke, and she clenched her eyes shut. "Oh, God. I should have gone first."

Everyone chuckled, and Gwen slipped a tissue into EJ's hand.

EJ dabbed her eyes, then touched it to her nose. She swallowed and focused directly on Jinx. "Jinx," she began again. "You are everything I've ever needed in a partner and a lover, and now a wife. You make me strong. You make me brave. You make me want to be a better person in everything I do. You're my rock, my inspiration, and my heart. I promise to always cherish you and to honor the love we share. I promise never to run in the hard times and never to take the goodness that you are for granted. I love and appreciate and admire you, and I'm so very blessed to be the one you've chosen as yours. And *I* choose *you*, Jinx, every moment and every day. I choose you." EJ's tears began to flow.

Jinx took her in her arms and held her close.

After a moment, allowing EJ to compose herself, Stacey asked, "May we have the rings?"

Reggie reached down and tugged the loose thread that held them in place on the pillow on Pete's back, then handed them to Stacey.

"A circle has no beginning or end and is, therefore, a symbol of infinity. It is endless, eternal, just like love." She gave one to Jinx and the other to EJ. "For many, the wedding ring is worn on the fourth finger of the left hand. This is because the vein in this finger was believed to lead directly to the wearer's heart. Jinx?"

Jinx took EJ's hand and slid the ring onto her finger. "With this ring, I marry you. I take you as my wife for as long as you'll have me."

EJ laughed, then stroked Jinx's fingers. "With this ring…"

Taylor's gaze drifted again to Gwen, and she found herself under the intensity of Gwen's as well. Her heartbeat quickened. Her blood raced through her veins. Her cheeks heated. But she couldn't look away.

Gwen gave her a soft smile, but it was a sad one. Then she looked back to EJ and Jinx.

Taylor felt the loss deep in her core.

"By the powers vested in me by the state of California, I now pronounce you wife and wife," Stacey said with a huge grin. "You may kiss."

Jinx swooped EJ up and covered her mouth with her own. She kissed her long and hard, then eased her back to her feet and sank into a deep, gentle one.

Reggie slapped Jinx on the back, laughing loudly. "Okay, lover, you have a whole honeymoon for that."

Taylor returned her attention to Gwen, trying to figure out that smile. What was there to be sad about? EJ and Jinx were married. Gwen had been excited about this moment for months. And yet, Taylor felt it, too. It circled around her. It lingered.

She pushed it aside and forced a smile. It'd have to wait.

There was celebrating to be done.

By the time the final pictures of the brides, their families, and the wedding party were finished, Taylor's face ached from all the smiling. She massaged her cheeks as they all made their way to the reception area, nestled into a cluster of trees where the guests had been enjoying cocktails and mingling as they waited.

The soft music the DJ had been playing silenced, and a smooth alto voice came across the speakers. "Ladies and gentlemen, please welcome our wedded couple, Jinx and EJ, and their wedding party."

The crowd cheered and applauded as the group filed past and took their seats at the head table. A team of servers appeared, balancing trays of flutes filled with champagne, and passed them out to all the guests as the DJ raised some chuckles with a few jokes, then introduced Sparkle to give the toast.

Sparkle rose and accepted the mic, then cleared her throat. "I've gotta say, I'm a little surprised to be the one doin' this, but then if I think about it, I'm the one who should because I had the most doubts about these two." She turned and cocked her eyebrow at Jinx and EJ.

The line and Sparkle's customary sardonic manner drew laughs.

"When this one," she gestured to EJ, "came waltzin' into our Jinxie's life, I was the first one to threaten that if she didn't treat her right, I'd hunt her down and kick her—" She winked at the crowd. "Well, you know."

More laughter.

She returned her gaze to EJ, her expression softening. "But I'm also the first one to admit when I'm wrong. Turns out Ms. EJ Bastien's the best thing that's ever happened to our Jinxie. And I have it on good authority our Jinxie's the best thing that's ever happened to her too."

EJ smiled and nodded.

"I've never known a couple more meant for each other, more suited to spend their life together, and more deservin' of a love that's changed them both forever. So let's raise our glasses to Jinx and EJ and their union and happiness."

Everyone toasted, then sipped the bubbly. Everyone but Gwen, that is.

Gwen downed over half her glass.

Curious, Taylor leaned in close to her ear. "You okay?"

Gwen stiffened slightly. "I'm fine," she said, her back still to Taylor.

"All right," Taylor said, easing away. "But if something's wrong, you know you can—"

"I'm fine."

Gwen's tone wasn't harsh, but it left no room for discussion. Taylor knew better than to push.

The DJ announced the first dance, and Jinx and EJ strolled hand-in-hand to the center of the floor. Jinx gently twirled EJ to the strum of a guitar, then pulled her into an embrace as Anne Murray began to sing her old country hit, "Could I Have This Dance for the Rest of My Life."

EJ looped her arms around Jinx's neck, and they gazed into one another's eyes.

The lyrics were perfect. As Anne continued singing about being partners every night and magic moments and falling in love, Taylor's eyes burned. She swallowed down emotion as she watched them dance and fall in love all over again. She cleared her throat. "Hey." She nudged Gwen. "If we had a song, what do you think it'd be?"

Gwen hesitated, then turned and slid Taylor an incredulous look. She smirked. "'The Wreck of the Day.'"

It was enough to free Taylor from the wedding quicksand that threatened to suck her under, but it stung some too. She wondered why as she laughed. It was a typical barb between them.

Gwen shifted around the rest of the way and slipped Taylor's champagne flute from her loose grasp. She took a deep swallow.

Taylor noticed Gwen's glass was empty. "Hey, take it easy. You haven't eaten much today. It's going to go straight to your head."

"All the important stuff's over. It won't matter." Gwen took another drink.

"But you've drawn the attention of several people," Taylor said quietly in a sultry voice. "You don't want to cloud your thinking, I'm sure."

Gwen glanced around. "I have not."

"Mm-hm. The guy straight across the dance floor. And that woman Chelsea who works here at Canine Complete that flirted with you at the Fourth of July party? Weddings are a bad place to lose your wits." Taylor teasingly elbowed her.

"Well," Gwen said, drawing out the word. "I'm with my best friend. I know she won't let me do anything stupid." She met Taylor's gaze with a puzzling expression. "Will you?"

It was an odd question for her to ask. Gwen didn't do stupid things, sober or drunk. Taylor studied her. "Of course not."

"And now, if the wedding party will join our happy couple on the dance floor." The DJ's voice resonated from the speakers.

"We're up." Taylor stood and held out her hand to Gwen.

Gwen stared at it like it was a suspicious life form.

"Come on," Taylor said, wiggling her fingers. "Everyone else is a couple. That leaves you and me."

Gwen didn't move.

EJ caught Taylor's eye from where she stood in Jinx's arms and waved them over as the rest of the party got into position.

"Seriously?" Taylor asked. "It's not like we haven't danced together before. Was it that bad?"

Gwen took a deep breath and chugged Taylor's remaining champagne. "No." She put her hand in Taylor's, then let her lead her onto the dance floor. "Remember. Nothing stupid."

Taylor shook her head. They definitely needed to talk.

As the music began, Gwen put one hand to Taylor's shoulder, while Taylor touched hers to the small of Gwen's back. They interlaced the fingers of their other hands and began to move in a slow circle. They *had* danced together before, many times, and they did it well. Usually.

But Gwen was stiff in Taylor's arms, her eyes cast down.

"Relax," Taylor said, running her hand up Gwen's spine, then back down in a soothing sweep. "As you said, all your wedding duties are finished. You can just have a good time now." She leaned in and pressed her cheek to Gwen's temple.

Gwen sighed, and the tension in her shoulders eased.

"There you go," Taylor whispered. The soft notes of a love song drifted around them as they swayed, and suddenly she realized Gwen had closed the small gap between them and was melded against her, their interwoven fingers tucked beneath Gwen's chin. What was up with her? Was the wedding really hitting her that hard? Taylor considered easing her away to quell a simmer of arousal deep in her own belly but caught herself. Maybe that was what she needed, a safe place to let down her guard. Taylor could handle it. It'd only be a few minutes. She shifted and tightened her hold.

When the song ended and one with a faster beat started, Gwen's only movement was to squeeze Taylor's hand more firmly.

Taylor took the hint and kept them moving in a slow, easy circle. It wasn't as though holding Gwen, feeling their bodies pressed together, breathing in the scent of her hair were hardships. Hell, she'd fantasized about moments like this, only in her fantasies, Gwen was feeling the same things she was, not having some emotional overreaction to whatever she was reacting to right now. But Taylor set everything aside and held her close.

At the end of their second dance, Gwen pulled away. She glanced into Taylor's eyes, then averted her gaze with a sheepish expression. "I think our duties as Maids of Honor are over." Her cheeks were flushed.

The music had picked up its pace, and couples from the surrounding tables had filled in the floor around them.

Taylor smiled and nodded. She held out one hand and ushered Gwen back to their seats.

Before she could settle into hers, the low tone of a woman's voice caressed her ear. "May I have this dance?"

Taylor turned to find a deeply tanned blonde, in her mid-forties, leaning a smidge too far into her personal space and flashing a confident smile. She looked slightly familiar. She must know Taylor, or at least know *of* her enough to know she and Gwen weren't a couple. Was she from Bad Dog or someone they'd met through Jinx? Taylor glanced at Gwen.

Gwen gave her a dismissive wave. "Go ahead. I'm fine."

Taylor hesitated. "Are you sure?" She didn't feel right about leaving her.

"Yep. Fine. Go." Gwen scanned the area as though looking for someone. "Have fun."

Taylor felt the blonde's fingers lace between hers, then a coaxing tug. She eyed Gwen as she took a step backward. She seemed okay. If Taylor hovered after being told Gwen was fine and to go, there'd be hell to pay. Then again, she *had* asked Taylor to make sure she didn't do anything stupid. Could Taylor do that if she wasn't with her?

"Go," Gwen said emphatically.

Taylor wavered another second. She could see her from the dance floor and could be back in a heartbeat. "We'll get some food when they're finished setting up the buffet. Okay?"

Gwen nodded without looking. "Sure."

Taylor and the blonde moved toward the throng of dancers, but Taylor couldn't shake her apprehensions about leaving Gwen. She cut a glance to their table and saw Chelsea easing into Taylor's seat. Taylor watched Gwen's lips shape the words, *no, thank you*, then curve into a soft smile. Letting Chelsea down easy.

Chelsea stayed, though.

Taylor let the blonde lead her onto the dance floor. The song that was playing was a fast one, saving her from having to make conversation. When it ended, though, the blonde moved closer.

Taylor shifted her gaze to the head table where Gwen had been. Both of their chairs were empty. A jolt of alarm shot through her. She searched the seating area and the rest of the dance floor.

No Gwen.

Where the hell was she? Then she spotted her in the line forming for the buffet.

She was chatting with EJ's boss and his wife.

Taylor calmed. *Good.* Gwen could use some food. Then again, was it a good idea to be talking to EJ's boss in the condition she was in? "I'm sorry," Taylor said to the blonde. "I need to go. Thank you very much for the dance."

The blonde blinked then stepped back. "Okay then." She turned, then said over her shoulder, "If you'd like to get together in the future, Andrea has my number."

Andrea's Christmas party! That's where Taylor had seen her. Taylor watched her walk away, simultaneously admiring the sway of her hips and wondering at her own lack of interest.

"Ms. Matthews," EJ's boss said in greeting as Taylor slipped into the buffet line beside Gwen. "Sarah and I were just commending Gwen on what a beautiful event this is. EJ says the two of you played a big role in the planning."

Taylor laughed at the idea. "She's being generous with my part. It was almost all Gwen and a little bit of EJ. I only provided moral support."

"Taylor's a good cheerleader, though," Gwen said, lifting her half-empty champagne glass in a mock toast. She swayed slightly.

Another one? Taylor inconspicuously steadied her with a hand to her back, remembering her promise not to let Gwen do anything stupid. Wasn't getting sloppy drunk in front of your boss's boss something stupid? "Gwen, could you come with me for a minute? There's someone I'd like you to meet. If you'll excuse us," she added to the couple.

"Of course," Sarah said.

Taylor grasped Gwen by the elbow and maneuvered her out of the line.

"Hey! I'm going to lose my place." Gwen leaned into Taylor. "And as you pointed out, I haven't eaten much today."

"Sit down, and I'll bring you some food," Taylor said as they approached their table. "And stay sitting. And don't drink any more of this until you get something in your stomach, or you're going to end up sick." She took the glass from Gwen and handed it to a server passing by.

"Didn't your new friend want to play?" Gwen asked, plopping down into her chair.

"No," Taylor said, her tone firm. "My new friend did *not* want to play with someone who's distracted keeping her best friend from being stupid. Now, sit here, and wait for me to come back with some food. *Don't* go anywhere."

To Taylor's surprise, Gwen obeyed, perhaps only because EJ and Jinx, along with Mandy and Russ, took a break from dancing to eat too.

Taylor set a plate of fettuccine alfredo, citrus glazed chicken, and a Caesar salad in front of Gwen, then sat beside her with her own meal, identical except for filet mignon medallions in mushroom gravy instead of the chicken. Taylor had been dying to taste the filet ever since Gwen had shown her the menu for the wedding. She noticed Gwen had commandeered another champagne and was well into it. At least she had food now. Maybe that would keep her from throwing up later.

They ate and laughed with their friends, enjoying the afterglow of the festive day. EJ and Jinx looked so happy and were perfect together. Everyone applauded as they cut the cake and toasted each other.

When Taylor returned to the table, this time with a piece of cake for her and Gwen to share, Gwen was gone. Taylor sighed in exasperation. She searched the crowd, looked to some of the buildings where the restrooms were open, checked the dessert table and the bar. Finally, she turned a full circle, scanning the outskirts of the grass area that was the center of the Canine Complete grounds.

Against the setting sun low on the horizon, she spotted a silhouette of a woman walking toward the footbridge that crossed a stream. She couldn't see her face, but it was Gwen. Taylor knew her shape, her walk, her carriage. She went after her.

Gwen stood on the bridge, watching the sunset, *two* flutes of champagne on the railing in front of her.

"Really?" Taylor asked.

Gwen glanced at her.

Taylor gestured to the glasses.

"I had food," Gwen said, then flashed a smile. "Besides, I didn't want to have to walk all the way back to the reception for the second one."

Taylor studied her. "What's going on with you? Why are you deliberately getting drunk? You don't drink this way."

Gwen rolled her eyes. "Can't I let loose once in a while?"

"Yes, but that isn't what you're doing."

Gwen turned back to the setting sun.

"When you let loose, you have a good time," Taylor said gently. "You dance. You laugh." She remembered their celebration of EJ's, and therefore Gwen's, last promotion with a smile. "You put straws on your teeth and talk like a walrus."

Gwen's lips twitched. "And you wonder why I don't do it very often."

"But that's not what you're doing today. Is it?" Taylor brushed the sweep of Gwen's hair from her cheek and curled it behind her ear, then trailed her fingertips across Gwen's nape.

Gwen sighed and tilted her head back, the tautness in her neck loosening under Taylor's touch. A whisper of a smile shaped her mouth. "That's nice."

Taylor slid her hand under Gwen's hair and began a gentle massage.

Gwen leaned closer and rested her head in the hollow of Taylor's shoulder. She let out a quiet moan that stirred deep in Taylor's belly. "I understand why women will do anything for you."

Gwen's statement came out in such a soft whisper, Taylor was sure she hadn't heard correctly. "What?"

Gwen shifted, lifting her gaze to Taylor's face. She said something, but Taylor missed it, her focus claimed by the warmth of Gwen's breath on her skin and the caress of her fingers toying with the pendant just below the hollow of Taylor's throat.

"Gwen." Taylor's voice was hoarse. She forced herself to still her hand on the back of Gwen's neck.

Gwen turned in the curve of her arm. "Don't stop." Then her lips were on Taylor's. Soft. Warm. Supple. It was a kiss. Not one like they'd shared before, not a hello or good-bye peck, or a quick "Happy birthday" or "Merry Christmas" brush. All Taylor would have to do to bring this kiss fully to life was move her mouth against Gwen's, slip the tip of her tongue inside. She could sense it, feel it in the press of Gwen's body against hers, in the thrum of desire in her own. This was Gwen, the woman she'd wanted for years but could never have. Then again, *this was Gwen.*

She couldn't. Not like this. Not with her drunk. Not without finding out what the hell was going on. She gripped Gwen's shoulders and started to ease her back.

Gwen threaded her arms around Taylor's neck, drove her fingers into her hair. She moved against her, her mouth covering Taylor's.

Taylor groaned, fighting her natural tendencies. *No.* No, she couldn't. But Gwen wanted it too. Right?

So why couldn't she?

CHAPTER FOUR

Gwen lay in the passenger's seat of her car, her head pounding each time Taylor crossed the reflectors to pass another vehicle. She'd done the hair-of-the-dog thing that morning and choked down a half of a glass of wine from EJ's refrigerator, almost thrown it back up, then started on some water to rehydrate.

Taylor made her some tea and toast before they'd loaded up to head home, and Gwen had been asleep or pretending to be, ever since. Mercifully, Taylor hadn't tried to talk to her about her behavior the past few days, but she knew it was coming. She just needed some time away from her, the wedding, and all things romantic to sort out her thoughts and feelings before she could figure out what to say about it all. She did have some explaining to do, though. Especially about the kisses they'd shared on the bridge.

Thank God Taylor had been true to their friendship and stopped things before they went too far.

Had Gwen simply reached her limit? Had all the nooks and crannies deep within her where she'd been stuffing her attraction to Taylor for years finally filled up? Was there no more room to hide? Or had all her crazy thoughts about Taylor, her fluctuating emotions only been the byproduct of a wedding that touched her so deeply—a wish for something similar for herself?

Whatever it was, Gwen knew she'd crossed a line the second her confession of having slept with a woman passed her lips. That part of her that had always wanted Taylor, that Gwen had always kept gagged and under control, had broken free. Of the few things Gwen had never told her, that was the one that would pique her interest the most.

And it had. That was when the looks had started when Gwen would glance up and catch Taylor watching her. And what about her own? There were times she didn't even know she was staring at Taylor, lost in thought until she found herself gazing directly into Taylor's eyes—like the look they'd shared in EJ's mirror.

Without EJ's presence in the room, there was no telling where that might have led—and not necessarily on Taylor's part. That was when Gwen realized she needed a plan. If they shared a moment like that when they were alone, she wouldn't be able to trust herself. And if *she* crossed the line that had been in place between them for years, how could she expect Taylor to honor it? And then it'd happened on the bridge. Thank God her plan had worked.

When the idea had come to her, she hadn't seriously considered it, merely passed right over it. It kept coming back, though.

If I'm drunk and make a play for Taylor, I know she won't let it go anywhere. Taylor wouldn't do that—with any woman, Gwen was pretty sure, but she was certain she wouldn't with her. So she'd started drinking the second she could. Not a good idea in general, considering she drank very seldom, but it'd worked.

Gwen had known she'd cross that line. She'd almost done it the night of the rehearsal dinner after they'd all gone to bed in separate rooms. She'd fallen asleep, had a dream—a vivid one—about sneaking into Taylor's room, into her bed, and had awakened with a start and an ache between her legs. She'd managed to remind herself that EJ was in the house with them and she'd taken care of her arousal herself, then forced herself to go back to sleep, but the night following the wedding, she and Taylor would be alone. EJ and Jinx were leaving straight from the reception for a three-week honeymoon at a rented beach house. Even sober, Gwen would have ended up in Taylor's bed. She had no doubt.

She'd needed help, so with excessive amounts of alcohol combined with making Taylor promise not to let her do anything stupid, she'd set off on a path she knew she shouldn't take. And it'd worked even better than Gwen had imagined.

When they'd danced and Gwen had pressed herself so closely to Taylor, they were surrounded by all the other wedding guests. But it'd felt so good. And when she'd kissed Taylor on the bridge, the reception was still in full swing, and EJ and Jinx hadn't left yet.

But oh my God...that kiss. Gwen had gone for it. But when Taylor had returned it, then dove in, demanding another, possessing Gwen completely, for a split second, Gwen thought the plan had backfired. She was going to get a hell of a lot more than a kiss. And in that moment, she didn't care. All she'd wanted right then was to drag Taylor into the bushes and fuck her brains out. The force of her need and urgency still made her tremble as she remembered it. She hadn't felt anything like it in a long time... *Not since—*

"Hey." Taylor's voice was low, her touch on Gwen's shoulder gentle. "Time to wake up. We're home."

Gwen let out a pained sigh. "Thank God." Thank all the gods... and goddesses...and Buddhas and divine, celestial, and supreme beings. Divinities, immortals, demiurges, numina. Avatars? She even threw in baby Jesus, the Greek Furies, and a few wood nymphs for good measure. She opened her eyes and gingerly sat up. Her head still hurt.

Taylor eased the car into Gwen's garage.

Gwen blinked. "What are we doing here? Your car's at your house." Her pulse quickened with apprehension at the thought of Taylor staying the night to take care of her. It wouldn't be unusual. They'd all done it for one another when one of them was sick. Gwen had helped both Taylor and EJ through many a hangover, and Taylor and EJ had taken turns throughout some of Gwen's overindulgences and illnesses, most recently a bad case of food poisoning from a questionable taco truck. It's what friends did sometimes. But she had to convince Taylor this was not one of those times. "I'm fine." She cringed inwardly. How persuasive. "Really," she added, trying to sound breezy.

Taylor watched the garage door lower in the rearview mirror. "I know you are. But you haven't eaten anything since that toast this morning, and I know you." She cut the engine and turned to Gwen. "The first thing you're going to want is a hot shower, so I'll make some food while you do that. Then once I know you have something in your stomach and can lie down and rest or watch a movie or something, I'll get an Uber. I don't want you driving home from my house by yourself when you feel like crap."

"Taylor, really. It's—"

"I'm not going anywhere until I know you've eaten and are settled in for the evening." Taylor shouldered her door open and climbed out.

Gwen glared at her back, then conceded the point. Taylor's offer seemed genuine, not like a ploy to allow her to pounce with her questions. And she was right. Gwen always did want nothing more than a long, hot shower when she got home to wash off any residue of her day, in this case, the film of alcohol she'd been imagining seeping from her pores, and having something in her stomach that she didn't have to make would be nice. "Fine," she muttered, never mind that Taylor was already pulling their bags from the back of the car.

Inside, Gwen opened the sliding glass door that led from the living room to the patio. She took a moment to admire several butterflies flitting over the lavender blossoms of her California aster and breathed in the fresh air as it chased out the stuffiness that had claimed her home in her absence. She felt suffocated in a closed-up house. Even during the colder months, she preferred leaving the windows cracked to inhaling dry, forced air heating. It was a quirk she'd picked up in defense of several years spent in Mrs. Brandon's overheated foster home.

Taylor crossed the living room and left her suitcase by the front door, then started toward the hallway with Gwen's.

"I'll take that." Gwen brushed a lock of hair from her forehead and forced herself to meet Taylor's eyes. Things were so awkward between them, and it was her fault. She only needed a little time, though, to sort out her thoughts. Then she could straighten everything out. "I'm going that way anyway for a shower. Right?" She lifted one shoulder in hopes of pulling off nonchalance.

"Okay." Taylor tipped the handle in Gwen's direction and waited.

Gwen grabbed it as she passed, then headed to her bedroom. She felt Taylor's gaze following her like a bloodhound on a scent. She eased the door closed behind her and leaned against it, then sighed. It felt good to be alone. Shower and food. Then she could be by herself for the rest of the evening.

When she stepped back into the living room twenty minutes later, she already felt better. The hot stream of water running over her bare skin had relaxed her stiff and tense muscles, the soapy caress of her own hands soothed her anxiety. She inhaled the aroma of tomato soup and grilled cheese, her favorite comfort food, and smiled as her stomach grumbled. Everything would be fine. This was her and Taylor. There wasn't anything they couldn't work out.

"Perfect timing," Taylor said from the open kitchen. She nodded to the dining table, where two place settings held bowls of soup and glasses of mint tea from Gwen's fridge. Taylor plated the sandwiches and served them just as Gwen pulled out a chair and sat.

"It smells delicious," Gwen said.

"I know what you like." Taylor's tone was light and teasing. "And I also know you always stock the makings of tomato soup and grilled cheese. Thank God because it's still about the only actual meal I can put together."

Gwen smiled. She'd been surprised and touched when Taylor had asked her to show her how to make it. She picked up her spoon as Taylor settled into the chair across from her, then took a bite of soup. She almost moaned at the rich flavor that coated her tongue and the warmth that flooded her mouth, then traveled down her throat as she swallowed. It was pure comfort flowing into her soul. She closed her eyes and sighed.

"That good, huh?" There was a hint of pleasure in Taylor's tone.

Gwen did moan with the second bite. "You have no idea." Taylor couldn't. Things didn't seem to affect her the way they sometimes did Gwen. Not emotional things. Or maybe it was simply that Taylor handled them differently, but for Gwen, she could only stuff her feelings down for so long before they all gathered together and turned on her, before they came raging to the surface, demanding to be dealt with. And this wasn't the first time it'd happened around the topic of Taylor and Gwen's attraction to her. She should have known better. But now she knew what she needed, and she'd take care of it.

They ate in silence, for the most part, Gwen thankful for the space Taylor was giving her. As Gwen cleared the table, Taylor tapped out something on her phone. When Gwen had loaded the dishwasher, she turned to face her.

"My ride will only be a few minutes. Then I'll be out of your hair," Taylor said quietly.

Gwen averted her gaze. She hated that she'd made Taylor feel she wasn't welcome to stay. "You're not—"

"It's okay," Taylor said, crossing to where Gwen stood. "I know you need to work something out. Just..." She lifted her hand as though to brush back Gwen's hair but stopped when Gwen eased away. She slipped her fingers into the front pocket of her jeans. "We're going to talk about this. Right?"

Gwen hesitated. Would they need to once she regained her perspective? *She* might not, but she did owe Taylor an explanation for how she'd behaved. She nodded reluctantly.

Taylor eyed her. "Promise?"

"I promise."

Taylor's phone pinged, and she glanced at the screen. "Wow, I guess the driver was closer than he thought. He's here."

Gwen walked her to the door.

Taylor grabbed her suitcase, then paused. She studied Gwen.

Gwen tensed under the scrutiny.

"See you at work tomorrow?" Taylor's statement rose at the end in question.

"Yes," Gwen said confidently. Some time to think and clear her head. A good night's sleep and she'd be fine by morning. "See you at work."

When Taylor had gone, though, it wasn't that easy. Gwen curled up on the couch, snuggled under her favorite throw, and let her mind navigate the rocky terrain of everything that had happened over the past four days, waiting for some conclusions to form. But the only one that came up over and over again was the very one that terrified her, the one that not only put her friendship with Taylor at risk but also her own heart.

She needed to talk to someone, needed help sorting this out, but the only ones with whom she'd discuss something like this were Taylor and EJ. They'd been the ones she'd gone to about everything for the past ten years. Of course, she couldn't talk to Taylor, at least not until she had some of her own answers. And there was no way she'd call EJ and interrupt her honeymoon. Although, she could already hear EJ's chiding when she got home for not if things went wrong between her and Taylor. She squeezed her eyes shut at the thought. But no, she wasn't going to cut into EJ and Jinx's time together.

She'd have to figure this one out on her own. And she had until tomorrow morning.

Taylor pulled into the parking lot of Bad Dog Athletic Apparel and scanned the front row. Gwen always arrived at work early enough to snag a premier spot closest to the building, but this morning her car was nowhere in sight. *Damn. She promised she'd be here today.*

Taylor made her way to the elevator, then stepped inside when the doors opened. It wasn't until they'd glided closed that she realized she'd been looking for the wrong car. She rescanned in her mind to check for Gwen's new ride but didn't trust her recall. Could she see that row of the parking lot from the conference room window on her floor? She frowned at her own absurdity. She *could* just call Gwen's desk to make sure she was there like a mature adult would do. Then she could see if she wanted to grab lunch later; Gwen would say, sure, and everything would be back to normal. And if Gwen wasn't there, Taylor could call her cell. She gave a slight nod of confirmation as she passed the HR counter and turned toward her own office.

"Good morning, Brenda," she said as she passed her administrative assistant's desk. "Anything pressing?"

Brenda rose and followed her. "You might not think it's such a good morning." She closed the door behind her. "One of your panelists for today—Walt, from marketing?" She waited for Taylor's nod of acknowledgment. "Can't make it. He has the flu."

Taylor groaned. She didn't want to have to postpone an entire day of interviews. "All right. Let me see if Gloria's available." She picked up her phone receiver and started to dial.

"And Gwen called," Brenda added as she waited in her customary efficiency. "She said to let you know she isn't coming in today."

Taylor froze, her fingers hovering over the number keys. She looked at Brenda. "Did she say anything else?"

"No." Brenda tilted her head slightly. "Not really."

"No? Or not really?" Taylor struggled to keep her irritation in check. This day was already getting on her nerves, and it hadn't even started yet. "Did she say anything else or not?"

Brenda straightened and squared her shoulders the way she did when she felt unduly challenged. It reminded Taylor of a bird ruffling its feathers. Brenda was an excellent admin assistant, and she and Taylor generally worked well together, but their communication styles were very different. Taylor was direct and to the point, whereas Brenda tended to be vague and obtuse at times, by Taylor's standards. Brenda, on the other hand, considered herself the clearer of the two.

The receiver still in her hand, Taylor rested her forearm on the edge of her desk. She softened. "I apologize." Nothing about her day or the weekend or her mood was Brenda's fault. "Can you tell me if Gwen said anything else, please?"

Brenda's auric feathers seemed to settle, but she loosely folded her arms. She smirked. "She said the wedding was beautiful and she wished I could have been there, that she hadn't forgotten she promised me the recipe for her special barbecue sauce at the picnic last month, and she told me a tidbit of office gossip that someone at your level doesn't get to know. Does that improve your mood?"

Taylor studied her, suddenly sidetracked. "Why can't I know?"

Without answering, Brenda turned toward the door. "Let me know if there's anything you need me to do for the panels today." She turned the knob and disappeared around the corner.

"I said I was sorry," Taylor called after her.

When Taylor had salvaged the schedule of entry-level interviews, she dialed Gwen's number.

The call went straight to voice mail. "Hi." Gwen's voice answered cheerily. "This is Gwen. You know what to do." It was the same message she'd had for years.

"Hey, it's me," Taylor said. "Where are you? Call me."

As Taylor moved through her day, she checked her phone for a return message at every break, ignoring anything from anyone who wasn't Gwen. She tried to reach her several more times with the same result, the tone of each of her own messages growing increasingly frustrated. As the hours passed, she put together the argument she thought had the best chance of getting her into Gwen's house after work and getting Gwen to talk to her. This was ridiculous. They were friends—*besties*, for Christ's sake. They should be able to talk about anything. Finally, just as Taylor was about to leave the office at five minutes to five, Gwen called.

"Where the hell have you been all day?" Taylor was surprised at the sharpness of her own voice. "I mean, I've been worried. Why didn't you answer or at least call me back?"

"Can you come over?" Gwen asked, as though she hadn't heard the questions and if she had, clearly she had no intention of answering them.

Taylor was caught off guard. With as much as Gwen had evidently been avoiding her, she would have expected to have to break her door down to find out what was going on. "Well, yes. Right now?"

"Yes. If you can." Gwen's tone held a mixture of nerves and resolve. The anxiety Taylor had been carrying throughout the day—hell, ever since the drive from EJ and Jinx's—began to ease. "Okay. I'll be right there." She grabbed her keys from her front desk drawer and stood. "I'll pick up something for dinner on the way over."

"I made something," Gwen said. "Just come over."

Gwen stepped out of her front door as Taylor pulled into the driveway. She stood on the stoop, her shoulders drawn up, hugging herself. She wore faded jeans and an oversized Bad Dog sweatshirt, the sleeves pushed up to the elbows.

The shirt was one Taylor used to have too, but now that she thought about it, she hadn't seen it in quite some time. The baggy fit on Gwen's small frame made her wonder. She slipped out of her car and started up the walk.

Gwen smiled, but it wasn't her usual bright and welcoming greeting. Her gaze shifted down, then quickly returned to Taylor's face.

Taylor almost missed a step. Had Gwen just checked her out? No. She didn't do that. "Hey," Taylor said as she approached.

"Hey." Gwen's answer was soft. She looked up into Taylor's eyes. "How was work? Did I miss anything?"

Taylor winked. "You missed me." Maybe they could just go back to their usual interaction.

The corners of Gwen's mouth tipped down slightly, and she bit her lower lip. "Don't do that."

Taylor faltered. Okay, the usual wasn't going to work. She should have known better after the kiss they'd shared at the wedding. She should let Gwen have the lead tonight. Clearly, there was something on her mind and she was ready to talk. "Sorry. Nervous energy." Taylor moved past Gwen and into the house. "I just don't know what's going on."

"I know." Gwen followed and closed the door behind them. "I owe you an explanation, but I want to have dinner first. I don't want any interruptions or distractions once I start. I just want to get..." She paused. "Can we just eat first?"

"Of course." Taylor was trying to be patient and supportive, but Gwen's unfinished sentence scared her. She hadn't said she wanted to get this over with, but that did seem to be what she'd held back. So this couldn't be good. Or was Taylor merely assuming the worst? And what would be the worst? Taylor tried to imagine. That Gwen didn't want to be friends anymore? That would definitely be the worst. And if Gwen's behavior over the past few days and that kiss meant whatever was going on with her would end their friendship, there *certainly* was no need to rush.

Dinner was amazing, as usual. There was something about Gwen. She could make sloppy joes taste like a gourmet meal. Tonight wasn't sloppy joes, though. She'd evidently wanted to make an impression. Dinner was a combination of some of Taylor's favorite dishes in Gwen's repertoire—baked lemon chicken, garlic broccoli pasta, and her special recipe ambrosia salad. Was this Taylor's last meal? Suddenly, she wished EJ were there. EJ would be able to keep whatever this was from going off the rails.

Gwen cleared the table but didn't load the dishwasher, something Taylor didn't think she'd ever seen, then poured each of them a glass of sparkling water and led the way to the living room.

Taylor stopped and arched her eyebrow at Gwen expectantly.

Gwen licked her lips. "Please, sit down." She gestured to the couch.

Taylor complied, then looked at Gwen again. She waited.

Gwen studied her, a plethora of emotions passing through her eyes. Finally, she turned away and crossed to the sliding glass door. She remained silent another long stretch as she stared outside. "I want us to talk about what's between us," she said finally.

Taylor watched her, hoping she'd turn around. She wanted to see her face, try to discern what she was thinking. "You mean what happened down at EJ's? At the wedding?" Suddenly, she remembered what seemed to have started everything, Gwen's allusion to having slept with a woman before. She thought back over moments in their friendship, particularly in recent years, that felt like more. Not simply the flirtatious banter that sometimes flew thick and heavy between them. That was all in fun. Or was it? There were other times…looks that smoldered, touches that lingered, embraces full-bodied and intimate. Maybe a little too intimate for friendship. Taylor knew her side of it, her feelings for Gwen she'd always kept tucked away for so many reasons. Was she about to find out that Gwen had feelings too? Her heartbeat quickened.

"No. Well, yes. Kind of." Gwen shifted and looked over her shoulder. Her gaze found Taylor's. "But more."

Taylor held her breath. "More?"

Gwen nodded slowly. "There's more for me, Taylor." She turned away again. "Before I go on, though, I need to know if there's more for you too. If there isn't, we don't have to have this conversation."

Without a thought, Taylor was on her feet, stepping around the coffee table, moving toward Gwen.

"I mean, it seems like there is, but if I've misread things…"

Taylor stopped behind her, uncertain what to do next. She wanted to hear Gwen out, see what she was going to say, but she also wanted to touch her, hold her, kiss her again—like that kiss at the wedding.

"…I can work it out. I don't want our friendship—"

"There's more." Taylor's body heated as she ran her hands up Gwen's arms and pressed against her backside.

Gwen gasped and stiffened, then relaxed into Taylor's hold and eased her head back against Taylor's shoulder.

"There's more," Taylor whispered in Gwen's ear. "Definitely more for me too." She trailed her mouth down Gwen's neck, drawing a soft moan from her that lit a flame deep within Taylor.

Gwen spun around, her cheeks flushed, her eyes hooded and a darker blue than Taylor had ever seen them.

Was this what Gwen in lust looked like—perhaps the only side of her Taylor had never seen? She'd tried to imagine it at times, but nothing she'd conjured came close to this sight and the feel of Gwen's body against her.

Gwen twisted her fingers into Taylor's hair and pulled her mouth down to hers. Her kiss was hot and hard, demanding.

Taylor sank into it. A wave of heat stirred deep within her, the need for Gwen that she'd tried to deny, to evade, to hide and keep buried came rushing to the surface. She couldn't stop it, couldn't control it. She swept Gwen into her arms and crushed her to her.

The kiss went on and on, as though they'd both been lost in the desert for days and each was the other's first drink of water.

Gwen moaned into Taylor's mouth, encircling Taylor's neck, and pulling her still closer. She nipped Taylor's lower lip.

Taylor sucked in a breath. "Gwen." She groaned. "Christ. Gwen." She ran her hands down Gwen's back, over her ass, then back up beneath the sweatshirt. When her fingertips grazed bare skin, pure need ignited in the pit of her belly. Wet heat pooled between her thighs. She pushed her against the glass door, then reclaimed her mouth in a savage kiss.

Gwen returned it with equal fervor. She arched into Taylor, drawing up one knee and wrapping her leg around Taylor's.

Taylor pushed hard into her.

Gwen cried out and tore her mouth free. She threw her head back.

With a primal surge, Taylor bit the delicate flesh of Gwen's neck. She couldn't stop herself. Her lust flowed rampant, like the churning flood of water suddenly released from a long-locked sluice. Then she felt Gwen's hands on her chest, on her shoulders, pushing, thumping.

"Taylor!" Gwen's voice rose and broke into Taylor's awareness. "Wait. Please." Her breath came in shallow rasps. "I can't...I want... Please. Wait."

Taylor forced herself still. Her mouth remained on Gwen's heated skin, her body kept Gwen trapped against the door, but she regained her conscious thoughts. What the fuck was she doing? She panted. "I'm sorry." She loosened her grip and tried to ease away.

Gwen held her tight. "No. It was me too. Just stay right here for a minute." She pulled Taylor's head down to rest on her shoulder. "Please. Just wait."

Taylor's pulse began to slow, her breathing evened.

Gwen's hold relaxed. She lowered her foot to the floor.

"I'm sorry," Taylor said again.

Gwen laughed softly. "It seems," she still panted slightly, "we have a lot of pent-up sexual energy."

Taylor chuckled and eased away. "Ya think?"

"Please, don't go too far." Gwen trailed her fingers down the sleeve of Taylor's blouse. "Don't leave."

Taylor met Gwen's eyes and saw the apprehension in them. She shook her head. "I won't. But I need to get away from you or I'm going to drag you down the hall, throw you on your bed, and fuck you into Leap Year." She took a full step back.

Gwen nodded.

Taylor kissed her fingertips, then pressed them to Gwen's lips before moving toward the couch.

Gwen blew out a breath. "Okay." Her cheeks and neck were flushed a deep red. "I guess it's established that there's a two-way attraction between us."

Taylor sat on the edge of the cushion and waited for more.

Gwen watched her, her gaze steady, her expression intense, but she said nothing else.

"But we knew that. Right?" Butterflies fluttered in Taylor's stomach, then flitted into her throat. "Haven't we known that for a long time?"

Gwen still stood against the sliding door, her shoulders pressed to the glass. At length, she nodded.

"So what's next?" Taylor asked, uncertain what she wanted to come next. The easiest thing for her to have done in the previous moment would have been exactly what she'd said, to drag Gwen down the hall to her bedroom and fuck her as long as she could hold out. That wouldn't have been enough, though. Nor would it have been right. As soon as they'd finished, Taylor would have been consumed by regret. She wanted more with Gwen, and yet, she had no idea how to do *more*. She'd never done it before, never even wanted it.

Gwen looked to the floor and shook her head. "I don't know."

Taylor considered her, astonished. Gwen looked nervous, tentative, in doubt. And Gwen was never any of those things. Well, there was the time she'd been nervous about reuniting with her mother, who she hadn't seen since she'd been nine, but other than that, Gwen was always sure of herself and confident. But tonight, it'd be up to Taylor to take the lead. She softened. "Will you come over here and sit down so we can talk about it?"

Gwen looked hesitant. "I don't think so. I think I should stay over here."

"Okay." Taylor drew out the word to stall for time, hoping something else would come to her.

As though deliberately coming to Taylor's rescue, Gwen inhaled deeply and squared her shoulders. "I need to say some things, and after I do, you might not want anything next."

There was the Gwen that Taylor was used to. "I doubt that," she said with a smirk.

"Just listen, okay?" The slight quiver of her chin belied her recovered composure.

"All right." Taylor sat back on the couch and crossed her legs. "I'm listening."

Gwen gave Taylor a long look, while she pursed her lips and narrowed her eyes in a thoughtful expression. When she seemed collected, she swallowed. "First of all, I want you, Taylor. I've been attracted to you and wanted you since the day we met, but I've also grown to love you as one of my dearest friends. And I don't know what I'd ever do without you."

Emotion rose into Taylor's throat, and she had to fight back the beginning of tears. "I feel the same way."

Gwen seemed to relax. "Okay. So no matter what comes of this conversation, even if we don't pursue our evident attraction, and especially if we do, I want our friendship to always come first. One of the main reasons I've never brought up any of this before is that I'm so afraid of losing that." Her eyes brimmed with tears.

"We won't lose it," Taylor said gently. "I'd never let that happen. Sex is sex. Our friendship is so much more than that." Even as she said the words, she knew she could never merely have sex with Gwen. Anything they did would always be so much more. But that was best left for another conversation.

Gwen let out a long sigh. "Good." The corners of her mouth lifted in a relieved smile. "All right, that said, I've tried to put my attraction to you aside, to bury it, to forget, to stuff it down deep where no one can see it for all this time, and I can't do it anymore. I want you, and it's just getting harder and harder to fight. So I want to sleep with you." She put her hands on her hips, then folded them in front of her. Then she shoved them into the back pockets of her jeans.

Taylor stifled a smile.

"I want to have sex with you," Gwen said with assurance.

The boldness of Gwen's words, the flash of lust in her eyes, her adorableness in Taylor's too big sweatshirt—never mind the fact that she was wearing it at all—combined to send a jolt of desire through Taylor's body. "I want that, too, Gwen. And I've wanted it just as long." She started to rise.

"Wait." Gwen held up her hand. "There's more."

Taylor dropped back into her seat.

Gwen glanced around the room, as though avoiding Taylor's gaze. "Even though we know each other *very* well, there are things I do, things I require from anyone I'm thinking about sleeping with." A blush crept into her face.

Taylor picked up her water to cover her chuckle.

"And just because I know you, I can't let myself disregard those things. I need the consistency." Gwen faltered. "I need to know I can still hold to who I am with you." She gave a single nod, clearly more to herself than to Taylor, and met Taylor's eyes again. "So even though I know you get tested frequently, and I'm sure you would have told me and EJ if you'd tested positive for anything, I need to see your most recent results."

Taylor stared at her, then, unable to hold on any longer, broke into a huge grin. "You're so fucking adorable."

Gwen gasped and planted her hands on her hips. "Are you mocking me?"

Taylor burst out laughing. "No, I'm just adoring you."

Gwen eyed her. "And that's another thing," she said adamantly. "You can't do *that*."

"Do what?"

"All that charming, flirty, pick-uppy stuff." She waved her hand in the air. "All that stuff I've seen and heard you do with hundreds of women."

Taylor smirked. "You've always been prone to hyperbole."

"And none of that." Gwen pointed a finger at her. "No cuteness or teasing, not like you do with all the other women."

Taylor smiled as she rose from the sofa. "Gwen Jamison, are you jealous?"

"Stay over there," Gwen said. "We aren't finished talking."

Taylor paused.

"And I don't stand in line for anyone, not even you," Gwen continued. "What I'm offering you in return for what I'm getting is well worth it." She flashed Taylor a sultry look.

Taylor raised her eyebrow in interest. "So what you're saying is that as long as we're exploring this with each other, I can't see any other women?"

A look of surprise passed through Gwen's eyes, then transformed into a decision. "That's exactly what I'm saying."

"Okay," Taylor said simply. She had no doubt it would be worth it.

"Okay?" Gwen's shock was evident.

"Okay," Taylor said again. "As long as the same applies to you, and not only women." She slowly crossed the room to Gwen.

Gwen's eyes never left Taylor's, a tiny smile playing at the corners of her lips. "All right." Just as Taylor reached her and leaned in to kiss her, Gwen turned around to look out into the darkness.

Taylor slipped her arms around Gwen's waist and pulled her back against her. "And what about your test results?"

Gwen ran her hands over Taylor's forearms and along the length of her fingers where they interlaced over her abdomen. "I have the results from when I tested after Richard and I broke up, and I haven't slept with anyone since." She tipped her head back and shifted to give Taylor a sidelong look. "Will that do?"

"Absolutely." Taylor brushed her lips across Gwen's temple. "I guess this means we aren't doing anything tonight."

"Noooo." Gwen nestled her head in the hollow of Taylor's shoulder. "I don't sleep with anyone on the first date."

Taylor released an exaggerated sigh. "All these rules." She breathed in the scent of Gwen's hair, then dipped her head to kiss her neck.

Gwen sucked in a breath between her teeth at the contact. "Seriously, Taylor, do you understand why I have them and why they have to apply to you, too?"

"I do, baby," Taylor whispered. "I know you very well."

Gwen moaned softly. "You can't call me that. I can't be just one of the many."

Taylor ran the tip of her tongue behind Gwen's earlobe. "Okay. I do, my passion fruit," she said emphatically.

Gwen laughed and slapped Taylor's arm.

"I've never called anyone that before," Taylor said.

"I'm sure." Gwen played with the rings on Taylor's fingers. "Maybe baby is all right," she murmured. "It's better than passion fruit."

Taylor chuckled. "I promise I'll never think of anyone else when I say it." *Ever again.* "Would that make it okay?"

Gwen hesitated, tilting her head and pressing her ear to Taylor's lips. "I think so," she said distractedly.

The room stilled, and the air between them warmed.

Gwen felt so good in her arms like this. Not as a friend, hugging good night, but as a new potential lover. Taylor didn't want to break this unimaginable spell that had so unexpectedly been cast over them, but she had to ask the next question circling in her mind. "Are you going to tell me about the woman *you* were with? You know all about mine."

Gwen stiffened in Taylor's arms, her hands stilling, her grip tightening on Taylor's wrists. "Not tonight."

"Another time?" Taylor asked tenderly.

A long pause filled the space around them.

"Maybe," Gwen said finally. "Maybe not. Is that a deal-breaker?"

"No," Taylor whispered, squeezing Gwen in her arms. "Nothing's a deal-breaker with you."

Gwen relaxed and molded into Taylor's embrace. "Good." She resumed her stroking of Taylor's hands. "Now, you need to go home before I make an even bigger fool of myself by losing all my resolve and taking you to bed."

"If I promise not to let that happen, can I kiss you again?" Taylor was *pretty* sure she could keep that promise.

Gwen turned in Taylor's arms and tipped her face up to hers. "I'm holding you responsible."

And there she was again—Gwen in lust. The dark blue of her eyes shone with desire. Her lips, still swollen from the earlier make-out session, were so close to Taylor's. Gwen's body pressed hard against hers, one hip nuzzled firmly into the apex of Taylor's thighs, coaxing the ache that used to reside deep in Taylor's core to the surface. She'd never wanted Gwen so badly in all the years she'd lusted after her, never wanted any woman this badly. She claimed her mouth, this time with a more tender kiss.

Gwen tangled her fingers in Taylor's hair and returned Taylor's passion with obvious need.

It was like no kiss Taylor had ever had before, and she somehow knew everything with Gwen would be that way. Yet, something nagged at her. It flitted around in the back of her mind like a gnat buzzing too close to her ear. An annoyance. A reminder?

But in the softness of Gwen's mouth, the movement of her body against hers, Taylor couldn't make herself care.

CHAPTER FIVE

Gwen checked her reflection in the full-length mirror in her bedroom. She was definitely dressed for a date, even if she hadn't been confident that's what the evening was. But of course it was.

She and Taylor had ended the previous evening at Gwen's front door with another bone-melting kiss, some murmured expletives of exquisite frustration, and whispered good nights. They hadn't made any further plans to see each other, though. They were Gwen and Taylor. Of course, they'd see each other. But then this morning, Taylor had called, obviously trying to sound casual and easy, and asked Gwen if she was free for dinner. The exchange had been weird.

Normally, Gwen would have answered the phone much later in the day to Taylor's brusque, "Hey. Want to grab dinner?" More likely, it would have been a text.

Gwen would have replied with something pithy, "If you're paying." But today, Taylor had led with, "How are you this morning?"

How was she supposed to answer that? She'd fallen asleep still reeling from the confirmation that Taylor wanted her as much as she wanted Taylor, the feel of being in her arms, the urgency and heat of their kisses, but then she'd awakened to the light of day and the terrible question of whether she'd done the right thing.

When they'd gotten home from the wedding and Taylor had left for her own place, Gwen had been committed to, once again, collecting all her feelings and her attraction to Taylor and locking them away. This time, though, it hadn't worked. Instead of being able to sweep them all together, like dirt and crumbs into a dustpan, it'd been like attempting to clean up spilled mercury. The more she tried to scoop them up, the more scattered and unruly they became. Finally, she'd realized that this time there might be no turning back. Now that this thing between them had been acted on, everything was different. You can't unring the bell.

The idiom was something Namastacey would say. Why hadn't Gwen thought to talk to Namastacey before taking it upon herself to implement her drunken plan to keep herself out of bed with Taylor? Namastacey was more evolved than most and wise. She'd started a ministry in prison and expanded it substantially since she'd gotten out. And she'd been right there at the wedding, officiating. Gwen had gotten to know her over the past couple of years since Namastacey's conviction for assaulting a federal officer had been overturned due to new evidence. She'd been released for time served on her drug charges and settled near Jinx to be close to a friend. She and Gwen had a lot of deep conversations, and Gwen had found her counsel sage and helpful on more than one occasion. So why hadn't she pulled her aside or thought to call her once she'd gotten home?

Namastacey's rich alto voice touched Gwen's consciousness in answer. *Because you didn't really want to do anything different than what you did. It's time you and Taylor work this out.*

And now, they'd taken it even further. They'd talked about it, confirmed it, all but planned to cross the line that had always been in place by agreeing to exchange test results.

A shiver ran through Gwen, tightening her nipples and her thighs. An image of Taylor in a low-cut blouse and snug, black jeans from some night in a club when Taylor had been on the prowl formed in Gwen's mind. When they were out on the town and Taylor was focused on other women, Gwen watched her, took her in, imagined. She'd often wondered what it would be like to be the object of Taylor's undivided attention. So this morning, after Taylor's call, she'd gone out on a quick shopping trip for a new dress and the sexiest pair of shoes she could find on short notice, and if the image in the mirror before her didn't do the trick, she was at a loss for what would.

Shimmery red fabric with sporadic slices of sheer mesh that revealed a hint of flesh wrapped her body from the high neckline at her throat to where the skirt fell mid-thigh. Gold and ruby hoops, a Christmas present from Taylor a few years earlier, adorned her ears, and the heels she'd found on the spur of the moment, while they didn't *scream* fuck me, did whisper a convincing argument. It was time.

When Taylor had asked where Gwen would like to go to dinner, Gwen had tossed out Rudy's Hideaway in an attempt to lighten the awkwardness between them. But Taylor had readily agreed.

"I was kidding," Gwen said. "You know you need reservations to get in, even on a weeknight."

"I'll take care of that," was all Taylor said.

And when Gwen had received a text later in the day, she'd expected it to say they'd have to go somewhere else. She was surprised to find: *Hideaway, 7 pm. Meet me there? Late meeting.*

Gwen had almost played the you-can't-take-me-anywhere-you've-taken-other-women card, but with as much of a player as Taylor was, she wondered if there was such a place. Besides, Gwen loved Rudy's and could only afford it for very special occasions. Like finally bedding her best friend after ten years. To settle her nerves at that thought, she grabbed her purse and strode out her front door.

As she stepped into the dimly lit bar, the aroma of steak and seafood, mingling with other delectable smells, made her mouth water and her stomach grumble. She'd deliberately skipped lunch to ensure she could fully enjoy Rudy's. When she spotted Taylor, leaning over the cherrywood bar, in lively conversation with the bartender, she second guessed that decision. As she took in Taylor's dark hair swept back from her face to reveal her irresistible smile, the low neckline of her sheer black blouse, and the cross of her sexy legs clad in smoky gray linen slacks, a different kind of hunger overtook her.

Taylor was gorgeous. And Gwen wanted to have sex with her, to know what it felt like to be had by her. She wanted more too, though. Then why hadn't she told her? Gwen had said she wanted more than what they had, to explore what else was between them, but when the implications went only so far as sex, she hadn't taken it any further. Why not?

Because Taylor didn't do that. But would sex be enough for Gwen? It had been with anyone else, with the several men she'd gone there with. But Taylor was a woman. Was Taylor capable of more, though, and if so, could she have feelings like that for Gwen?

Seemingly of its own volition, Gwen's gaze traveled shamelessly down the length of Taylor's body. Yes, Taylor was Taylor. And Gwen did want her, even if nothing else came of it. Gwen was so tired of fighting the attraction, trying to keep it hidden, pretending it didn't exist. She wanted her. If she had to do some emotional clean up afterward, it'd be worth it. At least, she'd have the memory of being naked in Taylor's arms, being under her, on top of her, inside her. And Taylor wouldn't promise anything she couldn't deliver. She let women down gently, and she'd be even more careful with Gwen. It'd be up to Gwen to hold perspective and not allow anything to ruin their friendship, and Gwen would protect that with her life.

So here they were.

Taylor turned, and her eyes met Gwen's. She stilled, and the laugh that had been on her lips died.

Gwen shuddered as Taylor's gaze moved over her as tangibly as a touch, traversing every swell, following every curve. Goose bumps spread across Gwen's flesh. A surge of arousal burned through her. She bit her lower lip, trying to collect herself, then called her body into check, and started across the crowded room.

As Gwen approached, Taylor slipped off the barstool, her attention riveted on Gwen. "Wow!"

Gwen smiled.

"Where'd you get that dress?" Taylor's quiet question was almost lost in the din of voices.

"That thrift store run by the nuns," Gwen said teasingly. "You can find all kinds of bargains there."

"Uh-huh." Taylor's expression darkened with evident lust as she lingered on one of the mesh strips and the bare skin beneath it. "I've heard the Catholics are getting more lenient."

Gwen laughed.

"Here you go," the bartender said, offering Gwen a strawberry daiquiri. "For the lady."

Gwen arched an eyebrow in surprise. "Why, thank you. My favorite. How did you know?" She eyed Taylor. "You told him, didn't you?"

"I know everything about you," Taylor said with a grin. "At least, I thought I did." Her focus returned to the dress.

"It's just a date dress." Gwen shifted her hip onto the barstool Taylor had apparently been saving for her.

"Oh, no." Taylor settled back into her seat as the bartender walked away to help other customers. "I've seen you get ready for dates plenty of times. You never looked like you do tonight."

Gwen took a sip of her daiquiri. "This must be a very special occasion then."

Taylor slid her hand into the cleavage of her blouse and made a thumping motion over her heart. "I was hoping I hadn't dreamed our conversation last night."

"Hey, Taylor," the bartender said quietly, leaning over the bar. "Justine says your table's ready, and you need to get there fast. She's held it as long as she can."

"Thanks, Dave." Taylor picked up her own drink, then held her hand out to Gwen. "Shall we?"

Gwen studied her, impressed but suspicious. "How did you pull off a table at a prime hour on such short notice?" She entwined her fingers with Taylor's and let her coax her from the stool.

"It pays to know people," Taylor said, ushering Gwen toward the small, intimate dining room off the bar. "Stick with me, and I'll show you all the finest places."

And *this* was Taylor on a date. It's what Gwen had told herself she couldn't do, and yet, being the object of Taylor's attention brought a huge smile to her face.

When they were seated, Taylor placed an order for garlic cheese bread, Gwen's favorite from the list of appetizers, then settled back and studied the menu.

Gwen set her own aside, having already decided on the scampi, and sipped her drink. She pretended to take in the décor and ambiance around her— the nautical theme, the portrait of Johnny Depp as Captain Jack Sparrow—but sneaked peeks at Taylor as often as she could. She couldn't believe she was really sitting across from her as her date, that she'd actually had the conversation with Taylor that she'd denied herself for so long. She let her gaze linger on Taylor's amber eyes, then lowered it to Taylor's mouth. The memory of the heated kisses they'd shared the previous night rekindled the smoldering desire in Gwen's abdomen and between her thighs. She swallowed a soft moan rising in her throat. Suddenly, she realized Taylor's lips had spread into a wide smile. With a start, she met Taylor's eyes.

"I'd love to know the thought behind *that* look," Taylor said, her tone sultry.

Gwen's face and neck burned with a deep blush. "I...uh..." She scrambled for a lie out of habit, then caught herself. She didn't have to lie this time. She could tell Taylor exactly what she'd been thinking, and more. But could she really? She'd spent so many years hiding those thoughts, making jokes about them. Could she make such an abrupt change merely due to a conversation? "I'm sorry. I shouldn't be looking at you so—"

Taylor leaned closer to the table. "You can look at me that way all night long. And you don't have to turn away anymore when I catch you," she added playfully.

Gwen couldn't help but laugh at the memory of all the times that exact scenario had played out. She relaxed. Yes, she could do this. She let herself be drawn in by Taylor's reassurance. She leaned in and rested her forearms on the table. "I was thinking about kissing you last night, and how good your mouth felt on mine."

"Mmmm. I've thought about that all day." Taylor's expression shifted into one of seduction. "And how much I'm going to enjoy doing it again." The tip of her tongue darted across her lower lip.

The quick movement drew Gwen's attention back to Taylor's mouth. Taylor was right. She didn't have to avert her gaze any longer. She enjoyed the images that full, sensual mouth conjured in her mind and her body's response.

"And now?" Taylor's voice was low and husky. "What are you thinking now?"

Gwen met Taylor's eyes again. This time she wasn't blushing. She could play this game. She gave Taylor her sexiest look. "Now..." She drew out the word. "I'm thinking about how good your mouth will feel everywhere else."

Taylor's lips parted and she inhaled sharply.

Gwen leaned closer. "On my skin," she whispered.

Taylor's eyes narrowed.

"Between my—"

"Okay." She held up her hands. "You win this round. I give. If we're going to get through dinner, I can't go there."

Gwen laughed, thrilled with the conquest. She'd always believed she could match Taylor in a full-on sexual spar, and it felt good to have it play out.

Taylor gave her a sidelong glance, then smirked. "I'm going to enjoy getting to know this side of you."

Gwen's deep affection for Taylor flowed through her and mingled with this new aspect of their relationship. "Me too," she said lightly. She lifted her drink in a toast. "To getting to know each other better." She grinned.

Over their garlic cheese bread and salads, Taylor pulled a folded slip of paper from the pocket of her slacks and slid it across the table. "I brought this so you'd know I'm serious about our conversation last night. All of it," Taylor said, her voice steady. "It doesn't mean I'm expecting anything tonight, though."

Gwen arched her brows teasingly. "You aren't?"

Taylor chuckled. "Well, don't get me wrong. If we end up there, I'm not going to argue. But if, you know, if you aren't quite ready, or whatever."

Gwen picked up the sheet, then hesitated. It'd seemed so important when she'd been pondering whether to have the conversation with Taylor, and certainly when she'd asked for it the previous night, but here in the restaurant, surrounded by people, with Taylor across from her in some ways like any other dinner they might share, she felt foolish. Taylor was diligent about being tested regularly and practiced safe sex since she was seldom exclusive with anyone. Gwen winced inwardly at the memory of telling her she expected exclusivity from her if they were going to explore this with one another. She'd been stunned Taylor had agreed to that.

"What's wrong?" Taylor asked, concern etching her features.

Gwen studied her. "Taylor, I'm sorry I asked for this. I know I can trust—"

"I'm not." She slipped her hand over Gwen's. "I know you never make the decision to sleep with someone lightly and that you always ask for test results. The fact that you asked me for this, tells me you're taking this seriously. That no matter what it is we explore together, it isn't just because I'm convenient and easy."

"And you want that?" Gwen asked. "Something serious?"

Taylor's fingers tensed where they covered Gwen's, and her eyes widened almost imperceptibly. "Well, you know...I mean...We don't really know what it's going to be until we try it. Right?"

Amused by the instant fear in Taylor's expression, Gwen squeezed her hand. "Don't worry. I'm not proposing." She smiled.

Taylor's cheeks pinkened. "No. I know. I just like that you're treating me like anyone else you'd become sexually involved with. That's all."

"And I like that you're *not* doing the same." She unfolded the piece of paper and read through what was on it, then handed it back to Taylor. "Thank you."

"And yours, Lady Gwen?" Taylor asked with the tone and nickname she used when jokingly addressing what she considered the high and imperious part of Gwen's nature.

Gwen smiled and retrieved her own lab results from her purse.

Taylor made a show of giving it a full perusal before returning it.

"Scampi," the waitress said, setting a full plate in front of Gwen. "And lobster ravioli for you," she added to Taylor. "Is there anything else I can get for you?"

"This is great, Justine," Taylor said with a wave of her hand over the food. "And thank you for getting us in."

Justine winked at her. "Any time, sweetie. Enjoy." She smiled at Gwen, then moved off to another table.

Gwen watched her for a moment and couldn't help but wonder. She turned to Taylor.

"Straight and married and a friend who does me a favor once in a while in exchange for Bad Dog shirts for her kids at Christmas," Taylor said, saving Gwen the awkwardness of asking.

Gwen softened. She had to stop thinking about all the women Taylor had been with and simply let herself enjoy what was between them. Taylor was who she was, and Gwen knew all about her going in. She needed to relax. She'd done the hard part, broached the long-forbidden subject and told Taylor what she wanted. She'd gotten the response she'd hoped for. All that was left to do was allow it all to unfold.

Taylor parked in Gwen's driveway as she'd done hundreds of times. Tonight, though, she sat and stared at the house. The porch light was on, as well as the rows of tiny lights that lined the walkway, but the rooms behind the curtained windows appeared dark.

Since Gwen had driven her car to the restaurant, she'd gone ahead, leaving Taylor to put in a to-go order for a slice of Rudy's decadent coconut cream pie and settle the bill.

At the door, Taylor raised her fist to knock, then paused, uncertain whether to simply walk in as she normally did when Gwen was expecting her.

Gwen saved her the decision by opening the door and pulling her inside. Her mouth was on Taylor's before any words could matter.

Taylor shuddered, then stiffened as her arousal sparked, caught, and coursed through her. She slid her free hand to the small of Gwen's back and drew Gwen against her.

The kiss was hot and hungry, but slow and tantalizing at the same time.

Taylor sank into it. She slipped her tongue between Gwen's lips and took control, but she kept to the languid pace Gwen had set. She moaned at the feel of Gwen's arms encircling her neck and Gwen's body pressing firmly into hers. She grazed her fingertips over one of the mesh patches of Gwen's dress and her pulse leaped at the heat of Gwen's skin. The desire that had been raging in her since the night before ignited into full need. She wanted to take Gwen to the floor right there in the entryway, but what if this was the only time they'd be together, the only chance they'd have to explore this heat between them? She wanted to draw it out as long as she could.

As though struck with the same thought, Gwen slid her hands to Taylor's shoulders, broke the kiss, and eased away. She was breathing hard. "Wait."

"Yeah." Taylor cleared her throat, then released Gwen.

Gwen smiled sheepishly. "I'm sorry. I've wanted to kiss you all evening, so I couldn't help it." She ran her fingers through her hair. "But I didn't mean to—"

"No problem." Taylor grinned and took Gwen in from her lust-darkened eyes all the way down to linger on her painted toes peeking out from the straps of her sexy sandals. She let her gaze roam freely back up to Gwen's face. "I have to say, I like you like this."

Gwen laughed softly. "I'm sure." She took the to-go bag and turned in the direction of the kitchen.

Taylor followed her through the living room and noticed the numerous lighted candles. "So this is why you wanted to get home first? To set up your seduction? You realize I'm a sure thing, right?"

In the kitchen, Gwen opened the refrigerator and set the pie inside. "I wanted it to be pretty." She closed the door and turned around.

Taylor stood inches from her and gazed into her eyes. "What else do you want?"

Gwen looked her directly in the eye and trailed her fingertips along Taylor's shoulders through the thin fabric of her blouse. "You know what I like." She eased closer. "You, me, and EJ have spent enough late nights talking about sex for you to know exactly what I like. Unless you don't remember."

Fuck. How could she ever forget? Taylor had gone to bed those nights on fire, imagining doing all those things to her. "I remember," she whispered. She lifted a tendril of Gwen's silky, blond hair and twirled it around her finger. "I mean, what do you want specifically, from me, tonight?"

Gwen licked her lower lip, then drew it between her teeth. She took a long time to answer. "I want you to undress me," she said finally. "Slowly."

Taylor playfully quirked her eyebrow. "As opposed to ravishing you with your clothes on?"

"Nooooo." Amusement tinged Gwen's voice. "As foreplay."

Taylor studied her sultry expression, looked into her hooded eyes. "I'm not sure what you mean," she said innocently. Of course, she knew precisely what Gwen meant and how much it turned her on. Gwen had talked about it many times, and Taylor had fantasized about it many more—slowly, excruciatingly undressing her, kissing her, admiring her languidly between each layer following each new reveal. "Could you demonstrate? You know, just a little?"

A knowing smile shaped Gwen's lips. "I could do that if it will help you out." She ran her hands up Taylor's arms, the heat of her touch leaving a trail of tingles through the sheer fabric of the blouse. Then she traced the neckline down to the first closed button. She toyed with it as she leaned in and kissed Taylor lightly on the lips. Then again. "Like this," she murmured.

Taylor felt the first button give way.

Each time Gwen's fingers grazed Taylor's bare flesh, Taylor's breath caught. Each time her mouth covered Taylor's more firmly, Taylor tried to capture Gwen's in return.

Gwen slipped the tip of her tongue between Taylor's lips, then sucked gently on the lower one, all the while dancing her fingers over Taylor's bare throat, her collarbones, the swell of her breasts.

Taylor moaned and twisted her hands into Gwen's hair. She crushed her mouth to Gwen's in a searing kiss.

Gwen kissed her back hard, letting Taylor take her for only a moment. Then she entwined her fingers with Taylor's and coaxed her hands down to her sides. She eased away, leaving Taylor gasping for air. Without a pause, she dipped her head and ran her tongue between Taylor's breasts, several more buttons of Taylor's blouse now open.

Taylor arched into Gwen, her blood roiling through her veins, arousal pooling between her thighs, need pounding in her clit. She had to get control or Gwen was going to have her on her knees, begging.

Gwen buried her face in Taylor's cleavage and moaned. She gripped Taylor's hips and began to tremble.

Taylor wrapped her arms around Gwen's waist and held her tightly. "Are you okay?" she asked, trying to calm herself enough to wait for the answer.

Gwen whimpered, panting, her breath hot on Taylor's skin. She nodded.

Taylor eased back, her pulse slowing some. She slipped her hand between them and lifted Gwen's chin until their faces were inches apart.

Gwen's eyes were closed.

"Gwen," Taylor said softly. "Are you okay?"

Gwen's eyelids fluttered open. It took her a moment to focus. Then she nodded again. "Yes. I'm so okay." She steadied in Taylor's embrace and her expression cleared. "But I want you slowly, Taylor. You have to help me keep it slow. Please? I want to relish every touch. Savor every taste. Enjoy every sensation."

Taylor blew out a breath. "I, I don't—"

"Please," Gwen said again.

There was a look in her eyes Taylor didn't understand—a pleading, a desperate need. "Okay," she said, having no idea how she was going to manage it. But standing there, holding Gwen in her arms, feeling that look deep in her soul, she knew she'd do anything for her. *Anything?* A swell of anxiety challenged her arousal, and a warning bell chimed, soft and distant, in the recesses of her mind, but her desire to be with Gwen was too strong to let anything else get through. "Okay. Slow. Just give me a minute."

Gwen smiled and laced her fingers through Taylor's. "Come with me." She led Taylor to the couch, then kissed her with a tenderness that weakened Taylor's knees.

The breakneck speed at which Gwen was shifting from lust-crazed and desperate to gentle and sweet made Taylor dizzy.

"Sit," Gwen whispered against Taylor's mouth.

Taylor's lust surged through her, and she bit Gwen's lower lip, but in an attempt to keep her word about slowing things down, she eased onto the sofa cushions, bringing Gwen with her.

Without hesitation, Gwen shifted sideways, then settled across Taylor's lap, her breasts brushing Taylor's.

Taylor groaned at the pressure of Gwen's body draped across her mound. "You are so sexy." Taylor heard only need in her own voice. "And not just a little bit of a tease."

Gwen grinned, her expression darkening. She wrapped her arm around Taylor's neck and pulled Taylor's mouth to hers.

They kissed long and deep, the heat between them igniting into full flames, but somehow, it made Taylor want to draw out the tantalizing sensations, made her want to set every inch of Gwen's body on fire a fraction at a time. She ran her hand up Gwen's back to grip the nape of her neck and slid the other up Gwen's bare leg, beneath her dress, stopping a mere breath away from where she assumed she'd find the allure of silk or lace. Then she made the trek down to Gwen's knee, over her calf, and to the strap around her slender ankle. She took over the kiss, her arousal ramping up at the whimper that escaped from Gwen's mouth into her own, and slowly—so damned slowly—removed Gwen's shoe. When it dropped to the floor, she took her time caressing and massaging Gwen's bare foot, all the while cradling Gwen and kissing her more thoroughly than she remembered ever kissing anyone.

"Mmmm." Gwen tightened her embrace and nuzzled Taylor's neck. "You feel amazing and smell so good." She inhaled a long, deep breath.

Taylor tilted her head back, allowing Gwen more access. She moaned at the sensation of the tip of Gwen's tongue making tight circles along the sensitive flesh as she trailed her fingers up the length of Gwen's other leg.

This time, Gwen parted her thighs in a clear invitation.

Taylor couldn't hold back an evil smile. "Oh, no." She grazed Gwen's inner thigh with her nails. "Slow is what you asked for, so slow is what you get." She followed the lines of Gwen's toned muscles to the back of her knee, teasing for a long moment and enjoying Gwen's soft mewl of desire and frustration.

Taylor slipped the shoe from Gwen's other foot and let her touch linger along the curve of Gwen's high arch. She'd given Gwen foot massages before—innocently, when Gwen had returned from backpacking trips that left her feet sore, and not so innocently, a few times when she'd pushed the boundary between them, but always amidst other friends, forcing Gwen to behave as though nothing out of the ordinary was taking place. Tonight, no one had to pretend. They'd both known from the beginning where the evening was leading.

Gwen squirmed in Taylor's lap, her rising arousal evident in every rotation of her hips, every clench of her thighs.

Taylor had to have more, had to see more, had to touch and taste. She slid her hand up Gwen's back, reveling in the pressure to her nipples as Gwen arched into her, then she unzipped Gwen's dress—ever so slowly, as requested.

Gwen groaned through gritted teeth.

When the garment opened, Taylor slipped her hand inside, finding Gwen's silky skin beneath her fingertips. Her clit throbbed in response, wrenching a long moan from her throat. It wasn't as though she'd never had her hands on this part of Gwen's body. She'd spread suntan lotion on her shoulders, rubbed Tiger Balm into sore muscles, even scratched some hard-to-reach itches for her a few times—but *this* was so very different. This was erotic and tantalizing. This was causing the most delicious responses in Taylor's body and pulling the sexiest sounds from Gwen's throat. She squeezed her thighs together as she returned her mouth to Gwen's and explored every inch of her back. At length, she released the hooks of Gwen's bra and caressed the skin beneath.

Gwen's body jerked.

Taylor slid her palm around to the side of Gwen's breast and gently kneaded it with the heel of her hand.

"Oh, God." Gwen's voice was low and husky, her breathing shallow. She shifted in an obvious attempt for more contact.

Taylor obliged, flicking Gwen's nipple, then thumbing it with more pressure.

"Oh, yes," Gwen whispered.

With every ounce of self-control she could muster, Taylor kept her caress light and teasing. She stroked Gwen's nipple gently until Gwen's moans became one long groan, then squeezed it and rolled it between her fingers.

Gwen gasped and cried out.

The feel of Gwen's nipple hardening made Taylor desperate to see it. She eased back and coaxed the neckline of Gwen's dress from her throat and tugged the bodice down her torso. She sucked in an appreciative breath at the sight of Gwen's breasts. She couldn't hold off a second longer. She lowered her mouth to Gwen's stiff nipple and closed her lips around it as she returned her hand to Gwen's thigh and made her way up under the dress once more. This time, she didn't stop, and when her fingers found no silk, no lace, but rather sank into hot, wet folds, her own groan tore from her throat. She sucked hard and pushed deep inside Gwen, then withdrew to set a rhythmic pace.

Gwen arched upward into Taylor's hand, into her mouth. Her breath came faster, her moans louder.

Taylor's desire and need rose, but it was Gwen's that held her captivated. Gwen's arousal coating her fingers, Gwen's swollen and pulsing clit beneath her strokes, Gwen's hard nipples in evident need of continued attention from Taylor's mouth. She quickened the pace of her hand, alternating between slipping inside Gwen and teasing her opening, between long, languid caresses through her folds and tight, fast circles around her clit.

Gwen threw her head back, lifting her hips and spreading her thighs wide. "Taylor!"

Taylor trembled with anticipation. She sucked Gwen's nipple harder, deeper into her mouth at the same instant she pushed inside Gwen and pressed her thumb to Gwen's clit.

Gwen came with a scream. "Taylor!"

And Taylor had never heard a more beautiful sound in her life.

CHAPTER SIX

When Gwen recovered from her second bone-melting orgasm on the couch, she sat up and straddled Taylor's lap, then ran her fingers through the lush thickness of Taylor's hair. She trailed the tip of her tongue between Taylor's parted lips. It took one moan and the hard grip of Taylor's fingers on Gwen's hips for Gwen to decide she'd need a whole lot more room to do all the things she'd been wanting to do for years. She eased to her feet, let her red dress and bra slide to the floor, and took Taylor's hand. Without a word, she led Taylor to the bedroom, then pushed the sheer fabric of Taylor's blouse off her shoulders.

Taylor's skin was hot. Her eyes smoldered.

"Now," Gwen whispered. "What do *you* want from *me* tonight?" She cupped Taylor's full breasts through the thin fabric of her bra and squeezed. Her own arousal surged again at the sharp intake of Taylor's breath.

Taylor tipped her head back and closed her eyes. "Anything. Everything." The words vibrated low in her throat. "Show me what you've been wanting to do to me."

Gwen dropped her hands to the waistband of Taylor's slacks and had them down around her ankles in a heartbeat. She loved being undressed slowly, but she couldn't wait another second to have Taylor naked and hers. Ten years was plenty long enough. As she reached around to unclasp Taylor's bra, she claimed her mouth. She couldn't get enough of those soft lips and that skilled tongue. She tugged the undergarment free, then pulled her down onto the bed. Taylor's weight on her, their bodies fully pressed together, Taylor's mouth appropriating the kiss brought Gwen's lust to full flame again. It wasn't as though she'd never been in this position before, but this was different. Very different.

The feel of full breasts and hips against hers, the sensuous slope of a female back beneath her hands, the silky smoothness of a bare thigh wriggling its way between hers sent her reeling into the past. It'd been so long since she'd felt a woman's naked body on hers. Actually, she'd never felt a woman's body. It'd been *so* long, she'd been a girl, and so had—

"Oh, God!" Gwen cried out and lurched upward.

Taylor's teeth lingered where she'd nipped the tender flesh of Gwen's throat, sending shards of pleasure straight to her clit.

Gwen sucked in a breath. Taylor was *no* girl. Definitely a woman. So was Gwen now, though. And it was *her* turn. She thrust against Taylor once. Then again. She twisted beneath her and flipped them, claiming the top position.

Taylor's eyes widened, then narrowed. A prurient grin shaped her lips. "Okay." She settled into the bedding and stretched her arms above her head. "Take what you want."

The words set Gwen on fire. She pressed down hard onto Taylor, ran her hands up Taylor's arms, and interlaced their fingers, then took her mouth in a bruising kiss.

Taylor moaned beneath her and lifted her hips, her thigh still nestled between Gwen's.

Gwen drew out the kiss, long and slow and hard, taking the time to revel in the pure femaleness of Taylor—the curves and swells of her body, the slenderness of her hands, the scent of her skin and hair, the taste of her mouth...*Damn!* Her taste! She had to taste her. She broke the kiss and started downward along Taylor's neck to the hollow of her throat.

Taylor groaned and arched into her. Her nipples brushed Gwen's.

A primal need clenched Gwen's belly with a strength she hadn't felt in years. She moved lower, grazed her teeth along Taylor's collarbone, then captured her stiff, engorged nipple in her mouth. She released Taylor's hands and dragged her nails down Taylor's arms as she sucked hard.

Taylor tipped her head back and began to move beneath her. Her breath came faster. "That's it, baby. Take what you want."

The rasp in Taylor's voice, the rawness of her surrender, brought Gwen's need to a pounding throb in her clit. She ground against Taylor's leg.

Taylor moaned deeply. "Oh, yeah."

But Gwen wanted more. She wanted this to last. She savored the feel of one of Taylor's hard nipples between her lips, the other between her fingers. She licked and sucked, fondled and squeezed, all the while thrusting her hips into Taylor's mound until Taylor writhed beneath her. As aroused as she was, she wanted this to never end. She was entranced with the sounds Taylor was making, her gasps for breath. Gwen glanced up into Taylor's face, mesmerized by her anguished expression. As well as she knew her, she'd never seen her like this. Then a sudden realization struck her. Taylor hadn't come at all yet. Gwen wanted *that*. To see her climax, to feel her, to hear her, to taste her. She broke free from her trance and moved down Taylor's body.

Taylor groaned in obvious approval. She twined her fingers into Gwen's hair and guided her between her legs. "God, yes."

Gwen wasted no time. She nestled between Taylor's splayed thighs and slid her fingers through Taylor's wet folds. The feel of her soft, slick flesh, the scent of her arousal, the sight of her swollen clit stole Gwen's breath. As she leaned in, she caught a glimpse of that single gray hair Taylor had freaked about the previous week, and she started to smile, but her giggle was muffled, then cut off completely, as she covered Taylor's center with her mouth and began to feast. Her mind reeled with memories, with fantasies, with all the times she'd imagined this moment and told herself it would never happen.

She ran her tongue up the length of Taylor's slit, drinking her in, then spread her lips wider with her thumbs. Gwen wanted all of it, everything. She plunged her tongue into Taylor's opening, lapping and exploring. When Taylor started bucking, Gwen wrapped her arms around her hips and moved to her clit, circling, flicking, relishing.

Taylor's breaths became gasps, her moans cries. Her grip tightened in Gwen's hair, holding her firmly.

Gwen closed her lips hard around Taylor's clit and sucked as she plunged her fingers into her. She stroked and sucked until Taylor screamed and thrust her hips up off the bed. Gwen rode out the orgasm through its final spasms accompanied by tiny whimpers that slipped from Taylor's throat.

Taylor loosened her grip, but let her fingers play in the strands of Gwen's hair. "Fuck," she murmured finally.

Gwen smiled and pressed a tender kiss to Taylor's sensitive clit.

She lost track of how many times they made love throughout the night, how many orgasms Taylor gave her, how many times she got lost in pleasuring Taylor to climax.

Now, as the morning light streamed into her bedroom through the slightly parted curtains and she lay curled in the crook of Taylor's arm, she remembered similar long-ago nights she rarely let herself revisit. There was no point. They'd served their purpose, though, along with what followed.

It'd all taught her to guard her heart, especially with women. She'd learned early in life that there was a line with women better left uncrossed when it came to love. EJ and Taylor had shown her that a woman's friendship could be counted on, but even her mother's love, the one love that's supposed to be true and trustworthy, had failed her. Twice.

And romantic love with a woman? That had been a hard lesson learned as well. Had she learned it, though? She shifted onto her back and stared at the ceiling. Here she was, so many years later, naked, cuddled up with a woman, and feeling…Was it love?

This was Taylor, though. Taylor was safe. For one thing, Gwen had entered into this with eyes wide open, knowing exactly who and what Taylor was. And she knew Taylor's fears and limits as well as the reason for them. Taylor never let anyone have too much of her because she made bad choices when she did. So even if Gwen slipped up, which she vowed she wouldn't, she could trust Taylor to keep things in balance.

"Are you going to tell me about her?"

Taylor's morning voice was husky and low, pulling Gwen from her thoughts. Normally, and especially after everything they'd just shared, the sound would have warmed Gwen, but the question itself sent a chill up her spine. She'd never told anyone anything about *her*, at least not until a week ago when she'd blurted out that she'd slept with a woman before. And that had opened the door, and here they were on the other side. She considered playing dumb. *Tell you about who?* But that would only buy her a few seconds. Besides, Taylor deserved better than that.

Taylor turned and raised onto her elbow. She rested her head in her hand and studied Gwen. "It couldn't have been only once. You know your way around a woman's body pretty damned well," she said with a wink.

Gwen felt a tiny smile tug at the corners of her lips. She appreciated Taylor's attempt to keep the conversation light, but she owed her a response. She just didn't know what to say yet. There was no short answer, and the full one would overshadow everything they'd shared. "Not now," Gwen said quietly. She met Taylor's gaze. "Maybe another time?"

The playful glint in Taylor's amber eyes softened, and she trailed her fingers lightly through Gwen's hair. "Okay."

Gratitude for Taylor's understanding and patience welled in Gwen's throat. "Thank you."

"We can talk about how incredible you were last night, though. Can't we?" Taylor grinned.

Gwen's cheeks heated. She didn't usually get embarrassed over sex. She shook it off and turned in Taylor's embrace. "Of course." She giggled. "We can always talk about that."

Taylor chuckled and kissed her lightly. "So did you get to do everything you've fantasized about us doing?"

Gwen considered the question, its obvious answer in opposition to her earlier concerns about how she was feeling lying here with Taylor. Perhaps, the smart thing to do would be to simply say yes—after all, they'd explored a lot—leave it all as a sexual fling between friends, and return to their usual dynamic, only with less tension built up between them. Her heart would be safe, and that was the thing that really mattered. The response that went with that answer wouldn't formulate, though. Instead, some of the things they *hadn't* done, and a few that she'd like to do again, swarmed her mind. New desire stirred low in her belly, and she wrapped her fingers around the nape of Taylor's neck and pulled her mouth down to hers. "Not even close," she whispered against Taylor's lips. "But someone has to get to work."

"And who might that be?" Taylor murmured. She trailed kisses along Gwen's jaw, then sucked gently on her earlobe.

Gwen shuddered at the sensation of Taylor's hot breath on her skin. "You." The word slipped out on a sigh.

"Uh-uh. I left a voice mail for Brenda on my way from the restaurant last night and asked her to clear my schedule today." Taylor nipped and licked her way down Gwen's neck between words.

Gwen closed her eyes and pressed her head back into the pillow in pure pleasure. Her pulse quickened, and she moaned softly. "A little presumptuous, don't you think?"

"Well," Taylor drew out the word. "I know you're free to take time off," her voice was low and husky, "when EJ's on vacation, like you did yesterday." She brushed her lips along the top of Gwen's shoulder, then lower, finding the swell of Gwen's breast.

Gwen moaned in expectation.

"And," Taylor picked up where she'd left off. "I had high hopes you might want me to do the same today. I confess, I even brought a change of clothes." She shifted, and her mouth was gone.

Gwen gasped. "Don't stop."

"No?" A smile played in Taylor's voice.

Gwen fluttered her eyes open to meet Taylor's teasing gaze. "No."

After a slight hesitation, Taylor dropped several light kisses into the hollow of Gwen's throat and grazed her fingertips over Gwen's bare stomach.

Gwen exhaled and started to settle back into the cloud of desire and arousal she'd spent so many hours floating on.

"First, you have to tell me the one thing we didn't do last night that you'd like to do the most," Taylor whispered.

Gwen blinked back to awareness and stared at the ceiling. A current of uncharacteristic shyness rippled through her, leaving a warm blush in its wake. She'd thought of it several times during the night and wished she'd prepared for it, but all this had happened so fast. "We can't do it now." She tried to look at Taylor but could only manage a glance. "Not here."

"I'm intrigued." Taylor eased down beside Gwen and rested her head on her own arm, but she continued slow circles on Gwen's abdomen. "Tell me more."

Gwen dragged her attention away from the touch. "Do you remember several years ago when you were in the hospital with pneumonia?"

"Yeah." Taylor paused. "You want to play doctor?" Amusement tinged her voice.

Gwen laughed and turned her head to meet Taylor's gaze. "That could be fun too, but it isn't where I was going."

"All right. So where are we going?" Taylor's caress inched upward with each circle.

Gwen closed her eyes, her nipples tightening in anticipation. "Remember, you sent me over to your place to pick up some things?"

"Mm-hm." Taylor sounded distracted as she trailed her fingertips between Gwen's bare breasts.

Gwen struggled to remain focused on the conversation. After all, it was something she wanted Taylor to know. "When I was looking for your earbuds, I opened the drawer of your nightstand, and I found your, uh…" She shot Taylor another sidelong glance but, again, couldn't hold it. She looked away. "Your strap-on." There, it was out.

Taylor stilled. She lifted her head, lust and curiosity mingling in her expression. "Really?" She grinned. "You want to do that with me?"

Gwen smiled and turned onto her side to face her. "Yes." She draped her leg over the slope of Taylor's hip, opening herself to her. "But I don't have one. We'd have to go to your place."

Pure need flashed in Taylor's eyes. "I guess we'd better get out of this bed then."

"Not yet," Gwen whispered, pulling Taylor's thigh firmly between hers. The arousal that had made itself known at Gwen's first conscious thought that morning began to build and edged toward its release. Hungry for more of everything, Gwen dipped her mouth to Taylor's nipple and sucked it tightly between her lips.

Taylor released a deep moan as she snaked her arm around Gwen's waist and pulled her hard into her.

Gwen's body responded as desperately as it had at Taylor's first touch the previous night, but her mind was busy conjuring images of the two of them and the toy in Taylor's nightstand she'd been fantasizing about for so long. She came once again with a sudden surge, but it wouldn't be enough.

Taylor felt like a horny teenager. She couldn't remember the last woman who'd gotten her this revved up. Had there ever been one?

After Gwen's startling revelation about Taylor's strap-on, they hadn't been able to get out of bed for the remainder of the morning. She wasn't sure why Gwen's announcement had surprised her; after all, Gwen had certainly enjoyed Taylor's fingers inside her and clearly liked penetration. And the mere thought of being inside her in *that* way had stirred Taylor on until they both had to surrender to hunger pangs. After one last round in the shower, they'd ventured out into the world for a leisurely lunch at Hop Sing Palace, their favorite Chinese restaurant. Now, with that need sated, the rest of the day stretched open and free before them.

As she maneuvered her sports car through the streets of Sacramento, a comfortable silence enveloped them.

Gwen's hand rested high on Taylor's denim-clad leg, her fingertips grazing the seam along Taylor's inner thigh.

Taylor's clit twitched with each movement, fanning the embers of her arousal back into flame. "Did you get enough to eat?" she asked merely to distract herself.

"Mmmm. I did." Gwen turned sideways in her seat and closed her eyes. "Now, I hear a nap calling our names."

Taylor smiled at the sleepy tone in her voice. A couple of hours with Gwen curled in her arms wasn't something she'd say no to, but there was one more stop she wanted to make. "Can you handle a little shopping first?"

Gwen cracked open one eyelid and squinted at her. "You hate shopping," she said suspiciously. "Unless it's wandering aimlessly through Bed Bath & Beyond, in which case, I'm definitely going to need a nap beforehand. And maybe some other things."

"It's not Bed Bath & Beyond. And I doubt this will take long. Humor me. We're already here." Taylor pulled into the parking lot and slipped the car into a spot.

"What?" Gwen sat up. "Where?" Her mouth dropped open when she saw the sign on the building in front of them. "A sex toy store?"

"An adult boutique," Taylor said with feigned offense.

Gwen rolled her eyes. "It's a *sex toy* store." She glanced around. "And it's broad daylight." She laughed.

Taylor smiled. "You can put on your sunglasses. And I think I have a hat here somewhere." She reached behind Gwen's seat and rummaged through the collection of items she kept there. "I've never known you to be afraid of anything someone might think, though." Her challenge was deliberate.

"I'm not *afraid*," Gwen countered predictably.

"Come on then." Taylor reached for the door handle. "Prove it."

Gwen grabbed Taylor's arm, stopping her. "I can't imagine there's anything in there you don't already have."

She had a point. Taylor forfeited the game and answered seriously. "You're probably right." She settled back into her seat. "But this trip is for you. You said you wanted to try my strap-on."

Gwen tilted her head, a clear invitation for Taylor to continue.

Taylor stared straight ahead unseeingly and tapped her fingertips on the steering wheel, stalling. This was going to be revealing, something she wouldn't consider doing under normal circumstances. There was nothing normal about this, though, and her mind was reeling from it. She weighed her words. "Look," she said, trying to sound casual. "I take good care of my toys and anyone I share them with by cleaning and sanitizing them between uses." She winced inwardly. She sounded like a safe sex testimonial. She glanced at Gwen.

Gwen pressed her lips together in a tight line, the way she did when she was suppressing a smile.

Taylor sighed. "What I mean is..." She looked out the windshield again. How could she say this without it sounding like Gwen was special? But Gwen *was* special. Taylor couldn't deny that, and surely Gwen already knew it. How could she not? Taylor steeled herself and forged ahead. "You said you didn't want me to treat you like the other women I've dated, so if we're going to use toys, and I absolutely have no objection to that, I want to get new ones that'll be only yours."

When Gwen didn't respond, Taylor slid a sidelong look her way.

Gwen's expression had softened, and there was a tender glint in her eyes. She leaned across the console and pressed a light kiss to Taylor's cheek. "Let's go," she whispered.

They walked into the store hand in hand, and Randy, the assistant manager, sent Taylor a discreet wave from behind the checkout counter.

Taylor gave him a small nod, hoping Gwen didn't notice, but Gwen rarely missed anything.

"They know you here?" Gwen asked.

Taylor lifted one shoulder with nonchalance. "As you pointed out, I already have most of what's here." She considered Gwen curiously. "You don't have any toys at all?"

"Some. I'm just more of an online shopper when it comes to..." She glanced around the store. "Personal items." Her cheeks pinkened.

Taylor made no comment about her coloring, not wanting to embarrass her any more than she might already be lest she bolt. Instead, she continued as though they were discussing gardening or the weather. "I started coming here years ago before there was such a thing as online shopping, so I want to stay loyal to them for being here when there was nowhere else to get..." She cleared her throat and leaned in close. "Personal items."

Gwen laughed and pushed her away.

"Besides, if we order what we were talking about earlier online, we won't get it for a couple of days." Taylor guided Gwen around an endcap that displayed a variety of types and brands of lube on sale and into the aisle of dildos and harnesses.

Gwen's step caught, and her eyes widened, turning a darker shade of blue as she scanned the array of shapes, sizes, and colors laid out before her. A salacious smile took shape on her lips. "My, my."

Taylor grinned. "See? And if we'd ordered online, we wouldn't be able to explore what you want this afternoon. After our nap, of course." She squeezed Gwen's hand playfully.

Gwen's gaze roamed the shelves like a cameraman's sweep of a vast panorama. Her grip tightened around Taylor's fingers. "I feel a second wind coming on."

Taylor chuckled. Knowing this was where they were going to end up had kept her wired all through lunch.

Gwen released Taylor's hand and moved tentatively along the row. She stared, clearly awestruck, at each item she passed. She stopped in front of a dark purple, ribbed dildo, her breath imperceptible, as though she might be holding it. "I've seen all of these on websites, but I've never touched one."

"You can touch anything on display." Taylor stepped up beside her and picked up the one that had drawn Gwen's interest. She squeezed it, tested its weight, and turned it over in her hands to demonstrate, then held it out to her. "Store policy is that you can't take anything out of the box."

Gwen's eyes were hooded, her lips slightly parted, as she cautiously felt the tip, then closed her hand around the width.

A charge of need shot like electricity through Taylor straight to her clit at the sight of Gwen's slender, strong fingers gripping the dildo. A quiet moan escaped her before she could stop it.

Gwen looked up at her, her pupils dilated, her face flushed. Taylor knew the color wasn't from embarrassment this time.
"Do you like this one?" Gwen's voice was low and husky.
Taylor couldn't think. "I, uh, you need..."
Gwen slid her hand up the toy, then back down and let the heat of her skin touch Taylor's.
The motion seemed almost unintentional were it not for the shift in Gwen's breathing. In desperation, Taylor closed her other hand over Gwen's and held it tightly. "You need to stop that." She was both teasing and urgently serious.
Gwen smiled lustfully. "I *need* to get you home." She kept up her slow stroke. "Which one do you want?"
Taylor swallowed hard and struggled to focus. "You should pick." She let herself sink into the brush of Gwen's skin, the pull of her grasp. "The size has to be comfortable for you, and I don't know what you like yet, in that way."
Gwen stilled, and a question formed in her eyes. She tilted her head and studied Taylor briefly. Then realization dawned on her face. Her smile widened. She slipped the dildo from Taylor's hold and returned it to the shelf, then looped her arms around Taylor's neck. "No. *You* need to pick it."
Taylor shook her head. "It needs to be the size you—"
Gwen silenced her with a deep kiss. She languidly probed Taylor's mouth.
Taylor sank her fingertips into Gwen's hips and pulled her hard against her.
Finally, Gwen broke the kiss and tightened her embrace. She gently sucked Taylor's earlobe between her lips, then whispered, "*I* want to fuck *you*. I want to come deep inside you."
Taylor's clit went hard. Her nipples stiffened. Her knees threatened to buckle.
"Is that okay?"
Taylor opened her mouth but couldn't make any words come out. She managed a fervent nod.
Gwen eased back and met Taylor's gaze. "Pick the one you want me to do that with."
All other thought fled Taylor's mind, replaced by the image of what Gwen had just said. She made a quick scan of the shelves and found

the one she wanted. She grabbed two. "One for your house and one for mine," she said in response to Gwen's broadening smile.

Gwen laughed. "This is so much more fun than Bed Bath & Beyond." She turned and took a step toward the harnesses.

"Wait." Taylor grabbed her hand, almost dropping one of the boxes. "I want one for you too."

Gwen paused, then without another word, picked up two of the larger purple ones.

Taylor cocked an eyebrow. "Really?"

Gwen winked. "What can I say? I know what I like."

They spent some time perusing the harnesses, Taylor choosing her standing favorite, then answering Gwen's questions about the various options and their benefits. Taylor's arousal intensified as she watched Gwen's expressions and the gleam in her eyes as she examined each display until finally, when Gwen selected the boxer brief style with the O-ring in the front, Taylor had to walk down the aisle alone to relieve some of the pressure of her jeans on the throbbing pulse between her legs. On the way to the register, she grabbed a vibrating bullet to slip into the little pouch of the tight shorts as a special surprise for Gwen, then managed to get through the checkout process by chatting with Randy about his mother's latest surgery.

In Gwen's bedroom, Taylor snaked her arms around Gwen's waist from behind and kissed her neck.

Gwen paused her rummaging through the shopping bag and pressed back into Taylor's body. She moaned quietly, then gasped as Taylor nipped at her flesh.

Taylor's arousal had ebbed some during the checkout process and on the drive home, but the mere taste of Gwen's skin, the scent of her hair, the feel of her in Taylor's embrace brought it rushing to the surface once more. She wished they were already back in bed. More than that, she wanted Gwen's whispered promise from earlier, ached to feel Gwen deep inside her. She eased away and let Gwen return her attention to the contents of the bag.

Gwen pulled out one of Taylor's harnesses, dropped it back in, then one of the toys Taylor had bought to use on Gwen. She tossed it into the chair in front of her, then pulled out one of the same harnesses. She huffed in obvious frustration and tried again.

Taylor laughed and took the bag from her. She dumped out the contents. "There. That should make it easier. And faster."

Without answering, Gwen scooped up the specific articles she'd been looking for and started to turn away, then halted. "What's this?" She retrieved the vibrating bullet.

"There's a little pocket it goes in. In these." Taylor indicated the harness briefs. "You want me to show you?" She grinned as she watched Gwen's expression change from curious to enlightened.

Gwen glanced at her knowingly. "I'm sure I can figure it out. *You*," she placed her hand against Taylor's chest and pushed her onto the bed, "get naked." She sashayed into the adjoining bathroom.

Taylor groaned as Gwen closed the door behind her. It'd been quite a while since Taylor had been on the receiving end of a strap-on, and it didn't happen often. Most women she'd been with who enjoyed that kind of play wanted her to do the giving, so to speak, even if they maintained control overall. Taylor never minded. She always aimed to please.

She undressed and stretched out on the bed. She envisioned Gwen up over her, then beneath her, Taylor riding the dildo Gwen would be wearing in only a matter of minutes. How quickly and unexpectedly things could change. If someone had told her only a week ago she'd be stripped bare on Gwen's bed, Taylor would have suggested that person check themselves into a mental ward. And yet, here she was.

"Oh, my God!" Gwen's voice was high pitched coming through the bathroom door. "How do guys deal with all this stuff between their legs?"

Taylor chuckled. "They're more used to it."

The door opened and Gwen stepped out. "I have to admit, I feel a little ridiculous."

Taylor's breath caught at the sight.

Gwen wore nothing but the boi briefs that nicely hugged her hips and tight little ass, her bare nipples stiff points accentuating the beauty of her small breasts and the dildo jutting from between her legs, making Taylor ache for the feel of it.

Taylor whistled low and long. "You don't *look* ridiculous."

"No?" Gwen asked shyly.

Taylor rose and crossed to her. She remembered how vulnerable she'd felt the first time she'd donned a strap-on and what had eased her self-consciousness. She slipped one arm around Gwen and pulled her close, covering her mouth in a searing kiss. With her free hand, she cupped the base of the dildo and rotated it gently against Gwen's clit.

Gwen gasped, then cried out as she thrust into the pressure of Taylor's movements. She gripped Taylor's shoulders.

"No," Taylor almost growled as she pulled Gwen to the bed. "You're hot as hell."

They eased onto the mattress, Gwen crawling up over Taylor as Taylor backed her way to the pillows. No doubt which position Gwen wanted. They slowed every few seconds to deepen a kiss or begin a new one.

Wet heat burned between Taylor's legs. She was so ready but wanted Gwen to set the pace. She reclined and palmed Gwen's breasts as Gwen lowered her full length onto Taylor's body, the dildo nestling between Taylor's spread thighs. They both groaned.

"I'm not going to last long," Gwen said, her breath coming quickly.

"It's okay. We have plenty of time for more." Taylor's steady tone belied the precarious hold she had on her own desperate need and the hard throb of her clit. She'd be lucky if she'd be able to stave off her imminent orgasm past a couple of thrusts once Gwen entered her.

"What do I do with this?"

Gwen's question served as a diversion, and Taylor glanced at the wireless remote for the vibrating bullet she hadn't noticed in Gwen's hand.

Gwen's eyes were hooded and dark with lust.

"I'll take care of that." Taylor took the remote and slipped it into the waistband of the back of Gwen's harness.

Gwen eased herself up onto her knees between Taylor's legs and without the slightest hesitation pressed the head of the strap-on into Taylor's wet, swollen folds. She grasped the shaft and glided the tip up and down, over Taylor's opening, then her clit, then back down. "Is this okay?"

A guttural groan tore from Taylor's throat, and she arched, thrusting her hips upward for more. But there was nothing there. She focused on Gwen's face to find her smiling seductively.

"So I'm not the only one?" she whispered, then tapped the head of the dildo against Taylor's clit.

Taylor jerked in response, and she clenched her jaw and gripped Gwen's thighs. "Oh, God! Do it, Gwen, please. I need you inside me."

"Oooooh, yessss." The words slid from between Gwen's lips like a soft caress, and she leaned forward, sliding into Taylor, an inch, then easing back. Then another, opening Taylor little by little until she was finally firmly seated inside her, filling her. She held still, supporting herself on her hands, gazing into Taylor's face from above.

They stared into each other's eyes, suspended in time for a long moment.

In Gwen's expression, Taylor saw everything she'd wanted for years. She wanted Gwen, not merely like this, not just giving each other pleasure, not just fucking, but all of her, every day. She wanted Gwen to belong to her and wanted to be owned by her in return. "Gwen, please," she said again, but this time she meant more.

Gwen squeezed her eyes shut and pulled back until the tip almost slipped out of Taylor, then she plunged back into her. She began a slow, steady rhythm, claiming Taylor fully with each thrust.

Taylor watched, touched, and felt.

Gwen's expression shifted as she rotated her hips each time she pushed into Taylor. She groaned as she ground her mound against her. She arched into Taylor's hands with each squeeze of Taylor's fingers around her nipples.

Taylor's need doubled, then again. The feeling of being filled always drove her over the edge, but to be staring up at Gwen and having Gwen be the one to do it…she had no words. She couldn't even form a coherent thought. All she could do was pant and groan and lift her hips to meet Gwen's quickening pace.

"Oh, God. Taylor!" Gwen's voice rasped with desperation. "I'm going to come." She drove into Taylor harder and deeper.

"Yes!" Taylor grabbed Gwen's ass and pulled her in tightly against her. She pumped hard.

Gwen screamed, her body arching and twisting, her thrusts short and sharp, but so deep, Taylor couldn't hold back.

Taylor's orgasm consumed her, the strong, hot spasms starting at her core, then raging through her like a wildfire. When Gwen collapsed on top of her, gasping for air, Taylor retained her hold, continuing to pump her hips until her body began to calm.

They lay motionless yet joined in perfect silence, Taylor's arms loose around Gwen's waist and one of Gwen's hands gently covering Taylor's breast, her cheek warm against Taylor's skin. Taylor wanted nothing more than for this moment to never end.

"I've always wanted to do that," Gwen whispered into the hush.

And I'm the lucky one you did it with. Taylor lifted her head and pressed her lips to Gwen's hair. "It was amazing."

"Was?" Gwen brushed her finger across Taylor's nipple. "Who says I'm finished with you?"

Taylor heard lingering desire in Gwen's voice and hissed in a breath at the teasing touch. "Ah, the challenges of a younger woman," she murmured with a chuckle. She felt Gwen's mouth curve into a smile.

"You knew what you were getting into." Gwen lifted her head and shifted on Taylor.

The movement increased the pressure against Taylor's clit and her inner walls. Taylor moaned.

"And I think you're up to it." Gwen ghosted her lips across Taylor's. "Besides, we haven't done anything with that other toy."

"You're right." Taylor dipped her chin in a slight nod. "My apologies. I got distracted." She slid her hand lower and found the remote control still tucked snugly in Gwen's waistband. Familiar with the buttons, she switched the power on, knowing the vibration would begin on low.

Gwen gasped and jerked. "Ooooh," she said after a few seconds, then settled in. "That's nice. Can you feel it too?"

Taylor studied Gwen's face. She loved how her expressions revealed her sexual responses. "I can." She was still so sensitive from her mind-numbing orgasm, the hum of the bullet made her clench hard around the dildo inside her.

Gwen jerked again, obviously feeling the tug. "Mmmmm. I'm definitely not finished with you." She placed her hands on either side of Taylor's head and pushed herself up, keeping their bodies joined by the strap-on.

New arousal and the beginnings of another climax stirred deep and low within Taylor. She cupped Gwen's breasts, then thumbed the nipples. She wanted to say something clever, but when Gwen's eyes met hers, the connection stole her speech and her breath, even any thought. In their depths, she saw Gwen's renewed lust and desire, but there was something else, something Taylor had never seen there before. It called to her. And to Taylor's astonishment, and a little to her horror, something deep inside her began to awaken, a yearning, a longing to answer that call.

She slid her fingers into Gwen's hair and coaxed her down until their lips met. The kiss they shared was tender and sweet, but it reignited the fire between them.

Gwen began to move in a gentle rhythm, and with each retreat and slow thrust back in, she drew Taylor closer to her.

Taylor kissed her fervently, hungry for more of what she'd wanted for so long but never thought she'd get to have. As Gwen moved inside her, returned her kiss, made love to her—*with* her—Taylor surrendered.

CHAPTER SEVEN

Gwen leaned back on her elbows and gazed up at the azure sky. Two white, puffy clouds drifted across it. The sun warmed her cheeks, but the slight nip of the dancing breeze announced the arrival of what little autumn central California experienced. She inhaled the scent of the wild grass that carpeted the meadow and listened to the trill of the birds from the surrounding trees. A gentle wave of tranquility washed through her.

Taylor touched her lips to the corner of Gwen's mouth. "What's the cute little smile for?"

Gwen sighed, enjoying Taylor's closeness. "I'm absolutely content, and I'm basking in it." As far as perfection went, the past two and a half weeks had been as close to it as anyone could expect from daily life. There was the morning they'd been faced with cold showers because Gwen's water heater had died during the night, but even then, all they'd had to do was move to Taylor's condo until it was fixed.

They'd spent every night together and had met for lunch many of the days Taylor had gone to work. Gwen had checked her and EJ's email and messages from home and had answered most since she knew what EJ's responses would be. She'd even put out tires at a couple of stores over the phone so EJ wouldn't have to deal with them the second she returned. The few times she did go into work, she made a pass by Taylor's office to say hello, or drop off a milkshake from Gunther's, their favorite ice cream parlor.

The fun thing about it all was that no one noticed anything had changed between them. Apparently, nothing they were doing was out of the ordinary, except maybe for the evening Gwen had lain across Taylor's desk and Taylor had gone down on her until she'd begged for mercy, but there were no witnesses. And the nights and weekends were pure decadence, pampering, and fun. Yes, perfection indeed.

"Only content?" Taylor murmured. She slipped her hand into the opening of Gwen's unzipped hoodie while she nibbled at the curve of Gwen's neck. "I think we can up that game, don't you?"

Gwen hissed in a breath. Nothing and no one had ever felt as perfect as Taylor. So maybe she should tell her that. But what else would that bring up? She had other, more pressing things on her mind right now. She eased down to the blanket, luring Taylor along with her. "I'd love nothing more than to get naked with you right here and feel the sun on our skin and your hands and mouth all over me."

Taylor groaned and slid her thigh over Gwen's. "If there's a but coming, you'd better say it quick."

Gwen didn't want to stop. Being with Taylor in this new way made everything else seem to disappear. These past couple of weeks, she'd enjoyed the luxury of not having to be anywhere at a particular time. She could simply sit and revel in what they shared. As of today, though, that was over. EJ and Jinx were home, and Gwen and Taylor were on their way down to the family post-wedding gathering and the opening of the presents. Come Monday, Gwen would be back at work, at her desk by seven thirty and focused on everything that kept EJ's schedule running smoothly. Gwen and Taylor would still have their nights and weekends, but the daytime hours would no longer belong to them. And they might as well start getting used to it.

"You're right." Gwen struggled to catch her breath and shifted from beneath Taylor. "As much as I'd like to stay here, I also want to get to EJ and Jinx's. I've missed them. And Pete." She ran her fingers through her hair, hoping to make it presentable in case any cars were passing by when they got back to the road. "And the sooner we get there, the sooner we can tell them about"—she wiggled her finger back and forth between them—"about us." They hadn't even discussed it between themselves. They still had a couple of hours left to the drive, though. Maybe that could be a topic of conversation.

"That's easy for you to say." Taylor's words came out as a grumble. She rolled onto her back and laced her fingers behind her head. "EJ's going to be all over me. And I hate it when she does that ear-thwack thing she uses on her kids. It hurts."

Gwen smiled, then leaned down to kiss the pout off of Taylor's lips. "Don't worry. I'll take the blame. After all, I started it. *I* kissed *you* at the wedding. Remember?"

Taylor scoffed. "You were hammered. She's still going to say it's my fault. That I took advantage of your innocence."

"No. I'll explain that you were a perfect gentlewoman at the wedding and afterward. And it wasn't until we got home and I propositioned you that you took advantage of my innocence." Gwen batted her lashes playfully. It'd astonished and amused her when one night's pillow talk revealed the frequency of conversations over the years in which EJ had warned, threatened, and even forbidden Taylor where Gwen was concerned. EJ *was* protective of her, but Gwen hadn't realized to what extent it went in their three-way friendship.

"Yeah, right," Taylor said with a smirk. "If EJ only knew what you're like in bed." In a quick movement, she grabbed Gwen and pulled her on top of her.

Gwen giggled and squirmed against her in a mock attempt to escape. "I wasn't aware you had any complaints about me in bed."

"Oh, no, baby. On the contrary." Taylor tightened her hold. "I just hate that ear-thwack thing," she added in a whine.

Gwen laughed and broke free. She knelt, resting back on her heels. Taylor sat up and smiled at her.

Something Gwen couldn't quite name glimmered in Taylor's eyes. "What?" she asked suspiciously.

Taylor hesitated, then gave a small shrug. "I was afraid if we slept together, we'd lose this. You know, our friendship and the fun we have." She held out her hand to Gwen. "I'm glad we haven't."

Gwen eyed Taylor's reach. "Is this a trick so you can pull me back down and have your way with me in front of all these birds and squirrels and little butterflies?"

Taylor chuckled and let her hand drop to her lap. "You're on to me." She slapped her thighs and stood. "Well, if I'm not going to get any here, we might as well pack up and hit the road." She bent and picked up the container that had held the fried chicken.

Affection welled in Gwen's heart. She slipped her fingers around Taylor's. "I'm glad we haven't lost our friendship and the fun we have too," she said softly.

Taylor squeezed Gwen's hand in return and started packing up the basket. "What made you think of a picnic today?"

Gwen took a slow survey of the meadow, the trees in their fall colors, the mountains in the near distance. She warmed at the beauty. "I've always wanted to have a picnic right in this very spot." She scooted forward and snapped the lids onto the bowls still containing remnants of potato salad. "And since you appear to be my I've-always-wanted-to experience, it seemed perfect."

"How'd you even know about it?" Taylor took the items Gwen handed her as they worked. "It's pretty far off the beaten path."

"If you stay on this road another twenty miles or so, you get to the turnoff for the Vippasana center I go to for my meditation retreats. I've always loved the drive through here."

Taylor was quiet for a moment. "I don't know how you meditate for ten days." She looked at Gwen with apparent admiration.

Gwen recalled some of the difficulties but smiled at the overall memories. She was due to schedule another sit soon. "It has its moments, but I always come home clear-headed and centered."

"I can't disagree with that. You're definitely the one who keeps us all on track." Taylor stuffed the paper plates and chicken bones into a small trash bag and tied it off. "I don't know how EJ and I managed not to screw up our lives before we met you."

There was humor in Taylor's tone, but beneath it lay a subtle truth. Gwen went with the humor. "You two were a hot mess before you met me. Admit it." She lifted the picnic basket and stepped aside, then watched as Taylor shook out the blanket and folded it.

"No argument here." Taylor winked. "EJ probably would have kept on running right past Jinx, and I might have ended up cut up into a million tiny pieces and stuffed into a pickle jar by some *Fatal Attraction* chick."

Gwen frowned, remembering several women Taylor had been drawn to that had set off Gwen's warning bells. One in particular, several months after Gwen had stopped Taylor from leaving a bar with her, had landed in the local news, arrested for stalking and trying to kidnap a woman who'd broken up with her. "I must be rubbing off on you." She looped her arm through Taylor's as they headed toward the car. "Your taste in women has gotten markedly better as of late."

"You could have rubbed off on me years ago instead of making me wait so long," Taylor said sulkily.

"You weren't ready until now." Even with everything new they'd shared, Gwen still loved their old banter and taking the superior position. "Besides." She giggled. "From what you've said about how strongly EJ's been protecting me from your wicked ways, we had to get her married off and focused on something else before we could slip under her radar."

In truth, Gwen would have no trouble thanking EJ for being a concerned friend and also gently reminding her that Gwen was a grownup. She'd assure her that she knew Taylor and understood the limitations of what they could have. She might even take the opportunity to share her own caution regarding getting involved with a woman and why. But then again, maybe not. Having kept that aspect of her thought system under wraps had enabled her to be the voice of encouragement for EJ when her feelings for Jinx became apparent. And after all, it wasn't that she believed *everyone's* heart was at risk being with a woman. Only hers.

"You want me to drive?" Taylor asked, tossing the blanket into the back of the car.

"No!" Gwen said excitedly. She placed the picnic basket beside their suitcases and closed the hatch. "I love all the twists and turns on this road. I want some more time putting my baby through her paces." She patted the top of the crossover affectionately.

"All right." Taylor strode to the passenger door. "Shotgun it is then."

Gwen checked her phone for a signal to send EJ an update on their arrival time, then slipped it back into the pocket of her hoodie. Reception was always sketchy through these hills. She'd text her when they got to the freeway.

"So," Taylor said, holding up the puzzle page from the morning paper in one hand, a gossip magazine in the other. "Crossword? Or stupid news?"

Gwen buckled her seat belt, then started the engine. "Crossword, I think." She smiled as she pulled into the lane and accelerated smoothly down the road and into the first curve.

"Okay, let's start with the no-brainers." Taylor opened the console and fished out the mechanical pencil Gwen always kept there. "Clean up, as in manuscript."

"Seriously?" Gwen shot her a glance.

"Edit," Taylor said, ignoring Gwen's ridicule of the ease as she filled in the squares. She scanned the page. "Ah, here's another one. Martial arts master, Bruce." She looked at Gwen expectantly.

Gwen sighed. "Lee. I want a harder one."

Taylor added the second answer. "Okay, let me find one." She tapped the page. "Here you go, Miss Smarty Pants. A combo track bet," she said in obvious challenge.

"How many letters?" Gwen asked.

"Six. The fifth is the 't' from edit." Taylor leaned back in her seat, seemingly settling in for a wait.

"Exacta," Gwen said.

"What?" Taylor sat up straight. "What's an *exacta*?" She examined the puzzle as though searching for an explanation there.

"It's a combination bet on the winning and second place horses in specific order," Gwen said matter-of-factly.

"How do you know that?"

"A guy took me to the track on a date once," Gwen said, slowing a little as they approached a blind curve. "Needless to say, I never went out with him again, but I learned a lot about horse racing and gambling that day."

Taylor chuckled. "Note to self." She scribbled in the margin of the newspaper page. "Never take Lady Gwen to the horse track."

Gwen laughed, then gasped as a mid-sized truck swerved into view directly in front of them. She stiffened and gripped the steering wheel, then wrenched it to the right.

Tires screeched. The world slowed. The truck skidded, the driver's expression stricken through the windshield. Taylor screamed.

Finally, impact. A blast of pain. Then blackness.

Taylor floated into consciousness. Something squeezed in on her. Her chest was constricted. She fluttered her eyes open, then clenched them shut against stinging wetness. She licked her lips—something bitter—the metallic taste of blood.

Everything flooded back. The jolt of the collision. The crush of the seat belt. The car rolling and rolling. A flash of Gwen yanking the steering wheel. The engine chugged, still running.

Gwen! Where is she? Taylor forced her eyes open and lifted her hand to swipe them clean. She fought against something. *Have to find Gwen.* She tried to push forward. Something pressed into her face.

Airbags. She began to focus. "Gwen?" Her voice croaked. She cleared her throat. "Gwen?" she said louder.

No answer.

Fear seized Taylor and overrode everything else. She fumbled for her seat belt release and twisted, only marginally aware of the pain in her ribs and her wrist. She pushed aside an airbag and let out a cry.

Gwen slumped in the driver's seat, broken glass caught in her hair and blood covering her face and chest. Her left leg bent unnaturally, angled by the crushed metal.

Taylor blanched, feeling faint. She gulped in air. She couldn't pass out. Then she heard a sparking sound, and the smell of gas filled the car. Her heart leaped. They had to get out.

She shoved open her door, losing her balance in the process. She tumbled out onto the ground. Sharp pain shot up her arm when she tried to lever herself to a sitting position. She cringed. *Have to get Gwen.*

She grabbed onto the edge of the seat and managed to get to her feet, then stumbled around to the driver's side, using the car for support. The world spun.

"Gwen?" she whispered, leaning close to Gwen's ear. "Can you hear me, baby?"

Silence.

"I've got to get you out. It might hurt." She slipped her hands behind Gwen's head and shoulders through the broken window and eased her forward to rest against the steering wheel. With one hand still on her to steady her, Taylor reached into the car and released the latch, then pulled. The door didn't budge.

The gas fumes grew stronger.

Hurry! The pounding of her heart throbbed in her head. She grabbed the outside handle with both hands and yanked hard.

A squeak and a groan from crushed hinges. The door creaked open an inch.

Panic swelled within Taylor, and she gripped the freed edge, gritted her teeth, and wrenched the door until it gave way.

She had to jump back quickly to get around it and almost fell again. What was wrong with her leg?

She bent and wrapped her arms around Gwen's waist and let her fall against her. Then she lifted. Thank God Gwen was small. And what if the car hadn't landed on its wheels? Taylor had a fleeting thought of going to the gym more regularly. She pulled Gwen free from the wreckage, falling backward into the dirt. Something sharp dug into her shoulder, but she held tight to Gwen. She scooted along, dragging Gwen with her. She couldn't stand again without something to grab onto. Little by little, she increased the distance between them and the car—and the running engine and the gas.

She should have felt relief and safety, but something was wrong. Why hadn't Gwen moved? Or made some kind of noise? Even unconscious, wouldn't the jostling and pulling hurt? Didn't people groan in pain even if they weren't awake?

Finally, Taylor bumped into something hard. A rock or a tree? Something. She panted. Her body ached. She had to stop. She shifted Gwen onto her back, then moved over her. She couldn't see. She wiped the blood from her eyes, but the blood on her hand only mingled with it. Her blood. Gwen's blood. There was so much blood. Would Gwen still be bleeding if she were…

Taylor couldn't bring herself to conjure the word. *She can't be.* She felt Gwen's throat, then pressed her ear to Gwen's chest. *Please.* Her eyes burned. Her head spun.

Then there were voices…people yelling. A loud explosion.

Dizziness overtook her. Then nothing.

CHAPTER EIGHT

G wen drifted in darkness.
No. It wasn't dark, but nor was it light. And there was no weight or mass or volume or breath. It was nothing, and yet it was everything. *She* was everything.

She couldn't hear, yet there were shouts and sirens. She couldn't see, but flashes and movement were all around her. There'd been a torrent of pain, and now, nothing. She had no body.

There were people. They were with her, surrounding her, and yet they weren't. She knew them or felt them. No, she *was* them—all of them. She was Gwen Jamison with Taylor Matthews, on her way to EJ and Jinx's. She was Taylor, nearby, head throbbing, fragile bones in her wrist broken, leg weak and swollen. She was the doctors—an intern who hadn't slept in thirty-seven hours, an attending whose husband was trying to get out of Afghanistan. She was the nurse whose wife and little boy were planning a surprise party for her twenty-eighth birthday, unaware she'd found the receipt for the cake order. She was the woman with red hair in the corner who'd only come into the ER to drop off dinner for a friend. She felt their fatigue, their fear, their joy, their shock.

She looked down. There was her body, so small on the table, torn and bloodied, hooked up to machines and stabbed with needles. Its eyelids were lifted, and a light shined in, a tube down the throat. But that wasn't her. She was everything else.

"She's in V-fib!"

A feeling from behind Gwen, a knowingness. She floated higher, turning. A light, beckoning her. She moved toward it.

It grew and brightened and then she was in it. No, again, she *was* it. And there was peace.

The light became blue. The blue turned to sky. She drifted downward, and trees came into focus beneath her. A grassy meadow appeared. And once again she had feet that touched the soft ground at the top of a hill. And in a shallow valley below, a cream-colored building called to her in silent welcome.

It seemed far away, made small by distance, but her first footfall landed soundly at the bottom of the steps leading to familiar double doors. Where had she seen them? They were painted the rich green of full spring, the handles shimmering golden in the brightness all around.

Gwen had to enter. A soft humming from within summoned her.

The doors swung open as she reached them.

She moved down a long hallway, more gliding than walking. Children's artwork decorated the walls, and the unmistakable smell of floor wax tickled her memories. The linoleum shone with a high polished gleam.

She knew where to go. One, two, three. She counted the doorways past where the corridor intersected with another, then automatically turned into the room with the number nine beside it.

She heard the chirping of birds through the open windows of her fourth-grade classroom and the tapping of chalk on the blackboard. The humming continued. She expected what she saw, and yet... She blinked. How could it be?

A woman, tall and slender with gray hair, stood at the front of the classroom, an open book in one hand, the other raised to the chalkboard. She looked exactly the same as the last time Gwen had seen her.

But that was almost thirty years ago. Would she still be alive? And how could she look the same? Gwen stared, overcome with emotion. "Mrs. Walker?" Her voice sounded small. It wasn't really a question. The actual question was, where was this place?

Mrs. Walker turned. "Hello, child." Her tone was warm and soft as it'd always been.

Then Gwen knew. "I'm dead?" A wave of uncertainty broke over her. She'd thought about death but hadn't ever come to any firm conclusions. Was she ready?

Mrs. Walker smiled gently. "In this precise moment in the world, you are. But not to worry. It isn't time for you to stay."

She'd been one of those rare adults who would actually answer a child's question, and Gwen had learned to rely on that. When Gwen had needed that kind of honesty the most, though, Mrs. Walker had no longer been in her life. She'd been Gwen's teacher the year Gwen had been put into foster care in another school district. It was the last she'd seen of her. But now, here she was once again to answer Gwen's questions.

Her presence comforted Gwen, as did the classroom in which she'd felt so safe. She took in her surroundings, the colorful bulletin boards decorated in paper fall leaves, the small tables and chairs, and the tenderness of the woman in front of her. "What happened?" she asked. "Why am I here?"

"You were in a car accident." Mrs. Walker set her book on one of the desks in the front row. "Do you remember?"

Gwen tried. At first, all she could comprehend were her current surroundings and the safety and solace she felt there. She didn't want to think of anything else. But then a burst of noise shattered the tranquility.

"Charge to three-fifty," someone yelled. "Clear."

Something pulled at Gwen, tugging her backward. She saw the truck coming toward her, heard a scream, felt the jolt of impact. The terror of that moment flooded her. She focused on Mrs. Walker. "Vaguely," she said in answer to the question. "But I don't want to." She walked to the window and gazed outside.

Instead of the meadow she'd first seen, a playground with its tetherball poles and basketball hoops stretched out until it became a grassy area where she used to sit at lunch. *Why did I come here?*

"This is a time and place you felt loved and cared for," Mrs. Walker said as though Gwen had asked the question out loud.

Gwen spun around. "How did you—"

"We're one here. The only reason you see me in this form," she said with a wave of her hand, indicating the room, "is to help you understand. And it's me and this place you're seeing so you won't be afraid."

"But I *don't* understand," Gwen said, feeling like a child all over again. "How are you here? How are *we* here? Does the school even exist anymore? And even if it does…" She looked around her. "This classroom is exactly as it was when I was nine. That can't be."

"All things can be as they are in all times simultaneously. Come, let's talk." Mrs. Walker held out her hand.

The gesture brought tears to Gwen's eyes. It was one she remembered well. When Mrs. Walker held your hand, you knew everything would be okay. She took it, and when they turned around, the wall of windows faded away and there was nothing but the playground, then the grass. Mrs. Walker sat, and with only a brief hesitation, Gwen followed suit.

"What would you like to know, child?" The warmth of the endearment she'd always used matched the smile she offered Gwen.

Questions filled her mind. What was happening? Why was she here? How did she return? Was Taylor all right? Gwen wasn't sure she was prepared for the answer to any of them. She flashed back to what she'd already asked. "You said in this moment in the world I'm dead, but that it isn't time for me to stay. What does that mean?"

"Your physical body is dead in terms of how the world defines death. Your heart has stopped beating. Your lungs aren't breathing. Your body isn't responding to stimuli, but as I said, it isn't your time."

Panic seized Gwen, constricting her chest. "How long do I have? I mean, before it's too late?"

"Time isn't the same here. We can talk until your questions are answered."

Mrs. Walker spoke of it all so matter-of-factly it almost confused Gwen more. She forced herself to concentrate.

"But your physical body has sustained serious injuries and needs to heal," Mrs. Walker continued softly. "And it can't heal without the presence of your essence, your consciousness. And *that's* the part of you that's here."

Gwen didn't want to think of her body, lying dead on the table in the emergency room with everyone scurrying around it, trying to bring it—her—back to life. Then the image of Taylor on a similar table flashed in her awareness. "What about…" She couldn't bring herself to finish.

"Taylor will be fine. She'll be there when you return, along with EJ and Jinx."

Gwen blinked in surprise. "How do you know about EJ and Jinx?" Or Taylor, for that matter. This was all too bizarre.

"I know about everything in your life, everything you've been through before and since that last day I saw you in my classroom." Mrs. Walker's tone was patient. "I know your mother left you and you went into foster care."

"When did you learn everything that happened?" This was all so confusing. How could she *know* any of it?

"Only now," Mrs. Walker said simply. "You have to remember, there isn't such a thing as time as the world knows it. There is now, and there is always, and they're the same."

Gwen squeezed her eyes shut, trying to make sense of it.

"As I said," Mrs. Walker went on, "you're only seeing me in this form because this is how you knew me, how you remember me. So what I'm here to tell you might be easier for you to hear."

Gwen wasn't certain how to continue. She took a moment to absorb her surroundings once more. It all seemed normal, and yet, something was so different. "It feels so good here. *I* feel so good here. It feels like…"

"Like love." Mrs. Walker's voice was rich and smooth like warm syrup flowing over pancakes.

"Love," Gwen whispered. Yes, like love.

"That's all there is where we are." Mrs. Walker gazed up at the sky, the light that seemed to have no source shimmering on her skin. "Love is all that's real, so when we're free of the trappings of the physical world, we recognize it's all we are."

Gwen studied her, amazed at her words and wisdom. "How do you know all of this? It feels right and true when you say it, but I can't hold on to that feeling. It keeps slipping away."

"I know it fully because no part of me remains in the physical world. But as I said, it isn't your time to stay here yet."

A stronger sense of the love Gwen felt washed over her. She closed her eyes and let it overtake her, then it ebbed once more. With reluctance, she opened her eyes again. "Can I stay if I want to?"

Mrs. Walker smiled with evident understanding. "Not now. There's eternity for that."

"Why not now?" Gwen wanted to keep this feeling, this sense of love. "And who decides?"

"Because you haven't completed what you set up for yourself in your current life," Mrs. Walker said, answering the first. She squeezed Gwen's hand. "And *you* determine it all."

Gwen sighed in frustration. "How do I do that when I don't know what's going on?"

"You do know. Just not in the way you're accustomed. As I've said, we're one. I am the part of you that knows everything."

"Ugh!" Gwen flopped down onto the grass. "Can't you just tell me then?"

Mrs. Walker's eyes sparked with what looked like amusement.

If she was a part of Gwen, she was an irritating part.

"I can tell you, but you still won't *know* it." Mrs. Walker considered her. "You have to experience something in order to truly know it. And the only place we can experience anything is in physical form in the physical world. That's what that world is for. It's like a classroom. It's where we go to learn."

"Tell me anyway." Gwen put a challenge in her voice. "You always said I was precocious."

Mrs. Walker laughed. "All right. You have to go back in order to learn to trust love. It's one thing to be able to feel it and accept it here, in a place where there's no alternative choice like fear or guilt, no past to draw on that says love can't be trusted. *Here*, you've never known anything else that you think says differently, but in the physical world, you've created a whole story that tells you differently, and it's your journey in this lifetime, or as many lifetimes as it takes, to work that out and see that love really is all there is *anywhere*."

Gwen's overload alarm blared in her head. She pressed her fingertips to her temples. "Oh, God! That didn't help at all."

Mrs. Walker patted Gwen's leg. "You see, child. There's a reason we don't know things until we're ready."

"But how am I supposed to do it when I don't understand any of this?"

"Don't worry," Mrs. Walker said, her tone as reassuring as ever. "You won't be alone. There is someone there to help you."

Gwen opened her mouth to release her next barrage of questions but was cut off.

"Why don't you relax here until your mind and heart settle more? Sit for a bit with what we've discussed before you go back."

"But—"

"And there's someone else here who would like to see you."

"There is?" Gwen sat up and gazed across the grassy meadow in the direction Mrs. Walker pointed. A white speck in the distance seemed to be moving toward them. Gwen squinted, but suddenly it was much closer—a beautiful dog, tongue lolling and gray ears flopping as he ran.

Her heart leaped, and she gasped. "Dexter!" She scrambled to her feet and raced toward him.

He barked wildly.

When they met, Dexter sprang into her arms, knocking her off balance. They tumbled to the ground.

"Oh, my God. Dexter, is it really you?" Tears flooded Gwen's eyes as heavily as the last time she'd seen him when she and her second foster mom, Connie, had to take him to the vet to have him put down. But these tears were so different.

He covered her face with wet, sloppy kisses until she grabbed him in a tight hug and held him to her. She inhaled, soothed by the comforting fresh scent of the oatmeal conditioner the groomer used. This place was so amazing.

He wriggled from her embrace and dashed around her, then lowered his front half to the ground, his tail wagging in the air. A Frisbee appeared out of nowhere—as, apparently, everything did here—on the ground between them, and he barked, his invitation to play.

Gwen got to her feet and started after him when he turned to run. Then she remembered Mrs. Walker. Were they finished? Could Gwen stay and play with Dexter? She turned to find yet another shift in this odd world.

Mrs. Walker stood in her classroom again, waving from an open window. "Go ahead," she said, her voice quiet in Gwen's mind. "You'll have a lot to deal with when you go back. Have some fun now."

Gwen took only a few seconds to think about it. A lot to deal with? She could only imagine. Somewhere in the far recesses of her consciousness, she heard a steady, high-pitched tone and someone yelling for another push of epi, but she was here now in this place of love, with Mrs. Walker, with Dexter, with a sense of freedom she'd never felt before. She ran like a carefree child after Dexter.

"Exacta." The voice was strong. Gwen's voice.

Taylor chuckled at the things Gwen knew, that she was willing to try. Horse races. Skydiving. Taylor.

"There's more for me, Taylor. Before I go on, though, I need to know if there's more for you."

The words swirled in Taylor's head as though on the stirring of a gentle breeze, but something else was there. A hard throb. An ache.

Taylor moaned as she drifted into consciousness, then sank again. She turned her head. Gwen covered in blood.

"Gwen!" Taylor bolted upright. Burning agony in her ribs stole her breath. Arms encircled her, holding her tightly but gently.

"Taylor, it's okay." EJ's voice. "You're okay." She rocked Taylor.

"Gwen." Taylor choked on the word.

"Gwen's alive," EJ said soothingly. "Try to calm down. You have injuries." She stroked Taylor's back.

Taylor clutched at her. Pain surged everywhere—her head, her middle, her wrist, her leg. She breathed in the familiar fragrance of EJ's perfume, nestling into the solace of her embrace. How was EJ here? Where was here? Taylor opened her eyes, then squinted against the stab of light. She was in a room, a bed. The smell of medicine and antiseptic hung in the air. Sunshine slipped between the narrow slats of miniblinds covering a window. "Where?"

"You're in the hospital," EJ said. "Do you remember anything?"

Taylor tried. All that came was the bloody image of Gwen, but EJ said she was alive. "Gwen. Blood."

"Yes," EJ said, easing Taylor back onto the bed. "You and Gwen were in a car accident. You both survived, though. Because of you." She caressed Taylor's cheek with her thumb.

Taylor blinked up at her, searching her face for more. Her head pounded.

"The driver of the truck that hit you and another man who stopped couldn't get down the hill to you in time, but they saw it all. They said you got out, then pulled Gwen from the driver's side before the car exploded. You have some bruised ribs and a broken wrist, and probably a concussion. And a tear in your anterior cruciate," EJ swallowed hard, "I don't know, a ligament in your leg, but…" Her voice broke. She began to cry. "Oh, God, Taylor." She covered her face with her hands.

Then Jinx was there, taking EJ into her arms.

EJ recovered quickly, wiping her tears and turning back to Taylor. "I'm sorry." She cleared her throat. "I don't know what I'd do if I'd lost you both. But you're here, and you're awake."

Something in EJ's demeanor alerted Taylor that there was more. "And Gwen? You said she's alive."

EJ exchanged a glance with Jinx.

Panic gripped Taylor. "EJ? Tell me, damn it."

"She's alive," EJ said weakly. "But she isn't awake yet. And her injuries are more severe than yours."

Taylor fought back her fear. *No. Please.* She'd just found her. "How severe?" she whispered.

"Her skull was fractured, and her left leg was broken in two places."

Taylor replayed the moment of impact. "Yeah, she yanked the steering wheel to the right, so the truck crashed directly into her door." The memory sickened her. "But she's going to be okay?" She looked imploringly at EJ. "Please? Tell me she is."

EJ swallowed hard.

"Taylor," Jinx said softly, stepping in. "They lost Gwen in the ER. She died, but they got her back. She had surgery on her leg and a subdural hematoma, but she has a lot of swelling in her brain, so they couldn't close her skull again. She's in the ICU, and they're watching her closely. As soon as the swelling goes down, they'll take her back into surgery."

Taylor's mouth was dry, and nausea crawled in her stomach. She fought back bile. "How long will that take?"

EJ took Taylor's hand and held it tightly. "They don't know, sweetie."

Taylor felt the strength of EJ's grip, but also detected a tremble. It hit her how hard this must have been on EJ, sitting and waiting to see if her best friends were going to live or die. She squeezed EJ's fingers, in the hope of offering her some comfort as well. "How long has she—have we —been out?" she asked. "How long have you two been here?"

"The accident was the day before yesterday," Jinx said, rubbing EJ's shoulders. "We came as soon as they called."

"How'd they know to call you? We were out in the middle of nowhere."

EJ bit her lower lip, clearly attempting to fully regain her composure.

Jinx went on for her. "Gwen's phone was in her jacket pocket, and amazingly, it was still usable. EJ's her emergency contact."

"Well, well. Look who's awake," a woman in light blue scrubs said from the doorway. She crossed to the bed and pushed a button on the side, elevating the head a bit more. "I'm Lydia, your day nurse. Let me take some vitals, then I'll get the doctor. He'll want to give you a once-over."

Taylor spent the next couple of hours being poked and prodded, undergoing tests and questions, even learned she'd been in surgery, too, for her wrist. She wore a cast on her left arm and hand that she'd been too groggy and preoccupied to notice when she first woke up, and her ribs were taped because two of them had sustained hairline fractures, probably from being jammed against the car door handle.

Dr. Avery was a pleasant, seemingly young, and soft-spoken man with freckles across his cheeks and bright red hair. He couldn't be as young as he looked, but he made Taylor feel old.

"Well," he said as he wrote something in her chart. "It looks like you'll be back on your feet pretty quickly. You'll need to wear a brace on that leg for a week or so before it'll be able to hold your full weight. I want to keep you here for observation for another day or two, but I don't anticipate any problems. Lydia will give you a list of things to watch for with the concussion. If you experience *any* of them, tell someone immediately, and if it's after your release, get back here right away." He finished scribbling. "Any questions?" He met her gaze.

"Can I see Gwen?" She'd asked earlier but had been put off in deference to her own well-being.

Dr. Avery looked at EJ and arched an eyebrow.

"Of course." EJ moved to Taylor's side and took her good hand in both of hers.

Surprised, Taylor glanced questioningly between EJ and the doctor.

"Okay," Avery said. "I'll make arrangements, but not until tomorrow." He closed the chart. "I want you to rest for the remainder of today." He was out the door before Taylor could protest.

The nurse had hooked her up to a morphine pump earlier, but the lingering pain still made her edgy. "What was that about?" she asked more grumpily than she'd intended.

"What?" EJ pulled the recliner she'd been sitting in during Taylor's examination up beside the bed and settled into it.

"The eye contact and you being the one to say whether I can see Gwen."

EJ covered Taylor's good hand with hers again. "I'm Gwen's legal and medical power of attorney. It falls to me to say who's considered family, among other things."

Taylor leaned her head into the pillow and sighed. "I guess I never thought about the fact that you must be that for both of us. Did you have to make any decisions for me I should know about? You didn't accept any marriage proposals for me while I was out, did you?"

EJ chuckled. "Well, there was this intern that had her eye on you, since you look so sexy with your head all bandaged up and in that hot hospital gown, but I shooed her off."

Taylor laughed, then coughed, then winced in pain. "Don't make me laugh," she said when she'd caught her breath.

"Sorry," EJ said, offering her a cup of ice chips Lydia had left on the side tray.

Taylor shook her head.

"I did sign the consent forms for the surgery on your wrist and gave them your medical history and insurance information. I also put Jinx down as an approved visitor." EJ's expression grew serious again. "We've been back and forth between your room and Gwen's in ICU. We didn't want either of you to be alone when you woke."

"You've been here at the hospital the whole time?" Taylor asked, astonished.

EJ's eyes brimmed with tears. She cleared her throat and swiped them away. "We got a hotel room nearby for when we need a quick shower, but so far, we've been here."

Taylor surveyed the room in curiosity. "Where's here? What hospital is this?"

"Community Regional Medical Center in Fresno."

Taylor could only nod. EJ sounded weary. Taylor studied her, noticing for the first time the dark circles beneath her puffy eyes and the fine lines aging her skin at least ten years. EJ sat forward in the chair, but her shoulders sagged under the weight of stress and fatigue. "You and Jinx should go to the hotel and get some sleep." Taylor was fading as well between the exertion of her exam and the morphine. She let her eyelids flutter closed.

"Now that you're awake, we probably will. But I can't let go of you yet." EJ tightened her grip on Taylor's hand. "I was so afraid of losing you. Both of you." She choked on a sob and buried her face in the bedding.

Taylor gave her fingers a quick squeeze, then released her and stroked her hair. "Shhh. I'm okay. And we just have to know Gwen is, too." She tried to take a firm stand on the last sentence, but she had to see Gwen for herself, touch her and talk to her, even if Gwen couldn't talk back.

EJ sighed.

Taylor didn't know if it was from the comfort of her touch or the despair and worry of not knowing Gwen's outcome.

"She won't wake up for a while," EJ said, her head still resting on the bed beside Taylor. "They have her strongly sedated until they can take her back into surgery to close up her skull."

Taylor clenched her jaw against the thought of Gwen lying in a bed somewhere so vulnerable. A stab of pain shot through her head as though someone had stuck a metal spike into her temple. She winced.

EJ sat up. "Are you all right?"

Taylor waited for it to pass, then tried to open her eyes. She couldn't. "I think I need to sleep."

"Sure," EJ said, grasping her hand once more. "I'll be right here."

Taylor wanted to tell her to go get some rest herself but was engulfed in blissful darkness before she could form the words.

The next time she stirred into consciousness, she was first aware of the beeps of the machines she was hooked up to. Slowly, she remembered. A hospital, a car accident, Gwen, EJ. She shifted and was instantly reminded she had fractured ribs.

"What's the matter?" Jinx asked.

She wasn't talking to Taylor, though. She couldn't be. Her voice wasn't nearby, and it was hushed. Taylor opened her eyes and saw EJ and Jinx seated together on a small couch across the room. EJ was pale, staring down at an open folder she held. A manila envelope lay in her lap.

"Yeah, what's wrong?" Taylor's voice croaked.

EJ jerked her head up, clearly startled. Her eyes were wide.

Jinx rose and crossed to the bed, blocking Taylor's view.

It seemed like a casual move, an accidental interruption of Taylor's line of vision, but Taylor knew better. Jinx had become EJ's guardian at the gate in the time they'd been together. She offered distraction when EJ needed a moment, held the world back for her when a bigger break was required. The tactic wasn't usually used on Taylor, though. Or Gwen. In fact, Gwen had developed her own version of it as EJ's admin assistant.

"Need some water?" Jinx asked as she stepped up to the side of Taylor's bed.

"That'd be great," Taylor said, her voice still raspy.

Jinx picked up the pitcher from the side table and filled the plastic cup beside it. She held the straw to Taylor's lips.

Taylor sucked in a mouthful, swished it around, then swallowed. She moaned. "Water's never tasted so good," she murmured.

Jinx retreated a pace, leaving EJ in sight again.

EJ had closed the file and was sliding it into the envelope. "You're awake again," she said with an obviously forced smile.

"What's the matter, EJ? What were you reading?" Taylor couldn't help but wonder if it was something important.

"Nothing pressing." EJ rose and left the envelope on the cushion.

"Good evening, everyone." A tall, heavy-set man who looked to be in his late thirties entered the room. "I'm Damian. Lydia has other pesky responsibilities like feeding her kids and dogs, so she left you in my capable hands for the night." He looked directly at Taylor. "I'll be your night nurse, so anything you need, just press that." He pointed to the call button. "And I'll come as soon as I can."

"Sounds like a deal." Taylor stifled her annoyance at his untimely entrance. What the hell was in the folder?

"For now, let me take your vitals," Damian said, busying himself. "Then they'll be bringing you some dinner."

EJ started gathering the things she'd had on the couch. "We'll head down to the cafeteria and grab something to eat so we're not in your way."

Taylor watched her. Whatever EJ had been reading had shaken her, but Taylor could wait. EJ needed rest. "Why don't you two go get some real food somewhere, then head to your hotel and get a good night's sleep. I'll be fine with Damian here." She flashed him as bright a smile as she could manage. "And you said Gwen won't be awake for a while."

EJ straightened and met her gaze. "Are you sure? We can stay until you've eaten and are settling in for the night."

"No. You need to take care of yourselves because I'm in no shape to do it right now if you get sick," Taylor said teasingly. Then gratitude overcame her. "Thank you for being at my bedside when I woke up and for being here through all this, but go get some sleep."

EJ smiled softly. "I could really use a shower."

"Exactly." Taylor waved her good hand in front of her face. "You both stink."

They all laughed and the tension in the room eased.

"All right. We'll be back first thing in the morning." EJ crossed to the bed and gave Taylor a gentle hug. "Sleep well."

Jinx stepped up after her and said good night with a quick kiss on the top of Taylor's head. "I'm so glad you're back," she whispered.

Taylor playfully pushed her away. "Get out of here before you make me cry."

Taylor watched Jinx slip a supportive arm around EJ and EJ sag into her as they turned the corner into the hospital corridor. Their relationship was one that was envied by many, Taylor included, if truth be known. But now, she had Gwen. Or she'd had Gwen. What if those few weeks were all the Universe was to grant them? A snippet. A tease.

Taylor thought of Gwen lying somewhere in the hospital, her skull open, her brain swollen, the rest of her body battered and broken. She couldn't stand it.

Gwen had to make it. She had to come back to Taylor. She wouldn't leave her now. Would she? Now that Taylor was so desperately in love with her and had admitted it—finally—to herself?

Taylor's heart ached. Why hadn't she told her? She knew why. She had to tell her tomorrow. She could only hope Gwen would be able to hear her.

Chapter Nine

Something flickered in Gwen's consciousness. A faint light? A sound? She drifted toward it.

Pain. Searing. Excruciating. It assaulted her, consumed her, tore at her flesh and bone. Her head, her torso, her leg. Everywhere. She wanted to scream, but something choked her. And the agony. She retreated. But there was that flicker again, tugging at her.

"Gwen. I'm here."

A voice. Distant. Familiar. It called to her, but she didn't want to go. Nor did she want to be where she was, in a thick, sooty fog. She wanted to be with Dexter and Mrs. Walker again. In the light and the love. She'd had only a moment when Mrs. Walker had appeared beside them as they lay in the cool grass next to the stream after running and playing for what felt like hours. And she'd known immediately.

It was time.

Gwen had hugged Dexter once more, then stepped into Mrs. Walker's tender embrace. Then a jerk, and the meadow had vanished, the woman and dog with it. The peace shattered.

"Clear!" someone had yelled.

She'd slammed back into her body just as lightning burned through it.

Since then, she'd been floating in and out of a dim awareness but never conscious. She sensed a surface she was beneath, a line that would need to be crossed at some point, but there was pain there. And the fog was thick and dark and kept her in its depths. But now, there was a voice, calling to her, luring her like a warm beacon in a frigid night.

"Gwen, can you hear me?"

Yes. She wanted to answer it. It was comforting. She wanted to go to it, but it was too close to the pain. That unbearable pain.

"Gwen. I'm right here, and I'll be here. You just rest and heal."

She relaxed. Her heartbeat slowed. She drifted on the solace as though it were a soft cloud carrying her. Where? *Someplace safe. No. Not safe.*

The memory was so vivid, she could feel every detail. Strong arms held her. A firm body pressed against her. She opened her eyes to a bright morning and frightened green eyes gazing at her.

"Gwen, you gotta get up. Into your own bed. Before we get caught."

"Fire," Gwen whispered. She ran her fingers through flame-red hair, its golden highlights sparking in the sunlight. But it couldn't be Fire. Fire was gone. She'd *said* she was here, though. Hadn't she? Hadn't it been Fire's voice?

"Gwen, c'mon. Hurry. Deborah's already up. We fell asleep last night."

Gwen heard the words. Their meaning registered, but Fire's skin was so warm against hers, their bodies so snugly fitted together in the single bed. Just one more second.

The door opened. "Okay, girls. It's time to get—" Deborah gasped. "What the hell?"

Gwen's heart leaped into her throat. Her stomach clenched. She couldn't speak.

"Deborah, it's not what you think," Fire said, a frantic pitch garbling the words. "Gwen had a nightmare."

Deborah yanked back the blankets. "And you both just happened to be naked? I'm not stupid." She grabbed Gwen by the arm and jerked her to her feet. "Get some clothes on." She shoved her toward her own bed on the opposite side of the room. "Both of you!" She scooped up the football jersey Fire slept in and threw it in her face. "I'm calling your social workers. I won't have this in my house." She stalked from the room.

"Shit!" Fire ground out the word.

Gwen bit back tears. "I'm sorry."

"It's not your fault, babe. We both fell asleep."

A dream. A nightmare. *No, no, no.* It couldn't be happening. Not again. A memory Gwen had kept locked away for years. The question that had always haunted her bubbled to the surface. Why didn't she move when Fire said to? If she'd even been standing in the middle of the room when their foster mother had opened the door, things would have turned out so differently.

Taylor's stomach churned as EJ replaced the receiver of the wall phone outside of the Intensive Care Unit and they waited to be admitted. She hadn't slept well, between the dull headache, the throb in her wrist, and the image of Gwen's bloody form slumped in the driver's seat every time she did manage to drift off. And she'd only been able to choke down four bites of bland oatmeal at breakfast because EJ wouldn't take her to see Gwen until she ate at least a little.

She swallowed her anxiety and a little bile at the back of her throat. Was she ready for this?

EJ had tried to prepare her by reminding her of Gwen's injuries, her surgeries, and some details about Gwen's appearance, but surely she couldn't look any worse than the last time Taylor had seen her.

The double doors in front of them swung open in a ghostly fashion, and EJ wheeled Taylor into a large room edged by three-sided cubicles, each holding a single hospital bed, a conglomeration of machines, monitors, and other medical equipment. Bags hanging on poles held blood and clear liquid that ran down through tubing into still and quiet bodies. Curtains at the ends blocked the view into some.

EJ didn't hesitate. She pushed Taylor past the nurses' station in the center, then turned at the corner. "Hi, Lori," she said with a quick wave to the woman behind the counter.

Lori smiled at her.

Clearly, EJ was no stranger here.

"You must be Taylor," Lori said, shifting her gaze. "I'm happy to see you up and around."

"Thanks." Was she really expected to socialize in a hospital gown? She wore a plush maroon robe Jinx had brought over it, but the whole situation still left her feeling exposed. She was out of her element and vulnerable. She folded her arms and hugged herself, tightening the robe around her.

"Can we go in?" EJ asked Lori.

"Sure." Lori glanced to the corner behind her. "Krista's in with her, but that'll be okay."

"Thank you." EJ slowed as they approached a cubical. "Ready?" she asked Taylor softly.

Taylor inhaled and nodded.

EJ eased back the curtain.

All Taylor saw at first were the machines, a half-full bag hanging from an IV pole, and someone leaning over the bed, blocking the view. The person was murmuring something she couldn't hear.

"Lori told us we could come in," EJ said, entering no farther, "But we can come back later if—"

The figure straightened and spun sharply. It was a woman in scrubs. She looked startled, then smiled and patted her chest. "I didn't hear you. You can come in now." Her auburn hair framed her face in a collar-length cut, its waves softening her slightly angular features. "And you're Taylor." She stepped away from the bed. "I'm Krista MacKenna, one of Gwen's nurses."

Taylor was supposed to say something, but she'd seen Gwen, and her attention was riveted. The blood drained from her face, and she grew lightheaded. *Christ!* She'd been wrong. Gwen *could* look worse than the last time Taylor saw her.

Pale and still, Gwen lay, tiny and frail, in the large hospital bed. She wore a cast that covered her left foot up to just below her knee and there were bandages around her thigh. The leg was elevated, suspended in some contraption. Her left arm was also wrapped. She looked fragile and broken. The worst, though, was her head. It, too, was swathed in thick gauze, but it was misshapen somehow, one side sunken, as though no bone protected the delicate brain matter inside.

Taylor swallowed hard. What had EJ said? Something about swelling and the surgeon not being able to close it? So they just left her like that?

EJ ran her hands over Taylor's shoulders, then squeezed them gently. "You're trembling. Are you okay?"

Taylor inhaled a shaky breath and nodded. She wasn't, but she didn't want EJ to take her back to her room. "Can I..." Unable to manage more words, she pointed to the side of Gwen's bed.

"Of course." EJ maneuvered the wheelchair into place and set the brake. She remained behind Taylor.

Taylor could only stare at Gwen's slack features, her pallor, the dark bruising coloring one cheek and temple. A tube ran from her mouth to a machine on the other side of the bed, a ventilator. It pumped and sucked air in and out of her lungs.

"You can talk to her, if you'd like," Krista said quietly.

EJ returned her hands to Taylor's shoulders, then rubbed her upper arms.

The touch fortified her. She cleared her throat. "Can she hear us?"

"No one knows for sure," Krista said. "But it's possible, so I always encourage patients' loved ones to talk to them."

Taylor let her gaze travel down Gwen's broken body as she listened, and it fell on Gwen's small, limp hand, its color almost as white as the sheet beneath it. She thought of the warmth of Gwen's touch, the caress of those fingers across her cheek. If only they could go back to their picnic, or one of their evenings cuddled up on the couch watching a movie. Why did time have to be so unforgiving?

Taylor shifted forward in the wheelchair and draped her good arm over the bedrail. She tentatively touched Gwen's hand, then grasped it gently. She looked up into Gwen's bruised and battered face. She had no idea what to say.

"I'll give you a little time," Krista said, moving toward the curtain.

"Thank you, Krista," EJ said. She stepped away, then appeared on the other side of the bed.

Everything seemed to be moving so slowly, and yet, every detail seemed crystalized with intense clarity.

EJ picked up Gwen's other hand and leaned over her. "Gwen?" she whispered. "Taylor's here to see you. She's going to be fine, and she's going to need you to keep her in line soon, so you have to wake up." She caught Taylor's eye across the stark bedding and smiled weakly.

Taylor got the message. She tightened her grip on Gwen's fingers and eased closer. "Yeah," she said, hearing her voice almost crack. She steeled herself and began again. "You'd better wake up before we got into trouble." She needed to say more, though, to tell Gwen she loved her and beg her not to leave her. But if she went down that road, she'd start crying, and if she started, she wouldn't be able to stop.

"Now that you know Taylor's okay," EJ said, "you can concentrate on getting back to us, put all of your energy into healing."

EJ sounded bright and confident, but it was forced. Taylor could hear it and was certain Gwen could too. "You have to fight, Gwen. You

can't give up." Her voice grew stronger. "I need you. We need you."
Tears burned Taylor's eyes and spilled onto her cheeks.

EJ was instantly at her side. She knelt and put her arms around
Taylor. "Shhh, it's okay. She's going to be okay."

Taylor nodded, unable to speak.

"Let's get you back to your room. You need more rest too."

As they emerged from the cubicle, Krista pushed off from where
she was leaning against the counter of the nurses' station. She shot a
concerned glance at Taylor, then looked at EJ.

Taylor's head pounded with pain. When had that started again?

"I think we're done for now," EJ said, easing the chair to a stop.
"Someone will be back to sit with her, if that's all right."

"It's fine," Krista said, starting to step past them.

"Where is it?" Taylor blurted the question without knowing she was
going to.

Krista paused.

EJ hesitated. "Where's what, sweetie?"

"The piece." Taylor's breath came in short, shallow bursts. "That
piece of her head?" What a ridiculous question. But no. It wasn't
ridiculous. It was important. "She needs it. Doesn't she?" Taylor looked
from one woman to the other. "Doesn't she need it to keep her brain in?"
She was losing it. She saw it in EJ's anguished expression.

Krista moved closer. "She'll be fine without it for a while," she said,
her tone reassuring, professional. "Her brain swelled during her surgery,
and the doctor has to wait for the swelling to subside before he can close
her skull again. But the incision's packed, and her brain's protected."

"But where is it?" Taylor struggled to control the irrational panic
threatening to consume her. Her voice rose. "Where's that piece of her?
You can't just take a piece of her."

Krista's demeanor transformed from removed professionalism to
compassionate. She squatted in front of Taylor. "It's with her," she said
comfortingly. "The doctor made a small incision in Gwen's abdomen
and tucked it in there to keep it surrounded by her own tissue so it'll stay
healthy and viable for when he puts it back. It's safe, and so is she."

Taylor met and took solace from Krista's steady gaze, the warmth
in Krista's green eyes offering a promise Taylor could trust. She began
to calm.

"Okay?" Krista asked.

Taylor sucked in a deep breath, then let it out slowly. She nodded.

Krista rose. "Why don't you try to get some sleep, and maybe you can come back later to sit with Gwen, if you want."

Another nod was all Taylor managed. Her headache raged, making her desperate for her morphine pump. Could Gwen feel pain in the state she was in? Was she scared? Of course, Taylor wanted to sit with her. Gwen had to know she was there, that she wasn't alone.

"Thank you, Krista." EJ sounded tired.

"Any time," Krista said as she headed back to Gwen's cubicle.

Once again in Taylor's room, EJ helped her into bed and gently tucked the sheet around her body. She smoothed her hand across Taylor's forehead as Taylor sagged into the pillow. "That took a lot out of you, didn't it?"

Yet another nurse, an older, roundish woman, reattached the line from the morphine pump to the port in Taylor's arm.

Taylor frantically pushed the button well past when the pre-measured dose would have been released. She closed her eyes under EJ's cool touch and heard the answer to EJ's question in her aching head. Yes, seeing Gwen like that had taken everything out of her. But she couldn't make her mouth form the words.

EJ stroked Taylor's face. "We have to know she'll be fine, Taylor," she whispered. "That she'll wake up and come back to us."

Tears filled Taylor's eyes, and she swallowed a sob. Thoughts of Gwen flooded her mind—her smile, her laugh, their banter for all those years before their first kiss, before they became what they are now. That kiss changed everything. All their kisses and their closeness and intimate moments since, changed everything.

Gwen always went on about *the Universe* and how it showed you what you needed to know, brought you things for your higher good, filled your life with love. How could *this* be for anyone's higher good? And how cruel could the Universe be to give them each other for such a short time, only to take it away again like *this*?

"What?" EJ asked. "I can't understand you, sweetie."

Taylor felt EJ's heat close to her lips.

"Can you say it again?"

Had Taylor spoken? She tried to gather strength. "So short." Her voice grated in her throat. It took everything she had. "Only got to love her...short..."

She faded into blissful oblivion, and unconsciousness consumed her.

❖

Taylor startled at the warmth of a hand covering hers. "Gwen?" She opened her eyes and looked around franticly but had to clench them shut against even the dim light in the room.

"It's me, sweetie." EJ's voice was quiet. Her fingers tightened around Taylor's. "I'm sorry. I didn't mean to wake you."

Taylor squinted, trying to focus on EJ in the chair beside the bed. Her scattered thoughts began to coalesce into memory. The accident. The hospital. Gwen in ICU.

"How do you feel?" EJ asked. "Do you need anything?"

Taylor swallowed, her mouth dry, her throat scratchy. "Water?" She moved to sit up but winced at the pain in her ribs and her head.

"Wait," EJ said as she rose. "Let me."

The head of the bed elevated smoothly. "That's good," Taylor said.

EJ poured a cup of water and handed it to her. "Do you feel any better?"

Taylor took stock of her body. "I think so. My head still hurts. And I'm stiff and sore, but all in all, not bad."

"Good." EJ sighed. "You scared me this morning."

"Yeah, sorry." Taylor took a sip of water, then let her head sink into the pillow. She closed her eyes. "I wasn't ready for that, but now I know what to expect. I'll do better next time."

"It's okay. It's hard seeing her like that." EJ slid the cup from Taylor's grip. "It's still a little hard for me to see you too."

Taylor lifted one eyelid slightly and considered EJ through the slit. "What do you mean?"

EJ smiled. "You haven't looked in a mirror yet, have you?"

Taylor stiffened but caught herself before she tried to sit up. "Why? Is there something wrong with my face?" She ran her fingers over her cheek, then her forehead. Her skin was puffy, and she grazed what felt like a bandage. She'd been vaguely aware of some soreness, but the pain in her head overwhelmed it so much, she hadn't given it much thought.

"Stop." EJ let out a small laugh and grasped Taylor's hand. "It's nothing that bad. Just one heck of a black eye and a butterfly bandage across the side of your forehead. But the doctor said there shouldn't be any scarring. All I'm saying is it's hard to see people we love bruised and battered, so I understand how upset you were this morning."

Taylor relaxed back into the bed. "I don't think I want to see myself yet."

"No. It's a good idea to wait a couple of days." EJ studied Taylor. "At least until the bruises fade a bit." She seemed distracted.

"Is there any change with Gwen?" If there were, EJ would have already told her, but Taylor had to ask anyway.

EJ shook her head. She returned to her chair and rested her elbows on the edge of the bed, then watched Taylor for another moment. "There's something I don't understand about this morning, though." She pressed the back of Taylor's hand to her cheek.

The tenderness of the gesture comforted Taylor in that way only a friend's touch could. She brushed her knuckles over EJ's skin. "What's that?"

"When we got back here to your room and you were falling asleep, you said some things. Something about loving her so short. Who were you talking about? At first, I thought it was Gwen, but that doesn't make sense. Did you meet someone and fall madly in love while I was honeymooning?" There was a note of humor in the last question. "But that doesn't make sense either."

Of course, it was Gwen. What did EJ think had been going on the past three weeks? Taylor opened her mouth, a snarky remark on the tip of her tongue. Shit! EJ didn't know. Taylor's head and emotions were so messed up, she'd forgotten she needed to be told. She stared at EJ, her mind racing. "I'm sorry."

EJ tilted her head with a confused smile. "For what?"

"We were going to tell you as soon as we got to your place, but then we didn't. Get to your place, I mean." Taylor faltered. Should she do this without Gwen? But she'd already started. EJ knew something was up and was waiting.

"Taylor?"

Taylor met her gaze. "EJ," she said a bit shakily. "Gwen and I... well. We're together."

"Together? You mean on the way down?" EJ's expression held only patience. "Yes, I know that. You were in the same car."

"No," Taylor said quickly. "I mean, we're *together* together." She paused, searching for words. "We're a couple, I guess." Were they? They hadn't talked about what they were.

EJ furrowed her forehead. "A couple?" She blinked quickly. "How? When?"

"It started at your wedding," Taylor said, watching EJ for signs of how she was taking this. "I mean, kind of, but not really."

"What does that mean?" EJ straightened in her seat. "You two were seeing each other like this before, and neither of you told me?"

"No. I just meant..." Taylor turned her hand in EJ's and held on. She didn't want EJ to pull away. "I've had feelings for Gwen for a long time. You know that."

"I've known you've wanted to sleep with her." EJ narrowed her eyes. "Is that what this is?"

"No, it isn't," Taylor said more sharply than she'd intended. "And, please, don't turn it into that. Listen to what I'm telling you."

"Then *tell* me. How did this all happen?"

"I don't really know." All of Taylor's own questions came flooding to the surface. Over the course of the last three weeks, she'd wished she'd had EJ to talk to about everything, but now that she did, it felt all wrong. It felt as though she was having to defend herself. "Something changed between us the weekend of your wedding. I think it started right before we got to your place when she told me she'd slept with a woman."

EJ's eyes went wide. "*Gwen?*" Her voice rose. "Slept with a *woman?*"

Taylor tugged her hand. "Shhh."

EJ glanced at the open door to the corridor, then looked back at Taylor. "Recently?" she asked more quietly.

"No. A long time ago." Taylor wished they'd gotten around to talking more about that. "I'm not sure when exactly, but before we knew her. But that isn't the important part. Something about her telling me, trusting me enough, seemed to open a door between us. And she kissed me at the wedding. And, oh my God, EJ. Kissing her and holding her felt more right than anything in my life ever has."

EJ only stared.

"Then the next day, all the way home, she avoided me. She wouldn't talk and would barely look at me. I told myself she was just hungover—which, Christ, she was more hungover than I've ever seen her. You know how she was always the one to take care of us?"

EJ made a twirling motion with her finger, a clear indication to move along.

Taylor refocused. "Right. But deep down, I thought our whole friendship had been ruined. Then Monday, she invited me over for dinner, and she said she thought it was time we admitted there was something between us and that she wanted to see what it was and if I felt the same way." Taylor shrugged as she remembered that evening. "So we did. And we have been. And…" She looked into EJ's eyes, hoping to find her best friend rather than Gwen's protector. "EJ, I love her. I'm *in love* with her, and I think I have been for a long time. We've spent every free second of the past three weeks together, which isn't that unusual, but it's been so different. Yes, we've had sex. Of course, we've had sex. But *that* attraction was the tip of a very large and very nice iceberg. We've talked about so many things, deeper things than even before, and you *know* how deep we've all gone with each other before."

EJ's skepticism showed in her expression. "But, Taylor, you don't fall in love."

"I know. But this is different. And we've shared so much and touched differently and made love." Taylor closed her eyes and swallowed the emotion rising in her throat. "EJ, I *made love* with Gwen. I don't think I've ever made love with anyone before." She opened her eyes and tears spilled down her cheeks. "Do you know what that feels like?"

"I do, honey."

And the catch in EJ's voice told Taylor she really did.

"But, are you sure that's how you felt then and not just now? I mean, the doctor said that concussions and traumas can cause severe emotional shifts and confusion. Maybe you feel this way now because Gwen's still in critical condition and you're afraid. I understand that, sweetie. I'm so scared too."

"No! You're not listening." The floodgates opened, and Taylor couldn't hold back the sobs. She *wasn't* confused.

"Okay. Okay." EJ leaped to her feet, her tone softening. She climbed onto the bed and took Taylor carefully into her arms. "Shhh. We don't have to talk about this right now. There'll be plenty of time now that you're awake. The important thing is for you to get better." She stroked Taylor's hair.

The tenderness and comfort of her best friend should have soothed her. Instead, it broke Taylor open. "But I didn't tell Gwen. Not any of it. I didn't tell her I love her." She choked on the words. "God! Why didn't I tell her?"

"It's okay." EJ held her close. "Things will get better. It'll all work itself out as your thinking gets clearer. And she'll get better too." EJ paused, then sucked in a shuddering breath. "She has to. She's still alive, and so are you, so everything is fine right now. Just stay in the now and keep loving her, the way you always have, and she has to feel it."

"That sounds more like Namastacey than you," Taylor said, forcing a slight smile.

EJ lifted one shoulder in a casual gesture, obviously equally forced. "What's the point of having a wise friend if you don't call her when you need her?"

Taylor let the words sink in as she clung to EJ. They *were* wise words, but more importantly, they were words Gwen would believe in. She drew solace from that, and eventually, she calmed. Just keep loving her.

They sat in silence for a long while, Taylor drifting through memories of Gwen, EJ seemingly lost in her own thoughts.

Finally, EJ shifted but kept a secure hold on Taylor. "Sweetie," she said hesitantly. "There's something I have to tell you."

A slight quaver in EJ's voice put Taylor on alert. She eased away to look into EJ's face. "What is it?" Caution crept through her, a whispered warning. Everything important to her was so precarious right now.

"Maybe I should wait. But I need to talk to Gwen's neurosurgeon about it, and I don't want you to hear about it the wrong way. You should hear it from me, not someone else…I think."

EJ was doing the rambling thing she did when she was nervous. It made Taylor nervous too.

"I don't know. Maybe you should be stronger," EJ rattled on. "I mean, a little clearer—"

"EJ, just say it." Taylor regretted her sharp tone, but her anxiety was already in the clouds. "Please," she said more calmly. "Say whatever it is."

"All right." With a sigh, EJ entwined her fingers with Taylor's. "But I'm telling you this because you're Gwen's other best friend, because we're all family."

There was a look in EJ's eyes Taylor couldn't decipher. What was she talking about? Of course, they were family. "Okay," she said cautiously. "What?"

"You know I'm Gwen's durable power of attorney." She rested a questioning gaze on her.

"You know I do." Taylor made a failed attempt to keep her impatience at bay.

"And do you remember that time we were all sharing what we'd want if something like this happened?"

A chill crept up Taylor's spine. "Yeah," she said warily. Did she want to know where this was going?

"Well." EJ bit her lower lip. "Gwen has a medical directive." She paused as though to let her words sink in.

Taylor went cold as they did. "That's what was in that folder you were reading yesterday."

EJ nodded, then glanced away before meeting Taylor's eyes. "It states that if she's incapacitated with no sign of meaningful recovery—"

Taylor drew back. "No."

EJ cleared her throat. "For twenty-one days..." She swallowed hard. "She wants to be taken off all life support."

Taylor's stomach rolled. Her mouth went sour as the image of Gwen lying in the bed in the ICU flashed in her mind. "What?"

"I know. I'm sorry," EJ said, slipping her arm around Taylor's shoulders. "I was going to wait to tell you, but like I said— "

"No." Taylor's voice broke, but she fought back more tears. "No," she said with a firm shake of her head. "You can't do that."

"Taylor," EJ said softly. "It's *her* directive."

"I don't care." Panic rose in Taylor like a flood tide. "*You're* in charge now."

"I'm in charge of carrying out her wishes." EJ's tone was strong, but her gaze was pleading.

"EJ, please." The tears broke through. "I can't lose her."

EJ encircled Taylor in a full embrace. "It won't come to that. I'm sure." She held Taylor close. "This is only the third day. She has a lot of time to wake up. I just wanted you to know so when you did find out, you wouldn't think I was keeping it from you. But I think there's plenty of time."

Taylor couldn't tell if EJ believed what she was saying, but Taylor had to. She couldn't face the alternative.

A quiet knock sounded at the open doorway.

"Are we interrupting?"

Taylor looked up to find Jinx and a woman in scrubs. She seemed familiar. She wasn't wearing a lab coat, so a nurse, maybe? Yes, Krista. Gwen's nurse from that morning. Taylor wiped the wetness from her eyes and cheeks. "No, come in," she said before EJ could answer. She needed a new topic.

Jinx crossed to the bed and kissed EJ lightly on the lips. "We have news," she said with a grin.

EJ's expression brightened. "Good news, from your smile." She glanced at Krista who remained just inside the door.

"I'll let Krista tell you. That way, it's official," Jinx said.

Krista smiled at EJ, then Taylor. "Yes, good news. The swelling in Gwen's brain has gone down, and she's being prepped for surgery for the doc to close her up."

EJ gasped and jumped off the bed. "Oh!" She covered her mouth with her hands, then pressed her palms to her eyes. "Oh, thank you!" She looked at Krista, then at the ceiling. "Thank you," she whispered, as though in prayer.

Taylor watched, astonished. She'd never seen EJ pray, not once. Ever. Then it hit her what the news meant. "Gwen's getting better?" She let out her own gasp. "She'll wake up now?"

"We'll have to wait and see what happens after the surgery," Krista said. "But this is a step in the right direction."

EJ rushed back to Taylor. "And, sweetie, there's still plenty of time," she said, all reassurance now.

Taylor focused on that. There was still plenty of time. She looked at Krista again. And this was a step in the right direction.

She had to hold on to those two things.

CHAPTER TEN

Voices. Gwen heard voices. Were they talking to her?
"It's been four days."
Anxiety and anger in one. Why? What was wrong?
"So much we don't know about the brain." A man. "We'll have to wait and see."
Whose brain?
"I'll be back to check on her tomorrow."
"Thank you, Doctor." A third voice.
Who were these people? Two of them sounded familiar, but Gwen struggled for anything more. The darkness pressed in on her.
"You said she'd wake up after the surgery." The angry voice was louder.
"Taylor! It isn't Krista's fault."
Taylor. Taylor. Who was Taylor? A faint image floated in front of Gwen. A woman smiling, amber eyes, dark hair.
"But *she* said Gwen would wake up, and that was four days ago."
"I'm sorry, but what I said was that the swelling going down was a step in the right direction. And it still is, but as Dr. Bingham said, there are a lot of unknowns about the brain."
This new voice was calm. It soothed Gwen.
"I need air," Taylor said.
There was movement, then a sigh.
"I apologize, Krista. She isn't usually like this. She's so scared."
Scared? Of what? Was there something to be afraid of?
"I know. It's okay. I see it all the time. The important thing right now is for Gwen's body to take the time it needs to heal."

A presence. Not a touch, but a presence. Close. Gentle and consoling. It reassured Gwen.

"We just have to wait," the voice named Krista said.

Wait? For what? For whom? A shiver ran through her. A memory. When you wait for someone, they never come.

Then, Gwen was far away. Another place, another time.

At nine years old, she stood in a drizzling rain at the top of the cement steps, holding open the heavy wooden door of the church. She looked back at the old, battered car, the green paint chipped and corroded.

"Wait for me here," her mother had said. From the driver's seat, she gestured Gwen inside the building with a sweep of her hand.

Gwen gave a reluctant wave, then watched her mother drive away. They'd lived in the car for a year, but her mother had never left her somewhere to go do anything, not to get food, not to buy drugs, not for a job interview like today. Gwen always waited in the car, maybe because there wasn't anywhere else to wait. But today, something wasn't right. On shaky legs, she went inside.

It was dark except for the dim light from the overcast day filtering through the stained-glass windows spaced along both side walls of the deep room. Pews filled the middle, leaving a center aisle. An enormous cross with the crucified Jesus hung above an elaborately decorated altar.

Gwen hadn't been in many churches, and ones like this, with the dead guy on the wall, creeped her out. She found a seat at the end of a pew where she could keep an eye on both him and the door and began to wait.

Time passed. Minutes? An hour?

A door behind the podium beside the altar opened, and a man wearing all black except for a thin white strip at his throat stepped into the large room. He paused, his dark eyes meeting Gwen's, his expression surprised.

Gwen's pulse raced with fear. Would he kick her out? Where would she go? How would her mother find her? She pulled the backpack her mother had given her that morning into her lap and quickly unzipped it. She rummaged through its contents, trying to look like she had a purpose. She heard the door close again, and when she stole a glance, the man was gone.

Just as she was beginning to calm, though, he returned with an older man dressed similarly with that same funny white thing around his neck.

They walked down the aisle toward her, both smiling, but Gwen's heart pounded harder with each step they took.

"Hello, there," the older man said as they stopped in front of her. "I'm Father Andrew." He extended his hand. "And who might you be?"

The sparkle in his eyes and the way they crinkled at the corners with his smile eased the tension that had stretched Gwen's body taut. But she considered him cautiously. She took his hand, thankful for its warmth as it engulfed hers. She hadn't realized how cold she was. "I'm Gwen."

His smile broadened into a grin. "Well, Gwen, you look like a fine young lady," he said, his grasp firm yet gentle. "It's a pleasure to meet you. What brings you here today?"

Gwen glanced at the younger man, then at the door she'd entered through. "I'm waiting for my mom. She'll be here soon." Could she sound any less sure? Why *wasn't* she sure?

"And where is your mom? Do you know?" Father Andrew released her hand, but his smile remained.

It was a nice smile, not pretend like some people's, but it didn't comfort her. "She went to an interview. For a job." She closed her arms around the backpack still in her lap.

"And she told you to wait here?"

"Yes." Gwen looked away. "She said there'd be good people here, so I wouldn't be alone." It was a lie, but she thought it might make her mother sound like a better mom. She'd grown used to trying to make her mother sound better because she was afraid someone would come take her away, like they'd taken her friend Britney, if her mom wasn't good.

"I see." Father Andrew clasped his hands in front of him. "Well, Gwen, is there anything we can get for you while you wait?"

She flicked her gaze up to his in surprise, then quickly averted it again. He wasn't going to make her leave? "No, sir. I'm fine."

Father Andrew hesitated. "All right, then. My associate, Father James," he indicated the younger man, "has some chores to do, so he'll be in and out of the sanctuary. If you need anything at all, just ask him."

Gwen shifted her attention to him.

He nodded, and the corners of his mouth lifted.

"Okay," Gwen said with relief. "Thank you, sir," she added quickly, remembering her manners.

"You're most welcome." Father Andrew turned, then looked back at her as though he might say something else. But he didn't. The two men strode back to the altar and disappeared through the same door where they'd entered.

More time. The light through the stained glass grew brighter, then began to dim again. The younger man came and went, each time performing a task. He smiled at her but didn't speak.

When her stomach growled, Gwen returned to the backpack and pulled out the brown lunch sack she'd seen earlier. Inside, she found a peanut butter and jelly sandwich, a bag of Doritos, and a small carton of milk. She studied the milk, and a wariness spread through her. It was chocolate. Her mother never let her have chocolate milk. And chips were rare too. Treats were expensive. Gwen ate in the solemn silence that surrounded her. Finally, she curled up on the cushioned pew, her backpack beneath her head, and fell asleep.

A gentle touch on her shoulder woke her, and she looked up to find Father Andrew and a plump, blond woman standing over her.

Father Andrew squatted beside the pew and took Gwen's hand in his. "Gwen," he said, those eyes that had sparkled earlier now as soft as his voice. "This is Mrs. Powell. She's a social worker, and she's going to take you to a place where you can eat some dinner and sleep in a bed tonight."

Gwen shot upright and clutched her backpack. "No! I have to wait for my mom."

Father Andrew patted her arm. "When your mother comes looking for you, I'll be sure to tell her where to find you. I have Mrs. Powell's phone number, and I'll call her."

Gwen started to protest again, but she could tell by Father Andrew's expression she didn't have a say. She was only nine. She nodded. Her mother would come. She swallowed hard and blinked back tears. Her mother would come, and Father Andrew would tell her. She would come.

More voices. Always voices. Most were familiar by now, and Gwen had names that went with some. When was now, though? How long had she been drifting? What had Mrs. Walker said? *Time is different here?* Was Gwen still where time was different?

There was Taylor who always sounded upset, even when she was talking about staying strong and coming back. Was she talking to Gwen? "Come back to me. Please, baby, come back."

Come back to where? And *from* where?

And EJ. Gwen was supposed to know her, but did she? She got glimpses of a wedding whenever she heard EJ, then a kiss. But it was Gwen being kissed, Gwen kissing. And somehow, she knew she wasn't kissing EJ, whoever EJ was.

And someone named Jinx who sat with her and sometimes read to her, sometimes talked about someone named Pete, sometimes told her jokes. "Knock knock." The voice named Jinx would wait.

Who's there? Jinx couldn't hear her. No one ever heard her. Even when she screamed.

"Howl."

Howl who?

"Howl you know unless you open your eyes?"

It was corny. All of Jinx's jokes were corny, but they made a smile swell deep inside Gwen. She liked the one named Jinx.

Sometimes, there were more than one, and they talked to each other as well as to Gwen. Sometimes, it was only one. Sometimes, Gwen could sense them there when she floated toward the surface, but she couldn't hear them.

Today, though, someone was crying, quietly and discreetly but unmistakably.

Gwen heard it at first from a distance. Then it grew closer, more discernible as someone in true distress.

"Baby, please. It's been two weeks. If you can hear me, please, open your eyes."

The voice was heavy and ragged, but it had to be Taylor. She was the only one who called Gwen baby. Gwen wanted to reach out to her, tell her she *could* hear her, but she didn't know how. She couldn't break through that surface that always separated her from everyone else. She'd thought it was because of the pain, that it hurt too much to be close to the surface, so she'd always backed away. That wasn't the case anymore, though. There was still some pain, but nothing like it had been. Now, when she became aware of others, she could drift right up next to the sound, brush the very edge of whatever separated the world they were in from wherever she was, but that was all.

And then there were the memories that came and went seemingly at random. But no, it wasn't random. Sometimes they came with that presence that comforted Gwen, the voice named Krista. Always so quiet, so soothing. And it took her back to places and people she could remember. And Gwen knew *it* somehow, that presence, that voice, that touch. It was a memory too.

Mostly, though, Gwen drifted in the dark fog, sometimes in its depths, other times so close to that surface, she thought she might be able to reach through to the other side. If only she could find her hands.

Taylor sat beside Gwen's bed, holding her hand, staring at her closed eyes. She'd been telling her about the lunch she'd had in the hospital cafeteria and the walk EJ had persuaded her to take afterward. Could Gwen hear her? Taylor had no idea. Krista said she might be able to, but she'd also said that she might wake up after that second brain surgery, and that had been almost three weeks ago. So what the hell did Krista know?

But Taylor couldn't take any chances. If there was the slightest possibility Gwen could hear her, Taylor had to keep talking. About the inane things as well as repeatedly telling her how much she loved her and begging her to wake up.

She took in Gwen's expressionless features and her pallor. Was she even in there?

The machines still showed brain activity, and her pupils reacted to light, but there was nothing else. No sign of comprehension that she was being spoken to, no indication of her waking up any time soon. Or ever.

Three weeks since the accident. Twenty-one days. Taylor squeezed her eyes shut to stave off the thought. Not yet. Only eighteen. There was still time. And surely, EJ wouldn't really do it, not after such a short period.

They hadn't discussed Gwen's directive since EJ had told her about it. It was a subject EJ seemed as reluctant to bring up as she was. For Taylor, any talk of it was too much like giving up on Gwen. She assumed EJ felt the same because of her silence on the matter, but every once in a while she caught a distressed expression on EJ's face when she was sitting with Gwen, something far different than the worry and concern expected in a situation like this. Once, Taylor came out of the ICU and found EJ crying in Jinx's arms, the antithesis of the strength she'd exuded through much of this.

Taylor should ask if EJ was okay, if there was anything she could do to help her. If it'd been back when she'd been both EJ's and Gwen's best friend, she probably would have been able to do that. She couldn't, though. She wasn't only that anymore. She was still EJ's best friend, certainly, but she and Gwen were more now. They were lovers. They were *in* love. At least, Taylor was, and she wouldn't be able to bear hearing EJ actually say she was considering carrying out Gwen's directive.

Gwen had come off the ventilator right after the doctor had closed her skull, and since she'd been able to breathe on her own, they'd been hopeful that she'd wake up. And her body had begun to heal. X-rays showed the breaks in her leg were mending properly. The bruises along her left side were faded. Even the stitches closing up her scalp had been removed, leaving the blistering red scar to lighten beneath the peachy fuzz of Gwen's hair beginning to grow back. The only life support remaining was the feeding tube that kept Gwen nourished. To remove *that*...

Taylor sickened at the thought of watching Gwen's body slowly starve to death. As much as Taylor dreaded it, she had to talk to EJ to find out what she was thinking. And surely with the change in her and Gwen's relationship, EJ would take her wishes into consideration.

"Hi, Krista," EJ said, her voice drifting into Gwen's cubicle from the nurses' station. "We brought you a treat."

"Oh, thank you." Krista's tone conveyed her customary calm and collected manner, while at the same time was cheerful.

Taylor clenched her teeth. She was so sick of her. Why couldn't she have kept her mouth shut about when Gwen might wake up instead of getting Taylor's hopes up? And she was always hovering over Gwen.

"Hey, Taylor," EJ said as she stepped up beside the chair. "We brought you a milkshake." She handed a Styrofoam cup to Taylor.

Jinx passed her a straw and a plastic spoon.

"Is that Krista's treat too?" Taylor muttered under her breath.

"Mm-hm." EJ glanced at her before leaning past her and kissing Gwen on the forehead. "Is that a problem?"

Taylor slumped in her chair and stuck her straw through the hole in the lid. "No." She sounded like a sullen teenager. "She just gets on my nerves."

EJ sighed. "Not again." She threw a look toward the center of the ICU, then lowered her voice. "She's amazing."

"She bugs me. She's here all the time."

EJ scoffed. "She works here."

Taylor lifted her gaze to find both EJ and Jinx staring at her questioningly. "All the other nurses work three days and then are off four." She should let it drop, but she'd already gone too far. She might as well continue. "She's here every day."

EJ shrugged. "She works a lot of overtime and comes in on her days off just to check on Gwen. She's a good nurse. She cares."

Taylor tensed with irritation. She slouched deeper into her chair and refocused on her milkshake. Why couldn't EJ see what she saw? "My nurses were good, and yet, not a single one took on extra shifts to come in and whisper to me all the time." She tried to keep the sarcasm out of her voice. Or maybe she didn't. "And that's another thing. She's always *whispering* to Gwen when I come in. It's creepy."

"Yes, you've said that."

Taylor didn't have to look up to see EJ's eye roll. It dominated the silent beat that followed.

"She's talking to her like she told all of us to do," EJ said.

Taylor recognized the tight tone she used when speaking to a subordinate at work who wasn't grasping a concept she thought should be self-evident.

"She's made a connection with Gwen." EJ sat on the arm of Taylor's chair.

"Yeah, and that makes sense for *us* to talk to her because she knows us. She doesn't have a clue who Krista is. It's probably confusing her." Taylor stabbed her straw into her milkshake again. She still hadn't taken a single sip. "There's just something weird about her."

"Well, I'm glad she feels a connection with Gwen. And with all of us. Whatever the reason. She's the one who's gotten permission for all three of us to be here together occasionally as long as we're quiet. She pointed out to the doctor that Gwen does better when we're here."

Taylor wanted to glare at EJ for defending Krista, but if they were to argue, she'd rather save it for the more important conversation about Gwen's directive. "She just bugs me," she grumbled again.

EJ slipped her arm around Taylor's shoulder, then leaned down and pressed her cheek against Taylor's hair. "Sweetie, there was a good chance Gwen could have woken up after her surgery, and Krista didn't say she would for sure. Don't hold onto that. We all need to stay positive."

"You're right." Taylor took a steadying breath. "It isn't really about her." Although, it was kind of. There was something not quite right about

Krista, but she couldn't nail down what it was. She abandoned the entire subject. "EJ, I need to talk to you."

EJ stiffened slightly, then loosened her hold around Taylor and straightened. She nodded, resignation in her expression. "Okay. Why don't we step around the corner?"

EJ had to know what Taylor wanted to discuss. What else could there be with only two and a half days left?

Jinx gave them both a cautious look.

"Will you stay with Gwen?" EJ asked Jinx quietly.

"Sure." Jinx squeezed Taylor's arm as she moved past her to take the vacated chair.

Even Jinx knew. Taylor sighed and gave Jinx's shoulder a gentle punch. Her blood coursed through her veins, and her palms dampened as she and EJ stepped into the corner of the ICU right outside Gwen's cubicle.

When their gazes met, EJ's was expectant and knowing.

"I need to know if you decided...No, I need to hear you say you're not going to give up on Gwen just because of some arbitrary number of days. I don't think you would, but I need to hear it." Taylor's words tumbled over each other like rocks in a landslide.

EJ paled. Then, in the moment it took her to open her mouth to speak, a flurry of emotions crossed her face. Grief. Horror. Anger. Guilt. "Give *up* on her?" she asked icily.

Taylor flinched. *Shit!* She hadn't meant to phrase it that way. "No. I'm sorry. I just meant—"

"Do you think this is easy?" EJ kept her voice low, but it remained hard.

Taylor held up her hands to try to stop what was coming. "No. I don't. I know it isn't. It can't be. I just need to know what you're thinking, and I'm so screwed up right now, I don't know the right words."

EJ's manner softened but only slightly. "*Those* weren't them."

"I know." Taylor sighed. "Can we start over?"

"All right." EJ folded her arms across her middle. "Go ahead."

Taylor looked into EJ's hard green gaze. She'd really messed this up. She searched for the right words, some sentence that didn't dump her worst fear onto EJ. They'd only begun to talk about it, but it felt as though the conversation had been going on for weeks. And maybe it had, maybe since they'd first become aware of Gwen's wishes. And that was it, wasn't it? These were Gwen's wishes. But how old had she been when she wrote them down and notarized them? She wasn't *that* old now. And who really knows what they want in this situation when they're young and strong and seemingly invincible? When life is sunny and good? She should just cut to the chase. "Twenty-one days isn't long enough. Jesus, her bones aren't even healed yet. Shouldn't she at least have as much time as they'd get?"

EJ's grip around herself loosened almost imperceptibly.

But Taylor saw it. Encouraged, she plunged forward. "She needs more time, EJ. I mean, I can understand her thinking twenty-one days would be enough. Can't you hear her saying one of her flukey things like 'It only takes twenty-one days to make something a habit, so if I'm not responsive by then, I'm probably not coming back?' That's something she'd say. Right? But people come back after much longer than that."

EJ turned her head and inhaled a shaky breath. When she looked at Taylor again, abject torment swam in her eyes. "I know. But it's what she said she wanted. And she might say it flippantly when we're all out for Mexican food and margaritas, but she wouldn't put it in a legal document unless she meant it." The argument was stronger than the delivery.

"I'm not saying leave her like this for years. Just longer." Taylor heard her own plea and knew what EJ's response would be. It would be Taylor's if the tables were turned.

EJ pursed her lips and searched Taylor's face. Tears spilled onto her cheeks. "But then, how long would be long enough? For either of us, Taylor? And what if we wait, and then she wakes up and she can't talk or understand anyone? What if she doesn't even know anyone or can't do any of the things she loves anymore?" EJ's pitch rose, along with her volume, as she ticked off the possibilities on her fingers. "How could I face her? She stated exactly what she wanted in her directive. And she trusted me with it."

A part of Taylor knew EJ was right, but the part that couldn't bear the thought of losing Gwen right after finding what they could have together couldn't take it. "What about me?" she yelled. "Shouldn't *I* get some say in this?"

EJ's attention shifted over Taylor's shoulder.

Taylor followed her gaze.

Krista and her supervisor watched them from the nurses' station, Krista with evident curiosity, the other woman with a warning glare.

"I don't know, Taylor," EJ said in a harsh whisper. "Maybe you should, but—"

"Hey! Hey!"

Jinx's voice barely registered in Taylor's awareness as she waited for the rest of EJ's statement.

EJ threw a startled glance toward the nearby cubicle.

"Her eyes are open!" Jinx shouted. "Gwen's eyes are open!"

The creases of a frown framed EJ's mouth, and she seemed to be trying to solve some puzzle.

Someone hurried past behind Taylor.

Gwen's eyes were open! The spell broke. Noise flooded in.

"She was just lying there," Jinx said excitedly. "Then she woke up."

"Page Dr. Bingham to ICU. Stat," the woman at the desk said sharply.

Taylor and EJ spun, bumped into each other, then hurried into Gwen's cubicle.

Jinx stood, her back pressed to the wall, her eyes wide.

Krista leaned over the bed. "Gwen? Can you hear me? Can you see me?" She spoke quietly but with a slight tremor.

Taylor held her breath. It seemed an eternity before she heard Gwen's voice. "Fire." It was barely a croak. Then louder. "Fire!" She raised her arms.

Krista caught Gwen's hands and held them to her chest. "Shhh."

Taylor's instincts took over. She rushed to the bed and wedged herself between it and Krista, breaking Krista's grasp on Gwen. "It's okay. There's no fire."

Gwen pressed her hands to Taylor's shoulders and pushed.

Taylor encircled her wrists. "There's no fire," she said more loudly, trying to get Gwen's attention. But Gwen was looking past her. "The car caught on fire, but we're not there now. You're safe."

Gwen struggled to free herself. Her eyes filled with tears. "Fire," she cried. Her breathing became shallow, her arms weaker. Then her lids drooped and closed again.

Dr. Bingham strode into the room. "Tell me what happened."

Krista made a sound, then stopped as though gathering her thoughts, but she seemed shaken.

"She just opened her eyes," Jinx blurted. "I was sitting with her and looking at her…and then she was looking back!"

"But I think she thinks she's still in the accident," Taylor said, franticly shifting her attention between Gwen and the doctor. "She kept saying fire, and she was staring off past me, like she couldn't see me but could see the car burning or something."

"She didn't recognize you?" Bingham asked.

Taylor's excitement at seeing the blue of Gwen's eyes after all this time faded at the realization. Gwen *didn't* recognize her. "I don't..." She shook her head. "I don't think so."

Krista cleared her throat. "Doctor?" she said tentatively. "I think she might have recognized *me*."

Taylor grimaced, her irritation spiking. Why was this woman in the middle of everything? And how in hell could Gwen recognize her?

"Fire is my nickname." Krista was still talking.

Taylor turned to her. What was she saying?

"At least, it was when Gwen and I knew each other."

Taylor could only blink, stunned into silence.

"So you think she was talking to you?" The doctor moved around to the side of the bed and retrieved his penlight from his pocket. "And she seemed to actually see you?"

"Yes, I think so." Krista kept her gaze riveted on Bingham as though actively avoiding everyone else in the room.

"All right," Bingham said, sounding noncommittal. "Let me check her out. Krista, I'm sure you have other work to take care of. And the three of you," he swept a glance over Taylor, EJ, and Jinx, "have a seat in the waiting room, and I'll come find you as soon as I'm finished."

"Thank you, Doctor," EJ said, a little breathless.

Taylor panicked. She couldn't leave now. "But what if she—"

"Taylor." EJ gripped her hand. "Let the doctor examine her." She pulled Taylor toward the exit.

Taylor complied, too dazed to argue. Why hadn't Gwen known her? And why *had* she known Krista? If she really did.

Who the hell was Krista anyway? And what the hell was going on?

CHAPTER ELEVEN

Gwen swam through darkness, but it was different. It wasn't the thick sootiness she'd almost grown used to, but lighter, more like sleep. Her arms felt heavy, but something or someone had touched them. Had she lifted them? And she'd seen someone, truly *seen* them, not in a memory or a dream. Several people. It wasn't much more than a flash before the strain of it all had overtaken her, but it'd happened.

Something brushed her cheek. Her eyelid was lifted, and a bright light shone in.

"Gwen? Can you hear me?" a man asked. He looked into her other eye.

She could. And she could see him too, only vaguely, but that was due to the light.

He let her lid drop again.

She fluttered her eyes open and stared up at him.

"Well, there you are," he said with a smile.

She blinked once, then again.

He picked up her hand from beside her on the bed. "Can you squeeze my fingers?"

What a strange thing to ask. She tightened hers around his.

His smile broadened. "Good. So you can hear me."

She considered the statement. *Obviously.* She tried to nod. It was jerky, and her head felt weird.

"Can you tell me your name?"

"Gwen." Her throat was dry and sore.

"What about your last name?"

She started an eye roll but winced and reconsidered when it hurt. "Jamison," she mumbled.

"Excellent. Do you know where you are?" He slipped the light into his jacket pocket.

She followed the movement, taking in details. White coat. Stethoscope. Beeping sound. Leg suspended by some metal bar. "A hospital?" Her voice was barely a whisper.

He nodded. "Do you remember how you got here?"

Gwen tried to think back to anything before opening her eyes to this man. A few pictures flickered—someone sitting beside the bed, Fire leaning over her, a dark-haired woman pushing Fire away. "Fire?" she asked the man.

"She's here," he said softly. "I have a few more questions, then I'll get her for you. Is that all right?"

"Okay." Gwen's voice grew stronger. Something was in her nose, though, distracting her. She brought her hand up to feel it and found plastic.

"That's an NG tube. We had to put it in to feed you," the doctor said. "We can get it out of there very soon. First, though, let me explain a few things."

Gwen shifted her attention back to him.

"You were in a car accident, and you sustained a head injury as well as some other injuries to your leg, arm, and torso. My name is Dr. Bingham, and I'm a neurosurgeon. I performed surgery on your brain to stop some bleeding."

Gwen struggled to make sense of what he was saying. It took a Herculean effort, and even then, not much sank in. A sudden fear struck her. She went cold. "Was Fire hurt?"

Dr. Bingham frowned slightly as though trying to understand. "No," he said, sounding cautious. "She's fine. She wasn't in the car with you."

Marginally relieved, Gwen tried to relax, but she was too agitated. "Can I see her? Please? I need to see her."

"Of course. But then we need to talk a little more. Deal?" Dr. Bingham arched an eyebrow.

Gwen studied him warily. She only wanted to see Fire. "Deal."

He went to the curtain at the end of the space that held her bed, some machines, and a recliner and spoke softly to someone on the other side, then returned to Gwen.

Gwen tried to remember who'd been sitting in that chair when she'd first broken free of that other place. Before anything came, someone opened the curtain and stepped up to the foot of the bed.

"Hi, Gwen." Her smile trembled, and her eyes shone with unshed tears.

It was Fire, but different. She looked older, her dark auburn hair collar-length, not its longer, layered style as it'd been that morning at breakfast; her body not as lean and wiry as last night when Gwen's hands and mouth had been all over it. And she wasn't in black jeans and one of the rock band T-shirts she almost always wore, tight over her firm breasts. Instead, she wore those things nurses and doctors wear. *Scrubs?* But still, it was Fire.

"Hi," Gwen said hesitantly. "I had to make sure you were okay."

Fire swiped the back of her hand over one cheek and drew in a deep breath. "I get that," she said as she walked around to Gwen's side. "We've been waiting quite a while to make sure *you* were okay."

We? Oh, yeah. "Is Deborah here?"

Fire's smile froze and she blinked.

"Who's Deborah?" the doctor asked.

Gwen was too caught up in an attempt to decipher Fire's expression to answer.

"Our foster mom...Gwen's and mine," Fire said, her gaze never leaving Gwen. Then she turned to Dr. Bingham. "In our teens." The last words were quiet.

"I see." His response was just as low. "Gwen," he said, shifting back to her. "Can you tell me how old you are?"

"Um." She had to think about it. Why did she have to think? "Sixteen." That sounded right.

"And where do you live?"

The customary self-consciousness Gwen felt when having to tell someone she was in the system swept over her. Her face warmed. She focused on her toes sticking out of the cast on her left leg and pursed her lips. "I live in a foster home with Fire and our foster mother, Deborah." She twisted the edge of her sheet between her fingertips. "And two little boys. Bryce and Bartie. They're twins." When no one said anything, she glanced up at Dr. Bingham, then Fire. "Right?"

Fire remained silent but looked across the bed at the doctor.

"What?" Clearly, Gwen had been wrong about something. Fire's appearance niggled at her. "Fire, what? You're scaring me."

"Go ahead," Dr. Bingham said to Fire.

She paused, then lowered the bed rail. She edged her hip onto the mattress and grasped Gwen's hand.

Fire's skin was warm and soft. Gwen loved her touch. It calmed her.

"Gwen," Fire said, meeting her gaze. "We don't live with Deborah anymore." She ran her thumb over Gwen's knuckles. "We aren't teenagers anymore."

Gwen waited for it to make sense, but it didn't. "What do you mean?"

"You aren't sixteen. And I'm not seventeen." Fire spoke slowly. "A lot of time has passed, and we've grown up."

Gwen clenched her jaw and scrunched her face against a spear of pain that shot through her head. "How old are we?"

"I'm thirty-eight. And you're thirty-seven." Fire watched Gwen closely.

"What?" Gwen couldn't comprehend any of this. Then she noticed some lines etched at the corners of Fire's eyes and more flesh to her cheeks. She looked down her torso again, taking in her defined arms and the depth of more mature cleavage. She focused on a scar across the back of Fire's hand that hadn't been there that morning, or yesterday, or whenever the last time had been that Gwen had actually seen her. She lifted her gaze to meet Fire's again. "That's why you look different."

"Yes." Fire sighed. "That's why I look different." She appeared relieved.

Gwen pondered everything she'd been told in the past several minutes. A car crash. A head injury. The passage of time. No, the passage of *years*. She couldn't do the math in the state she was in. "How long have I been here?"

"A little less than three weeks," Fire said, still stroking Gwen's hand.

"Three weeks." And what about all the rest of that time? "So I haven't been asleep for years? Right?" She looked between Fire and the doctor.

"No," Dr. Bingham said. "Just since the accident."

Gwen took in Fire again, the changes in her appearance, her more mature demeanor. They did have a plan, or *had* had one back then, to be together when they aged out of the system.

"Do you remember anything past the age of sixteen?" Dr. Bingham asked, interrupting her thoughts. "Anything at all?"

Gwen searched her mind. There were memories of her mother, good and bad; some other foster homes before Deborah's; and lots of Fire from the day they met and the following year, but nothing more. She shook her head. "I'm sorry."

"That's okay. Just relax," he said. "Can you tell us the last thing you do remember?"

Gwen closed her eyes. She took in a breath, held it, then released it. An image began to focus like a developing photograph. "Breakfast. This morning." She looked up into Fire's face. "You were wearing your Blink-182 T-shirt and..." She let her words trail off at Fire's troubled expression. "Right," she said. "That wasn't this morning, was it?"

"No," Fire said. "It wasn't."

"That's okay," Dr. Bingham said. "Sometimes with a head injury like yours and brain surgery, there can be some initial memory loss that comes back with time. We'll wait and see. In the meantime, you're awake, which is excellent, and you know who you are."

No, she knew who she used to be. She swept her gaze over Fire. "Why do I remember back then but not the years since?"

"I can't answer that." The doctor wrote something in Gwen's chart, then closed it. "There's still so much we don't know about the brain. You do have some current friends here who are anxious to see you. That could trigger your more recent memory. Are you up to it?"

"Friends?" Gwen tensed. Was she up to it? "What if I don't remember them?" She met Fire's eyes, hoping for reassurance.

"That'd be okay," she said, squeezing Gwen's hand. "I'm sure they'll understand, but it's worth a try, isn't it?"

"Who are they?" Gwen asked. It was so strange to be meeting people she didn't know that were supposedly her friends.

Fire glanced at the doctor.

He nodded.

"Well, there's EJ; her wife, Jinx; and Taylor," Fire said, watching her. "Taylor was in the accident with you, but she's fine. You, EJ, and Taylor all work together, which is how you met."

"Jinx!" The name came out as a squeak fueled by Gwen's excitement. "I remember Jinx."

Fire gasped. "That's great!"

Then an image of a beautiful, exotic bald woman with gold bands around her toned biceps floated up from the depths of Gwen's mind, and disappointment crashed in on her. "Oh, wait. That's the super villainess who's the leader of the Fearsome Five. Probably not the same one waiting to see me." She searched Fire's face for confirmation.

"No," Fire said, but she smiled affectionately. "You did enjoy your comics."

"Why don't we bring them in, and we'll see what you remember. Okay?" Dr. Bingham turned and started toward the curtain. "I'll go fill them in on where things stand, and, Krista, you can remove Gwen's NG tube. I'm sure she'd rather have some real food, even if it is from the hospital."

Fire smiled. "Will do, Doc."

"Krista?" Gwen eyed Fire. "No one calls you that. Not without getting their ass kicked."

Fire laughed. "Everyone calls me that now, and I don't kick too many asses anymore. You can still call me Fire, though. If you'd like. I'll be right back. I need some scissors."

Gwen watched her leave with wonder. Fire not kicking ass? Things *had* changed. Gwen had so many questions for her. Where did they live? Clearly, Fire had become a nurse, but what had happened to her dream of learning to fly and making her living in the sky? And what did Gwen do? Right now, though, she was too nervous about meeting their friends, oddly for the first time. And how many other first times awaited her about her life?

Taylor paced the waiting room.

Gwen's awake! The thought resounded in her mind. *Or, at least, she was.* But that was still good, right? She *had* awakened. Taylor *had* seen the blue of her eyes after almost three weeks, after almost twenty-one days. She shuddered at how close it'd come. What had EJ been about to say right before Jinx had called to everyone? Had she almost told Taylor she'd decided to remove all life support and Taylor didn't have anything to say about it? And what about Gwen? Did Gwen truly not recognize Taylor? Taylor quickened her step. And Krista. What the hell?

"Taylor," EJ said from the chairs along the wall. "Will you please sit down? You're making me anxious."

Taylor halted in mid-turn and stared at her. "*I'm* making you anxious? What about you and—"

"Please?" EJ patted the seat beside her. "Gwen's awake now. We don't have to think about her directive anymore."

"We don't know that. Her eyes were closed again when the doctor kicked us out." Taylor wasn't ready to make nice, but she did sit down with EJ and Jinx.

EJ frowned. "I choose to believe she woke up again. Otherwise, I think Dr. Bingham would have come to talk to us by now."

As though conjured out of the ether, Bingham strode into the waiting room. He indicated for them to follow him with a tilt of his head toward the corridor.

Taylor almost felt guilty as the family members of other ICU patients watched her, EJ, and Jinx rise to leave.

Bingham waited in the hallway and pursed his lips as they approached.

"Did she wake up again?" Taylor asked, already impatient.

Bingham nodded solemnly. "She did. And physically, she seems fine."

"Physically?" EJ asked before Taylor could utter the word. EJ clutched Jinx's hand.

"She doesn't remember some things," Bingham said, then added quickly, "which isn't uncommon following brain trauma and surgery and certainly not after an extended period of unconsciousness. A lot of patients have some memory loss in similar circumstances, and often it turns out to be temporary."

"So she'll get it back," Taylor said, trying to reassure herself more than anything else.

"I can't say for sure," Bingham said. "But that's the hope."

"Does she know who she is?" EJ asked.

"She does know that," Bingham said thoughtfully. "But she's confused about *when* it is."

"What do you mean?" Jinx released EJ's hand and slipped her arm around EJ's waist.

"She thinks she's sixteen." Bingham paused and glanced from Jinx to EJ, then to Taylor. "And while she remembers things about her life at that age, she doesn't seem to have any recollection of anything since. That's why she recognized Krista. Apparently, they knew each other in their teens."

"What?" The word exploded from Taylor's lips like a car crashing through a wall. Gwen had shared a lot with Taylor about her teen years, feeling so alone and being in all the foster homes, but she'd never said anything about a Krista. Or Fire. "And Krista never mentioned that?"

Everyone turned and looked at Taylor blankly as though the point she'd just made was irrelevant.

"I think the important thing is that Gwen does remember Krista," EJ said finally. "So she might remember us when she sees us again now that she's fully awake." She returned her attention to Bingham. "Yes?"

He smiled at her. "That's the ideal. I'd like to hold back on actually telling her much, though, to give her time to allow real memories to come back to her, rather than simply learning things about her life from what people say. Some basics of how you all know each other and maybe where she was going when the accident happened, things like that would be okay. But nothing too detailed about her life, and specifically about the time between her teens and now. I'll request a consult with our neuropsychologist and get some input about how to proceed. Maybe even have Gwen do a few sessions, if needed." He turned and started down the corridor. "For now, let's try not to tell her anything too startling or upsetting, if there's anything like that."

Taylor fell into step behind EJ and Jinx as they all followed like sheep. What would be too startling or upsetting? The fact that one of her best friends for a decade that she doesn't remember had recently become her lover? Especially if she and Krista were…Taylor's gait caught, and she came to a halt. What *had* Gwen and Krista been to one another? Was Krista the woman Gwen slept with?

EJ glanced over her shoulder at Taylor. "Are you all right?"

Taylor focused her thoughts. "Fine," she said, catching up with the group. "What kinds of things would be too upsetting?" she asked Bingham.

He arched an eyebrow at her. "You're her friends and family. You'd know better than I would. Trust your instincts, and maybe let her lead."

She nodded as they stopped outside the large door to the ICU, and he flashed his access card in front of the reader.

EJ cast a nervous look at Jinx, then at Taylor.

At least Taylor wasn't the only one feeling daunted by the responsibility of not saying the wrong thing and possibly making things harder for Gwen.

When they entered the cubicle they were all so familiar with, they found Gwen sitting up in bed. The feeding tube was gone, and her cheeks were pink. She blinked at them with wide eyes, her expression apprehensive.

"Hi," EJ said, sounding hesitant. "It's so good to see you."

"Thanks." Gwen's voice trembled. Her gaze landed on each of them in turn, first EJ, then Jinx, and finally, Taylor. Then she looked back to Jinx. "I remember you."

"You do?" Jinx grinned.

Taylor's heart leaped into her throat. If Gwen recognized Jinx, wouldn't she have to know Taylor and EJ too?

"You were sitting there when I woke up." Gwen pointed to the chair beside her bed.

"Yeah, I was. You really surprised me." Jinx laughed softly.

A tiny smile lifted the corners of Gwen's mouth.

"That's great," Krista said from the other side of Gwen's bed. She patted and stroked Gwen's hand.

She'd been there, right beside Gwen, since they'd come in. For support? Encouragement? But Taylor had managed to disregard her presence until now. It should have been Taylor giving Gwen support and encouragement. She tamped down the anger that tried to force its way from deep in her gut. Why was Krista even here? Didn't she have other patients?

Taylor remembered how Gwen had cried out Krista's name, or rather, her nickname, when she'd first seen her, and realized now that Gwen had been flailing and fighting against Taylor not because she was seeing the burning car and trying to get away from the fire. She'd been fighting against Taylor, trying to get to Krista. Her stomach clenched with fear, and emotion choked her. She swallowed hard against it. She could remember Taylor. She remembered Jinx. She could remember everything.

"Do you know Jinx from before you saw her in the chair?"

Krista again. Shut up. Shut up. Shut up. The doctor said to let Gwen lead. Really, though, the reason Taylor wanted Krista, or anyone else, not to push Gwen was that she wanted to stave off hearing that Gwen didn't know *her* for as long as possible.

Gwen studied Jinx for a long moment, then shook her head. "But you're Jinx?"

Jinx nodded. "I am."

Gwen dropped her gaze to where Jinx's fingers were interlaced with EJ's, then lifted it to EJ's face. "So that means you're EJ."

"That's right," EJ said, sounding hopeful.

"Is something coming back to you about her?" Dr. Bingham asked.

"No." Gwen's tone was impassive. "It's just that Fire said earlier that Jinx was EJ's wife and they're holding hands."

"At least, your thinking is clear," he said with an encouraging lilt. "That's good."

Gwen gave him a small smile, then looked at Taylor. She made a perusal of her as though taking in every detail, considering each on its own merit, then moving on in search of something more interesting.

Taylor held her breath.

"And you're Taylor," Gwen said, her attention lingering on the cast encasing Taylor's left wrist.

"Yes," Taylor said flatly. There was no hint of recognition in Gwen's voice, expression, or demeanor.

"You were in the accident with me?" Gwen asked.

"Yes."

"Where were we going?" Gwen continued studying Taylor, her eyes slightly squinting.

Taylor tensed. How should she answer? "We were on our way down to EJ and Jinx's. They just got home from their honeymoon, and everyone was getting together to watch them open their wedding presents." She sighed with relief when Gwen simply nodded, seeming satisfied with the answer. Her relief was short-lived, though.

"What do you mean *heading down*?" Gwen asked. "I thought we all work together. Don't we live in the same place?"

Taylor froze. "Uh…"

EJ squeezed Taylor's arm, then stepped forward. "We used to, but when I met Jinx, she was living in the city where my son and daughter-in-law live, and her business is there, so when we decided to move in together, I relocated to be with her. I travel all over the state as regional manager for Bad Dog Athletic Apparel, where you, me, and Taylor work, so I split my week between home and our office in Sacramento. That's where you and Taylor still live and work."

"Oh." Gwen sighed as she seemed to take it all in. She glanced back to Taylor, then to Jinx and finally rested her gaze on Krista. "Where were you? Why weren't you going to EJ and Jinx's with us?"

Krista missed only a beat, then quirked her lips and lifted her shoulder. "Working."

Gwen smiled softly. "I'm glad. Otherwise, you could have been hurt too, or even…" She visibly tightened her grip on Krista's hand. "I couldn't stand it if anything happened to you." She returned her attention to Taylor. "And I'm really glad you weren't hurt seriously."

Her tone was so innocent it broke Taylor's heart. The doctor had told them not to tell Gwen too much, but it felt as though they were all lying to her.

Gwen leaned her head against the pillow and gently closed her eyes. "I'm sorry," she said quietly. "I'm suddenly so tired."

"That's perfectly understandable," Dr. Bingham said. "You've had a big day. I'll schedule a neuropsychologist to come talk with you in the morning about your memory loss and confusion, and I'll be around to see you tomorrow also. For now, we'll let you get some sleep." He gestured toward the opening to the cubicle. "Ladies?"

Krista started to ease her hand from Gwen's, but Gwen stiffened and pulled it back. Her eyes opened wide. "Can't you stay?"

Krista moved closer. "It'll be okay," she whispered. "One of us will always be here at the hospital, and whatever nurse is on shift will know how to reach us. EJ's made sure of that." She glanced at EJ, and Gwen's gaze followed.

EJ smiled and nodded.

"The most important thing right now is for you to rest," Krista continued.

Gwen sank back into the bed as she relaxed.

Taylor had to acknowledge that Krista knew how to calm someone down. And as much as she hated to admit it, she was glad. As conflicted and worried as Taylor was, even though Gwen was awake, Taylor would be useless right now at helping Gwen much at all. She turned and left.

Outside the ICU, Taylor stood in silence with EJ, Jinx, and Krista. Everyone seemed just as much in need of a minute to catch up. The past few weeks had felt like an eternity, waiting and wondering what would happen to Gwen, like time had stood still.

As though orchestrated, they all released a long breath at once. Then they all laughed.

EJ slid her arm around Taylor's waist and pulled her in tight. "I'm so relieved," she said, still laughing but suddenly through tears.

Taylor turned and drew her into a full hug. "Me too." She kissed EJ's temple, stealing an instant to finish absorbing it all. "Me too."

"So I guess we should go get something to eat while she's sleeping," Jinx said, rubbing her stomach. "Then we can figure out who wants the first shift of the brand-new hospital watch." She grinned, clearly unable to hold back her happiness.

EJ stepped away from Taylor with a final squeeze. "That sounds great. Krista, would you like to join us, or do you still have a few hours left on your shift?"

Taylor looked at Krista in surprise. Krista *did* have some hours left on her shift. The night nurses didn't come on until seven. Krista had stopped and said something to her supervisor on the way out, but why had she left? And she'd made it sound to Gwen like she wouldn't be taking care of her anymore.

"I'd love to," Krista said to EJ. "But I need to go talk to the director of nursing to see if I still have a job here."

"What?" EJ asked.

"Why?" Jinx followed up.

Krista's cheeks pinkened, and she looked right at Taylor. "I'm sure you're wondering why I never told anyone I knew Gwen when we were young."

Good. At least, Taylor wouldn't have to ask. She gave a curt nod.

Krista pursed her lips as though preparing for what she was going to say. "I'm a traveling nurse, which means I move from hospital to hospital, working usually three- or six-month contracts. It's a nice way to see and live in different cities. The night I saw Gwen brought into the ER was the second to last night of my contract here. When I'd confirmed it was really her, I asked the director if I could stay on an as-needed basis."

"So the director knows you used to know Gwen?" EJ's question was more confirming than inquiring.

Krista's light blush darkened to full red. "No." She broke eye contact with Taylor and looked to the floor. "I was afraid if I told her that, she wouldn't let me care for Gwen as a patient. There's a policy in some hospitals against patients being treated by family members or friends. It might not have applied with Gwen and me, given the number of years it's been since we knew each other, but I didn't want to take any chances. It's been so long…" Her voice broke, and she sucked in a shaky breath.

"I lost her once. I mean, literally. I couldn't find her when I came back." She began to cry.

EJ moved to her and rubbed her shoulder.

Jinx pulled a package of Kleenex from her back pocket and handed it to Krista.

Taylor just stood there, waiting for the rest of the story. She'd known early on, or at least suspected, that Krista wasn't simply the caring nurse everyone else thought her to be. There'd always been something sketchy about her.

"Thank you." Krista blew her nose, then handed the rest of the packet back to Jinx. "Anyway." She brushed her tears away and inhaled deeply. "I knew the hospital was short-staffed, so I asked the director if it'd be helpful if I stayed a while longer to assist until some new nurses came in." She focused on EJ. "I know it wasn't honest, but I couldn't bear the thought of finding her again only to be shut out."

EJ smiled sympathetically.

"I've made a lot of friends here," Krista continued, seemingly bolstered by EJ's apparent understanding. "So I called in a few favors and traded shifts with someone so I could work in ICU while Gwen was in there. With all that, I'm sure the director isn't going to be very happy with me. And now that I know Gwen's okay, whatever the consequences are, it'll be all right." She looked directly at Taylor again. "And I can be on my way."

Taylor realized she was glaring at Krista. She glanced away and tried to soften her demeanor. None of this was Krista's fault. If Taylor had somehow lost Gwen for so many years, then unexpectedly found her again, she'd do anything she could to be able to talk to her. But she was in love with her. Did that mean Krista had loved Gwen in that way too?

"You can't just leave. Not now."

The words and the shock in EJ's voice drew both Taylor's and Krista's attention.

"You're the only one Gwen remembers, the only one that can give her any comfort. That was clear in there." EJ's gesture toward the door to the ICU was frantic. "You have to stay, at least until she regains more memory or gets to know *us*, so she knows she isn't alone." She glanced at Taylor, then Jinx. "Don't you agree?"

As much as Taylor wanted to send Krista packing, EJ was right. How terrifying would it be for Gwen to have the one person she knew in all this disappear? Especially since she clearly had no memory of Krista leaving her before. What would happen when that came back to her? "EJ's right. You can't bail now. You have to stay, at least for a while."

Krista considered Taylor for a long moment. "Are you sure?"

Taylor was aware of what Krista was asking, knew that Krista knew Taylor was in love with Gwen. She had to know Taylor's fear. No. She wasn't sure at all. She balled her fists to steady herself. "It's best for Gwen."

"All right, then." Krista dipped her head. "I would really like to stay, so thank you all. Let me go talk to the director and get that part cleared up, then I can check on Gwen, if you all want to go get something to eat at a real restaurant for a change."

EJ laughed and hugged Krista. "That would be wonderful, but I don't want to go too far. Feel free to join us in the cafeteria when you're finished."

"Thanks. I'll do that."

Taylor watched Krista walk away, and a knot twisted tight in her stomach. She'd thought all that needed to happen for her world to right itself was for Gwen to wake up. How wrong she'd been. She'd meant what she'd said, though. Krista staying *was* best for Gwen. And *that* had to be the focus for them all. Taylor loved Gwen, so that had to be *her* focus.

She closed her eyes, drew in a deep breath, and let her new mantra drift through her mind. Whatever was best for Gwen.

CHAPTER TWELVE

A tall woman with dark skin and a white lab coat over a turquoise blouse open at the neck stood at the foot of Gwen's bed, writing in a notebook that lay on a rolling bedside tray. A silver and turquoise heart pendant hung just below the hollow of her throat, repeatedly pulling Gwen's attention to it for no reason Gwen could grasp. There was so much she didn't know, didn't understand. She felt the same as she had that day in the church when she was nine. Small. Alone. Lost.

The woman had introduced herself as Dr. London, the neuropsychologist consulting on Gwen's case due to her memory loss. She'd already asked Gwen all the questions Dr. Bingham had, then moved on to the topics Gwen had to admit she'd only been told.

"So you don't have any actual memories of your friends EJ, Taylor, or Jinx?"

Gwen sighed. "Just from when I woke up yesterday."

"But you do have actual memories of Krista MacKenna, or Fire, as you call her?"

Gwen nodded. "But only from a long time ago. Nothing from now or the years in between."

The doctor jotted something down, then glanced back to another page in her notebook.

What was she looking at? They hadn't been talking long enough for her to have many notes. Had she already spoken to the others?

"I see," the doctor said. "And what about any family? Do you remember them?"

Gwen shifted, nervous at the new subject. It was far from her favorite. "I remember my mother, but I haven't seen her since I was nine."

"Did she pass away?"

In her mind, Gwen saw the taillights of that old car. Of all the memories to be crystal clear, why did it have to be that one? "No." She heard the bitterness in her voice. "She drove away."

"And you have an actual memory of that?" Dr. Landon sounded encouraged.

"Yeah," Gwen said with a humorless laugh. "Lucky me."

Dr. Landon's expression softened.

Was that pity? Gwen's anger flared. She hated pity. She glanced away to get control. "It's no big deal. I got over it." When she returned her gaze to the doctor, she almost believed it as she *almost* always could convince herself she did. "Besides, I only remember it from when I was nine to sixteen. Right? Who knows? Maybe sometime between seventeen and thirty-seven we've had a wonderful reunion and she's on her way here right now." The words rang empty, though, deep in her soul. And that was confirmed by Dr. Landon's only response being patient observance. Gwen felt like a newly discovered germ being studied under a microscope. "Can we move on?"

"I'm sorry," Dr. Landon said. "I know this is difficult, but it's important—"

"I know." Gwen waved her hand in dismissal. "It's important that I remember things for myself." She repeated what she'd already been told several times. "So what's next?"

Dr. Landon hesitated. "Your father? Or siblings?" She held her pen poised to write.

The warmth in her dark brown eyes belied her almost curt demeanor and consoled Gwen. "No. I never knew my father, and I don't have siblings."

Another note. "All right. What kinds of things do you enjoy doing?" Landon flashed a smile, clearly as glad to be done with the previous topic as Gwen. "Activities? Hobbies?"

Gwen searched the contents of her mind. "I like comic books," she said finally. "But you probably mean more adult stuff." She gave the doctor an apologetic look.

Landon paused in her writing and focused on Gwen. Her expression was gentle. "There are no right or wrong answers. We're just starting a record of what you do and don't remember to see where we stand in putting together a treatment plan. Try to stay relaxed as best you can."

Gwen's attention drifted back to the doctor's necklace.

"You keep looking at this." Dr. Landon touched the heart. "Does it remind you of something?"

The question was unexpected. Did it? Gwen concentrated, but nothing came. "No."

The doctor must have seen something in Gwen's response because she lifted her eyebrow. "Does it make you feel something?"

Gwen shrugged. "I don't know." She did, but it was stupid.

Dr. Landon's gaze was intense but encouraging.

"It kinda makes me feel…" *God, it's* so *stupid.* But she'd already begun. "It kinda feels like safety." She forced the words out. "And…"

Dr. Landon waited. When Gwen didn't go on, she asked, "And?"

"And love," Gwen blurted as her face burned. She looked at her hands in her lap. *Stupid.*

"That's good," the doctor said as she made more notes.

"It is?" Gwen glanced at her, not letting herself look at the pendant anymore. "Why?"

Dr. Landon rested her arm on the tray. "Anything you have an emotional reaction to could hold some significance to you and, therefore, could be attached to a memory. That's one of the reasons for all these initial questions, to try to find things that have meaning to you even if we don't understand, for now, what that meaning is."

"Oh."

The doctor smiled. "Let's move on and see if anything else comes up."

They continued with what felt like hundreds of questions about seemingly random things, then Dr. Landon had Gwen look at different shapes and objects and try to draw them. She had her read a passage from a book and memorize a limerick, then recite it back. By the time they were finished hours later, Gwen was exhausted.

She'd just woken from a nap and was staring out the window of her new room on the general ward when EJ walked in carrying a shopping bag.

"This is a lot nicer than the little cubicle in ICU," EJ said, her smile bright.

She looked rested and more relaxed than the last time Gwen had seen her. Gwen hadn't seen any of her *friends* since they'd left the ICU after her colossal failure at remembering any of them. She'd slept through the rest of the day and night and had been involved this morning with Dr. Landon.

"Is it?" Gwen surveyed her surroundings. It was certainly more spacious. She'd been so busy when she woke in the ICU, trying to make sense of what'd happened and who everyone was, she hadn't noticed a lot. "I wasn't in there very long."

An emotion Gwen couldn't discern passed through EJ's eyes, and her smile softened. Her expression held a mixture of amusement and affection. And was there a hint of sadness there?

"Oh, yeah," Gwen said, warming with the heat of a blush. "I guess I was in there quite a while, wasn't I? And *you* spent a ton of time there."

"I did," EJ said, her tone tender. "We all did. And since it means you're awake and getting better, I'll be happy to never set foot in there again." She dropped the bag she carried into the chair at the side of the bed, then leaned against the railing. "How was the neuropsychological evaluation?"

Gwen eased back against her pillows. "Trying so hard to remember things I can't is exhausting."

"Maybe don't worry about trying then. Let things come back to you as they do."

Gwen sighed. "It's so difficult, though, not knowing things I should."

"I'll bet." EJ reached toward Gwen's hand but withdrew before making contact.

Was that the kind of friends they were? Was a gesture like that natural between them? Gwen wished she could feel it, wanted a comforting touch, but it felt weird when she thought of EJ, a stranger, consoling her that way. She cleared her throat. "I wish I could just ask someone to tell me everything I don't remember. You know, bring me up to speed on my life? But Dr. Landon told me it'd be more confusing that way because then when I start remembering on my own, I'd have other people's versions of things that happened as well as my own, and my brain wouldn't be able to tell the difference. And that would make everything even more complicated than it is now."

"Yes, she told us that too."

Gwen considered EJ. "So she talked to all of you?"

"Yes," EJ said. "Last night. She and Dr. Bingham."

Gwen remembered Dr. Landon's notebook and how it seemed fuller than it should have. "I thought so."

"Is that okay?" EJ asked.

Gwen shrugged. "Sure. Isn't that what adults do? Talk *about* kids instead of *to* them?"

EJ tipped her head to one side. "I hadn't thought of it that way. I'm sorry. Dr. Landon was trying to collect some general information about you and your life. We were trying to help."

Sincerity shone in EJ's eyes. For some reason, the green of them made Gwen think of the heart pendant Dr. Landon wore. That feeling of safety and love flowed through Gwen. She frowned, regretting her words and tone. "I'm sorry. I didn't mean to imply you did anything wrong. Besides, I keep forgetting, I'm not a kid anymore. It's so confusing. I keep slipping back and forth between feeling sixteen and feeling something else I don't recognize. My thirty-seven-year-old self, I guess."

This time, EJ took Gwen's hand and squeezed it. "You don't need to apologize. You're going to be given a lot of slack for as long as you need it."

"Thanks." Gwen liked EJ, what little she knew of her, and even without any memory of her, she trusted her. She tightened her fingers around EJ's before letting go. It was awkward but somehow felt like the start of something.

"Has anyone mentioned your team meeting this afternoon?" EJ asked.

Dr. Landon had told Gwen about her, her doctors, and those close to her all getting together to discuss what came next, but Gwen wasn't sure who fell into that last category. She hated feeling so lost. "Yeah." Gwen tried to keep her annoyance from her tone but failed. "I'm not wild about having to leave my bed in this, though." She looked down, indicating her wrinkled and flimsy hospital gown.

EJ chuckled. "I'm glad to hear that. The Gwen *I* know would *never* agree to that, which is why Taylor and I went shopping for you this morning and got you these." She picked up the bag and retrieved something from it. "I don't know if you'll like them now, but men's pajamas, mostly the tops, have been your favorite thing to sleep in since I've known you." She held up a pair of brand-new, factory-folded light blue pj's.

An immediate feeling of comfort flooded Gwen. She ran her hand over the fabric, and its softness caressed her fingertips. The touch eased an anxiety she hadn't fully identified. "Thank you," she whispered. She couldn't wait to get them on. She hadn't realized that part of how vulnerable she felt was due to what she was wearing.

EJ laughed. "You're welcome. I'm glad there are things you remember even if you don't know it."

"Yeah. I'll have to tell Dr. Landon about this. She said it's important to note things I have emotional reactions to even though I don't know why." She glanced up at EJ. "How do you know what I sleep in?"

EJ started unfolding the pajamas and removing the cardboard they were wrapped around. "You and I and Taylor are best friends. We all know a lot about one another. And as soon as you get your memory back, you'll find that *you* probably know far more about us than we do about you because that's one of your strengths. You notice everything and file it away for future reference."

"What about Jinx?" Gwen hoped she was good friends with Jinx too. There was something about her that put Gwen at ease.

EJ shook out the pajama top and began smoothing out the creases. "You met her a few years ago when I started seeing her, and while you haven't known her as long, the two of you have become very close."

And Fire? Surely, Fire was friends with them all too.

EJ finished unbuttoning the garment and held it out to Gwen. "There." When Gwen took it, EJ turned around. "If you need help, let me know. Otherwise, I'll give you privacy."

Gwen loosened the tie at the back of her neck and slid the hospital gown down. Excited, she leaned forward and slipped one arm into a sleeve and winced at the pull at the still healing slash in her bicep. Then she tugged the shirt around her. The material against her skin felt luxurious. What the heck had EJ bought? Silk? "Okay," she said as she began to work the buttons. "I'm good."

As EJ turned, she scooped up the bag again and pulled something else from it. "We didn't think you'd be able to get the pants over your cast, so we got you a robe too." She yanked a tag from the sleeve.

Gwen studied the blue, black, and white plaid flannel. Something flickered in the back of her mind. "That seems familiar."

"Good." EJ smiled. "You have one like it. We were hoping this one might trigger something. Or, at least, make you feel a little," she shrugged, "I don't know. More at home? If anyone can feel at home in a hospital."

"That was thoughtful," Gwen said, touched by the consideration. "Thank you. For all of this." She ran her hand down the front of her pajama top. "I already feel more secure."

But something wasn't right. It was there, skirting the edges of her awareness but still just out of reach. EJ and Taylor thought it would make her feel at home. And it was EJ and Taylor who went shopping for her. But where was her *home*? Wasn't it with Fire? And where *was* Fire? And there it was. "Why didn't Fire go shopping for me?"

EJ glanced up as she stuffed the detritus from the new garments back into the bag. "I'm sorry?"

"Why didn't Fire, or Krista," Gwen corrected herself, "get me all this stuff? I mean, she's my partner. Or wife, maybe. Right?" Since EJ and Jinx were married, things must have changed for gay couples during the time Gwen couldn't remember. "*She* should be the one here taking care of me. Now that I think about it, she hasn't even come to see me today. Where is she?"

EJ stilled, then straightened. She opened her mouth, then closed it. She blinked, then parted her lips again.

Gwen couldn't help but think of a fish. Why could she remember what a fish was but not her best friends?

"Okay, who's ready for a ride?"

Gwen jumped at the deep voice that shattered the silence starting to become awkward. She turned to see a thin, bald guy in his twenties, push an empty wheelchair up to her bed.

"Transport is here. I'm Tony," he said with a broad grin. "Your chariot awaits."

Still wanting an answer from EJ, Gwen turned back to her, but EJ had moved on.

She smiled at Tony and laid Gwen's robe across the foot of the bed. "I'll get out of your way so you can get her leg unhooked. And, Gwen, I'll be right back to help you into your robe."

"No problem," Tony said. "I'll get her situated, and we'll meet you at the doc's office."

"Oh, thank you," EJ said without so much as a glance in Gwen's direction. "That's so nice." *Then* she turned to Gwen. "I'll see you in a few minutes." She smiled and was gone.

Gwen stared after her. What had she said that freaked EJ out so much? She didn't understand. *Weren't* she and Fire together? The frustration she'd been struggling with since she woke from unconsciousness gave way to anger. Never mind what the doctors said, she had questions, in particular about the significant people in her life. And she'd have most, if not all, of them in the same room together very shortly. She intended to get some answers.

CHAPTER THIRTEEN

Taylor sat in one of the chairs in front of Dr. Landon's desk and listened as EJ relayed her conversation with Gwen.

So Gwen thought she and Krista were still a couple? That was going to be a big problem in about fifteen minutes. They'd come up with a plan for Gwen's care when she was released from the hospital that they intended to talk with her about during the meeting, and it *didn't* involve her going home with *her wife,* Krista.

"I can't imagine why she'd think they're together," EJ said to Landon. "It doesn't make any sense. Gwen's straight. She's always dated..." She looked at Taylor.

Taylor gave her a weak smile.

EJ leaned back in her chair. She lowered her head and massaged her temples. "I can't wrap my head around any of this yet." She sighed, then returned her attention to Taylor. "So is Krista the one Gwen slept with?"

Taylor's heart ached at even the possibility. "I don't know. She never said who it was, but I'm thinking yes."

"Could someone tell me in? Quickly, since Gwen is likely to be here before long?" Landon's voice was patient despite her request for speed.

Taylor hesitated, unable—no, unwilling—to be the one to have to put it into words.

EJ took the lead. "The whole time we've known Gwen, she's dated men. She never once mentioned having any interest in a woman, until just a few weeks ago when she told Taylor she'd slept with a woman before." She turned her focus to Taylor. "And she said it was a long time ago, right?"

Taylor nodded.

"So it could very well be Krista," EJ said, once again talking to Landon.

Dr. Landon flipped a couple of pages in the notebook on her desk and pursed her lips as she read. When she looked up again, her manner was confident. "All right. This is something we're going to have to tell her. It would be a betrayal if her best friends let her believe she's in a long-term marriage, and when she finds out she isn't, her trust in all of you would be destroyed. And she needs you all right now. So since we don't have a lot of time, here's what I recommend." She looked at Jinx. "Ms. Tanner, could you please intercept Gwen with transport and take her for a short walk around the grounds? Give us fifteen or twenty minutes."

Jinx leaped up from her chair on the other side of EJ. "On it." She was gone without another word.

"Do we know where Krista is?" Dr. Landon asked.

"She should be here any minute," EJ said. "She didn't plan on being included in the meeting, but she wanted to see Gwen before and after."

At that, Krista's voice drifted in through the door Jinx had left open. "Hey, where you going in such a hurry?"

"She'll need to be in here." Dr. Landon rose and stepped out of her office. When she returned, she had Krista in tow.

By the time Jinx arrived with Gwen, the other doctors had joined them, and everyone and everything was in place.

Gwen sat in a wheelchair, wearing the robe Taylor had picked out for her. Her cheeks were flushed pink, presumably from her first venture outside in weeks, and her eyes were bright.

The sight of her so much like the old Gwen, except for the hard cast on her left leg and the fine layer of what only now could be considered hair rather than fuzz covering her head, took Taylor back to their picnic in the meadow right before the accident. Their banter. Their closeness. Their kisses. *Oh, God. The kisses.* How Gwen could kiss. And the way she snuggled against Taylor after they made love. And now she didn't even know her. Grief rose in Taylor's throat like high tide and threatened to drown her.

It didn't help that Dr. Landon had rearranged the seating so Gwen wouldn't be alarmed that Krista, *her wife*, wasn't the one sitting on the other side of her from EJ before they had a chance to ease into the first topic of conversation. Krista now occupied the seat where Taylor should be, where she *had* been only moments before, even as Gwen's other best friend, but certainly as her lover. And Krista? She wasn't *anything* to Gwen. Not now.

Taylor clenched her jaw. She could do this. For Gwen. It wouldn't be long before she, EJ, and Gwen would be leaving and Krista would be out of the picture.

"Hello, Gwen," Landon said with a smile. "How are you feeling after your nap?"

Gwen broke into a grin. "I was a little groggy, but Jinx stole me away for a walk outside, and the air and sunshine felt amazing."

"Good," Landon said, her tone gentle. "Well, we have a lot to cover, so is everyone ready to get started?"

A murmur of ascent went around the room, and Gwen fidgeted.

Landon settled her soft gaze on Gwen. "Before we get to what we're actually here to talk about, there's something else we need to discuss."

Gwen fixed her attention on the doctor as though Landon was the only other person in the room.

What was she thinking, or feeling? Taylor could only imagine what it must be like to be sitting in a room full of people you didn't know and waiting for them to tell you what they had planned for you. But then, hadn't that been how Gwen had described what it was like being in the foster care system throughout her pre-teens and adolescence? She'd also told Taylor how terrifying it was. Was she scared now?

"Do you remember us talking about the importance of you giving yourself time to see what you can remember on your own?" Dr. Landon asked.

Gwen squinted ever so slightly.

She already knew something was up, Taylor could tell.

Gwen nodded.

"But I also said that if anything came up that we felt was imperative for you to know, we wouldn't keep it from you?" Landon folded her hands in front of her on her desk. Her gaze never wavered from Gwen's.

Gwen hesitated before another nod.

"All right." Landon offered a smile.

She obviously meant it to be reassuring, but Landon didn't know Gwen the way Taylor did. The more this got drawn out and built up, the more frustrated and apprehensive Gwen would get. In fact, she already looked scared. Taylor stepped in. "Gwen."

Gwen jerked her head to look at Taylor, her expression that of a wary animal.

"EJ told us you had questions about why EJ and I went shopping for you instead of Krista," Taylor said before Gwen could respond. "That's what we want to tell you." She paused. "We know you well enough to know you'll be getting worried, and we don't want that. Okay?"

A beat passed as Gwen studied Taylor. Then she sighed and visibly relaxed.

Had that been a spark of gratitude she'd sent Taylor's way?

"Good," Gwen said, returning her attention to Landon for only an instant. "That's something I'm interested in knowing." She fixed an expectant stare on Krista.

Wow. Landon had called that one. She'd said Gwen would need to hear it from Krista. That worked for Taylor. If Krista was stupid enough to have had Gwen and then let her go, she *should* be the one to explain herself.

"So?" Gwen said. "What's going on?"

Krista's expression seemed to fluctuate between dread and relief. She took a deep breath. "I…" She faltered. She cleared her throat and began again. "EJ and Taylor went shopping for you because they're your best friends. They know you."

Gwen waited, but Krista didn't go on. "And?"

Krista bit her lower lip, then ducked her head. She straightened and met Gwen's eyes. "We aren't together," she said firmly, clearly determined to push through. "I'm sorry. I should've told you first thing."

She sounded so miserable. Taylor almost felt sorry for her.

Gwen's jaw slackened, and she blinked. "Oh. What…" Her gaze drifted as though she was trying to process the information. "What hap—"

"Deborah caught us in bed together."

And there was the answer to one big question. Taylor's stomach knotted with anxiety. When Gwen had told her she'd slept with a woman before, Taylor had assumed a one-night stand, a short fling maybe. Not something that would make Gwen think she and the woman could still be together so many years later.

"And our social workers split us up," Krista continued, her voice trembling, "and assigned us different placements." She swallowed hard. "I hadn't seen you since that day, until you were brought into the ER three weeks ago."

Gwen considered her for a long moment. She didn't speak. She didn't move. Was she even breathing? At length, she looked down at her hands in her lap and began rubbing the tie of her robe between her fingertips, a tic Taylor recognized that soothed Gwen when she was anxious. Or pissed. "What about our plan?" she asked finally.

The pain in the question rang so much louder than the words. It crushed Taylor. She wanted to rush to Gwen, take her in her arms, hold her. She wanted to tell her it didn't matter if she and Krista weren't together, that she wasn't alone, that Taylor was right here. That she loved her and would be beside her through it all. But she couldn't. Landon had said it would be better for Gwen. She'd said they needed to be patient with her recovery. Too much, too soon could overwhelm her, possibly cause a psychological fission.

What's best for Gwen. Taylor gripped the arms of her chair and forced herself to stay seated.

"You only have...I mean, had...two months left." Gwen went on. "Then you were going to find a job and get us a place to live while I was in the system for my last year. And I was going to keep saving what I made from my part-time jobs, so we could have a new start together. We had it all worked out. You were supposed to come back for me on my eighteenth birthday." She stared at Krista. "You didn't come back?"

To give Krista her due, she looked stricken.

Christ. Taylor couldn't imagine how horrible she must feel.

Dr. Landon cleared her throat. "If I may interject..."

Gwen turned to her, her expression startled, as though she'd forgotten anyone else was in the room. She hesitated, then nodded.

"Do you remember when we talked "

Gwen blew out an obviously exasperated sigh and held up her hands. "Could everyone, please, stop prefacing everything with *do you remember?* I remember everything that's happened since I woke up. As you've all told me, I *am* an adult. Stop treating me like a child."

"I apologize," Landon said softly. She held Gwen's gaze for a few beats, then continued. "Are you sure you want to know more about what happened right now?"

Gwen's eyes narrowed.

Uh-oh. Taylor knew what was coming. She'd been on the other end of *that* look.

"Do *you* know what happened?" she asked Landon, then pinned Krista with a glare. "Did you tell everyone what happened and just let *me* think we were still together?"

"I wasn't sure what you thought."

Taylor winced. Oh no, no, no. Wrong answer. Gwen was going to have her way with that one.

Gwen's features hardened. "So when I asked you yesterday why you weren't with Taylor and me on our way down to EJ and Jinx's and you said you were working, you didn't understand that I thought we were *all* friends, because surely since you were at my hospital bedside, you and I must, *at the very least,* still be in each other's lives as very good friends, if not as a couple like we'd planned?" Her normally cool blue eyes blazed.

There wasn't the slightest stir in the room.

The only response from Krista was her pounding pulse, visible at the base of her neck.

Gwen turned back to Dr. Landon with the air of a cutthroat attorney finished with a useless witness. "What were you going to say?"

"I was asking if you're sure you want to hear all the details of what happened right now," Landon said, as calmly as though she'd never been interrupted, as focused as if Krista wasn't about to have a stroke right in front of her. "Or maybe, you'd like to wait to see if it all comes back to you naturally at a time when you're ready for it."

Gwen sighed, sounding exhausted. "You're right. I don't want to know the rest." She glanced at Krista again.

But it wasn't the dagger Taylor would have expected. It was a much softer look, laced with disappointment. In Krista's place, Taylor would have preferred the dagger.

"I have enough to deal with right now," Gwen said. "Can we get to whatever this meeting is really about?"

"Yes. Of course." Landon opened the file in front of her.

Krista started to rise. "I'll get out of the way."

Gwen clasped Krista's wrist before she could fully straighten. "No. I want you to stay."

Really? Taylor was stunned. After finding out Krista abandoned her at the very time Gwen was being sent out into the world on her own, Gwen still wanted her around?

"Really?" Krista asked with echoed astonishment. "But you're mad at me."

Gwen rolled her eyes.

That cute eye roll Taylor loved so much being directed at another woman, at *Krista*, who didn't deserve Gwen after what she'd done, seared Taylor's heart. If you got that adorable eye roll when Gwen was mad at you, it meant she already knew she'd forgive you, even if she made you pay a little before she did.

"I *am* mad at you," Gwen said. "But more than that, I feel stupid. Like we'd still be together after twenty-one years." The derision in her tone was apparent. "That isn't how life is. Not for me." She lifted her gaze to Krista's. "You should have told me. Immediately."

"I know. I'm sorry." Krista's desire to touch Gwen, maybe hold her, shone brightly behind the unshed tears in her eyes.

Or maybe Taylor was simply reading that into the scene because it's what she'd want to do, always wanted to do when she'd done something to piss Gwen off and Gwen forgave her.

"The fact remains, though," Gwen said, still talking to Krista. "You're the only person here I truly remember so, as nice as everyone seems to be, that buys you a vowel. I want you to stay." Gwen finished in a whisper.

Krista's relief radiated in the visible relaxing of her shoulders and her knees giving out, landing her back in her chair, but most of all, in the tear she managed to swipe away before it got halfway down her cheek. The look that passed between Krista and Gwen shattered Taylor's world. She had to get out of there. Certainly, Gwen wouldn't care if *she* left. Before she could get to her feet, though, Dr. Landon was talking again.

"Okay," she said. "First, let me explain the purpose of this gathering."

Taylor gauged her ability to move to the door without disrupting the conversation but realized she couldn't without bringing the meeting to a halt. She'd have to endure.

Landon invited Dr. Avery, the orthopedic surgeon who'd treated both Taylor and Gwen, to begin, and he explained that the breaks in Gwen's leg were healing well and he could clear her for release from the hospital. She'd be able to arrange the physical therapy she'd need wherever she was living. Bingham followed with a similar summation of her brain surgery and the ensuing complications, then recommended she work with a neuropsychologist or a psychiatrist when she got settled with the goal of recovering her full memory. He also cleared her for discharge. When Dr. Landon came to the end of her report, she added her own clearance for Gwen's release.

Taylor had watched Gwen's face grow a little paler each time her leaving the hospital was mentioned. Now, Gwen sat stiffly with her lips pressed together and her eyes round.

"Where will I go?" she asked, her voice shaky. "I mean, where do I live? And how will I get around with this?" She waved her hand over her bandaged and casted leg. "And how do I get by when I don't know anything about my life?"

Taylor couldn't bear seeing her so vulnerable. It was so un-Gwen. Again, she wanted to jump in with the answer, but it wasn't her place. It'd be EJ, the one Gwen had chosen as her Person, who'd discuss it with her.

"Well, you're awake now and fully alert and capable, so the decision is completely yours." EJ slipped her hand over Gwen's on the arm of the wheelchair. "But as your family, we've come up with a couple of possibilities, if you'd like to hear them. But it *is* entirely up to you," she added quickly.

"Yes." Gwen turned her hand beneath EJ's and tightened her grip. "I definitely want to hear them. Thank you."

At least Gwen was starting to feel more comfortable with someone *other* than Krista. Taylor would have her chance too. As soon as they got settled somewhere, Taylor wouldn't leave Gwen's side, and with EJ no longer calling all the legal shots and Krista having moved on with her life, Gwen could gradually get to know Taylor again, and surely, she'd get her memories of them back.

EJ smiled. "You do have a house in Sacramento. That's where you live, and you can go there if you want. We'll make any arrangements you need for in-home care."

"But I'd be alone there?" Gwen sounded small.

"Oh, no, sweetie," EJ said, her voice almost a croon. "Whatever choice you make, someone who loves you will always be nearby. Taylor lives full-time in Sacramento too, so she'd be with you a lot, and I'll arrange to be there at least half the week, more if I can. I promise, you won't be alone through this."

"What about you?" Gwen asked Jinx, her expression anxious.

"I'll be there as much as I can too. We all will," Jinx said, sounding sincere in that way unique to her.

Gwen looked down to where EJ's hand clasped hers, then back to EJ's face. "You said whatever choice I make. What's my other one?"

"Well…" EJ glanced around to Jinx, then Taylor.

This was the option they'd put the most thought into and the one they hoped Gwen would pick. Although Dr. Landon had said it might be beneficial for Gwen to be in her own home surrounded by her things, she also agreed that having regular contact with all the people thirty-seven-year-old Gwen considered her family could have as strong an impact.

"You can come home with us, to the town where Jinx and I live." EJ paused again, watching Gwen. "We all have other friends there. Sparkle, Reggie, and Namastacey? And you're friends with my son and daughter-in-law." Her tone and one eyebrow lifted in obvious question.

Gwen simply shook her head.

"Sparkle and Reggie are Jinx's business partners, and the three of them own and run a beautiful facility for dogs called Canine Complete. It's like a dog spa and resort. And on the grounds, there's a large farmhouse where you'd be staying. Reggie and Sparkle used to live in it, but since they built a new home on the back lot of the property, the farmhouse is used for guests. It's lovely and big. You'd have no trouble getting around while you're in your wheelchair. And the grounds are gorgeous. There are dogs everywhere, some of whom you've already met and are friends with." EJ chuckled. "Our dog, Pete, will be waiting for you, I'm sure. He loves you. Jinx will be around every day."

Gwen met Jinx's gaze again.

Jinx grinned. "We can go for walks all over the grounds whenever you want."

Gwen laughed softly.

Taylor wondered what private joke had been created today when Jinx was stalling Gwen's arrival to the meeting. She couldn't shake the fear and anxiety that crept in every time she saw Gwen connect with someone when she hadn't even looked twice at her.

"Taylor's already arranged for a leave of absence from work for a while," EJ continued, "and there's plenty of room in the farmhouse for her to stay with you and still give you your own space and privacy."

When Gwen locked her gaze on Taylor, Taylor's heart jumped, and she realized how little actual interaction they'd had since Gwen woke up. *God, I miss you, baby.*

"You can do that?" Gwen asked, the worry in her expression having lessened with each revelation of the plan.

"I already have. I won't leave you alone in the world—" She had to cut herself off to keep the *baby* from passing her lips. From the corner of her eye, she saw Krista flush a bright red. She hadn't meant to draw a comparison but wasn't sorry she had. She couldn't imagine how devastated the eighteen-year-old Gwen had been when Krista hadn't shown up on the day she was booted out of the system. Gwen had told her how difficult that day was with such an unknown future and no family to lean on, but now, Taylor knew she'd left out the worst part.

"I do have to go back to work at least part-time," EJ said, pulling everyone's attention back to the main topic. "But I'll also be there for you. Jinx and I won't be staying at the farmhouse, but our place is nearby. And for your actual physical care, we'll hire professionals no matter where you choose to be."

Gwen began working the tie of the robe again as she worried her lower lip between her teeth. "What about Fire?" she asked finally.

Fire. The tone in Taylor's mind was smug. *Fire will be gone.* And Taylor would be glad. She and Gwen would have plenty of time to be together in the farmhouse, and Gwen could gradually get to know her again.

EJ and Krista exchanged a glance.

Alarms rang in Taylor's head, loud and shrill. What was that look?

"I mean," Gwen said, "you're all great, and I can tell I'm lucky to have you all for friends, but Fire's still the only one I actually remember and know."

"Yes," EJ said. "We thought about that, so if you'd like, she can come stay with you too."

What? Taylor almost leaped from her chair. She clenched the arms hard.

"The farmhouse has three big bedrooms, plus a parlor downstairs where we can set you up. So Krista and Taylor could both stay there with you and take care of whatever you need."

What the hell? When had *that* been discussed?

As though reading Taylor's mind, EJ said, "Krista and I talked about it this morning."

Taylor didn't even try to keep her fury out of her glare and was rewarded when EJ winced slightly in response.

"Would you?" Gwen asked Krista.

"Yes," Krista said matter-of-factly. "My contract here is finished, and I haven't signed another one yet. I was going to head home for a month or two, but I want to be with you, Gwen. I want you to have everything you need. And I can handle any nursing or home care duties if you're comfortable with that."

Gwen let out a deep sigh and rubbed her forehead. "All right. Let's go to this farmhouse."

"Excellent," Dr. Landon said. "I can have my assistant put together a list of doctors and home care agencies in the area for you before you leave, and we'll schedule your discharge for tomorrow."

"Thank you, Dr. Landon," EJ said.

"Yes," Gwen said, a bit shakily. "Thank you."

In the hallway, Krista eased Gwen's wheelchair to a stop. She'd been the one to slip behind Gwen and grab the handles before anyone else, before Taylor, could even get to her feet. Now, she stood like a potted plant several feet away from the other three gathered around Gwen. She seethed.

"God, I feel like such a wimp," Gwen said. "I felt great going in there, and one meeting takes me down. I'm so tired."

"That's understandable," Krista said. "A lot of important things were discussed, ones that had emotional charges for you. It's no surprise you feel drained."

Her calm reassurance could have soothed Taylor and her concerns along with Gwen's had it not been for the rage pumping through her veins. She was so mad she didn't know for certain who she was mad at. Krista, for showing up at the exact worst time after not being where she should have been twenty-one years ago? EJ, for leaving Taylor out of the loop time and time again? Jinx, for…Well, at the moment, wasn't it enough that Jinx was simply married to EJ?

"Taylor?" Someone spoke her name.

Taylor's fog of fury parted, and she found Gwen looking up at her tenderly. Taylor melted when Gwen looked at her that way. She melted now, but she couldn't speak.

"Thank you for stepping in and telling me what was happening. You must know me well to have picked up on my anxiety when everything was being dragged out." She offered Taylor a small smile. "I appreciate your help."

A lump of her own gratitude, relief, and love swelled in Taylor, closing her throat. She wanted so much to be the person Gwen looked to for comfort and solace, and whatever else she needed, in the way Taylor was pretty certain they'd been heading before everything went to hell. She swallowed her emotion. "You're welcome," she said as steadily as she could. "I could tell you were getting scared."

Gwen's smile widened a bit. "Thank you," she said again.

Their gazes held, suspending time between them.

This is what I want. If only the moment could never end.

"Are you ready to head back to your room?"

Fucking Krista. Taylor flexed her fists. She wanted to scream, but for Gwen, she stifled the urge. But their moment was broken.

"Yes," Gwen said. She pulled her attention from Taylor and glanced to EJ, then Jinx. "I need to sleep for a while."

Taylor watched, feeling pathetic and helpless, as Krista turned Gwen around and wheeled her down the corridor.

EJ blew out a breath. "That went well."

Taylor spun on her. "It went well? You mean, it went according to *your* plan. Yours and *Krista's.*"

EJ frowned. "Taylor, I know you're upset—"

"Upset? No. I passed upset quite a while ago when you wouldn't listen when I said there was something hinky with Krista. And since yesterday when I realized you weren't going to allow me even an opinion on removing Gwen's feeding tube—"

"Taylor, that's over. Gwen's awake and doing well. We don't have to make—"

"Fine." Taylor stepped closer and pointed her finger in EJ's face. "Let's move to today, this morning, when you apparently discussed with *Krista* her coming to stay with me and Gwen. Without a single word about it to me?"

"Do you know why I didn't include you?" EJ's voice hardened, but she kept her volume low. "Because I knew you'd react like this. But this is best for Gwen, and if you'd calm down for just one second, you'd be able to see that."

"Yes, I would. And if you'd talked to me about it this morning, you're right, I probably would've reacted like this, but I would have come to the same conclusion then too." Taylor's pulse pounded in her temples. "But now, this isn't about that. It's about you repeatedly discounting my involvement with Gwen. You haven't once taken our relationship into account from the moment I told you things have changed between us. Of course, I would have concluded that having the one person she remembers with her would be best for the woman I love, even if that person isn't me. *Because* I love her."

EJ lowered her head and covered her face with her hands. "Taylor." She drew out the word like a moan. "I haven't seen any of that. How am I supposed—"

"You don't have to *see* it." Taylor could barely keep from shaking her. "I *told* you what you needed to know. All you had to do is *listen* instead of taking over and just making all the decisions unilaterally."

Jinx stepped up to EJ and ran her hand over EJ's back, then sent Taylor a sympathetic look.

EJ jerked her head up. Anger flared in her eyes. "It was my responsibility to make the decisions. Gwen appointed me."

"Not today it wasn't. You said it yourself in there." Taylor pointed toward Landon's office door.

EJ stiffened. "We could go round and round about this forever. The fact is that Gwen appointed me her power of attorney, and yes, she's no longer incapacitated, but she still needs help, and she doesn't remember what you and she are, whatever it is. So I'm going to keep doing my job until she tells me otherwise. And I'm done with this conversation."

Taylor stilled, her rage molten in her veins. She'd seen this side of EJ many times and knew there was no use in any further discussion or argument. Besides, she needed to get out of there. She turned and started down the hallway.

"Where are you going?" EJ called after her.

"Out of here," Taylor shouted over her shoulder. "I need some time and space away from *you*."

"Wait. I want to talk to you about something else." EJ hurried to catch up to her.

"Seriously?" Taylor stopped abruptly and spun around, causing EJ to come to a screeching halt. "Why would I listen to another word you have to say?"

"Because it's about Gwen."

"So you'll acknowledge my feelings for her when it suits you?"

"You'd do this for her as her best friend," EJ said, her tone settled into its normal range and volume. "I know you would."

Taylor's frustration forced a ragged breath from her lungs. "Fine. What?"

"Gwen's going to need clothes and toiletries," EJ said as calmly as though they hadn't just been at each other's throats. "We could buy her all that new, but she was so comforted by the mere feeling of vague familiarity of the pajamas and robe we got her, I think it might help her to have some things from her house. You know, some of her favorite clothes and maybe that throw blanket she loves to snuggle into and watch movies? Her own perfume and shampoo and soap. And maybe even some pictures of all of us together."

"Okay. Okay. I get it." Taylor ran her hand through her hair, smoothing it into place.

"And since you said you need some time away from me," EJ eyed her, "I thought a drive up to her place and an overnight rest at home might do you some good."

"You mean it'd be good for me not to be around so you and Krista can get her settled." Taylor glared at EJ.

"No. I don't mean that." EJ tentatively touched Taylor's arm. "I mean what I said. I think it would be good for you, for you and me, to take some time away. And I honestly believe it would help Gwen to have some of her own things around her. And when you get back, which will only be a day or two, and Gwen is all settled, maybe you and I could go out to dinner or something. These last few weeks have been hard on both of us. We need to reconnect."

Taylor still seethed. EJ was right, but Taylor wasn't finished being mad yet.

"I didn't mean to hurt you. I promise," EJ said. "Please, believe that."

The sincerity in EJ's expression softened Taylor, much to her irritation. EJ would never deliberately hurt her. Tears threatened her composure. She couldn't let go here, though. If she did, everything she'd been feeling and struggling with since she woke after the accident would overwhelm her. She'd never get control. She bit back the tears. "All right. I'll go." She turned away toward the exit.

"Are you okay driving?" EJ called to her. "I mean, after the accident and all? Should we hire a car and driver?"

"I'll take care of it. I'll rent a car, and I'll be fine," Taylor said without looking back but loudly enough to be heard. "I'll see you in a couple days."

Taylor hadn't driven since the accident, but then, she hadn't been the one driving either. She'd be fine. She'd have to be. She couldn't take being cooped up in a car with a stranger. The harder part would be being in Gwen's house with all the new memories Taylor had there. EJ might not be able to get her head around their new relationship, to accept that things were definitively different between them, but Taylor was achingly aware. And if Gwen ended up not remembering what they had together and Taylor had to go back to being only friends, even best friends...

Christ. That would destroy her.

Taylor ducked into a bathroom and locked the door. She slumped against the wall and let the tears fall.

CHAPTER FOURTEEN

Steadied between Jinx and Fire, Gwen balanced on her good leg. The Xanax the doctor had given her before she'd left the hospital had alleviated the worst of her anxiety at getting into a car and allowed her to sleep for much of the two-hour trip from Fresno. Now, somewhat rested, she gazed around her in awe. EJ had been right. The Canine Complete compound was gorgeous.

Lush green fields extended in all directions, the expanse only interrupted by the beauty of pristine white fencing that created smaller sections. Some held colorful equipment like hurdles and ladders, while others waited empty, perhaps space for running and playing ball. She could imagine dogs and trainers working in them and would love to be able to watch. Several buildings dotted the opposite end of the fields, a din of barking arising from a large, fenced, circular area connected to one. In the distance, a small footbridge caught and held her attention. The ghost of a thought no, a feeling—she couldn't quite grasp whispered to her. She tilted her head to listen more closely.

"Are you tired?" EJ asked as she moved the wheelchair behind Gwen.

Gwen dragged her focus back to the moment. She shifted, leaning more heavily on Jinx, and glared down at the chair. She didn't want to be stuck in it, but it was better than another bed. Besides, Dr. Avery said she needed to follow her directions while her leg was still healing and do her physical therapy diligently if she wanted to be able to do everything she used to. She had no idea what *everything she used to* entailed, but she did want a full recovery so she could choose any activity.

"I know you slept on the way down," EJ said, "but do you need more rest?"

The touch of the cool afternoon breeze and the sunshine on Gwen's face exhilarated her. "No." She bent and reached for the arm of the chair. Fire and Jinx tightened their grips and helped her ease into it.

"I want to stay outside. I want to explore."

Fire chuckled. "Of course you do." She stepped away and opened the back door of her car.

Gwen, EJ, and Jinx had driven in EJ's Lexus, followed by Fire in her own car, a Subaru of some kind. It was disconcerting seeing Fire with such an adult life. Looking so different. Owning a car. Working, and not just in a job but a career. In nursing, of all things. So much responsibility. And it meant she had to have gone to college. How had she done that? When they'd known each other, Fire skipped school every other day and hadn't been able to keep even a part-time job due to her somewhat volatile nature. And neither of them had known how to drive.

Gwen flushed, unsettled. She couldn't seem to keep the two timelines straight. "Is that normal for me?"

"When I knew you, it was," Fire said with a smile. She lifted the small case that held Gwen's pajamas and robe, along with a couple of pairs of sweatpants and a few tops EJ and Taylor had bought on their shopping trip.

Gwen looked up at Fire. Her hair was darker than it used to be, more auburn than the flame red of her teens, but its golden highlights still glowed like embers in the sunlight, giving her face a subtle radiance. She was still beautiful. Laughter and optimism had always sparkled in her eyes despite everything she'd gone through, and that glint remained. What had she gone through in the years since? Hell, what had Gwen gone through since?

"And it's true of you now. You'd almost always prefer to be outside," EJ said, running her fingers lightly over Gwen's shoulder. "So that's something you know is your true nature."

A burst of thunderous barking exploded through the open windows of the house in front of the cars, making Gwen jump.

"Hold on," a raspy voice shouted over the noise. "Let me get the door before you tear it down."

When said door flew open, a large gold and brown dog hurled himself out and leaped off the porch steps.

Gwen startled and gasped, but when he slid to a stop in front of her, tongue lolling, she relaxed and laughed. "Well, hi there."

He excitedly began a thorough investigation of her, his frantic sniffing beginning at her bare toes extending from her cast and traveling up her leg. At her knee, he stopped and tentatively sniffed at the wheelchair. A low growl rumbled in his throat.

"I know, buddy," Gwen said. "That's how I feel about it too."

The dog looked up at her and cocked his head, then resumed his examination, starting over with her other foot.

Gwen giggled at his enthusiasm. "Let me guess. You're Pete?"

The dog sat on his haunches and gave a final bark. His entire body quivered as he seemed to wait for something else.

Jinx chuckled. "Yes, this is Pete. He usually leaps into your lap. You taught him bad habits when he was a puppy," she said with obvious humor as she ruffled the fur on his head. "But I think he knows something's up with your cast and all."

"Awww, what a sweetheart." Gwen could tell Pete was one of those dogs that was almost human. "I bet he'll do it gently." She patted her thigh. "You want to come see me?"

Pete sprang to all fours but instantly calmed, then eased closer and rested his big head in her lap. His weight and warmth filled Gwen with a sense of comfort and that unconditional love so many dogs exude.

"I can tell we were friends," Gwen murmured, stroking the softness of one ear, then the other. "Or should I say *are* friends?"

He let out a deep sigh that ended in a low grumble and turned his head in her lap so he was more directly beneath her hand.

She laughed. "I guess you know what you want." She obliged and scratched gently.

A woman squealed. "Oh, my God!"

Gwen looked up with a start to find a small, bleached blonde standing on the porch with a heavy-set woman with dark cropped hair behind her. They stared back at her with wide grins.

The blonde pressed her hands to her cheeks, and tears spilled from her eyes. "Oh, damn. I promised myself I wouldn't cry, and now look at me blubberin' away."

The larger woman chuckled and wrapped her arm around the blonde's shoulders. "That's all right, sweet pea. We were all worried about our girl. Let it go."

As Gwen sat with Pete's big bear of a head in her lap, surrounded by all these women, an awareness that such scenes were known to her unveiled itself. Not a memory. More of a knowing. And yet, something wasn't quite right about this one.

"Oh, darlin'," the blonde hurried down the steps, "I know you don't remember me. EJ told us. I'm Sparkle, and I just..." Her tears were flowing more freely now. "Can I give you a little hug?"

A smile bubbled up from deep within Gwen. She didn't remember Sparkle, this was true, but she somehow knew she loved her hugs. She nodded and sank into the embrace that seemed to have been coming with or without her consent.

Sparkle's arms were strong yet gentle. She stroked Gwen's short hair as she rocked her tenderly. "You gave us such a scare, girl," she whispered.

Gwen's eyes flooded in a sudden rush of emotion as, for the first time since she'd woken, it hit her that she'd died. That she could have so easily not come back. That, whether or not she remembered them, she had people who loved her, more than she'd ever had in her life, even when she'd had her mother.

"Oh! Oh, no!" Sparkle released her. "Did I hurt you?" She ran her thumbs beneath Gwen's eyes, wiping away the wetness. "I'm so sorry."

"No," Gwen said, catching Sparkle's hands and squeezing them. "I just realized how lucky I am." She looked up at the woman still on the porch. "You're Reggie?"

"Yes, ma'am." Reggie gave a single nod. "Welcome to your new and temporary home."

Another swell of emotion at the generosity in the greeting threatened to overtake Gwen, but she swallowed it down. "Thank you." She glanced around her. "All of you. Thank you."

But something was missing. Some*one*. Taylor. Gwen hadn't talked with her as much as she had with EJ or Fire, but somehow in this moment, she knew Taylor was integral to scenes like this one and to Gwen's life. EJ had said she'd gone to Gwen's house to get some of her things. She'd be back tomorrow. Then everything would be complete.

"So," Sparkle said, having regained her composure. "Do you want something to eat or drink? Or maybe you want to lie down? We have your room all set up."

"No. I want to be out here in the sunshine and the air," Gwen said, filled with a surge of life. "Jinx, can you take me for a walk? You promised me lots of them. I want to be out there where everything is so green." She gestured to the fields.

"I'd be happy to," Jinx said. "But we'll have to stay on the paths. I don't think your wheelchair can handle the meadows."

"We can take care of that," Reggie said, beaming. "Hold on." She disappeared into the house and returned with a second chair, similar to the one Gwen sat in, only the wheels were much wider, almost like small tires. "When we saw this in the medical supply store, Sparkle said you had to have it." She grinned. "All-terrain. The four-wheel drive of wheelchairs."

After Sparkle had proudly shown everyone the accessibility ramp Reggie had built off the far end of the porch, working late into the previous night so it was finished for Gwen's arrival, Gwen transferred into her new ride, and she, Jinx, and Pete took off into the gorgeous afternoon. While her memory of the past three weeks was limited to the last couple of days, she felt the layers of artificial light and recycled air waft away under the day's freshness and warmth. She turned her face into the soft breeze and reveled in its caress. She sighed in contentment. Life was so good.

Jinx followed a curved path around to the buildings Gwen had seen. She walked slowly, pointing out various things along the way and telling Gwen all about the history and growth of Canine Complete. Her pride and joy were evident.

The more Gwen learned about Jinx, the more she liked her. She listened, rapt at the story, and stroked Pete's head each time he nudged her hand with his nose as he pranced along beside her.

As they got closer to the circular fenced area she'd noticed earlier, the barking that had been the backdrop to the afternoon grew louder, and she could see between the wooden slats of the fence. A group of dogs raced around, playing with each other.

Jinx moved the chair farther around and stopped in front of a gate through which the view was unimpaired. "This is the exercise yard for the dogs being boarded. If they're sociable, they get to play with the others. If not, a staff member brings them out individually and plays ball with them or takes them for a run."

The sight lifted Gwen's spirits even higher. After she'd chosen the option of coming here for further recovery, she'd had second thoughts. Maybe her own home would've been better. Now that she was here, though, surrounded by so many kind people and all these dogs and beautiful grounds, she had no doubt she'd made the right decision.

"Oh, look!" She laughed at a stubby-legged wiener dog chasing a huge Rottweiler. Every so often, the Rottweiler would turn sharply and make a tight circle around the dachshund, then the dachshund would yip and nip at the bigger dog's feet. Then they'd be off and running again. "They're so cute."

Jinx smiled. "That's Dylan Thomas and Shatzi. Dylan's the Rottweiler. They're best friends when they're here together."

Gwen heard the love in Jinx's voice. "Do you know all the dogs?"

"Pretty much," Jinx said, still watching the antics in the yard. "There are some that have started training while I've been gone, but I'll get to know them now that I'm back."

Once again, a realization struck Gwen. EJ, Jinx, and Taylor had given up their lives for the weeks she'd been unconscious. And now, Fire was doing the same, and Taylor had taken a leave of absence from her job for who knew how long while Gwen finished recovering. "I'm sorry you all had—"

"Hey," Jinx said with a quick jerk of her head in Gwen's direction. "Don't you do that." She dropped to one knee beside her. "No apologies. We're all here for you because we love you. None of us want to be anywhere else until you're back on your feet. Literally. That's why EJ and I wanted you to come here, so we can see you more and help take care of you."

Gwen gave her an embarrassed smile, then nodded. She wanted to believe her because if it weren't true, Gwen would feel horrible. "Thank you."

Jinx squeezed her hand. "So where do you want to go now?"

Gwen glanced around. "I want to be surrounded by green. Can we go out into the fields? Maybe over by those trees." She pointed to a cluster across the grassy meadow.

"You got it." Jinx rose and turned Gwen's chair around. "Let's see what these all-terrain wheels can do."

At the end of a bumpy ride that had them both laughing, yellow, red, and brown leaves crunched under the tires of the wheelchair, and the afternoon sunlight filtered through the ones that remained on the branches above. As they came to a stop at the far edge of the cluster, Pete began racing around in circles and jumping into the air.

Gwen laughed harder. "What's going on with him?"

Jinx set the chair's brakes, then hesitated, her eyes meeting Gwen's. "This is where we play Frisbee," she said softly, but she sounded distracted. "Can I…" her voice broke a little.

"Jinx, what's wrong?" Gwen ran her hand down Jinx's forearm. "Are you okay?"

"I just…" Jinx blinked rapidly. "Can I hug you?"

Touched, Gwen smiled. "Of course."

Without another word, Jinx slid her arms around Gwen and held her close.

A rush of pure comfort swept over Gwen. She sighed and hugged Jinx back, resting her head on her shoulder.

Neither said anything.

Finally, without letting go, Jinx spoke. "I thought we lost you." Her words were quiet. Her voice quavered. "I can't imagine our family without you here. Thank you for coming back."

Gwen couldn't answer. A surge of emotion clogged her throat and cut off her breath. All she could do was tighten her hold.

"I should've done this as soon as you woke up," Jinx continued. "We all should have. But I think we were so worried about overwhelming you since you didn't remember us, we held back. But when I saw Sparkle do it, I couldn't wait anymore." She sniffed. "Thank you." She inhaled deeply, then started to ease away.

Gwen clung to her. "Not yet." Her voice shook as much as Jinx's. "It feels good. I'm just beginning to understand how lucky I am to have all of you."

Jinx gave her another gentle squeeze. "You do have us. Every single one of us. Whether you remember or not, we're all family. And you haven't even met all of us yet." She let out a small laugh.

Reluctantly, Gwen let go and relaxed against the back of her chair. "Thank you, Jinx. You're so sweet." She watched as Jinx straightened and took in her striking features—the laugh lines at the corners of her deep blue eyes, her lips that always seemed to be on the brink of a smile, her overall manner that emanated warmth and reassurance. Jinx's voice returned to her from a deep, sooty fog. *Knock knock.* Gwen giggled. "You know, I do remember you."

Jinx's eyes widened. "You do?"

"Not from way before, but from when I was unconscious."

Jinx tilted her head with a questioning look. "Really?"

"I think." Gwen shifted her gaze to the expanse of the meadow.

Pete still dashed around, stopping randomly to see if Jinx was paying attention. He barked.

She turned and pulled something from her pocket, then shook out a folded, canvas Frisbee, sending Pete into delirium. She threw it, sailing it over his head.

Pete spun and raced after it.

"I think I heard all of your voices when you were talking to me," Gwen said, searching her mind. "I think I even put your names with each voice, but when I woke up, all that was gone. All I actually remembered then was Fire."

Pete ran to Jinx and dropped the Frisbee at her feet.

"But now that I'm with you all," Gwen went on, "and getting to know you, I seem to know things."

"Like what?" Jinx sounded eager. She scooped up the dog toy and threw it again.

Gwen's thoughts were sketchy. She focused hard. "Well, like jokes. I think you tell jokes?" Her statement turned into a question.

Jinx's eyebrows shot up. "Yes!"

"And did you tell me jokes when I was unconscious?"

Jinx flushed a light pink. "Well, yeah. Taylor told me not to torture you with them while you couldn't get away, but you always seemed to like bad jokes before, so I thought it might make you feel better. Was it horrible?"

Gwen's heart filled with affection, for Jinx and her attempt to help her through such a tough time, and for Taylor for trying to protect her. "No, I liked it." Gwen looked out across the field. "Did you talk to me about Pete too? I think I remember hearing about him, but I didn't know who he was."

"I did! I told you everything Sparkle and Reggie said he'd been doing when we had our check-in phone calls. I thought since you love him so much, you'd like hearing all that."

"I did like it, even though I didn't know him." Gwen spotted Pete in the distance flipping the Frisbee high into the air and catching it himself. As she watched, another dog came to mind, this one lighter in color, almost white. He was running in the field too, not this one, but one as beautiful. He'd run toward her, and when she'd recognized him, she'd fallen to her knees and thrown her arms around his neck. *Dexter!* But where had she seen him? And when?

"Gwen?" Jinx's voice cut into her thoughts. "You all right?"

"Yes." Gwen said tentatively. "I just...I saw this dog."

"You mean Pete?"

"No, a different one." Gwen felt as though she were in two places at once, here with Jinx and Pete, and somewhere else. "Dexter."

"The dog you loved from that foster home when you were twelve?" Jinx asked.

Gwen's heartbeat quickened with excitement. "You know about him?"

Jinx laughed. "We all do. You've talked about him a lot. He sounds like a great dog."

Gwen smiled, thinking of him. "He was."

"But you saw him?" Jinx glanced around the meadow.

"Not here," Gwen said. "Wherever I was. He was there."

"You mean when you were unconscious?" Jinx knelt beside Gwen.

Gwen recalled the gray, dark fog she'd drifted in, that place where she could hear the voices but couldn't see anything. "No, somewhere else."

"Where?"

Gwen set her mind free, let it soar. "Another field. And there was a school." A scene started coming back to her. "And my teacher," she added as the image of Mrs. Walker sharpened.

"A teacher?" Jinx sounded confused.

"Yes, my fourth-grade teacher," Gwen said, knowing none of this was making sense to Jinx. It barely made sense to Gwen. "She was my teacher the year my mother left."

"Oh." Jinx settled onto the grass. "So this was a long time ago?"

"No. It doesn't seem like it." Gwen's mind raced. "I mean, yes, it was a long time ago since I was in fourth grade. And Dexter, well, Dexter was a great dog at one of my foster homes, and we had to put him to sleep. So he's..." Gwen gasped.

"What?" Jinx sat up straight and grabbed Gwen's arm.

Gwen turned slowly as awareness dawned. "I was with Dexter and Mrs. Walker when I was dead. But I wasn't dead. Mrs. Walker said my body was dead in that moment but that *I* was in a place with no time. But I had to come back." She stared into Jinx's eyes, eyes as astonished as hers must have been.

"You mean in the ER?" Jinx blinked. "They said they lost you and had to restart your heart."

Gwen scrunched her forehead, trying to think. "I guess." Then she remembered. "Yes. There was a light. Just like they say." She grasped Jinx's hand. "And I knew to follow it. And then a building that was my school. And Mrs. Walker. And we talked. Jinx, it felt so good there."

"What did you talk about?" Jinx asked.

In a flash, everything rushed back. It hit her like a gale force wind. She slapped her hand to her chest. "So many things. About how I could be dead and there at the same time. And that year and how I just disappeared from school one day. About that place we were in and how it felt so amazing, so peaceful. And—" She winced. "Oh, God! Jinx, I wanted to stay there." After finding so many people obviously important to her, who clearly loved her, she was astounded at the idea of not wanting to return.

"But you didn't," Jinx said, derailing her train of thought.

Gwen shook her head. "I didn't." Mrs. Walker's voice came to her. "She said I had to come back."

"Your teacher? Did she say why?"

"She said I hadn't finished what I came here to do. That I needed to learn to trust love." Bewildered, Gwen leaned back in her chair.

"That's so cool," Jinx said enthusiastically.

"But I do trust love." Gwen's mind swirled in confusion. "I mean, I had trouble when my mother left me behind, but when I found Fire"—she met Jinx's gaze—"I realized it was just my mother's love I couldn't trust. I love Fire so much. And I know she loves me. I can trust…No, wait. That was when I was sixteen." And now she was thirty-seven, and they weren't together. There was that damned twenty-one years. She searched Jinx's face. "What happened?"

"I don't know," Jinx said softly. "You'd have to ask her. I don't think anyone else knows."

Gwen considered the suggestion, then decided. "No. Dr. Landon said it'd be better for me to remember on my own, so I'm going to try." Mrs. Walker drifted back in. "And my teacher told me we can't know things until we're ready. She did say, though, there'd be someone here when I returned to help me. Maybe *that's* Fire." She looked at Jinx once more, this time for potential agreement.

"Uh, I don't know." Something that might have been concern passed through Jinx's eyes before she averted her gaze. "You want to go back to the house?"

Jinx might not know what happened between Fire and Gwen so many years ago, but she clearly knew something. Gwen chose not to press. She wasn't even sure if she wanted to know more right now. Whatever had happened, Gwen had obviously recovered. Did she want to relive any pain or guilt she might have felt going through it? Maybe if she waited until she was truly ready, it could all come back to her without that. "Sure," she said. "But, Jinx?"

"Yeah?" Jinx sounded cautious.

"Could you not tell anyone about all this? I want time to process it." It all felt too personal, and not just a little weird. She'd know when the time was right, and she wanted to be the one to share it.

"Of course." Jinx got to her feet. "It isn't my story to tell."

Tension Gwen hadn't realized she was holding lifted. "Thank you. But you have to promise to bring me out here again," she added to bring the conversation back to the ease that had developed between them.

Jinx laughed. "Any time you want."

As Jinx pushed the chair across the meadow toward the farmhouse, Gwen's attention was inexplicably drawn again to the footbridge at the far end of the field. There was a surge of images and sensation. Warmth flowed through her. Colors of a sunset glinted off water. The excitement of something new tingled low in her belly. She almost asked Jinx about the bridge, if Gwen had ever been on it, where it led, but there'd be another time for that. She'd already said something that had made Jinx uncomfortable. Why add to it?

Besides, her memory of where she'd gone when she'd died had left her with plenty to ponder, things to figure out. And who was here to help her with it all?

CHAPTER FIFTEEN

Taylor stepped through the doorway at the back of the farmhouse and into the kitchen. No one was in the room, but the lingering scent of baked apples and sugar, along with the pie cooling on the counter, were telltale signs that Sparkle had spent part of the morning there.

Taylor had always loved the cozy feel of this kitchen with its red and white rooster décor and bench seat corner dinette. Sparkle and Reggie's new home was beautiful, but prior to their move and turning the farmhouse into a guest house, sitting at this bar helping Sparkle prepare meals for the group had quickly become one of Taylor's favorite places to be when they all got together here. She'd missed it. Taylor was no cook. She simply liked the room and Sparkle's company.

Sparkle was direct and to the point, the call-it-like-you-see-it type, and she'd called Taylor on her feelings for Gwen repeatedly since the day they'd met. Not just the physical attraction but what she truly felt. And not the way EJ did, with warnings and threats, but with actual interest and sometimes encouragement. Something Taylor appreciated, even if she didn't ever follow Sparkle's advice to go for it. Taylor had always given in to her fears, her certainty, of what would happen if she surrendered to those feelings. She'd lose herself in Gwen, in her love for her, and she'd promised herself she'd never let that happen again.

She thought back to the previous night, being in Gwen's house, in her bed where she'd slept alone, but not alone. All the memories of being there with Gwen, touching her, kissing her, being far more than their friendship had allowed for so many years consumed her, and she'd realized at around two in the morning how far down that rabbit hole she'd fallen. She'd actually had the thought that maybe it'd be better if Gwen never remembered what they'd had for those three short weeks. Maybe if she only remembered their friendship. Then Taylor could back up, gather all those feelings that had been on the verge of pouring out, tuck them away again, and retreat to the safety of her life as it'd been. She bit her lip. But did she want to?

She moved through the bottom floor of the farmhouse, pulling the rolling suitcase she'd packed for Gwen behind her and listening for any sounds that indicated someone was there, but only silence greeted her. She didn't want to call out in case Gwen was sleeping.

Someone had to be around, though. There'd been a Subaru she'd never seen before parked out back. Krista's perhaps? Taylor clenched her jaw slightly before she caught herself. That was another recurring rant that had kept her awake the previous night. *Krista.* But she'd finally resolved to accept everything that was, and that included Krista's continued presence. She was a nurse. She could take care of Gwen in ways the rest of them couldn't.

She strode through the foyer and poked her head around the corner of the doorway to the old parlor and took in the hospital bed that filled the space once occupied by a pool table, but it was empty and neatly made. The robe Taylor and EJ had bought for Gwen lay draped across the back of an overstuffed chair. The room felt as homey as it always had, but the bed with its hanging trapeze lift and metal railings served as a harsh reminder of Gwen's condition. The reality triggered images of the truck barreling toward them and their car careening down the embankment. The memory of the stench of burning leather and rubber turned Taylor's stomach. She drew in a sharp breath and shook the scene from her mind. It still haunted her dreams, but she'd be damned if it'd take over her daytime hours. She breathed deeply.

Taylor crossed to the bedside, lifted the suitcase to the mattress, and opened it. It didn't hold many of Gwen's favorite clothing items—a lot of those were in the bag that had burned with the car—but the familiarity of these still might trigger some memories. She returned to the foyer and retrieved some hangers from the coat closet, then started unpacking Gwen's things.

A floorboard creaked overhead.

She glanced at the ceiling. It had to be Krista. Anyone upstairs would have heard Taylor pull into the back parking area, and anyone *else* would have come down to greet her. Perhaps Krista wasn't any happier about Taylor being there than Taylor was about Krista's presence.

Taylor hadn't considered that. Maybe after finding Gwen all these years later, Krista resented Taylor's newfound relationship with her as much as Taylor did the past Krista and Gwen shared. Or maybe it was simply the timing of it all they both resented. Either way, the idea of Taylor getting on Krista's nerves as much as Krista got on Taylor's was childishly gratifying. Regardless, Taylor was here and had a job to do. She wanted to have all Gwen's things in place by the time she got back.

As Taylor emptied the suitcase, she arranged Gwen's sweats, underwear, and socks in the drawers of the nightstand that, presumably, Sparkle and Reggie had moved from a bedroom upstairs. Then she slipped Gwen's blouses and pants onto hangers and hung them on the metal bar of the trapeze lift. They'd have to go in the coat closet in the foyer, but that would be okay. There'd always be someone around to get things for Gwen.

At the bottom of the suitcase, Taylor found the soft T-shirts she'd wrapped around a few of Gwen's favorite pictures and carefully retrieved a couple. In a framed snapshot of Gwen, EJ, and Taylor at Gunther's, the much-loved ice cream shop they frequented, Gwen sat in the middle, smiling widely, with an arm draped around each of her best friends. It'd been Gwen's thirty-second birthday. A five-by-seven photo showed Gwen and EJ toasting one another at the party celebrating EJ's promotion to executive regional director and, consequently, Gwen's to administrative assistant to an executive. They'd all gotten so drunk that night they'd left the party in a taxi and made it only as far as Taylor's condo. Gwen had to race inside to throw up, so Taylor had paid the fare, and EJ and Gwen had stayed the night. They'd all passed out in Taylor's king-size bed, none of them remembering how they'd ended up there.

Taylor chuckled at the memory of Gwen's wide eyes and heated blush the next morning when she'd realized where she was and whom she was pressed up against. She placed the two pictures on the nightstand, then unbundled the rest.

A small collage frame held four pics of Gwen with her hiking friends on various backpacking trips, and a professional portrait of EJ, Jinx, and Pete they'd given to all of their friends when they'd announced their engagement was mounted in silver. Finally, she gazed at a snapshot of Gwen and her mother. She hadn't been sure about bringing this one since, while at thirty-seven, Gwen had made peace with everything that had happened, at sixteen, where her mind was stuck, she had no idea their paths had crossed again.

"Knock knock?"

Taylor smiled and looked up, expecting to find Jinx delivering one of her bad jokes.

Instead, Krista stood in the doorway, her hands stuffed into the front pockets of her jeans, her shoulders slightly hunched beneath a Raiders black and silver football jersey. "Hi," she said tightly. "Need any help?"

Taylor held the smile a beat for show, then turned away. "That's okay." She set the last photo on the nightstand.

"I can put these in the coat closet." Krista's voice was close.

Taylor jumped. She grabbed the hangers from the lift before Krista closed her fingers around them. "I've got them. Thanks." She hurried to the foyer. When she returned, Krista was still beside the bed.

"How was your drive down?" Krista asked.

Chitchat? Really? Taylor searched her mind for a snarky retort but relented. Krista was making an effort. The least Taylor could do was be nice. But what could she say about her drive today? She might tell EJ or Jinx how she'd gripped the steering wheel so tightly her hands cramped when she'd passed the off-ramp that led to the site of the accident. But not Krista. Nor would she tell her about the picnic Gwen had packed for their trip and how they'd lain on the blanket in the meadow talking and making out. That last memory of Gwen before Taylor's world had gone to hell had flooded her so violently she'd had to pull to the side of the freeway until she could stop sobbing. "It was fine. Not much traffic."

"That's good," Krista said. She glanced at Taylor, then around the room.

Taylor winced. The tension between them was as thick as sludge. They had to find something to talk about. "So where is everyone?" she asked. "I mean, everyone else. Because you're here."

Krista laughed softly. "I knew what you meant." She leaned her hip against the edge of the bed. "Gwen had an appointment with the psychiatrist Dr. Landon set her up with, and EJ and Jinx took her to it."

"Oh. That was quick." Taylor relaxed slightly.

Krista folded her arms and trailed her fingers along her bicep. "Apparently, Dr. Landon called ahead and filled the new doc in on the situation, so he agreed to see Gwen today even though it's Saturday." Her gaze moved from Taylor's face to the window behind her, then swept over the pictures Taylor had arranged on the nightstand. Her eyes widened, and she leaned forward. "Is that Gwen's mom?"

Taylor automatically followed her stare. "Yeah. How'd you know that? You didn't know her. Did you?"

Krista picked up the photo and studied it. "No, but Gwen had a picture of her when we first met."

Taylor flinched. "She did? When *we* met her, she said she didn't have any."

"No," Krista said absently, still absorbed. "A guy that was at our foster home when Gwen got there burned it because she wouldn't…" She looked at Taylor. "Well, it was the only one she had." She returned the frame to the nightstand. "How old is Gwen there?"

Taylor tried not to think about what the guy might have wanted from Gwen. She'd heard about some of the things Gwen had to deal with in the system. "She was thirty when she found her mom."

"Gwen went looking for her? *She* didn't come find Gwen?"

"Yes. She hired a private investigator."

Krista frowned. Sadness passed through her eyes, followed by a flash of anger.

Taylor gave her a moment to process the implications. Clearly, Krista was aware of the impact it'd had on Gwen that her mother never came looking for her. Gwen had fought with herself, wanting to be strong enough not to care, not to be the one to search. It'd hurt her so badly. In Krista's silence and her expression, Taylor saw how deeply she'd known Gwen and how genuinely she must have been affected by Gwen's pain. Taylor still wasn't thrilled about her being there, but she now understood that Krista was as protective of Gwen as the rest of them, and that made a difference.

Krista finally pulled her attention from mother and daughter and focused on Taylor. "EJ never mentioned getting in touch with Gwen's mom after the accident. Has she passed away?"

Taylor shrugged. "Who knows? She only stuck around for about six months." How much should she tell her? "Gwen didn't go after her again."

Krista's expression darkened. "Was Gwen okay?"

"She's okay with it now. She worked it through, but…" Taylor hesitated. "I think it'd be better for Gwen to tell you the rest when she remembers it."

Krista nodded. "Sure. I understand."

"But since you do know the basics now," Taylor said, looking back to the array of pictures. "Do you think I should put that one away until Gwen does remember the reunion they had? I brought it because she does technically remember her mother, but I hadn't considered the fact that it might be hard on her if the picture only reminds her that her mother left her again and not that she's healed from it."

Krista sighed. "This is so hard, trying to figure out what's best for her."

"Yeah," Taylor said, thinking back through all the doubts and questions she'd had when she was trying to decide what to bring from Gwen's house. It felt good to have someone to bounce this off of given that EJ wasn't around.

"It might be better to put it away for now," Krista said finally.

Taylor didn't hesitate. She plucked the framed photo from the arrangement and cupped it in her hand. "I'll keep it in my room for now. And speaking of which, I'm going to get my bags from the car and get unpacked." She started toward the door.

"When you're finished, could you come back down?" Krista asked. "I'd like to talk with you about something."

It was inevitable. They'd have to address the proverbial elephant in the room at some point. Better to do so before Gwen had to settle in with them both in the same house. "Okay," Taylor said. "I won't be long."

"No rush," Krista said, easing away from the bed. "Gwen won't be back for a while. You just missed them by a few minutes."

Taylor moved into the foyer, and Krista caught up with her.

"Have you eaten?" Krista asked as she fell into step. "Sparkle made butternut squash raviolis for dinner last night and left a plate for you in the fridge with some garlic bread. Said it's one of your favorites. Want me to heat it up for you?"

Despite her decision to try to get along with Krista, she wanted to say no. No, thanks, that is, to be polite. Maybe with a shrug of indifference. Getting along with her was one thing, but letting her heat things up for her, wait on her... But oh, my God! Sparkle's garlic bread? And yes, her raviolis were definitely a favorite. She faltered. She *was* starving. And it wasn't like Krista would probably pick up on her cool nonchalance. She didn't know Taylor hadn't eaten since last night, that she hadn't wanted to take the time this morning to even go through a drive-through. She'd wanted to get here to be with Gwen. "That would be nice of you," Taylor said, surrendering. "Thank you."

When Taylor returned to the kitchen after unpacking and getting settled, she found Krista removing a covered plate from the oven. She blinked in astonishment. "You didn't have to go to all that trouble. Nuking it would have been fine."

Krista smiled. "Food doesn't stay hot as long when you reheat it in the microwave. And this way, the pasta doesn't get tough." She waved her free hand in the direction of the corner dinette where a place setting of cutlery and a folded napkin waited along with salt and pepper shakers and a container of parmesan cheese. The gesture was clearly an indication for Taylor to sit.

Bewildered, she obeyed.

Krista set the plate in front of her, then returned to the oven. She retrieved a foil packet and brought it to Taylor. "Lemonade? Sparkle made that last night too," she said on her way to the refrigerator, as though she already knew the answer.

And, of course, she did. Anyone who'd ever tasted Sparkle's homemade lemonade would know the answer. "Sure," Taylor said, more dumbfounded with each passing moment.

Krista grabbed a glass from the cupboard, filled it from a pitcher, and brought it to Taylor. She sat on the corner bench across from her and curled her legs beneath her.

Taylor studied her, not knowing if she looked like a cuddly puppy settling in for a nap or a coiled snake ready to strike.

Then Krista smiled.

Taylor narrowed her eyes. "Oh, crap. You're going to make me like you, aren't you?"

Krista let out a hearty laugh, true humor lighting her eyes. "Would that be so bad?"

Taylor considered her answer.

"Here's the thing." Krista's expression became serious. "I know you don't want me here, and this could get awkward if we don't work it out."

"Do you want *me* here?"

Krista looked thoughtful. "It's not that I don't want you here. It isn't my place to say who can or can't be here. It's just that I wish you were still only friends with Gwen."

Taylor rested her elbows on the table and leaned forward, her empty stomach of secondary interest for the moment. "That's honest," she said, impressed. "So I'll be honest too. I'm torn about you being here. On one hand, I know it'll be good for Gwen to have your nursing skills so readily available, but also, as much as I hate to admit it, because EJ was right. It's important to have someone here Gwen knows. Or, at least, thinks she knows." Taylor paused to see if Krista would object to the qualification.

She simply dipped her head in acknowledgement.

"On the other hand, I hate that you're the only one she thinks she knows, and I was hoping once we left the hospital, we'd be done with you." Taylor cringed inwardly at the harshness of the sentiment. "No offense," she added.

"None taken." Krista remained impassive. "And I'm sorry my presence upsets you. Normally, I don't stick around where I'm not wanted, but there's no way in hell I'm going anywhere as long as Gwen wants me here."

Taylor frowned but nodded. She understood completely. She hated the next question clawing at her to get out, but it had to be asked. And answered. "Do you plan to try to get Gwen back?"

Krista pressed her lips into a firm line, and her eyes clouded with emotion. She held Taylor's gaze so hard and for so long, it surprised Taylor when she averted hers and it became distant. "I wouldn't try to sway her on anything until she has her memory back, and once that happens, you won't have anything to worry about. She'll remember that I didn't come back for her and won't want anything to do with me."

Taylor recalled Krista's flash of anger at the revelation that Gwen's mother hadn't been the one to find Gwen and had to wonder. "Why didn't you?" It wasn't her business, *at all,* but the words were out before she could stop them.

Maybe it was the bluntness of the question that snapped Krista back from wherever she'd drifted to. When her gaze landed on Taylor again, her eyes were misted with a light sheen of tears. She swallowed hard, then gave a sharp shake of her head. "When I tell that story, I want it to be to Gwen."

Taylor nodded, feeling almost sympathetic toward Krista. She obviously regretted whatever had happened, what she'd done to lose Gwen. She softened. "Maybe you won't have to."

Krista frowned. "I don't want her to not get her memory back just so she doesn't know I failed her. I'm not *that* person."

No, she wasn't. Taylor had seen enough of her to know that. "I only meant maybe when she remembers, everything will come back at once, and she'll remember the why along with the fact that she worked it through."

"That'd be great," Krista said with a wry smile, "except that she never knew why. All she knew is that I left her and never came back, exactly like her mom. Did she work *that* through?"

Taylor's mind spun. Gwen's mother *and* the first girl she'd slept with, possibly her first love, had both walked out on her with no explanation? That could certainly break someone's heart, especially at such a young age. Was that why, if Gwen had been attracted to women all this time, she'd never revealed it? Was that why she dated men even though she didn't seem to ever want them around for long? Taylor struggled to process it all. "I don't know. She's never said anything about you."

Krista let out a bark of a laugh. "Well, that says it all, doesn't it?"

It pretty much did, but Taylor didn't want to say it. Krista felt bad enough. She didn't need her face rubbed in it. The sound of a car pulling up to the back of the house saved her from having to comment further.

Krista edged aside the curtain and peered out the window.

"Is that them?" Taylor asked.

Krista shook her head. "Someone in an old Mini Cooper." She flexed her fingers in a tiny wave. "A blonde in tie-dye?" She arched her eyebrow.

Taylor grinned and jumped up. "Yeah!" She hurried to the door and yanked it open. "Namastacey!"

Dressed in a loose-fitting tunic with a blue, green, and purple spiral design, navy leggings, and neon pink high-tops, Stacey bounded up the porch steps and into Taylor's outstretched arms. "Can I hug you? I don't want to hurt your ribs?"

"They're doing okay." Taylor couldn't help but pull her in close. "Just be a little gentle."

She encircled Taylor's waist and snuggled into her embrace. "Oh, honey." She rocked her and inhaled deeply. "It's so good to see you." She eased away and held Taylor at arm's length. "Are you okay? Are you all healed?" She ran her hands down Taylor's ribcage and around her torso.

Taylor laughed. "What is this? A pat down?"

She scoffed and gave Taylor's shoulder a playful slap. "I just need to see for myself that you're intact. You and Gwen have no business giving us that kind of scare." She pulled Taylor into another tender hug.

Taylor held her close. "I'm good," she whispered. "I promise." She breathed out a deep sigh, soaking in the comfort Stacey always exuded. She sank into the embrace, suddenly aware of how long it'd been since she'd been hugged like this. Most of her hugs came from EJ and Gwen, and with things the way they were between her and the former, and the latter not even remembering her, she'd been coming up far short of the four-hugs-a-day minimum she'd heard somewhere was necessary for one to thrive.

"We need to talk, honey." Stacey gently rubbed Taylor's back, then eased away. "But that wasn't you peeking out the window, so who's here with us?"

Taylor stepped back and ushered her into the kitchen.

Krista was getting to her feet just as they crossed the threshold.

"This is Krista," Taylor said, beginning a formal introduction, but she was immediately stumped. "She's, uh…"

"Gwen's nurse from the hospital." Stacey offered her warm smile, her dimples winking in her cheeks. She extended her hand.

Krista shook it. "That's right. And you're Namastacey?" She furrowed her brow. "That's an unusual name."

Stacey laughed. "It's a nickname. I did some spiritual study when I was serving time, and some of the girls started greeting me with"— she pressed her hands together in prayer position and bowed slightly— "namaste, Stacey. That's my real name, Stacey Evans," she said quickly. "Then, before long, it became just"—she touched her palms together again and dipped her head—"Namastacey." She straightened and winked. "Just some jailhouse fun. It gets a little boring in there sometimes."

Amusement sparked in Krista's eyes. "Whichever you prefer, it's nice to meet you."

And Namastacey had struck again. It fascinated Taylor that, even though she always introduced her prison time right up front, Stacey could win over practically anyone quickly and easily with her openness, warmth, and charm. The dimples probably helped too. They were adorable.

Stacey smiled, her face lighting up, making her look as though life had been far kinder to her than it had. "I answer to both."

Taylor shifted, growing impatient. She wanted some time with Stacey—or in this case, Namastacey, since she could use the wisdom and counsel that side of Stacey was known for—before the others got back.

"Well," Krista said, glancing at Taylor, "it sounds like you two have some things to discuss, so I'll give you some privacy."

Appreciative of her perceptiveness, Taylor gave her a nod. "Thanks."

"Is that your lunch?" Stacey asked when Krista was gone.

"Oh." Taylor took in the place setting and food absently. "I forgot all about that."

"Come on, then." Stacey crossed to the table and sat. She patted the seat beside her. "We can talk while you eat."

Taylor complied and opened the foil packet to find the garlic bread Krista had promised. She took a bite and moaned.

Stacey laughed. "I know. Right? It smells fabulous. Do I detect Sparkle's butternut squash raviolis in there?" She pointed at the covered plate.

"Yeah." Taylor removed the lid and inhaled the savory steam that drifted up. "Want some?"

"No, thank you," Stacey said gently. "You enjoy. And tell me how you're doing."

"I'm fine." Taylor stabbed a ravioli with her fork. "Everything's healed accept this." She lifted her still casted wrist. "And the doctor in Fresno said it's mending perfectly. My injuries weren't nearly as bad as Gwen's."

"That isn't what I meant." Stacey paused. "I'm talking about *you*. How are *you* doing?" She pressed her hand to her heart. "In here."

"I'm doing okay." Taylor took the ravioli into her mouth and chewed. It wasn't exactly a lie. She could be doing worse. "I mean," she shrugged, "it's not easy having one of my best friends completely forget me." When Stacey didn't respond, Taylor ventured a sidelong look. She froze with a slice of garlic bread halfway to her mouth when she met Stacey's level gaze.

Stacey stared at her, lips tight in a knowing smirk. "One of your best friends? Is that really what she is still?"

It was. Wasn't it? Gwen was still one of her best friends. In fact, maybe more so with the deeper intimacy they'd shared. But that wasn't what Stacey meant. Or was it? She faced her fully. Did she know? How could she? "Did EJ tell you?" She heard the hope in her voice before she felt it in her heart.

"No, honey. Jinx." Stacey drew up one knee and wrapped her arms around it. "She said she's worried about you not having anyone to talk to about all this since you and EJ aren't seeing eye to eye. And Jinx needs to be there for EJ, so she filled me in and asked me to check on you."

A weight settled in Taylor's chest. Of course, EJ wasn't concerned about Taylor. That would require her acknowledgment of the change in Taylor and Gwen's relationship. And even then, it'd be Gwen she'd be upset about, thinking Gwen needed to be protected from the big, bad player.

But Taylor hadn't realized how encouraged she'd been at the mere prospect that EJ might have come around while Taylor was gone. "Right. Jinx." Taylor sighed. "At least, *she* believes Gwen and I..." She still didn't know what she and Gwen were.

"So you are?" Stacey grinned. "You and Gwen are a couple?"

Taylor stared down at her plate and pushed the raviolis around in the sauce. "I don't know if we're a couple. But we kissed at the wedding. And then we talked about it." She turned back to Stacey, unable to keep from blurting out everything. "The three weeks after the wedding were so good, Stacey. We spent every night and weekend together and even took some time off work. We explored the attraction that's always been between us. We talked about things we'd never talked about before." Memories of that first kiss, so many intimate touches they'd freely shared, the look of pure ecstasy and joy on Gwen's face when she'd come deep inside Taylor, and Taylor's pure surrender to everything she felt for Gwen in that moment flooded her mind. Her throat closed, and tears burned her eyes. "And then that fucking truck." She bit her lip to keep from outright crying.

Stacey ran her hand up and down Taylor's arm, her touch soothing.

"And then after three weeks of not knowing if she was going to live or die, to have her wake up and not remember any of it. Not remember me." The tears broke loose on the last word.

"You've been through a lot, and there's still more to come for both of you." Stacey looped her fingers around Taylor's wrist and squeezed it. "I don't believe you've taken all this time to get together just to lose it so quickly. There must just be more that needs working out before you can be what you're going to be to each other."

The confidence in her voice steadied Taylor. "You think so? Like what?" Taylor sniffed and wiped her eyes with her napkin.

Stacey shrugged. "Who's to say?" She looked to the kitchen doorway that led to the rest of the house and squinted. "Maybe Gwen and Krista have unfinished business. Jinx said they used to know each other."

"Oh, God." Taylor dropped her fork and rubbed her hand over her face. "Don't say that."

"It doesn't have to be a bad thing. It could simply be something that needs clearing up before Gwen can be completely free to be with you," Stacey said reassuringly. "It can't be a coincidence that Krista showed up at this exact moment after so many years. And there has to be something there, given that Gwen never mentioned her to any of you in all the time you've known each other."

Taylor frowned. She wanted to believe that, but could she?

"I'm just saying, this isn't over yet." Stacey patted Taylor's hand. "There's more to play out, and I have to believe it'll all be all right. Don't give up hope."

Taylor forced a small smile. Stacey was usually right. "I suppose I'm going to have to trust you on it. If I don't, I'm going to drive myself insane worrying about losing Gwen."

Stacey leaned back and shook her head sagely. "Anyone with eyes can see that you and Gwen belong together. Most of us have merely been waiting for the two of you to figure it out."

"What about EJ?" Taylor asked.

"What about her?"

"*She* doesn't think we belong together." Taylor pushed her plate away, her appetite ruined by her anxiety. "I'm so mad at her. And I don't think I'm her favorite person right now either. We've had disagreements before but never like this. I don't want to lose our friendship, but I don't think—"

Stacey cut her off with a dismissive wave. "I'm sure deep down she knows. She has to. She knows the two of you better than any of us. You and EJ are having a fight."

Taylor scoffed. "A big one."

"If you say so."

Taylor resisted a retort. She respected Stacey's wisdom, but she had a feeling she wasn't going to like this next part. "What's that mean?"

"Anything is as big or small as we say it is. If you say you and EJ are having a *big* fight that you can't get past, so be it. You might as well walk away now."

Taylor flinched. The words stung. "I didn't say I was walking away."

"No, but you can't give up in your heart either." Stacey leaned close. "You and EJ love each other, and sometimes we fight with the people we love."

Taylor's anger flared. "She was going to pull the plug on Gwen without taking my feelings into account at all."

"Was she?" Stacey arched her eyebrows. "Did she say that? Or is that what you heard in your fear and grief?"

Taylor stiffened, determined to stay mad. But what *had* EJ said? "She said those were Gwen's wishes and that Gwen trusted her to carry them out." Her tone was harder than Stacey deserved, but her emotions from that conversation with EJ had broken loose. "And she said she didn't know if I should have any input."

"Now that Gwen's awake, can you try to put yourself in EJ's position?" Stacey asked. "Would you have been clear on everything? Those are big decisions to have to make for someone else."

"But she wouldn't even listen." Taylor clenched her jaw, remembering the time at the hospital. "Not even about Krista. I told her there was something about her that wasn't right, something she wasn't telling anyone. And then EJ talked to *her* about Gwen's discharge and Krista coming with us without saying a word to me."

"Honey." Stacey wrapped her arm around Taylor's shoulders and pulled her close. "You were both in difficult positions, and those particular situations don't even exist anymore. Gwen's awake now and healing. She doesn't need anyone to decide for her if she's going to live or die. She's here for the rest of her recovery by her own choice. And everyone knows that she and Krista used to know each other. Gwen doesn't need anyone to make her decisions for her anymore. But she does still need you both in other ways. And the two of you can better serve her if you're not arguing."

"EJ thinks I'm no good for Gwen, that I'll never settle down with one woman, and that Gwen deserves better than me." Taylor threw out the words with no thought.

"Are you sure those are EJ's doubts and not your own?"

"Mine? Stacey, I love Gwen." Taylor was dumbfounded, and yet, somewhere deep within her, Stacey's words rang true. And her own ignited a slow burn of the terror she'd kept buried for so long, a terror of the mere possibility of love. She'd felt it stirring at times during the weeks she and Gwen had together, but each time, she'd stuffed it back down. But now, it'd been said, acknowledged. And not only by Stacey, someone to whom she could deny it. She'd acknowledged it herself without meaning to. The stirring became a simmer, then a boil. Her body heated. Her face burned. Her deepest, darkest secret that she'd only ever told Gwen and EJ was about to be exposed. Not that she'd spent four years in prison; hell, a lot of people knew that, including Stacey, but how and why she'd landed there. Taylor leaped up and began to pace.

"I believe wholeheartedly that you love her, and it clearly scares you to death for some reason. I've heard you say yourself that you aren't meant to settle down with one woman."

Stacey's tone was gentle but matter-of-fact. And she was right. Taylor had said those very words so many times throughout her adult life. "But I was wrong," Taylor said. "This is different. This is Gwen."

"Then fight for her." A challenge flashed in Stacey's eyes. "Better yet, fight for the love all three of you share as hard as you're fighting right now to be right, and no one has to be wrong. The three of you can come through this with your relationships intact. Whatever they are."

Taylor hesitated. Could she do that? Could she just let go of everything that'd happened in these past weeks?

"Give yourself and EJ some time to move through the stress and emotions of the whole situation," Stacey said, clearly knowing Taylor's thoughts. "You love each other. You'll get through this. And give Gwen some time to recover what memory she can. She's only been awake for a few days."

Taylor sighed. Stacey was right about one thing for certain. Taylor *did* love EJ, no matter how mad at her she was. And they both loved Gwen. As for *who* didn't trust Taylor with Gwen? Taylor had to get honest with herself about that. EJ might think Taylor couldn't settle down and fully commit to one woman, but Taylor *had* been the one to convince her of that.

It wasn't EJ she had to prove wrong. It was herself.

CHAPTER SIXTEEN

Gwen breathed a sigh of relief as EJ wheeled her into the entertainment room of the farmhouse.

She'd done it. She'd made it to the psychiatrist's office and back in the car without anxiety meds. Granted, EJ had to stop twice on the way and once coming back for Jinx to help her out of the back seat for air, but still, no Xanax. She was determined to take as few prescription drugs as she could during her recovery. She wasn't sure why, but a voice deep within her told her it was important. Even for the remaining pain from her injuries, Ibuprofen was working well enough. But she *was* shaken by the car ride.

She would have liked to have asked EJ to take her to her room for a short nap. It didn't take much to exhaust her, and today's outing had done it. When they'd pulled up behind the house, though, EJ had said the cute little sports car parked beside Fire's Subaru belonged to Taylor, and Gwen had an almost desperate desire to see her. She'd been irrationally disappointed when Taylor hadn't arrived before it was time to leave for Gwen's appointment.

Fire rose from one of the plush brown sofas nestled amid several recliners and a couple of loveseats in the large room, and the country music video on the big screen TV went mute. "Hey there." She set the remote on an end table. "How'd everything go?"

"Pretty well." Gwen trailed her fingers over her temple and along the side of her head, a gesture that would have made more sense if she had enough hair to comb away from her face. She'd noticed she did it when she was either flat-out lying or telling a partial truth, like now. A tell? She swallowed her frustration. It was so disconcerting knowing so little about herself. The truth was she had hoped the psychiatrist would have a better idea than simply waiting around to see how much of her memory returned on its own, but the fact that two doctors said the same thing probably meant it was best.

"Hungry?" Fire asked before Gwen had to elaborate.

"No. Thank you," she added distractedly. "Do you know where Taylor is?" Her need to see her was growing exponentially.

"She's upstairs. She wanted to lie down for a little bit." Fire planted her fists on her hips.

It used to be a stance she took when she felt awkward. Did it still mean the same? Gwen's own anxiety plowed the question aside like a bulldozer. "Oh."

"I'll get her, though." Fire headed toward the foyer and the stairs. "She said she wanted to know as soon as you got home."

The thought quelled Gwen's agitation. Taylor wanted to see her too. That had to mean something. More importantly, Gwen's eagerness to see her had to mean something as well. Why had Taylor's absence affected her so strongly? She'd known Taylor was coming back and would be staying with her. With her and Fire. And why did that last part feel weird? She stretched her neck and rubbed the back of her skull, trying to ease a burgeoning headache.

EJ pressed her fingertips to Gwen's shoulders, then began a gentle massage. "Are you okay, sweetie?"

Gwen nodded, startled. She'd forgotten EJ was there. "Just tired."

"You should probably rest for a while." EJ gazed down at her, concern etched into her features.

Her watchful presence and the care she gave Gwen—God, she'd even tucked her into bed the previous night—soothed Gwen like she finally had the mother she'd always dreamed of having. Even when her mother had been with her, she'd never been focused on Gwen and nurturing her the way EJ was. Gwen had always been more of an afterthought, a begrudged responsibility. She'd made sure Gwen was fed and clothed and had a roof over her head, even if for a year it was the roof of a car, but Gwen always turned to her teachers or the counselors at the free programs her mother dropped her off at during the summer months for the attention and encouragement that kept her trying in school and life. Then when she'd lost Mrs. Walker, she'd turned her back on everything. Until she met Fire. Fire's energy, her spark, and eventually her love brought Gwen back.

"She'll be right down," Fire said as she re-entered the room. Gwen blinked, finding herself still staring at EJ.

EJ smiled. "Where'd you go?"

"Just…" Gwen looked from EJ to Fire, then back, trying to re-acclimate to the present. They were both so old. No, EJ was older, perhaps old enough to be Gwen's mother. Her mother had Gwen at sixteen. But Fire was Gwen's age. And Gwen was…Jeez, thirty-seven. She still couldn't comprehend that. "I don't know," she said to EJ. "Just thinking."

"Gwen?" The voice was tentative.

Gwen turned to face Taylor standing by the doorway. She warmed as her instant smile overtook her rather than it being an action she performed. Taylor was here, but Gwen had no idea why that felt so good. She took her in, her bronze skin, the shimmer of her lustrous, dark hair, the tense set of her mouth. But what entranced her were Taylor's eyes, tawny in their color, hesitant in their cast. "Hi," Gwen said, hearing all of her relief and solace at finally seeing Taylor in that one word.

Taylor must have heard it too. She grinned, then laughed. Her entire being seemed to relax. "It's so good to see you out of the hospital and someplace familiar."

And safe. It hadn't been said, but Gwen didn't doubt it's what would have come next had Taylor continued.

Taylor ducked her head and did an almost convincing job pretending to scratch her eye.

But Gwen saw the sheen of tears before Taylor turned away. "It's all right," she said softly. "*I'm* all right."

Taylor let out a snuffy laugh. "I'm sorry. I still get emotional around everything that's happened. And I'm just so glad you woke up."

Gwen smiled.

Taylor cleared her throat and met Gwen's gaze. "So you did okay on the trip down yesterday?"

Gwen laughed. "With drugs. I was out of it most of the way. But this morning, I made it to my appointment without any." Her cheeks heated, and she glanced at EJ. "With a few stops for me to regroup, of course."

Taylor worried her lower lip between her teeth. "I understand. I had to pull over a few times for a breather, driving up to Sacramento and back. It's not easy being in a car after what happened."

EJ took in a sharp breath. "Oh, Taylor. We should have gotten you a driver."

Taylor shook her head. "I was fine. I stopped when I needed to. I think it was good for me to face it."

Gwen admired Taylor's courage. She didn't remember the accident at all, yet she'd trembled as they'd approached EJ's car outside the hospital. How much did Taylor remember? She could only imagine what it was like for her and she didn't want to risk upsetting her by asking. "I'm glad you're here," she said instead. "And that you're staying."

Taylor tilted her head and lifted her eyebrow slightly. "Yeah?"

Soft wings fluttered in Gwen's stomach, and her heart skipped. The look was familiar, as was Gwen's reaction. It was how she felt when Fire smiled at her a certain way, or it *had* been. Was it still? She flicked her gaze in Fire's direction. But no, *this* was about Taylor. Was she crushing on Taylor? She was so old. But that didn't matter. Gwen thought of her ninth-grade history teacher, Ms. Daniels. She was old, forty maybe, and that hadn't stopped Gwen from having all kinds of reactions to her. But then, who wasn't old when someone was sixteen?

Wait. Gwen's head spun, and she closed her eyes and buried her face in her hands. She wasn't sixteen. Why couldn't she keep that straight?

When she lifted her head, EJ, Taylor, and Fire were crouched in front of her, their faces pale, and eyes wide.

EJ spoke first. "You need some rest."

"EJ's right," Fire said. "You should lie down."

Taylor's gaze remained fixed on Gwen, as though she was waiting for Gwen to say what she needed rather than telling her.

It settled Gwen. She couldn't look away. "I think so too," she said in answer to the others, then to Taylor, "Will you help me?"

A hopeful look passed through Taylor's eyes.

Those beautiful amber eyes. The next instant, Gwen was somewhere else, on her back, gazing into them above her.

"Of course," Taylor said with obvious surprise.

Gwen snapped back to the farmhouse, the room, the wheelchair. Her injured leg ached, and fatigue engulfed her. "Thank you."

Taylor rose and angled the chair toward the door.

"Be careful," Fire said as they began to move. "Use the lift belt to get her out of the chair."

Her tone was possessive, territorial, a side of Fire that had always irked Gwen. She couldn't address it now. She was fading, and she had to talk to Taylor. Besides, why would Fire be jealous of Taylor?

"I've got it," Taylor said stiffly.

Gwen closed her mind to whatever was going on between them, then her eyes. They'd have to work it out. She had enough to deal with.

In Gwen's room, Taylor eased the chair alongside the bed, stepped back and studied it, then started to adjust it.

"Turn me around so my good leg is alongside the bed," Gwen said, recreating in her mind what Fire had done the night before. "Then back me up a little."

Taylor complied. "Like that?"

She seemed far more amenable to Gwen's suggestions than she'd been to Fire's. "Perfect." Gwen locked the chair. "Now, we need that." She pointed to the lift belt lying across the foot of her bed.

Taylor retrieved it. "I'm sorry I didn't learn all this before we left the hospital." She glanced at Gwen, then looked away, clearly embarrassed.

"There wasn't much time." Gwen smiled. "And there wasn't a reason. There were plenty of people to do this in the hospital."

Taylor chuckled. "It seems you haven't lost your impressive logical thinking." She held up the belt. "What do I do with this?"

Gwen leaned forward. "Put it around my waist."

"How's that?" Taylor asked after slipping it behind her and down to the small of her back.

"Good." Gwen straightened and tightened it, then fastened it with the Velcro. "Now, take these." She indicated the leather loops at her sides. "And help hold me up with them when I stand."

Taylor's eyes widened. "But your doctor said you're not supposed to put any weight on your leg until you've done some physical therapy."

"I won't. Don't worry." Gwen inched forward in her seat. She wanted this done so she could talk to Taylor, then go to sleep. Who'd have thought she'd ever miss being able to simply stand up and get into bed? "My weight will be on my other leg, but it's weak from me being inactive all that time, so you'll have to help hold me up. Okay?" She looked into Taylor's face and saw hesitation.

Taylor swallowed and nodded.

"Do you want to get Fire or EJ?" Gwen asked, hoping she didn't. Being with Taylor felt right. "If you're uncomfortable—"

"No," Taylor said sharply. "I mean, I want to be careful, that's all."

"Okay. Good." Gwen gripped the arms of the chair. "I'm going to get up, and I need you to lift and steady me." She leaned forward as Fire had shown her, then pushed. Every muscle in her arms strained, and she gritted her teeth. She trembled under the effort. The morning had kicked her butt. Then she felt the pull at her waist and Taylor's strength and support, even and sure. She glided into a stance on her good leg. She groaned at the relief of being able to stretch her body.

"Oh, my God! Did I hurt you?" Taylor encircled Gwen's waist. "I'm so sorry."

"No, no," Gwen said quickly. "I'm fine." The sudden shift from Taylor's release of one of the loops, though, threw her off balance. She pitched forward. Instinctively, she grabbed Taylor's shoulders and held on tight.

"I'm here," Taylor said softly. She slipped her other arm around Gwen. "I'm right here."

Their bodies melded together, fitting perfectly, and the light scent of something sultry teased Gwen's senses and tickled some deeply buried recollection. The combination made her want to turn her face into the warmth of Taylor's skin at her open collar and breathe in whatever it was about Taylor that seemed to be trying to set her free. She slid her arms around Taylor's neck and pressed into her.

Taylor stiffened, then tightened her hold. "I'm right here," she whispered again.

Gwen relaxed into the embrace. Yes, right here. She could stay right here a long time. She inhaled Taylor's scent once more. Was Taylor's cheek against her hair? Gwen blinked rapidly, trying to focus and became aware that if she tilted her head back, she could touch her lips, the tip of her tongue, to the pulse point at the base of Fire's neck. It drove Fire wild when Gwen licked and nipped that spot. No, not Fire. Taylor. This was Taylor. *Damn it!* She jerked away and straightened, her face and ears flaming hot. "I need to sit." She avoided Taylor's gaze. "Can you turn me?"

Taylor moved, pivoting Gwen so she sat on the edge of the bed. "Like that?" Taylor's voice was husky.

"Yes." Gwen eased sideways to rest on her elbow, then lowered herself to the pillow. The soft bedding cooled her cheek, and the support and comfort of the mattress coaxed a long sigh from her.

Taylor gently lifted Gwen's legs and carefully aligned them, bent-kneed, with her body.

"Thank you." Gwen could barely force the words from her throat. She shifted to her back and released another long breath as she stretched out her good leg.

Without hesitation, Taylor lifted Gwen's casted foot and straightened that leg as well. Then she pulled the light blanket folded across the end of the bed over Gwen. "Comfy?"

Gwen nodded. "Thank you."

"If you don't need anything else, I'll let you rest," Taylor said, stepping away.

Gwen started to drift, then remembered. "Wait!" She grasped Taylor's wrist. She still needed to tell her what she'd realized the previous day. It didn't seem like much now, but maybe it would ease Gwen's tension from what had just happened, whatever that was. "I want to tell you something." She made herself look into Taylor's eyes.

Taylor waited with an expectant expression.

Gwen collected her thoughts. "I wanted to tell you that yesterday I realized you're very important in my life." She winced. It sounded ridiculous outside of her head.

Taylor's face lit up. "You remembered something about me? About us?"

"No. Not exactly remembered." She struggled for the right words. "When I first got here and met Sparkle and Reggie and everyone was so loving and happy I was out of the hospital and here, it all felt so wonderful. It was like a family, and I was a part of it. I haven't ever felt that before, at least not that I can remember right now."

Taylor's expression softened, and she squeezed Gwen's hand. "We *are* a family, and you're most definitely part of it. An important part."

Gwen swallowed the emotion that rose in her throat and wrapped her fingers around Taylor's. "And that's what I wanted to tell *you*." Her voice broke. "Even with how good it felt with everyone around me yesterday, I knew something wasn't right. Something was missing. And it was you. And it told me that even though I can't remember a lot, I know you're very important to me."

A huge smile deepened Taylor's laugh lines, and her eyes shone with affection. And something else. Appreciation? She pressed the fingertips of her casted hand to the back of Gwen's. "I wish you could know how happy that makes me."

Gwen smiled, then some framed photos on the nightstand drew her attention. "What are those?"

Taylor glanced to them but didn't release her hold. "I brought a few of your favorite pictures from your house. Dr. Landon said it might help your memory to have some of the things you love around you."

Gwen squinted, trying to make out the one closest. "Is that us? You, me, and EJ?"

Taylor shifted and picked it up, breaking their connection.

Gwen missed it immediately, its absence a chill on her skin.

"Yeah. It was your birthday." She passed the photo to Gwen. "You *had* to have ice cream, even though we'd already eaten ourselves sick at your favorite restaurant."

Gwen studied the picture, then caught Taylor's tone. Was she teasing her? She'd been so serious at the hospital. She cut her a glance. "You're smiling awfully big for someone who's sick," she said, indicating the picture.

"That's not a smile. It's a grimace," Taylor said with a smirk.

Gwen laughed and returned her gaze first to Taylor's image, then EJ's, and finally her own. "We look happy," she said wistfully.

"Hm. It was a fun evening." Taylor watched her, as though waiting for something.

Waiting to see if she remembered. It was the way everyone watched her. As she stared at the picture, taking in each face, each expression, she noticed how her arms were draped over each of their shoulders, how theirs cradled her between them. In her mind's eye, she saw all of them somewhere else. She blew out a candle on a cupcake. The low lighting in the room revealed nautical instruments as décor and a portrait of Captain Jack Sparrow on the wall. She strained for more, but exhaustion consumed her, and her eyelids fluttered closed.

"I love Rudy's," she whispered before drifting into sleep.

Taylor pressed her back to the wall outside Gwen's room and stared at the ceiling.

Had she heard correctly? Did Gwen say she loved Rudy's? She'd mumbled it, but Taylor had been close. And it was clear. Yes! She'd heard right. Gwen remembered Rudy's.

"Taylor? What's the matter?"

EJ's grip on Taylor's arm pulled her attention from her elation before the question registered. She looked into EJ's fearful expression and grinned. "She remembers Rudy's."

"What?" The concern in EJ's eyes gave way to confusion.

"Gwen remembers Rudy's," Taylor said again, her voice rising with excitement.

EJ squinted, as though trying to solve a puzzle.

"Rudy's Hideaway," Taylor added for clarification, although she didn't need to. They all knew Rudy's.

EJ's gaze drifted into Gwen's room, hope and doubt mingling in her features. "Did she say something about it?"

Taylor looked over her shoulder at Gwen's sleeping form. She'd stood beside the bed for at least ten minutes, stunned into immobility by Gwen's last comment. She'd wanted to wake her and ask her to repeat those beautiful words and find out exactly what she remembered. Was it only that night from the photo, or was it *all* the times she'd been there? Taylor's heart leaped. Had she remembered that last time when *they'd* been there?

"How do you know?" EJ asked, interrupting Taylor's joy yet again. To avoid the risk of waking Gwen, she took EJ by the wrist and led her through the foyer. The low tones of music from the entertainment room told her Krista was probably still in there, so she towed EJ to the kitchen. "She said she loves Rudy's," she said in a rush as soon as they entered.

EJ stared at her. "Out of the blue?"

Taylor huffed with exasperation. "No," she said, her impatience ringing in her tone. "She asked about the picture of all of us at Gunther's that I brought from her house. I told her we'd gone out for dinner at her favorite restaurant, then went for ice cream. She said we all looked happy. Then when she was falling asleep, she said, 'I love Rudy's.'"

"Did you *say* Rudy's?" EJ asked, still being obtuse.

Taylor grabbed her shoulders and squeezed. "No!" She drew the word out for emphasis.

EJ gripped her forearms. "Okay, stop. I get it."

Finally. Happiness flooded Taylor. "She remembers Rudy's!" she said in a high-pitched trill, no longer able to contain her emotions.

EJ laughed, and her eyes shone with genuine pleasure, the shadow of worry and dread that had lingered there for weeks at least momentarily gone.

Taylor hugged her. She hadn't seen this EJ since the wedding. God. The wedding. The kiss. That's when everything had started.

EJ held her tightly.

"This is good," Taylor said, savoring the moment. "Right? This is good?" She needed to hear EJ say it, to be in it with her. She needed everything she was feeling, hoping for, to be real.

"Yes, it's good," EJ whispered.

But her slight hesitation told Taylor what she really thought. She pulled away. "You don't believe it."

EJ sighed. "I want to," she said, searching Taylor's face.

What was she looking for? Agreement with her doubt? Taylor wouldn't give it to her. "You think I'm lying?"

"Of course not," EJ said quickly. "It's just that it might not last once she wakes up, and I don't want either of us to get our hopes up only to be disappointed. I think we should stay prepared for any possibility. Dr. Stafford, the psychiatrist Gwen saw today, said there's no telling how long this could take."

Taylor clenched her jaw and shook her head. "Why can't you be with me in this, let me feel like she might come back to me? Why can't you be on my side for just one minute?"

"Because this isn't about you, Taylor." EJ's eyes frosted. "This is about Gwen, and it's *you* who should be with *me* in this. She needs both of us on *her* side to get through this."

Hadn't Stacey said basically the same thing? And they were both right. Gwen would need both of her best friends. And they'd need to be working together *for* Gwen, not fighting behind the scenes. As for her and EJ personally, they *did* love each other. She dropped any further argument. "You're right. I'm sorry. We'll wait until she wakes up to see if she really remembers."

EJ's gaze warmed. "Thank you. I don't want us to fight anymore." She tentatively touched Taylor's arm, then ran her fingers down to grasp Taylor's. "Can we go somewhere like we talked about to maybe reconnect?"

Taylor hesitated. "I'd rather stay here." She held onto EJ's hand to try to reassure her. "I'd like to be here when Gwen wakes up. Could we sit out on the veranda and talk?"

The hope in EJ's expression dulled, but she nodded.

When they'd settled in the Adirondack chairs outside the back door, they sat in a familiar, comfortable silence for several moments as they looked out across the fields of the Canine Complete grounds. Without effort, without explanation or discussion, without a single word, the chasm that had grown so wide between them seemed to close. Would it have been this easy all along? Had all they'd ever needed to do been to simply shut up?

Taylor exhaled a long breath, relaxing in the cool breeze and the distant barking of the dogs. "Is Jinx at the exercise yard?" How long had it been since she'd asked EJ such a mundane question? No lives at stake. No accusations.

"Mm-hm. She missed the dogs while we were gone." EJ tipped her head back and closed her eyes. She seemed to be soaking up the returning easiness between them as much as Taylor was. "I've missed *you*," she added softly.

Taylor, EJ, and Gwen had all been best friends for ten years, but EJ had been at Taylor's side for over twenty. They'd seen each other through so much. They were like sisters. She reached across the space between their chairs and laid her hand on EJ's. "I've missed you too."

There was probably more to be discussed, not the least of which was EJ's acceptance, or lack thereof, of the change in Taylor and Gwen's relationship, but for now, this was good.

CHAPTER SEVENTEEN

Gwen sat on the back porch in the chilly fall morning snuggled up in cozy sweats and her favorite hoodie, one she'd snagged from Taylor that was faded and worn and too big on her, but she loved it. The air was crisp, the sun risen but still low above the horizon as she sipped from a steaming mug of peppermint tea.

She didn't know if she'd liked the drink prior to the accident, but she assumed so since someone had stocked it in the house supplies and no one else drank it. Plus the fact that no one had asked her if she wanted to try it but rather just brought it to her.

In the two and a half weeks since she'd left the hospital, that had happened frequently. Things simply appeared in front of her, and she liked them. She didn't know if anyone was aware of what they were doing, but that didn't matter. Whether a conscious act or not, it told her the people around her knew her and she belonged with them.

She was starting to get to know them too. Every day, she learned new things about EJ, Taylor, and Jinx and discovered she had excellent taste in friends, and while she'd assumed she still knew Fire, she was finding her even more interesting as an adult than when they were teens. She seemed more mellow, even reserved. There was a discipline about her that Gwen never would have expected. She cooked. She was tidy. She was a nurse, for crying out loud. Gwen still couldn't guess how that had transpired. Fire didn't talk about herself much, which gave her an air of mystery, and Gwen didn't ask a lot about her because she didn't want to accidentally venture into places she wasn't yet ready to go, like why Fire hadn't come back for her. Something within her told her, for now, she was happier not knowing.

All and all, though, Gwen hadn't remembered a thing. She'd gotten glimpses, or more like nigglings, but still hadn't had a single true memory bubble to the surface from any time after the age of sixteen. Dr. Stafford said it might be because Fire was the first person Gwen saw and recognized when she woke, and it had taken her back to a time she'd felt safe. She could see that, kind of. After all, back then, she *had* felt safe with Fire after navigating the twists and turns of the foster care system alone since she'd been nine. Surely, though, her life after Fire, her life in such a loving and close-knit family with EJ, Jinx, and Taylor had given her safety as well. So why couldn't she remember that?

The first day Taylor had been back, apparently Gwen had murmured something in her sleep about some restaurant they all liked, but when she woke, she couldn't recall a thing about it either from her mutterings *or* her experience. Taylor had looked so devastated, Gwen had felt guilty, but still nothing more had surfaced.

Today felt hopeful, though. Not on the memory front, but physically, there was something to celebrate. After diligently doing every rotation of her physical therapy exercises the past fourteen days, she was strong enough to support her weight on her good leg. She was graduating from her wheelchair to crutches. Walt, her physical therapist, would be bringing them and showing her how to use them after breakfast. She'd learned to maneuver the chair efficiently during her time in it, but she could hardly wait to be up on her feet again. At least one foot.

The hum of engines and the crunch of gravel under tires drew her attention to EJ's Lexus, followed by Jinx's Jeep Cherokee, coming around the far corner of the house into the parking area. Gwen smiled and waved.

"Good morning," EJ called as she climbed from behind the wheel and closed the car door. "Ready to walk today?"

Her attire, chocolate brown dress slacks, an emerald silk blouse, and tan low heels, reminded Gwen that EJ was heading up to her office in Sacramento for the beginning of the week. It was the first time she'd be there since before EJ and Jinx's wedding. She'd been working remotely from home or the farmhouse since they'd all left the hospital. *Our* office, EJ had called it. That had set off a sense of longing in Gwen. Would it ever be her office again? And could she miss it if she never remembered it? And yet, something about EJ dressed this way *was* familiar.

"I'm more than ready," Gwen called.

Pete barked a happy hello as he jumped, tail wagging, from the back seat of Jinx's SUV.

Gwen set her tea on the redwood table between the chairs and braced for his morning exuberance. He was still cautiously gentle with her, but sometimes the combination of his eagerness to see her after a night away and her awkwardness as her body healed ended in something spilled or broken. "Hi, puppy," Gwen said in a croon when he snuggled his head into her lap. "Did you sleep well?" She stroked his ear.

"The important question is, did *you* sleep well," EJ said, ascending the steps of the veranda. "Or did your excitement about today keep you awake?"

"A little of both." Gwen sighed at the calming wave that always washed over her when she ran her fingers through Pete's fur. "I fell asleep right away, but I woke up early, wanting to get started on the day."

"Was anyone up to help you?" EJ asked as she settled into the chair beside Gwen's.

"I was, but she didn't call me." Taylor pushed through the screen door, carrying a tray holding a carafe and some coffee mugs. "She's little Miss Independent."

Taylor's tone was the teasing one Gwen was getting used to. "You weren't up. I could hear you snoring all the way downstairs." The banter developing between them seemed natural. Had it been?

"Psh. I don't snore." She set the tray beside Gwen's cup on the table. "That must have been Krista."

Gwen still couldn't bring herself to call Fire Krista. She laughed at Taylor's easy quip and looked up at Fire stepping from the house with a second tray covered with plates of sliced fruit and bagels. There had been no snoring. Gwen only said that in hopes of avoiding any chastisement from EJ about taking risks.

Fire gave her a quiet smile as though to say, *I know what you're doing.*

And Gwen was sure she did. Fire knew all of Gwen's tricks for staying out of trouble. What was different here was Fire's reaction to Taylor's taunt. The Fire Gwen used to know would never let anyone say anything mocking or derisive about her, even in jest. Her flares of temper in such circumstances were largely what inspired her nickname. That and her red hair.

"What time is Walt coming?" Jinx asked as she rested her hip against the railing of the veranda on the other side of EJ. "I want to try to be here to witness those first steps."

Gwen grinned at her. Jinx had become her most fervent cheerleader. She frequently spent her lunch break assisting Gwen with her PT exercises and brought her a set of dumbbells to help her regain her arm strength. Not to mention the daily walks around the grounds and up the road. Jinx even let her sneak some time on her good leg when they were alone, as long as she had a tight hold on her.

"Oh." EJ drew the word into a long whine. "I wish I could be here for that. I can't believe the timing of you graduating to crutches being on the first day I absolutely have to make an appearance in the office. Jinx, you *have to* take a video."

"I will, baby." Jinx ran her fingers through EJ's hair. "I told you that all three times you asked this morning and the two last night while you were packing."

"And I'll get lots of practice in the next few days while you're gone," Gwen said, "so by the time I come over to your house on Thursday for Thanksgiving dinner, I can really show off for you."

"Speaking of Thanksgiving," Fire said as she finished spreading cream cheese on a bagel. She handed it to Gwen.

Gwen took a bite, then a sip of tea.

"I can make some of the side dishes ahead of time," Fire continued, "and bring them over when we come, if that would help."

"That's between you and Jinx. She's the holiday chef." EJ speared a variety of fruit slices onto a plate, then added some grapes. She slid it over to Gwen.

After the first week, Gwen had told them all they didn't have to wait on her, but they continued anyway. When she'd said it a second time, EJ had said, "Please, let us. At least, for a while. It makes us feel good. We almost lost you." Her voice had trembled on the last sentence, reminding Gwen that she wasn't the only one that had been through something traumatic. And if she were completely honest, she liked being so cared for. She assumed it would end naturally at some point.

"Are there any dishes that are unique to you or your family that you want to share?" Jinx asked Fire. "Namastacey's bringing her cranberry goulash, and Reggie left us a pot of her Texas chili even though she and

Sparkle are in Tahoe for the week. You can bring anything. It doesn't have to be about the holiday."

Fire looked thoughtful, then smiled and blushed. "Not really," she said, picking up another bagel. "But I can bring one of the regular dishes like yams."

"Oh, c'mon." Jinx grinned. "What did you think of just then?"

Gwen looked from Jinx back to Fire, wondering herself. Then she saw Fire at the kitchen counter in their foster home. She gasped.

Fire glanced at her and laughed. "Should I?"

"Oh, my gosh, yes! It's delicious."

"What?" Jinx asked eagerly.

EJ and Taylor sat silently, focused on the exchange.

Fire laughed. "I could make my grandmother's Spaghetti-O casserole."

"*That's* interesting." Jinx sounded fascinated.

It was one of the things Gwen loved about Jinx. She had such a childlike quality about her. But Gwen was too shocked at Fire's mention of her grandmother to think about Jinx for more than an instant. No one but Gwen knew where Fire's Spaghetti-O casserole recipe came from. Fire *never* talked about her grandmother to anyone but her. Had she made peace with that demon from her past? Or was Fire feeling as safe and comfortable as Gwen did in this new family they'd found?

"It's settled then," Jinx said, slapping the table. "Spaghetti-O casserole is on the menu."

Fire chuckled, then passed a gentle smile to Gwen, perhaps lost in one of her own memories of what they'd shared.

"And what about you, Taylor?" Jinx continued. "Want to bring a specialty pizza like last year? That chicken tikka masala one was good."

"Sure," Taylor said in her casual manner. "I checked the online menu for Pizza Fusion last night, and they've added a moo shu vegetable pizza. Should we try that?"

"Excellent." Jinx rubbed her hands together. "We're all set then."

Gwen's mind drifted as she ate, and the conversation took on a more meandering cadence. EJ's meeting that afternoon. Taylor's upcoming doctor's appointment to get her cast off. Jinx and Fire's plan to go to the bicycle shop to look for a bike for Fire so she could start riding with Jinx. Gwen's excitement about her own day vibrated through her as she ate, the sweetness of the fruit heightening her mood even more. She bit into a piece of pineapple and quivered at the flavor coating her tongue. "Mmm. I love pineapple."

Someone chuckled, and EJ squeezed Gwen's arm.

"That's why I got it," Taylor said.

But Gwen was somewhere else. "Oh, my God. Remember how good it was in Hawaii? It was so fresh and sweet. And we could get it anywhere. Even McDonald's." She laughed. "Remember? It was on the sides menu alongside French fries?" When no one answered, she looked up from her plate.

Everyone stared at her.

"What?"

"You remember Hawaii?" EJ asked.

Gwen blinked, then gasped. She *did*! "Yes!" She started to shake.

Fire grabbed her plate and set it on the table.

EJ knelt beside Gwen. "What exactly do you remember?"

Gwen searched her brain. Images flashed. "The pineapple. We went to that pineapple grove and learned that a mother pineapple plant takes two years to produce one pineapple. I remember thinking, how can there be so many pineapples in the world at that rate."

EJ laughed. "That's right. You said that."

Elation flooded Gwen when more came. "And I remember going on the tour at Pearl Harbor and all the bullet holes still in the buildings. And the memorial for the USS *Arizona* and how sad that was." Then an image of EJ came, her hands on her hips, pacing. They hadn't known whether to be pissed or worried. "And Taylor disappeared for two days with some woman she met at the Polynesian Culture Center." She looked at Taylor. "We were scared something happened to you."

The wide smile on Taylor's face vanished. "I know. And I was sorry."

EJ patted Gwen's leg. "That was eight years ago, and since then, she's always made sure we know where she is," she said with a smirk. "We told her she couldn't travel with us if she didn't."

Taylor nodded, looking chagrinned.

Genuine fondness for her warmed Gwen's heart.

"Do you remember anything else?" EJ asked gently.

Gwen poked around in her mind again, waiting to see if any more pictures or thoughts surfaced. Nothing came. She shook her head.

She looked at Taylor again, finding a mixture of hope and disappointment in her eyes, then at Jinx who grinned. When she met Fire's gaze, she found pure terror.

Fire looked away.

"Gwen." EJ's voice was hushed. "You remembered our trip to Hawaii when you were twenty-nine."

She sounded in awe. The full impact of her meaning slammed home. Gwen's mouth went dry. She'd remembered something that *wasn't* prior to sixteen, that involved her best friends, her family.

That had to mean there was more. That there *would be* more.

She scanned the faces around her. EJ's wonder. Jinx's joy. Taylor's conflict. It was Fire's fear that tore at her, though. What waited for her in that memory?

Taylor stood by while Gwen carefully lowered herself onto the couch in the entertainment room. The physical therapist had recommended someone stay nearby for the first few days she was on her crutches given the severity of her fractures. While her good leg was strong enough to support her weight again, if she were to slip or lose her balance and land on the injured one, it could do new damage.

Gwen shifted onto the cushion, then leaned back. She rested the crutches against the armrest.

"You want me to take those?" Taylor asked.

Gwen shook her head, never taking her eyes from them. She ran her hand over one as though caressing it. "I want them right by me." She grinned. "What a great day."

Taylor smiled. "It really has been. Do you want anything before we start the movie? Something to drink? Popcorn?" Gwen's love of all things buttery remained unwavering.

"No, thank you. I'm still full from dinner. Everyone here is such a good cook." She rubbed her stomach. "Well, except you. But you're a great dishwasher."

They'd all agreed when they'd set up house together that whoever made the meal didn't have to clean up, and Taylor ended up on KP more often than anyone else.

The corner of Gwen's mouth lifted in a teasing half smile.

Taylor loved that the playful dynamic they'd had for years had returned so easily even without Gwen's knowledge of its prior existence.

"Hey." Taylor sat on the other end of the sofa and stretched her arm along the top. "I made you tomato soup and grilled cheese yesterday, and I didn't hear you complaining." In fact, she'd heard a couple of genuine moans of pleasure while Gwen was eating. And they'd nearly killed her. She'd had to get up from the table and insist on doing the lunch dishes despite the fact that she'd prepared the meal, to ward off images of Gwen naked in bed, enjoying Taylor's touches and caresses.

Gwen laughed. "That's true. They were *very* good. I especially liked the seasoning and the tomato slice on the sandwich."

"That's how I learned to make it," Taylor said without thinking.

"Who taught you?" Gwen asked, shifting more in Taylor's direction. "Your mother?"

Taylor laughed. "Uh, no. My mother had a personal chef. She didn't even make toast." She considered Gwen's question and the answer. She was still sometimes unsure what was okay to tell Gwen and what might not be, other than the big stuff anyway. What could this hurt, though? "You taught me."

Gwen's eyes widened, and her brows arched. "I can cook?"

Taylor chuckled. "Yes. You're a great cook."

"Hm. I wonder when *I* learned. And how?"

Taylor knew these answers, but they fell into the category of Gwen's personal memories, not hers. She remained silent.

"Fire never knew how to cook before either, except for the Spaghetti-O thing," she said wistfully. "I wonder when she learned."

"Speaking of Fire," Taylor said, thinking it was time for a subject change before the conversation drifted into dangerous waters. "I wonder what happened to her. Didn't she say she wanted to watch the movie with us?"

"She did," Gwen said, still sounding distant.

"Maybe I should go check on her. See if she changed her mind." Taylor would have preferred to have more time alone with Gwen, but it was the nice thing to do. She started to rise.

"Wait a minute," Gwen said.

Taylor paused and looked at her.

"Today when I remembered being in Hawaii with you and EJ?" Gwen said it as a question.

Taylor nodded, then settled back into her seat.

Gwen bit her lower lip. "I really felt how close we all were," she said, searching Taylor's face. "I was scared that something happened to you. I could feel it, like it was happening today. We must be even closer now, all these years later."

Taylor's heartbeat picked up its pace. "We are." She had to keep this on track. Gwen was talking about the three of them, not her and Taylor the three weeks before the accident. "All three of us are very close friends."

Gwen cut her a sidelong look. "Why can't I remember that?"

Taylor scooted closer and took Gwen's hand. "You will." She held on tightly. "Today was only the beginning. The rest will come."

Gwen looked down at their intwined fingers, then into Taylor's eyes.

When Gwen looked at her so directly, so deeply, it felt as though she could see Taylor's every thought, her every secret. And these days there were more secrets than ever.

"I know you aren't supposed to tell me anything about my own life, and I don't want you to, but could you tell me some things about you?"

Taylor relaxed. This was all right. Surely, she wouldn't ask about the two of them. "Okay, but you already know the most important thing about me. Where I learned how to make such a great cheese sandwich," she added when Gwen cocked her head in question.

Gwen laughed. "Well, yes," she said lightly. "But what about something more trivial like why you aren't married or with someone. I mean, I assume you aren't since you haven't mentioned anyone."

A lump rose in Taylor's throat. What did she say to that? Was she with someone? Had she and Gwen been together? It didn't matter. She couldn't say it even if it might be true. "You assume correctly."

"I can't believe that," Gwen said. "You're so beautiful. And smart. And fun." She blushed. "Is it okay to say that? I know we're just friends, but I can still think those things, right?"

Taylor couldn't help but chuckle. In her thirty-seven-year-old persona, one rarely got to see flustered Gwen. "It's fine. And thank you," she said with a hint of flirtation simply because it was automatic.

"Why then? Have you ever been in love?"

This one Taylor could answer with no danger of slipping into areas they shouldn't go. Plus, it was something she'd already shared with Gwen. It didn't seem likely she'd react differently than she had before.

Gwen at sixteen seemed as open and nonjudgmental as the adult Gwen. "I have," Taylor said, wanting to keep it light. "When I was nineteen, I fell truly, madly, deeply in love as they say."

"And it didn't work out?"

"No. But more than that, it made me stupid." Taylor hadn't been down this path for a long time. It was part of her story, but it seemed so foreign. "I got into the drug scene with Jimmy, my boyfriend, and after a year or so, he started dealing. I was so gone over him, I'd do anything he asked. And one day, he asked me to go down to Mexico and pick up a shipment for him. He said it was a small one, no big deal. I knew better. He didn't usually ask me, but his regular guy was sick." As she spoke, the anxiety that had churned in her stomach that whole day so long ago ate at her.

Gwen's gaze was riveted on her.

"Anyway, as you've probably guessed, I got caught."

"How?" The word was only a whisper.

Taylor shrugged. "Bad luck, I thought at the time. But now, I don't believe in luck, good or bad. I do know that even though I served four years in prison for it, it was one of the best things that could have happened."

"Why?" Gwen asked with obvious astonishment.

"It got me straight." Taylor caught herself and smirked. "Not in all ways. Prison *was* where I first discovered the pleasures of women. But straight in the sense that I learned I wanted a better life. And it gave me the conviction to create one when I got out. It also got my family out of my life, which was fine with me. I never fit in there. My arrest was the final straw for them."

Gwen was quiet, staring down at their still linked hands.

Taylor should have let go, but Gwen's hand in hers felt so right.

"And you've been afraid to let yourself fall in love again for all this time?" Gwen asked finally.

What? Taylor was stunned. Was that another memory coming through?

"It makes sense. If you fell in love so deeply that you'd do anything for him, and then it led to that." Gwen lifted her gaze to Taylor's. "That'd make anyone afraid to fall in love."

Taylor stared into the deep blue of Gwen's eyes, then shifted to her lips, soft and parted. What she wouldn't give to be able to kiss them again. But no, not a memory. Only a conclusion, a logical one that, of course, Gwen would draw. "Well, maybe someday."

Gwen smiled. "Thank you for sharing that with me. I want to get to know all of you as much as I can in case I don't remember everything. You're all so amazing. I don't intend to lose any of you."

"No chance of that," Taylor said confidently. "And think about it. We're already making new memories together."

Gwen laughed. "That's right! I hadn't thought of that."

"So." Taylor stretched and stood. "I'll go find out what happened to Krista so we can get this movie started."

"You know what?" Gwen said, reaching for her crutches. "If it's okay with you, can we reschedule the movie for tomorrow night? I'm tired all of a sudden. I think my big day caught up with me."

"I'm not surprised," Taylor said, moving into position to spot her as she got to her feet.

After helping Gwen get settled in bed, Taylor headed upstairs. At the top, she noticed Krista's bedroom door slightly ajar. What *had* happened to her tonight? Taylor knocked gently, and it eased open.

Krista stood at the closet with an armful of clothes, and a half-filled suitcase lay open on the bed.

"What are you doing?" Taylor asked, stepping into the room.

Krista spun around. At the sight of Taylor, she grimaced. "Ever heard of knocking?"

"I did knock. What are you doing?" Taylor asked again. She could guess, but the idea was so appalling, she had to hear Krista say it.

Krista's expression hardened. "I can't do this." She dumped her bundle beside the case and started folding a blouse.

Taylor went cold. "Can't do what?"

"I can't sit around and wait for Gwen to remember what I did to her," Krista said, her back to Taylor. "I can't face her when she does."

She was really going to leave? Now? Taylor reached her in two angry strides and grabbed her arm.

Krista whirled and twisted from her grip. "Don't touch me." Her eyes blazed.

"You can't just leave," Taylor said through gritted teeth. She wanted to yell but didn't want to risk Gwen overhearing.

Krista whipped back around and returned her attention to packing. "Yes, I can. This isn't your business."

Taylor moved between her and the bed and yanked the shirt from her hands. She threw it to the floor. "Yes, it is my business. Gwen is my business. And she wanted you here, *needed* you here, because you're the only one she knows."

Krista stepped back and folded her arms. "I *was* the only one she knew. She's gotten to know all of you some since we've been here, and now she remembers you all. And she never knew me as who I am today."

"Really?" Taylor's anger shifted to disgust. "After everything you did, manipulating your way into being her nurse, lying about knowing her and what you were to her, wriggling your way into coming home with her to be with her, *now* you're going to bail on her *again*?"

Krista narrowed her eyes. "I didn't lie."

"Whatever. We're not going to argue semantics."

Krista's shoulders slumped, and she blinked several times. Her eyes were red, and tears brimmed at the edges. "I can't face her when she remembers. I can't be here."

"You have to be," Taylor said more gently. "Be here for her this time."

Krista squeezed her eyes shut and shook her head.

Taylor shoved the clothes and suitcase aside, then touched Krista's shoulder to coax her to sit on the bed.

Krista jerked. Her eyes snapped open, and she thrust her arm up in a defensive stance.

Taylor raised her hands in surrender. "Okay." Jesus. What had happened to her? "Just sit with me for a minute."

Krista studied her with evident skepticism. After a long moment, she conceded.

They sat in silence, Taylor waiting to see what Krista would say next.

About the time she thought Krista wasn't going to speak at all, she drew in a deep breath and looked at the ceiling. "She already knows, and remembers for herself, everything about me she ever knew." She swallowed hard. "Except when we got caught by Deborah and what came after. And as soon as she remembers that, she's going to hate me."

Taylor thought about that. "I doubt it. That isn't the Gwen I know." What was she doing? This was her chance to get rid of Krista. And all she'd have to do was let her finish packing. She considered what Namastacey had said about fighting for Gwen, though. At the time, she'd taken it to mean fight for her love and to be with her. But wasn't trying to make sure she had everything she needed to make a full recovery regardless of who she ended up with, if anyone, wasn't that fighting for her too? She sighed with resignation. "The Gwen I know will probably feel the emotions around the memory like she did today when she got mad at me remembering my disappearing act in Hawaii, then in a bigger case like yours, she'll most likely want some answers. And how's she going to get those if you're not here?"

"You don't get it," Krista said, sounding despondent. "She remembered you on a nice vacation."

Taylor scoffed. "Yeah, and what an asshole I can be." She didn't want to share the earlier conversation that memory had sparked between them, but she did want to offer Krista some encouragement. "Gwen's generally an extremely forgiving person, especially if she can make sense out of a situation. With all the lengths you've gone to since you found her again, I doubt you didn't come back for her in the past just because you woke up that morning and said, 'Naw, I don't want to go. She can deal with it.'"

Krista gave a sardonic laugh. "Hardly."

"So doesn't she deserve to know the reason?"

Krista bowed her head.

Taylor waited, but no further response came. She rose. She'd done the best she could without knowing the details, and she'd done far better at being a good person than she'd have thought she could given the circumstances. She started for the door.

Maybe one last ditch effort. Based on Krista's earlier reaction to Taylor butting in and to her anger, maybe a different approach was better. She stopped. "You know," she said carefully. "I thought you were pretty tough throughout everything, able to take whatever came. But now that it comes down to the hard stuff, maybe you just don't have the guts." From the corner of her eye, she saw Krista's head jerk up and felt her glare burning into her back as she left the room.

As much to her own surprise as it would be to anyone else's, she'd done everything she could think of, short of tying her to the bedposts, to get Krista to stay. If it didn't work, when Gwen remembered that day Krista didn't show up, she'd still have Taylor, EJ, and Jinx to support her, as well as Namastacey, Sparkle, and Reggie. And Pete, whom she would likely count on the most. And at least now, they all knew about Krista, so they'd be able to be there for Gwen in a way they'd never been able to before.

She hoped Krista would stay to give Gwen an explanation that might give her a peace she'd never had before around something that had to have been devastating. If not, though, Gwen would be okay. They'd all make sure of that.

Taylor smiled as she went to her room. Everything would be okay. Gwen had had a memory.

CHAPTER EIGHTEEN

Thanksgiving morning had dawned clear and brisk, but Gwen had woken with a heavy cloud shrouding her. Had she had a bad dream that left this sense of grief? Whatever it was, something wasn't right, and it had lasted into the late afternoon.

She hadn't felt quite right all week, ever since she'd remembered the trip to Hawaii. No, *that* day had been fabulous, between a bona fide memory surfacing and regaining more independence via her crutches. Dr. Stafford had been thrilled when she'd told him about it at her appointment on Tuesday and had said she maybe could expect more breakthroughs now that one had come. But the past two days were off, and not only for her. Fire had come downstairs the morning after she'd mysteriously disappeared following dinner. She'd been even quieter than usual, and it almost seemed as though she was avoiding eye contact with Gwen. And the look she'd given Taylor could have frozen flames. But Taylor had only smirked.

Something else had happened as well. EJ had called and said a couple named Ken and Brandy from Gwen's hiking club would be passing through on their way back from a holiday visit with family and wanted to know if she'd be up to seeing them. Gwen remembered the names from when Taylor had gone through the rest of the pictures she'd brought from Gwen's house and that Taylor had said Gwen had hiked part of the Appalachian Trail with them one summer.

The more Gwen learned about her life, the more amazed at it she became. She had fantastic best friends and so many people who loved and cared about her. She had a job in which she was so highly thought of that she'd been assured it would be there for her whenever she was ready to return. She was the kind of person that vacationed in Hawaii and hiked the Appalachian Trail. Coming only from what she could recall from the age of sixteen, how could she have imagined that kind of life? And yet, she must have at some point because she'd created it. Although she was nervous, she wanted to meet Ken and Brandy. As Taylor had pointed out, she was making new memories.

But what she felt today was linked to the past. She had no doubt. She tried to present a smile and enjoy the get-together, but she wasn't fooling anyone. EJ looked concerned, Jinx kept eyeing her curiously, and Taylor had outright asked her three times if she was okay. Even Pete followed her wherever she went, attentive to her every movement. Fire still kept a slight, yet conspicuous, distance.

This thick cloak of sadness that weighed her down reminded her of the dark, sooty fog she'd floated in for the weeks she'd been unconscious. *That* was something she wished she could forget. She shivered every time she thought of it. Gwen should fess up, but what could she say? *I feel sad.* How childish would that sound? Besides, it had to pass soon.

When they were seated for dinner with all the delicious aromas drifting around them, the scene couldn't have been more beautiful. As each person offered what she was thankful for, the blessings were the same. *We're all together. We're all alive.* That was fair. Gwen was certainly happy to be alive, and when she met Taylor's eyes, those beautifully hypnotic eyes, Taylor's own gratitude for her own life, her own survival, linked them. Was that the strength of the bond she felt with Taylor, their shared experience of the accident?

She met and held each woman's gaze, whispering heartfelt thank-yous. When she got to Namastacey, though, she stopped. An image came to mind, a large, dimly lit room with thirty or forty women seated on mats in lotus position or in special chairs. Namastacey sat two rows in front of Gwen and a couple of people over. Gwen recognized it all. The meditation hall at the Vipassana retreat center. She and Namastacey had attended a ten-day sit together.

It came to her the same way the memories of Hawaii had. She swallowed hard and bowed her head, "Namaste," she said softly.

Namastacey broke into a wide grin. She pressed her hands together and dipped her chin. "Namaste," she said knowingly.

Everyone else smiled. They recognized what had happened. Another memory had bubbled into Gwen's consciousness.

Gwen didn't want to address it, though. She shuddered. Something else was coming. She didn't know what or when, but it was coming. And it wasn't good.

"Let's eat," Jinx said, her tone bright. "We have a lot to be grateful for."

Gwen picked up the mashed potatoes in front of her and scooped a spoonful onto her plate, then passed them to Fire beside her. She took the stuffing from EJ. When the Spaghetti-O casserole made it to her, she looked into the pan. It appeared exactly as she remembered it, the circular noodles, the tiny hotdogs, the tomatoey red sauce, melted cheese throughout, and a potato chip crust on top. She'd loved it when Fire made it for her before, but her stomach turned at the sight, and a hint of tears stung her eyes.

She blinked them back. She glanced around and found Fire watching her, a slight smile on her lips and a hopeful look in her eyes. She forced her own small smile, then served herself a hefty spoonful before handing the pan to Fire.

Gwen ate as much of the other menu items on her plate as she could before trying Fire's offering because every time she moved her fork to it, a wave of nausea made her stomach clench.

"You don't have to eat it," Fire said when Gwen once again diverted to another choice, her voice low in Gwen's ear.

Gwen startled. She looked up from her plate.

Taylor watched from across the table, her brows drawn together.

Why did everyone always have to be staring at her? Her head pounded at the invasion. Without thinking, she scooped a forkful of the casserole into her mouth. At the first taste, she gagged, and the contents of her stomach threatened an encore. She choked the food down, but everything else raged to the surface.

The images from her eighteenth birthday broke through. Clear and sunny but with a slight chill, the morning had held the promise of Gwen's only dream, to be with Fire again. She'd waited in their favorite park, watching, from shortly after dawn until well after dark, as people appeared in the distance, elevating her excitement, then dashing it when they weren't Fire. Her exhilaration that the day they'd be together again had finally arrived turned to utter devastation as she walked the dark streets to find someplace to stay for the night when she'd realized it wouldn't be in the cute little apartment Fire had assured her would be ready.

The memory of the long, slow hours she'd sat in that same park for so many days following kept coming in detail. First, the possibility Fire simply got held up, maybe at her new job. Or perhaps the new home she'd created for them was in another city, and the car she'd bought and learned to drive had broken down or run out of gas. Or an accident that didn't kill her, of course, because that would be too cruel, had her in a hospital for a few days, and, naturally, Fire had no way to reach her. It took countless days and nights spent in that park and in the cheap, fleabag motel she'd found before the unthinkable crept in. Fire wasn't coming. She changed her mind and started a life without Gwen. She saw the taillights of her mother's car from the church steps in her mind. It had happened again.

The resurgence of that realization hit Gwen as violently now as it had then. The room spun. Her stomach cramped. Her mouth filled with saliva. She shoved away from the table, doubled over, and wretched, just like she'd done her last day in that park. She never went back. Ever.

EJ and Fire leaped up on either side of her.

"Oh, God!" Gwen cried. "I'm sorry."

"Shh. It's okay." EJ rubbed her back.

The memory of lying on the faded, stained motel bedspread, feeling exactly as she did now, flooded her mind. Then everything else came, the days and weeks that followed when she'd only been able to get out of that bed occasionally to stumble next door to the convenience store and force down a hotdog or nachos and replenish her stock of packaged junk food. She didn't talk to anyone, didn't shower, didn't think of anything except how Fire wasn't there and the only life she'd planned for was gone.

Her stomach clenched, and she heaved again.

Taylor was there, where Fire had been, with a cool, wet towel. She pressed it to Gwen's forehead, then gently ran it over Gwen's face.

Gwen gulped for breath. "I need air," she said between gasps. "Outside."

Without a word, EJ and Taylor rose, bringing Gwen up between them, then helped her to the French doors at the end of the dining room and out onto the patio.

Gwen leaned back on the lounge chair they settled her into and closed her eyes. She never wanted to open them again, didn't want to face anyone. She inhaled deeply.

"Here's some water in case she wants it." Jinx's voice was quiet.

Who else had followed them out? Gwen cracked an eyelid open. Only the four of them. No Namastacey. And, more importantly, no Fire. A sharp pain pierced her heart. Never Fire again. Fire was gone. She'd left Gwen long ago.

As she sat beside Gwen, Taylor lay the cool towel across Gwen's forehead. "How's that?"

Gwen nodded slightly. She owed them an explanation. "She left me." She had the strength for only a whisper. "She left me alone in the world."

"Yeah," Taylor said just as softly.

"I remember it." Gwen almost choked on the words. "I remember it all." The tears came, and she curled onto her side. "It hurts so bad."

Taylor wrapped her arm around her and pulled her close.

Like a drowning child, Gwen grabbed her and held on.

"I know." Taylor lifted Gwen into her lap and hugged her fully. "But you're not alone now. You have all of us."

Gwen could only burrow deeper into the embrace and cry harder. She soaked in all the love in Taylor's tone and words and the truth of them she'd felt every second since she'd woken after the accident. Fire *left* her all alone in that park. Without a message, with no clue, with nothing and no one to lean on.

"Gwen?"

It was her. That's right. She was here now.

Gwen buried her face in the front of Taylor's blouse. "No." Her answer came out on a sob.

"Gwen, please." Fire's voice broke. "Let me explain. Please."

No. Not Fire. But yes, Fire. Past and present. Fire and Krista. Thoughts and images tumbled and cascaded through Gwen's mind. So jumbled. So confusing. "No. I can't see you. Can't look at you. It's too much."

"Come on," Namastacey said. "Give her some time. I'll take you back to the farmhouse."

"Gwen, I'm so sorry."

At the sound of retreating footsteps, Gwen relaxed, but she didn't relinquish her hold on Taylor. Nor did Taylor on her.

Taylor was strong. Taylor was safe. Taylor was here, and Gwen had a feeling she always would be.

❖

Taylor rested on the double lounge chair with Gwen in her arms. This was how it should be every night and every morning. Not because Gwen was in emotional shambles from remembering one of the worst times in her life, though. But because they were in love and had finally realized it and had begun a new life together.

Why had everything gone to shit?

They'd been lying there for some time with EJ in another chair beside them and the sounds of Jinx cleaning up the detritus of the ruined dinner drifting through the open French doors.

Gwen loosened her hold around Taylor's waist but didn't move away. She simply shifted slightly so the back of her head nestled snugly in the hollow of Taylor's shoulder.

Taylor allowed herself to travel back in time to the evenings they'd spent exactly like this on one of their couches watching a movie, a luxury she hadn't often indulged in since the accident because coming back to their new reality hurt too damned bad. Tonight might be a game changer, though. Would Gwen remembering that Krista had left her, and how, mean Krista would be going on her way? But even if that were the case, would the impact of the memory of that keep any memories of what she and Taylor had started from coming to the surface? Taylor had been knocked off center by how brutally the recall had hit Gwen. She'd known it would be hard on her but hadn't guessed anything like this.

Gwen stared into the distance, transfixed.

Taylor hadn't wanted to make her talk before she was ready, but something in Gwen seemed to have shifted. She went with her gut. "What are you thinking?"

Gwen didn't answer for a long moment. When she did, her voice was soft. "I was thinking about the moon."

Taylor followed Gwen's gaze to the celestial body that hung low in the evening sky, bright and almost full. It reminded her of standing on the footbridge with Gwen after the wedding and watching the sunset. And then the kiss. Her throat closed with the pain of the promise of that moment and then the loss of it. She forced herself back to the present. "What about it?"

"I feel like the moon." Gwen folded her arms around her middle. "It looks so bright and shiny, like what I see when I look in the mirror. My hair growing in, my complexion getting more color as my body heals. But there's a whole dark side I can't see, that I don't know anything about. Anything can be waiting there."

Her tone was forlorn, almost despondent. Taylor couldn't stand it, but could anything she said make a difference? She tightened her hold in an attempt to comfort Gwen. "I think more will come back to you now that it's started. Isn't that what your psychiatrist said?"

Gwen scoffed. "Yes, but if there's more like tonight, I'm not sure I want it to. I mean, I still have to remember *why* she didn't show up without a word. And what if that's even worse? The worst I guess would be that she died, but that obviously isn't the reason, so it can only be that she just didn't want to be with me."

"Not necessarily." Taylor caught a quick movement from the corner of her eye. She looked to find EJ staring at her in apparent surprise. Taylor's own shock struck her mute. Who was this other person inside her that kept giving Krista the benefit of the doubt? It'd been one thing to try to keep Krista here until Gwen remembered what happened, but did she have to defend her now that Gwen had? But no, she wasn't defending Krista. She was one of Gwen's best friends, and they'd all counted on each other for help sorting things out when needed. And if there'd ever been a time Gwen needed help, it was now. "There could have been something that happened that kept her away for a while, and then she couldn't find you when she did come."

Gwen twisted to look into Taylor's face. "Do you know what happened?" Her tone held a menacing edge. "Did she tell you?"

"No," Taylor said quickly. The last thing she wanted was to get on Gwen's bad side in all this. "I did ask her why she didn't come back, but she wouldn't tell me. She said if she told that story, it should be to you. I respect her for that."

Gwen's expression turned pensive, and she settled back in against Taylor. "You guys aren't supposed to tell me anything I could remember on my own, so does that mean I never knew why she didn't show up?"

Uncertain as to whether even that might be too much to say, Taylor looked to EJ for help.

EJ only watched her, wide-eyed, as though enthralled in the story and waiting to see what happened next.

Left on her own, Taylor sighed. "No, you've never known. And you'll have to ask her if you want to find out because no one else knows."

"I don't want to," Gwen said too quickly, like the obstinate teenager Taylor had come to know over the past couple of months. "Do you think I should?" she added cautiously.

"Yes. I think you need to know." Taylor stroked Gwen's hand where it lay across her stomach, then squeezed it. Stacey's words that had scared her so much raced in. *Gwen and Krista have unfinished business.* She struggled for a way not to say what came next, then relented. "I think you need to know so you can put it behind you and move forward with what you want. Whatever that is." She closed her eyes and sank her teeth into her lower lip. She refused to say any more.

Gwen remained silent for a long time. "I don't want to talk to her," she said tentatively. "I can't. Not until it doesn't hurt so much."

Taylor relaxed. A reprieve.

"Do you think she'll stay?" Gwen asked after another pause.

Taylor considered the two times Krista had already had to be convinced to stay and how upset she'd been after Gwen had remembered Hawaii. "I don't know."

Gwen shivered. "I don't know how I'm going to face her tonight when we go home." She threaded her fingers between Taylor's.

Taylor opened her eyes a slit and looked down at their hands, then up to Gwen's face. Did Gwen know what she'd done?

Gwen stared into the darkening sky. "I don't want to see her tonight."

"You can stay here." EJ scooted to the edge of her chair and leaned close. She ran her hand over Gwen's hair. "Do you think you'll be able to sleep?"

Gwen tipped her head back. "God, I hope so. I'm exhausted." She looked at EJ. "I don't want to be a lot of trouble, though. I already ruined your Thanksgiving dinner."

"Don't worry about that." EJ waved her hand. "Jinx loves to cook. And Christmas is only a month away. This will give her some leverage in wrestling it away from Sparkle."

Gwen smiled weakly. "Thank you. And thank you for inviting me to stay the night. I really don't want to see…" She inhaled a shaky breath. "I don't want to go home yet."

"You don't have to, sweetie." EJ hugged her. "You're welcome here as long as you want. Do you want to stay out here a while?"

"I'm beat. I think I'd like to go to bed."

EJ rose. "Okay, let me get your crutches, and I'll show you the guest room." She paused and met Taylor's gaze, a soft glint in her eyes. "You'll stay too?"

Taylor's breath caught as their connection that seemed to have weakened with all the strain they'd been under whooshed through her. As it settled into the empty space in her heart its absence had left, she let herself feel how much she'd missed it. A flood of emotions swelled in her throat, stealing her response. She nodded. Everything was right again, at least with EJ.

After EJ and Gwen went inside, Taylor sat in the quiet evening and tried to make sense of the day. So many things were different than they'd been only that morning. This was how things would be for a while, wasn't it? One minute Gwen not remembering something so they couldn't talk about it, the next a memory crashing in and they'd have to walk through a minefield, carefully testing what was safe to say. And there didn't seem to be any rhyme or reason to the order in which things came to her. When would she remember something about the time she and Taylor had spent together as lovers? Did she have to get things straight with Krista before she could do that? And what if she got things *too* straight with Krista? In that case, would she never remember her time with Taylor? Her head ached from all the questions and unknowns.

Footsteps drew her attention back to her surroundings.

EJ stood beside her with two mugs. "Hot apple cider?" She handed one to Taylor.

"Thanks." Taylor took a sip, then blew out a breath. "What a day, huh?"

"I'll say." EJ sighed. "Gwen was asleep before I finished hanging up her clothes. That had to be horrible for her."

"Keep an ear out for her tonight," Taylor said, not wanting to rehash the details. "She cries out in her sleep sometimes."

EJ tilted her head, inviting more.

"She doesn't wake up, but sometimes if you talk softly to her, she calms down faster." Taylor hated that she wouldn't be the one listening for Gwen tonight. She examined the contents of her cup to keep EJ from seeing it in her expression. "Or you can rub her head. You know, the way she likes when she's sick? That calms her too."

"Would you like to sleep on the couch upstairs in my office instead of in the living room?" The hint of a smile tinged EJ's voice.

Taylor cut her a glance and saw the teasing spark in her eyes. "Do you have to ask?"

EJ laughed. "No. Jinx is making that one up for you as we speak."

Taylor sat up straight. "She doesn't have to do that. I know my way around your linen closet."

EJ patted her arm. "Stay. She doesn't mind." She left her hand in place. "I want a little time with you."

"Yeah?" Taylor eased back into her lounge chair.

"Yeah." EJ smiled, but her tone was serious. "You were wonderful with Gwen tonight. Not that you aren't always great with both of us when we need you. But tonight was different."

"How so?" What could have been different? Taylor had been just as lost as she'd been since she woke up in the hospital, never sure what to say or do or where she stood with anyone.

EJ shook her head, her expression reflective. "I've never seen you like that with anyone before. Not even Gwen." She studied Taylor as though trying to solve a riddle. "Usually, even when you're helping someone or taking care of them, you're still kind of snarky and flippant. In fun, of course," she added quickly when Taylor opened her mouth to object. "But tonight…" EJ trailed off. Her demeanor softened. "Tonight, I think what I saw was what you've been telling me. That you're truly in love with Gwen."

Taylor sighed, exasperated. "I *am* truly in love with Gwen. How many times do we—"

"Don't." EJ tightened her grip. "Please, don't take this the wrong way. I'm trying to apologize."

Taylor blinked. She couldn't have been any more unprepared for that. "You are?"

EJ smirked. "You don't have to sound so surprised. I can apologize when I'm wrong."

Taylor snorted. "Not often."

"I'm not often wrong."

EJ delivered the response in the regal tone she saved for making her most important points. It made Taylor smile, but she opened her mouth to argue.

"But I was this time," EJ cut her off again. "And I want you to hear that. And my apology. I'm truly sorry." The haughtiness in her voice gave way to sincerity. "I'm sorry I didn't trust what you were saying. I should have. My God, you've been my friend almost half my life. I should have listened."

Taylor hesitated, then nodded. "I hear you. And I accept your apology." She had to ask. "So what did you see tonight that made such a difference?"

EJ settled further into her chair and gazed into space. "I saw my two best friends snuggled together like it was the most natural thing in the world. One of them who's been so terrified of losing the first love she's found in…what? Almost thirty-five years? Putting her fears aside and telling the one she loves that she needs to listen to what her ex-lover has to say, even though, I'm guessing, that conversation is the very root of every fear she has." EJ paused and arched her eyebrow at Taylor, an obvious request for confirmation.

Taylor only gave her a slight shrug.

EJ smiled knowingly. "And I saw my other best friend, who can't remember hardly anything about her adult self or any of her adult friends, cuddling into you in a way she's never done with either of us in our closest moments or even with the boyfriends she's had. And holding onto your hand like a lifeline, just knowing somehow that you're the one to turn to for comfort and safety in the middle of the shit storm that hit her today. Even if she doesn't consciously remember you, Taylor, she does know on some level that you love her and—again, guessing—she loves you."

Tears sprang to Taylor's eyes, and she clenched her teeth, trying to hold them back. "God, I hope you're right."

"I'm ninety-nine percent sure I'm right," EJ said softly. "Whatever changed between you and Gwen while I was gone—and I *do* want to hear about it when you can tell me together—trust it. You and Gwen gave me some really great advice when I wasn't trusting in me and Jinx, and I listened. And look where I am now." She smiled. "So listen to me now. Trust in you and Gwen."

"Knock knock."

Taylor groaned.

"No, don't worry," Jinx said, stepping onto the patio. "Not a joke. Just didn't want to barge in unannounced."

"You know what, Jinxie?" Taylor said, using Sparkle's endearment for her. "I could use a joke right now."

EJ burst out laughing. She looked up at Jinx. "You've got her now. Make sure it's a really corny one."

Jinx chuckled. "Are you sure?" she asked Taylor. "I don't want to take advantage of you in a low moment."

"It's okay," Taylor said. "I give you permission. But can it at least be funny?"

Jinx grinned. "Let's see." She rubbed her hands together. "Okay, I've got one. Knock knock."

"Who's there?" Taylor asked.

"Mikie."

"Remember, it has to make me laugh."

"Mikie," Jinx said again.

"Mikie who?"

"My key doesn't fit the lock. Let me in."

Taylor laughed. "Okay, that one *is* kind of funny. Either that, or I'm punchy from the long day."

"Oh, you liked it," Jinx said, letting EJ pull her onto the lounge chair beside her. "Admit it."

Taylor chuckled. "All right. Since it's just us tonight, and no one will believe you if you tell them, I confess, I do like some of your jokes."

Jinx pumped her fists in the air. "Yes! I knew it!"

Pure joy shone in EJ's eyes as she beamed at Jinx.

Taylor had missed scenes like these so much over the past few months. The laughter. The teasing. The love that so easily flowed between all of them. But this scene wasn't complete. And no scene ever would be without Gwen. Taylor prayed EJ was right. Even though they'd never said the words out loud, she prayed that deep down Gwen knew they loved each other.

Chapter Nineteen

Gwen braced herself with one hand on the fencepost and threw the Frisbee as hard as she could with the other. She loved watching Pete run, ears flapping, tail wagging.

He raced across the grassy field and leaped into the air to catch the toy. He started back her way, then spotted Jinx leaving the exercise yard connected to the kennels. He dashed off to greet her.

Gwen laughed. The cool morning had called to her when she'd woken from the dream of her mother, and she'd wasted no time getting dressed and into the clean air to clear last night's remnants. Sometimes what came to her in dreams weren't full memories, but this one had landed like one. She'd check with someone, but she'd bet money, if she had any, that she really had reunited with her mother at some point long enough to lose some personal items, including an expensive watch and a very nice television, and have her checking account cleaned out when her debit card went missing.

Oddly, the information didn't bother her. It almost felt as though it had happened to someone else. Some memories had a specific feel to them, like they weren't actually part of her, but neither were they ever far away. Kind of like her shadow.

She retrieved her crutches from where she'd leaned them against the fence and started toward the paved path to intercept Jinx and Pete. Taylor had been standing on the veranda of the farmhouse for most of the time Gwen and Pete had been playing, on the phone for a while, but mostly watching them. There was something about Taylor that made Gwen feel like everything would be okay, no matter what. It'd been present with her from Gwen's earliest interactions with her in the hospital, but Gwen had been much more aware of it since Thanksgiving. The way Taylor had held her while she'd cried, so securely, yet soothingly. She'd been so honest and direct about what she thought Gwen should do while never trying to take the decision away from her. And Gwen still hadn't made it.

She couldn't bring herself to talk to Krista, who'd left the farmhouse anyway. She'd said she couldn't do it until the memory didn't hurt so badly. In the five days since, much of the pain and shock had diminished. So what was she waiting for?

"Hey there," Jinx called as Gwen neared the path. "Look at you all out and about on your own."

"Not really. I have my secret service." Gwen nodded toward Taylor as she kept pace with Jinx. She'd gotten pretty darned good on her crutches if she did say so herself.

"We're *all* watching you, but you weren't supposed to figure it out." Jinx leaned close. "Even Pete," she whispered.

Gwen giggled. "No! Pete hangs out with me because he loves me." She made kissy noises at him when he looked up in response to his name. When she lifted her gaze, she met Taylor's across the gravel parking area. Her breath caught.

In her black jeans and dark gold top, her light bronze skin glowing in the bright morning light, and the sun touching the silver threads in her jet-black hair, Taylor was stunning.

It wasn't the first time Gwen had been struck by her beauty, but Taylor was her friend. She shouldn't be ogling her. She turned to Jinx. "Do you know if I've seen my mother as an adult?"

Jinx missed a step. "Uh…"

"Oh, it's okay." Gwen had to focus on her own footing more now that they were on the gravel. "I had a dream last night that I think is a memory. We were in a house together. I think my house, maybe."

"That's great." Jinx smiled. "Yeah, you did find her a while back, but it was way before I was around, so I can't tell you much more than that. You should ask Taylor. But before you do," she caught Gwen's arm, "give me and Pete a kiss good-bye. We have puppies to train."

Gwen kissed Jinx on the cheek and Pete on the top of his head. "Go forth and tame the wild ones." She watched fondly as they raced toward the main office building.

"Ask me what?" Taylor reached down and took the crutches from Gwen. It was a system that had evolved over the past week.

Gwen gripped both railings and hopped up the three steps. "I had a dream about my mother last night that felt like a memory. We were together, but I was an adult." She took her crutches back and crossed to the chairs. She plopped into one. "Did that happen?"

"Yes," Taylor said without hesitation. "What else was in your dream?"

"We were making dinner," Gwen said, then waited. That wasn't quite right. "*I* was making dinner. She set the table, though." She let her mind's eye survey the room. The open plan kitchen and dining area was decorated in blues and white, the kitchen walls bearing the mere suggestion of color brought out by an accent wall of the dining room. Hand-painted thin swirls decorated intermittently spaced counter tile and a country style light wood and tile table finished the casual yet classy ambiance. "I think it's my house. I hope it is because I really like it."

Taylor's lips quirked. "What do you like about it?"

"The kitchen is blue." Gwen closed her eyes, trying to see more detail. "And the canisters are white with the same pretty swirls that are on some of the countertop tiles." She looked at Taylor. "That's so cool that they made them match."

"You did that." Taylor lowered herself into one of the other chairs.

"What?"

"You made them match. You hand painted those little wispy lines."

"Really?" Gwen struggled to remember when she'd learned something like that. She'd had no hint of artistic ability in high school, and the aspects of her life following that had continued to surface over the past couple of days didn't mesh with painting or home decorating. It'd been only the secretarial skills courses she'd taken at the community center and her appeal to middle-aged businessmen that had allowed her to land a job that would pay her rent. But she wasn't yet ready to revisit that train wreck part of her past. "So that *is* my house?" she asked excitedly.

"It is," Taylor said, watching her closely.

"And my mom? She looked different than I remembered before." In the car, in front of the church, her mother had still looked young, a little life-worn and hungover, but still young. "But I guess she was quite a bit older if I…"

Taylor remained silent.

Then it hit. Everything swarmed in at once. The private investigator she'd hired had found her mother at a homeless shelter in Southern

California. It hadn't been difficult. It had taken Gwen far longer to decide to look for her than for the PI to track her down. Gwen had kept waiting for the knock on her door that would tell her that her mother had some regrets about leaving her daughter for strangers to care for. Finally, one morning, it was time.

When she'd called the shelter and left a message and her number for her mother, her phone had rung a mere thirty minutes later. It'd been awkward at first, but before long a meeting was planned. Everything had gone smoothly, and a short while later, her mother came to live with her.

As all the glimpses of scenes and snippets of information began to congeal into a bigger picture in her mind, Gwen waited for the emotional onslaught, something similar to what had followed her remembrance of her eighteenth birthday. And even if it didn't have as devastating an impact, wouldn't there have been some sadness or disappointment that *she'd* been the one who'd had to do the searching? She remembered being determined that she'd never do that. But there was nothing like that, only the satisfaction of trying and succeeding. But what about the money she'd started noticing missing from her wallet or her favorite gold earrings she thought she'd lost until the matching necklace also vanished? No anger? No self-recrimination for thinking it would be different? Maybe at first, but not now.

"Are you okay?" Taylor asked gently.

Gwen sighed. "Yes." She met Taylor's sympathetic gaze. "Interestingly, I am."

"Do you remember everything?" Taylor looked as though she wanted to move closer or touch Gwen, or something. But she remained where she was.

Gwen fit the earlier pieces she'd gotten with these new ones and found a whole scenario. "You mean that she left again one day while I was at work and this time with the contents of my jewelry box and bank account, along with my TV and stereo?"

Taylor nodded. "And don't forget the car."

The image of a silver 2008 Corolla flashed in Gwen's mind. "Ah, yes. The car." She rolled her eyes. "In all fairness, though, I did buy that for *her*."

Taylor laughed. "Yes, you did."

"Why isn't this upsetting me?" Gwen asked, confused.

Taylor arched her eyebrow. "Isn't it?"

Gwen laughed in amazement. "Not really. How can that be?"

"You did do some therapy," Taylor said.

"Before, during, or after?"

"That about covers it."

"That bad, huh?"

Taylor shrugged. "I think because you were already working on your childhood stuff when you decided to start looking for her, you had a jump on things when they started falling apart."

Gwen pondered the idea. "So you're saying I already had closure before I lost the memories, so now the closure comes back with them?"

Taylor smirked. "Well, if you want to put it in psychobabble."

Gwen smiled. She looked out across the grass fields and the pens and let her mind roam to see if anything else came. A name drifted in. "Monica." She tested it and saw a woman with short, dark hair seated in an overstuffed chair. A notebook lay in her lap, and a tiny blue parrot hopped around on her shoulder. "My therapist?"

"Yep. Good job." Taylor reached over and took her hand.

"What's with the bird?" Gwen asked.

"I don't know. You never said." Taylor stretched out her legs and crossed her ankles. "You liked him, though. His name was Toby."

"That's a cute name," Gwen said, but her thoughts had moved on. Could it be she was so at ease with the memory of her mother coming back into her life, stealing her stupid, and disappearing again because she'd already dealt with it in therapy? If so, that would mean, presumably, she'd dealt with her mother's first vanishing as well since sitting here today, she no longer felt any energy around that either. So in contrast, she must *not* have worked on anything around Fire. She caught herself. Around Krista. She'd vowed never to call her Fire again. Fire had been someone she could count on and trust. Krista was someone she didn't know.

Still, though, Krista was the only one who could tell her what had happened to Fire, where she'd gone, why she hadn't come back. Was Taylor right? Did Gwen need to know the why of it? She now knew why her mother had left her at that church. She'd been a mess and couldn't handle a child and all the responsibility. Her mother's words. That was so weak, though. Surely, that hadn't made much of a difference in Gwen's emotional closure on that part of her life.

Something Namastacey once said came to mind. She'd told Gwen that all unhealed relationships return to be made Holy, or healed. It wasn't from Buddhist teachings but from the other path Namastacey studied, *A Course in Miracles*. At the time, Gwen didn't have a clue what it meant. Now, though, it made sense. Her mother had come back and stayed long enough for Gwen to get the closure she needed to be at peace with having a mother for whom she'd be hard-pressed to find a Hallmark Mother's Day card that applied. Yet, she truly was at peace with it. And now there was Krista.

"You really think I need to talk to her?" she asked Taylor.

"I think, if you don't, it's going to be a lot harder for you to come to terms with it." Taylor answered as though she'd been doing nothing for the past five days other than waiting for that exact question.

Gwen swallowed, her mouth dry. "Why do I need to come to terms with it? I haven't yet, and my life seems pretty damned fantastic." Taylor's pause was so long Gwen tugged lightly on her hand. "That wasn't rhetorical."

The corners of Taylor's mouth lifted in the tiniest smile Gwen had ever seen, and it didn't reach her eyes. Her gaze remained fixed on something distant. "I can't tell you that."

It sounded ominous, but deep in Gwen's soul, it rang true. Like it or not, she had to talk to Krista. "She's still here?"

"Yes."

Taylor's tone wasn't at all what Gwen expected. It wasn't happy, or excited, or even merely satisfied. It held a note of resignation. "Okay," Gwen said, more to herself than Taylor.

She hadn't seen Krista since Thanksgiving. Krista had left EJ and Jinx's after Gwen had said she wouldn't talk to her, and she hadn't been at the farmhouse when Gwen and Taylor returned the following afternoon. Gwen had thought maybe she'd gone completely and was relieved, but then, inexplicably, bristled and almost cried. Then she'd heard Taylor on the phone telling someone to give Gwen time. It had to be Krista, but Gwen hadn't been able to ask. It had all been too much. "Where is she?"

"Staying with Stacey." Another immediate answer.

Of course, she'd known all along. "Can we call her?"

Taylor retrieved her cell phone from her back pocket. "Do you want to ask her to come over or do you want me to?"

"I'll talk to her," Gwen said, unsure if she wanted her over at all. Couldn't they talk on the phone and be done with it? How long could it take for Krista to say she changed her mind once she got out into the big, exciting world?

Taylor held out the phone to her.

Gwen eyed the thin rectangle with all the little pictures on the screen. "I don't know how to work that," she said, her cheeks heating. She'd watched the others make and take calls over the weeks, and she'd talked on Jinx's or Taylor's a few times when EJ had called while in Sacramento, but the last call she remembered placing had been a long time ago when cell phones looked nothing like this one.

"Sorry." Taylor tapped the screen several times, then handed the device to Gwen.

Gwen listened to the ringing on the other end.

"I'll give you some privacy," Taylor said as she stood.

Before Gwen could object, Krista's voice sounded in her ear. "Taylor? Is everything all right?"

"Um." Gwen cleared her throat. She was vaguely aware of Taylor opening the screen door and disappearing into the house. "This isn't Taylor. It's me. Gwen."

The silence that followed hung heavy with the weight of all the years, all the unshared moments, all the unanswered questions that lay like corpses between them.

"Hi," Krista said finally.

Gwen swallowed. "Hi."

More silence.

"Gwen, I…" Krista faltered. "I…" She tried again. "I don't know what to say to you."

Gwen pulled her lower lip between her teeth and bit down hard. Was *she* going to have to navigate this conversation? Anger simmered in her belly.

"No, that's not true," Krista continued in a rush. "I know what I want to say, but I don't know if it's what you called to hear."

Gwen's vision blurred. She'd thought she'd run out of tears, but here were more. She flashed back to the park, the cold of the metal bench through the worn denim of her jeans, and all those days of waiting. "I only want to know why."

"Gwen, please." Krista's voice broke. "It's not a simple answer. Can we please sit down together and talk?" The words came out in gasps as she started to cry.

The sound tore at Gwen's heart. She'd heard Fire break down only once, the night she'd gotten the call that her grandmother had died. Gwen had held her in her arms while she sobbed like the little girl she truly was. It was the first time Gwen had realized Fire wasn't unbreakable and invincible, that how she presented to the world wasn't the real Fire. Or, now that Gwen thought about it, maybe it was the true Fire, just not the real Krista. That had been the first night they'd shared a bed.

Could she do it? Could she meet with Krista and hear her out? Didn't she owe her that, owe them both that? What if the why was what Taylor had said, something happened that kept her away? What if Gwen had been right in one of her own conjured scenarios?

"Shhh," Gwen breathed into the phone. "Okay. Shhh. We can talk." Krista calmed as Gwen whispered softly.

It was the first time Gwen had considered that she wasn't the only one who might have been in pain. A stab of guilt caught her by surprise. How could she have been so self-absorbed? Maybe she should have talked to someone about it, maybe Monica, or EJ, or Taylor. Surely, someone would have told her she was being a self-centered jerk. "We can talk," she said again.

"Thank you." Krista's voice was hoarse. "When? You name it. I'll be there."

"Are you up to it later today?" Gwen asked cautiously. "I want to get—" She cut herself off. After making Krista endure five days of waiting and not knowing, did she have any grounds to say she wanted to get it over with? "I'd like to do it today."

"What time?"

"After lunch? One o'clock?" Gwen wanted to think, to process everything she'd remembered about her mother, and to spend some time with Taylor. She'd enjoyed their past few days together with Jinx and EJ dropping in for lunch or dinner. It was like playing house. And then there was what she might need to say to Krista.

"Perfect." Krista sniffed. "I'll see you then."

"Okay. Bye." Gwen tapped End Call and set the phone on the table. She heard Taylor moving around in the kitchen. "I'm finished," she called out.

"That was short," Taylor said as she set a cup of tea in front of Gwen. She returned to her previous seat. "How'd it go?"

"Thank you," Gwen said for the drink. "We didn't actually talk yet." She took a sip. "She's coming over at one."

Taylor fidgeted with something in her hands.

"What's that?" Gwen asked.

"Something I thought you might like after our conversation earlier." She held it out to Gwen. "It's a picture of you and your mom the first time you met after you found her. I brought it from your house."

Gwen took the framed photo and studied it closely. She traced her mother's face, her eyes so much like Gwen's, the way they twinkled. She smiled. "I remember this. We met at a Denny's in San Diego."

"That's right." Taylor's tone was low, almost reverent.

Gwen looked up from the picture and into Taylor's eyes. Those eyes. What was it about those eyes? Sure, they were gorgeous, that amber color, but there was something else. "Why do you say it that way?"

Taylor's expression remained soft. "It was just a really nice day. You were so happy." Her gaze drifted slightly as though she was lost in the memory, then it sharpened. "Well, you enjoy your tea. I'm going to clean up the kitchen since you've invited company over without checking first." She stood and pressed the back of her hand to her forehead. "A housewife's work is never done." She started to turn toward the door.

"Taylor?" Gwen crooked her finger, beckoning her.

Taylor leaned down.

Gwen slipped her hand around the back of Taylor's neck, enjoying the silky smoothness of her hair between her fingers. She pulled her close and brushed a kiss across her cheek. She let her lips linger longer than she should have. When she eased away, Taylor was opening her eyes. "Thank you," Gwen whispered.

Their faces only inches apart, Taylor arched her brow. "For?"

Gwen released her hold. "Everything."

Taylor straightened, her focus still on Gwen.

"For this." Gwen lifted the picture. "For talking with me and helping me figure out all this stuff. For listening when I just need to get things out. For washing throw up off my face." She grimaced.

A teasing glint flashed in Taylor's eyes. "Someone has to keep you cleaned up."

Gwen glimpsed Taylor in a black pencil skirt and suit jacket walking toward an elevator and Gwen calling her back. Without a word, she straightened the collar of Taylor's teal blouse, then smoothed a couple of strands of hair back into place. She squinted at Taylor. "I'm starting to get that that's not the way things typically are."

"Uh-oh. I'm going to have to warn EJ that our little tyrant is coming back," Taylor said as she let the screen door slam behind her.

"I'm sure I'm not a tyrant," Gwen called after her. "Maybe a benevolent dictator but not a tyrant." She giggled.

She set the photo on the table in front of her and considered everything that had come back to her about her mother from her dream and her talk with Taylor. She'd already remembered everything she could about why she and Krista weren't still together, and by the end of today, she'd presumably know the hows of that as well. And those were the big things, right? So what was it Taylor said she couldn't tell Gwen? When Gwen had asked why it was important for her to come to terms with Krista not coming back for her, Taylor had said she couldn't tell her. And there'd been such sadness in her eyes.

What else could there be?

CHAPTER TWENTY

Gwen started fidgeting at twelve fifteen, the fluttering in her stomach turning to nausea by twelve forty. She hadn't been able to eat much of the turkey sandwich Taylor made her for lunch and wished she'd eaten breakfast. At twelve fifty, she began to pace the entertainment room, if one could call her clump-swish gait on her crutches pacing.

Why had she wanted to wait until after lunch? Krista had sounded like she would have come over immediately if Gwen had asked. All Gwen had done in the time between was get increasingly stressed about the conversation.

The sound of a car entering the gravel parking area behind the house made her jump. Show time. Taylor had said she'd make them something to drink and let Krista know where Gwen was, so Gwen sat on the couch and waited. She listened to the low voices as Taylor and Krista greeted each other in the kitchen. Then footsteps.

Krista slowed as she came through the doorway, a mug in one hand and a glass in the other, and gave an uncertain smile. "Taylor made you some tea," she said in place of a greeting.

Not surprising. She had to be even more nervous than Gwen.

Krista stood awkwardly at the far end of the couch and stared at her.

"Would you like to sit down?" Gwen asked.

"Oh." Krista moved closer.

Gwen accepted the cup from her as she sat beside her.

Krista took a swallow of her drink, then set the glass on the table in front of them. She glanced anxiously around the room, "I'm sorry. I know I asked to talk to you, but now that I'm here, I don't know where to start."

Gwen averted her gaze. She understood. And she would have liked to have been able to help her out, but she still wasn't sure how she felt about her now that she'd experienced the full impact of Krista disappearing when they were supposed to have been starting a life together. "Then can I ask a couple of questions?"

Krista sighed, looking grateful. "That would be good."

Gwen steeled herself. "I think I remember the morning Deborah caught us together. I saw it somehow when I was still unconscious. And you referred to it when you were telling me that we weren't together anymore."

"That's right." Krista said, her voice taut.

"And you said they separated us?"

Krista nodded.

"Where did we go?" Gwen still had no memory of anything between that day and what had come to her beginning on her eighteenth birthday.

"I went to a group home." Krista rubbed the scar on the back of her hand as though it ached. "I don't know where you went. I tried to find out. I went back to Deborah's to ask her, but she wouldn't talk to me. She said if I came back, she'd file a complaint. I tried your social worker, but she wouldn't tell me anything either. I even hung out around our old school for a while, hoping you were still going there, but I never saw you."

"A group home?" Gwen had heard the rest, but those words had snagged her like a fish hooked on a line. They still terrified her from her own short stay in one when she was thirteen. She'd been jumped one night in the bathroom and beaten into unconsciousness because she'd let it slip that the older girls had sneaked out in the middle of the night to meet some boys.

"It was all right." Krista met Gwen's eyes for the first time since she'd sat down. "I was only there that last two months until I got cut from the system."

Of course, Krista didn't have to ask about Gwen's reaction. "So what happened after that?" Gwen asked, gently, yet firmly, snicking the door in her mind shut on any threads of thoughts or memories of group homes. "With you, I mean." That *was* what they were there to talk about, after all.

Krista looked sick. "Well, I started with our plan, trying to make sure everything was ready for you when *you* got out. I used the money you gave me while we were preparing as much as we could." She turned her head and looked out the window as though searching for an escape. "You said to use it to get some place to live while I found a job. But nothing was like we thought it'd be. It wasn't easy to find a place for the amount I had." She let out a laugh that held no humor. "We thought it was so much. And I was only eighteen, *barely* eighteen, with no credit history. All I could find was a room in a guy's house. His name was Fernie, and when I ran out of money, he said I could stay if I fucked him and his friends on a regular basis."

Gwen couldn't stop the gasp that slipped between her lips.

Krista didn't seem to notice. "And a job?" She met Gwen's eyes, sadness and apology in hers. "Let's just say there's a price to pay for screwing up so many times. All those bosses I called assholes and all the fights I got into with coworkers? I learned that stuff follows you."

Gwen had no idea what to say. She'd been so selfish, thinking only how *she'd* been affected. Guilt seeped into her heart like a cold, damp fog.

"Anyway," Krista said, picking at a jagged spot on her fingernail. "When the money ran out, I didn't have anywhere to live, no address to put on job applications. I started panhandling and hanging out in parking lots, washing people's windshields. I stole a purse someone left in their unlocked car." She leaned forward, her elbows on her knees, and rubbed her forehead. "And through everything, all I could think of was I was letting you down."

Gwen clenched her eyes shut. "Oh, baby, I put so much pressure on you." She reached for Krista and pulled her to her, cradling her head in her lap.

Krista's shoulders shook.

"I'm so sorry," Gwen whispered, trying not to lose control of her emotions. "I had no idea. I'm so sorry."

"No," Krista said, shifting to look up at Gwen, her face wet "I'm not telling you this to make you feel bad. I just need you to understand that I tried." She choked on the words. "I really tried. I just couldn't do it. But I never left you, Gwen. Not in my heart. I've always loved you."

A dam broke. All of Gwen's feelings for Krista she thought she'd sealed away forever hit her like a tidal wave. Sobs racked her body. Tears flooded her eyes and poured down her cheeks. She folded herself over Krista and covered her mouth with hers.

She kissed her hard with every ounce of love and desire she'd ever felt for her, every sorrow, every regret. Krista's taste, her scent, the fullness of her lips called up images and sensations from intimate moments of connection and passion, true memories of times they'd shared.

Krista reached up and threaded her arms around Gwen's neck, arching to deepen the kiss.

Then, Taylor was there. Not in the room or the house. But, somehow, in the kiss. In Gwen.

She sat up, twisting to press against Gwen. The heat of her body penetrated their clothing.

Gwen leaned back into the plush couch cushion, bringing Taylor with her, holding Taylor tight. More memories. Kissing on another couch. Undressing. Taylor's hands all over Gwen's skin. Memories? They couldn't be. Lying in a meadow, those amber eyes gazing down at her. A surge of arousal coursed through Gwen, thrumming between her thighs. It writhed, long pent and aching for release. A low moan vibrated in her throat.

Another answered. Another kiss. Gwen caressed the back of Taylor's neck, twining her fingers in her hair. No, not Taylor's hair. A different texture. A shorter length. Gwen fluttered her eyelids. Red not black. Her thoughts reeled. What was she doing? "Wait!" She wedged her hands between her and Krista and pushed. "Please, wait."

Krista pulled away. "Oh, God. I'm sorry. Did I hurt your leg?"

Gwen leaned her head back and gasped for breath. "No. And don't be sorry. That was amazing. I'm just a little confused." She blinked at Krista, into her green eyes, taking in her swollen lips. "Make that a lot confused."

"I know. I shouldn't have lost control. It's just, when you kissed me, it felt so good." Krista straightened and turned, her feet back on the floor. She ran her fingers through her hair.

Gwen remembered the feel. Then thought of Taylor's. What was happening?

"It did feel good," Gwen said as her breathing slowed and her body began to calm. "But I can't just pick up where we left off twenty-one years ago."

"No. I know that." Krista flopped against the back cushion of the sofa. "It was an emotional moment, and we got caught up in it. If you want me to leave, I understand."

Gwen grasped her wrist in case she tried. "I don't. I'd like to hear more if you're up to it."

"Sure," Krista said, but something flickered in her eyes.

In her *green* eyes, Gwen noted. *Not* amber.

"Do you want me to make you some more tea?" Krista picked up the cup. "This is probably cold."

"I can do it if you'll carry it back for me."

"Let me." Krista rose. "I haven't gotten to take care of you in days. I've missed it."

"Okay, but I'm getting spoiled with all of you around." Speaking of around, where was Taylor? Had she seen or heard what happened between her and Krista? Gwen watched Krista leave and listened. No low voices this time. Where had Taylor gone and why? And why did it matter?

If Gwen were going to wonder something about Taylor, how about why was she fantasizing about her? Is that what that had been? How could she fantasize about her best friend that way? And if she really had that strong of an attraction to her, being around her on a daily basis had to be hell. So no. The whole episode had to be connected with the flood of emotions and her physical response to Krista.

When Krista returned and Gwen had taken a couple of swallows of her new tea, she had to ask. "Is Taylor still in the kitchen?"

"No, I didn't see her. Her car's still here, though, so she can't be far." Krista returned to her spot beside Gwen, a little closer than before. "So," she drew out the word humorously, but there was an edge to her voice. "You said you want to know more. What in particular?"

"Everything that's happened to you since we got separated," Gwen said seriously. "But I'm really curious how you became a nurse."

Krista nodded. "For that I have to start pretty much where we left off."

"Okay." Gwen took another swallow. "I'm listening."

"Looking back on it now, it was kind of cosmic." Krista settled in. "When I ran out of money, I didn't have a job or anywhere to live, so I ended up on the streets for a while. One day, I'd wandered into a part of town I didn't know, and I came across an Army recruitment office."

Gwen's eyebrows shot up, seemingly of their own volition. "You? In the army?" Her voice squeaked.

"I know. I thought you'd get a kick out of that. Even as I signed the paperwork, I thought, Gwen isn't going to believe this." Krista didn't look at her, though. "It was only three months until I was supposed to meet you, and I had nothing. So my plan was to enlist, go through boot camp, be finished in time to get leave to come meet you, and then we'd live wherever I was stationed."

"So what happened?" Gwen asked.

Krista looked at the floor the way she did when she was embarrassed or felt guilty or ashamed.

Obviously, something had gone wrong. Gwen stroked the back of Krista's hand. "It was a long time ago, and we're both here now," she said softly. "What happened?"

"*I* happened. Again," Krista said with a shrug. "I got into a fight, not the first since I'd signed up, and did some time in the stockade. My leave got canceled, and by the time I could travel and got home, you were long gone."

Gwen thought about how many days she'd returned to the park and waited. She wished she knew exactly, but they'd all blurred together in her grief and fear. "How long was it?"

"About six weeks," Krista said with a sigh. "I couldn't get leave right away."

Gwen nodded. No sense worrying about it now. "Then what?"

"I worked stocking inventory at the base hospital for a while." Her tone was flat. "It was boring as hell. And all I did on my off time was drink and beat myself up for screwing up again and losing you. Then I met a woman named Captain Destiny."

Gwen snorted.

Krista smiled. "I kid you not," she said. "Actually, Captain Bradford is her official title, but Destiny is her first name, so that's what most of us who knew her *unofficially* called her off duty."

"And what did Captain Destiny do for you?" Gwen took another sip to hide anything her expression might reveal. She wasn't sure she wanted to know what Captain Destiny did for Krista.

"She believed in me. And she encouraged me. And whenever I needed it, she gave me a good chewing out." Krista turned her hand and took Gwen's in hers. "She was a lot like you."

Gwen blushed under Krista's sentiment and touch. "I'm glad you had her."

"She convinced me I was smart enough to be a nurse. Even a flight nurse." Krista leaned forward and retrieved her glass. Some of her air of confidence had returned with that revelation.

"You're a flight nurse?" Gwen asked, a little awestruck.

"I was. I'm not now, obviously."

Gwen flashed her a wide grin. "You did it! You got to make your living in the sky." She held up her mug for a toast. "Here's to you."

A bit sheepishly, Krista tapped it with her glass. "Here's to me."

"Where were you stationed?" Gwen asked.

"The first several years I was in North Carolina at Fort Bragg. Once I became a nurse, I put in for Iraq."

Gwen gasped. "You were in Iraq? Wasn't that dangerous?"

Krista chuckled. "It *was* a war zone, so, yes."

A chill ran through Gwen at the realization that she could easily have never seen Krista again. Never had this conversation. Never known what happened to her. She softened. "I'm glad you made it home."

"Me too," Krista said. "Especially now." She raised Gwen's hand to her lips and kissed her fingers. "And I'm glad you survived that car crash."

"There's something I've been wondering about since I woke up," Gwen said, thinking about the accident and being taken to that particular hospital.

"What's that?" Krista looked wary but didn't shy away.

"You said your contract was about to end when Taylor and I were brought in, and you were planning to go home for a few months before you signed another one."

"Mm-hm."

"Why were you there in the ER? And how did you recognize me? It sounds like I was a mess."

Krista paled as she studied Gwen, as though seeing her again. She turned in her seat to fully face her. "You were. It almost destroyed me when it sank in that it was really you." She touched Gwen's cheek, then her hair, as though she suddenly didn't trust that Gwen was truly there. "I thought I'd found you after all these years only to watch you die."

"Did you recognize me?"

"No. When I saw you, you were…" Krista paused, clearly choosing her words carefully. "I saw your name on the board first, where all the patients and their locations in the ER are listed. I stared at it for the longest time. I couldn't believe it. Then I ran to your bed, and they were working on you." She huffed out a laugh. "No one could have ever guessed I had any training. I froze. All I could do was stand in the corner and watch."

The scene hit Gwen like an icy wind. It wasn't a memory, not like the pineapple or the meditation hall or even the cold metal park bench. More like knowledge, the way she'd *known* that night. "That was you. The redhead in the corner. You brought your friend dinner."

Krista stared. "How did you know that?"

"I saw you. And I felt you." Gwen tried to piece it together. "I mean, I didn't know it was you. I was only aware of what you were feeling. Your shock. But I didn't know what you were shocked about. There were others too, like one of the doctors whose husband was in Afghanistan. She was scared."

"Dr. Rink," Krista said, her expression bewildered. "Her husband was missing."

"But they found him?"

"What?"

"You said was. Did they find him?"

"Yeah," Krista said absently. "Yeah, he's been home for a few weeks." She still watched Gwen. "How do you know that stuff?"

"I'm not sure." Gwen had tried without success to figure out her time in the hospital. "I wasn't in my body, I don't think. I was kind of floating, and then I went somewhere else."

"You were really dead." The impact of the realization was clear in Krista's tone and pallor.

Gwen remembered being dead. Dexter. Mrs. Walker. All that peace. It was really too bad so many people were afraid of it. What Mrs. Walker had told her drifted back into her consciousness. *It's not your time. You need to learn to trust love. Someone will be there to help you.* Was it Krista? Is that why, with all the hospitals in the country Krista could have been in as a traveling nurse, she was in the one Gwen had been brought to that day?

"I don't want to lose you again," Krista said abruptly. She grabbed Gwen and pulled her into an embrace. "I can't. Even if we can't be together like we were, promise me we'll be in each other's lives."

"I promise." Gwen wrapped her arms around Krista. "I feel the same way. I've missed you so much."

"Oh, my God, I've missed you too," Krista said into Gwen's hair.

Gwen held her, soaking in their new connection, but there was still so much more she wanted. She eased away. "Now that we both know everything that happened, or at least everything I can remember at this point, we have a lot of catching up to do. Will you come back and stay here at the farmhouse again?"

Krista hesitated. "Shouldn't we check with Taylor?"

Taylor? "Why would we need to check with Taylor? She was fine with you being here before. Besides, she's the one who pushed me to call you this morning to have you come over to talk." Something niggled around in the back of Gwen's brain even as she said the words. But of course Taylor wouldn't mind if Krista came back. "She'll probably be thrilled to not have to do all the work around here. And I *know* she missed your cooking. We both did."

Krista laughed. "All right. I'll go pick up the things I took to Stacey's, then I'll be back to make some of that honey balsamic chicken she loves for dinner."

"That should win her over," Gwen said, only half teasing.

When Krista had gone, Gwen waited in the entertainment room, assuming Taylor would come in to check on her as she always did. As time ticked by, though, Taylor didn't come. Finally, Gwen got up and went to the kitchen, saw that the downstairs bathroom door was open, checked the study, and glanced into her room where she'd found Taylor a time or two changing the sheets on Gwen's bed or putting away her laundry.

"Taylor?" she called up the stairs. But she got no answer. She considered trying to climb them. What if something had happened to her up there and she needed help? But the staircase was long and narrow, and Gwen wasn't sure she could navigate it safely on her crutches.

She went outside onto the veranda, followed it all the way around the house and scanned the surrounding fields and pathways of the Canine Complete property.

No Taylor.

Her car was still there, but Taylor was gone.

It hit her like a punch in the gut. Taylor hadn't left her side since they'd come to the farmhouse. Her absence now left a void.

But shouldn't it be Krista's absence that left her feeling empty? She'd just made up with her after being apart for so long. Hell, she'd just made out with her. But that was an emotional moment, as Krista had said.

And Gwen had been thinking of Taylor throughout most of it.

She looked around the grounds again. Where *was* she? She couldn't be far without her car. Why did she leave? Had she seen Gwen kiss Krista? The thought struck Gwen as odd. Why would it matter? No answer came, but for some reason it *did* matter.

Gwen didn't want Taylor to think she was still in love with Krista. But why?

CHAPTER TWENTY-ONE

Taylor followed Jinx from the grooming salon into the reception area of the main Canine Complete office, Pete beside them. The staff T-shirt Jinx had given her so she could help with Charlie's bath clung to her, and her black jeans were soaked. The standard poodle had seemed so calm. How had she ended up drenched?

She smiled at Marie, the secretary she'd had a couple of dalliances with since EJ and Jinx had gotten together.

"Hey, Taylor. You're wet," Marie said with a wink.

Taylor chuckled. "Jinx put me to work," she said, ignoring the double entendre.

"You loved it," Jinx said. "I told you it'd cheer you up."

"It was fun," Taylor said. "I admit it."

They entered Sparkle's office, and Jinx rounded the end of the desk and plopped down into the high-backed, swivel chair. "There's nothing like playing with dogs in water to put a smile on your face." She woke the computer and clicked the mouse several times.

Pete settled on the floor beside Taylor.

She loved how he always knew who needed him. But she was better now. She reached down and scratched behind his ear. "So that's the helm of Canine Complete?" she asked, motioning to Sparkle's chair.

"Yeah. You want to sit in it?" Jinx jumped up.

"No." Taylor elongated the word for emphasis. "That has to be like sitting in the president's chair in the Oval Office. It's just not done."

Jinx laughed and sat down again. "I sit in it all the time."

Taylor cocked her eyebrow in challenge.

"Okay," Jinx said with a shrug. "Only when she's gone. And I can't eat in it."

"And because she loves you almost more than Reggie."

The door of the private entrance from the customer parking lot swung open and EJ strode in. "Hello, wife. Hello, bestie." She kissed Taylor on the cheek, then lingered on Jinx's lips until she got a low moan from her.

"All right, all right." Taylor covered her eyes. "Have mercy on the celibate."

"Oh, I'm sorry. I forgot." EJ finished with a peck on Jinx's cheek, then straightened.

"Yeah, right." Taylor glared at her.

"You know what? That's something I wish I'd connected when I was doubting what you were telling me about your feelings for Gwen." EJ came around the desk again and sat on the front edge. "We were in the hospital all that time with all those nurses and female doctors, and you didn't hook up with a single one."

Taylor was outraged. "You think I'd do that with Gwen in the condition she was in even if I weren't in love with her?" She folded her arms. "I loved her before too, you know."

"I've known you when you would have. In addition to other things, you've always used sex for stress relief. No offense," EJ added quickly.

Taylor frowned. How could she be offended when it was true? "Well, I wouldn't now, even for stress relief. And I was plenty stressed."

"That's what I'm saying." EJ's gaze went soft. "I meant it as a good thing."

Taylor loosened her hold around her middle. "What are you doing here anyway? It's the middle of the afternoon."

EJ leaned back on her hands and sighed. "I finished up in Fresno early, so I decided to put my visit to the San Jose store off until tomorrow afternoon so I could have dinner with you, Gwen, and Jinx, and then have the night to cuddle with my new wife. What are you doing over here? And who's with Gwen?"

"I needed to get out of the house." Taylor plucked the wet fabric of her shirt away from her skin. "Krista's with Gwen."

EJ sat up straight. "Krista's back?"

Taylor nodded. "Gwen was ready to hear her out."

"Oh!" EJ's pitch rose. "That's good, right? You told her yourself you thought it would be good for her to know what happened."

"Yeah," Taylor said. "It will be."

"But you're worried it will go too well?"

Taylor swallowed. She couldn't make herself say the words. She looked at Jinx across the desk.

EJ followed her gaze.

"She saw them kiss," Jinx said for her.

EJ turned back to Taylor. "Ooooh." She was quiet for a minute. "What kind of kiss?"

"A *real* kiss," Taylor said, using the term she and EJ coined for a heavy duty, headed-for-sex lip-lock back in their clubbing days.

EJ's eyes widened. "They did that in front of you?"

"No. They don't know I saw." Taylor shifted in her seat. The wet waistband of her jeans chafed her skin. "They were in the entertainment room, and I went upstairs to put some laundry away. You know how the stairs line up exactly with that doorway. So when I came down, I couldn't miss it."

EJ pressed her lips into a firm line, clearly thinking. "It won't matter," she said finally.

Encouraged, Taylor let her hopes rise. "Why do you say that?"

"Because I've seen her with you. Last week, when she was reliving possibly the worst day of her life, it was you she wanted. Even when she'd calmed down, she stayed glued to you."

"I hope you're right." Taylor tried to keep her tone neutral, but EJ would see through it even if she succeeded. It was more for herself, though. And for Gwen. After Taylor had left the house, she'd gone for a walk to think before she detoured to the grooming salon to hang out with Jinx, and she'd promised herself she wouldn't jump to any conclusions. Gwen needed time to sort things out, and Taylor would give it to her.

"I am right." EJ slipped off the desk and circled behind Taylor. She started a gentle massage of her shoulders. "She might not know consciously that she's in love with you, but some part of her knows it, so she's going to remember."

Taylor tipped her head back and groaned. "God, that feels good. Harder."

EJ dug her fingers in. "You're as knotted up as a gnarled rope. You should get a massage."

"I am getting a massage. Don't stop."

The ringtone from Taylor's phone blared into the room.

"Grrr." Taylor lifted her hip and pulled it from her back pocket.

EJ slowed her movements.

"No, keep going." Taylor checked her screen.

"Krista?" EJ said, obviously reading over Taylor's shoulder.

Taylor's pulse lurched, and she bolted upright in her chair. She answered the call. "Krista. Is Gwen okay?"

"No!"

Gwen's voice rang loud in Taylor's ear, and she pulled the phone away.

"Gwen is *not* okay." She articulated every syllable, now through the speaker. "Where are you? And why am *I* the only one without one of these phones? I've had to sit here and wait for Krista to come back to begin to track you down. Surely, I have one. Where is it?"

"I was wondering when she was going to realize that," EJ whispered.

Taylor wrenched around and scowled at her. "I'm over at the office with Jinx and EJ," she said to Gwen. "And I don't know where your phone is. Mine was in the car when it caught fire." She silently gagged on the memory of the stench of burning rubber and leather and hot metal as she did whenever she thought of the accident.

"I have your phone, Gwen," EJ said, picking up the conversation. "It's in a bag of your and Taylor's things they took off you both when you got to the ER."

"Oh," Gwen said, a little calmer. "Well, I would like it."

"Of course. I'm sorry," EJ said, sounding sincere. "I hadn't thought of it before now. I'll look and see what else is in the bag."

"Thank you." Gwen paused. "Is Taylor still there?"

"I'm here," Taylor said. She cleared her throat to recover from her reaction to the memory. "You're on speaker. We can all hear you and talk to you."

"Oh." Another hesitation. "Can I talk to you when you get home?"

"Sure. I'll be right there."

"Okay. Good-bye. End call?" The last was muffled, then the line went dead.

Taylor slumped in her chair. "You could have prepared me for that," she said to EJ. "That could have happened when you weren't around, and I wouldn't have known what to tell her about the phone."

"I really did forget about it." EJ sat in the other guest chair in front of the desk. "I mean, I looked through the bag and used it in the beginning to contact people I thought she'd want notified. Then I put hers back in the bag to keep with her other things. I didn't think about it again until we got here, but I decided to hang onto it because I remembered there are a bunch of pictures of her and her mom on it, and she hasn't remembered that yet."

"She has now," Taylor said, getting to her feet. "That all came through this morning. It's what led to the conversation about talking to Krista."

"Wow, she's had a big day." EJ tugged the hem of Taylor's T-shirt down from where it had hiked up over her hip. "Did you talk with her again about letting Krista tell her why she didn't come?"

"Yep, so I have nobody to blame but myself if she falls for her again." Taylor recalled the times she'd kept Krista from leaving and a part of her wished she hadn't. "Krista was going to leave the night after Gwen had that first memory of Hawaii. I didn't tell you that, did I?"

EJ shook her head. "Did you stop her?"

"I did." Taylor scrubbed her fingernails over her thighs. They were starting to itch. She had to get out of these wet clothes.

"She's going to remember you, Taylor," EJ said, giving her an encouraging look. "And you're the one she's going to fall in love with again. How could she not?"

Taylor gave a tiny smile. "Thanks. If nothing else, it's nice to have you in my corner again."

EJ stood and hugged her.

"I'd better get back to the house," Taylor said. "I've been summoned."

"And you love it," EJ said with a self-satisfied smile.

Taylor drew in a deep breath, then slowly expelled it. "God help me, I do."

EJ and Jinx laughed.

"I think we've reawakened the tyrant in her, though." Taylor walked toward the door. "This could have been our chance to tame that little beast."

"But then she wouldn't be Gwen," EJ said, edging her hip onto the corner of the desk.

"So true." Taylor rested her hand on the doorknob. "You two are joining us for dinner?"

"Yes. We'll be there soon," EJ said. "I need to talk with Jinx about something."

"Uh-huh." Taylor scanned the desktop, flashing back to the night she and Gwen had made use of Taylor's desk for highly inappropriate and non-OSHA approved purposes. "By the way, before you decide to give Gwen's phone back to her, or look through her pictures yourself, you should know there are some pics of her and me in there."

EJ scrunched up her face. "Thanks for the warning."

"And watch out for that." Taylor pointed to the stapler. "It can pinch as well as poke. Trust me on this."

EJ gasped in obvious mock offense, then opened a drawer and slid it inside.

Taylor laughed and walked out.

Krista made a light, early dinner for all of them, and EJ and Jinx were eager to get home as soon as the kitchen was cleaned up. Marie had thwarted their plan to defile Sparkle's office by insisting the computer needed to be scanned for malware and she would need to check it periodically. So they'd shown up at the farmhouse just in time to save Taylor from having to hear about Gwen and Krista's earlier conversation. It was inevitable, but with the image of Gwen and Krista kissing still fresh in her mind, she wasn't ready to hear about anything else.

Taylor was grateful the evening was ending. The itching that had begun in Sparkle's office had gotten worse and spread up onto her torso. The only one who'd seemed to notice had been Gwen who'd been watching her all evening. Or maybe she hadn't noticed since she hadn't said anything, but then, why had she been watching?

At this point, Taylor couldn't care less. All she wanted to do was get up to her room, strip naked, and scratch. She started across the foyer toward the stairs.

"Taylor?" Gwen called from her room. "Can we talk for a few minutes?"

Taylor's step faltered. "Is it something that can wait until morning? I'm kind of tired."

No response. The only sound came from the entertainment room where Krista was watching TV.

Taylor peered into Gwen's room.

Gwen perched on the edge of her bed, a thoughtful expression shaping her delicate features. "I'm sorry. I was thinking about if it could wait. I don't think I'll be able to sleep, though, if I don't talk to you first. Would you mind?"

"No. I don't want you not sleeping." Taylor's side itched, and she gave it a last discreet swipe, then crossed to where Gwen sat. "What's up?"

"I need to tell you something," Gwen said seriously.

"Is something wrong?"

"No." Gwen looked down at a tiny bleach spot on the thigh of her sweatpants and ran her fingertip over it. "I don't think so."

Taylor waited for her to say more. Another itch stretched across her stomach right above her waistband. She'd changed into dry clothes when she'd gotten back to the house in the hope that would solve the problem, but it seemed to be getting worse. She scratched one end of the itch and waited until Gwen looked away to nonchalantly go after the other. She gritted her teeth. The middle was driving her nuts.

Gwen's gaze roamed over the collection of pictures on her nightstand. She stopped on one and drew her eyebrows together.

Taylor looked at the photos. "What's the matter?"

"That's Thomas Jefferson Rock," she said quietly.

"What?" Taylor darted her glance from one frame to the next until she found the one with a rock in it. Gwen and her hiking friends stood close together, grinning like used car salesmen in the bright sunshine. Each carried a backpack and wore hiking boots. It was one of Gwen's Appalachian Trail trips.

"I know that!" Gwen's excitement bubbled over. "And not because you told me, but because I remember." She turned back to Taylor, the blue of her eyes bright and shining. "That's in Harpers Ferry, West Virginia. It's the psychological midway point of the whole trail, but the actual midway point is in Pennsylvania farther north."

Gwen's exuberance made Taylor smile. For a moment, she forgot the itching.

"Oh, Taylor! It's so beautiful. This is that place I told you about where the Potomac and Shenandoah Rivers come together."

Taylor started laughing, enjoying Gwen so much her heart ached. And this was how Gwen had come home from that trip, elated and ready to go again.

Gwen stopped suddenly and stared at her. "But you know all of this already. Because I already told you."

Still laughing, Taylor nodded.

"And I told you I wanted to take you there. I still want to take you there." Hope danced in Gwen's eyes.

"What did I say before?" Taylor asked, surrendering to her physical torment and scratching both sides of her stomach, working her way toward the middle.

"You said you didn't hike." Gwen glanced down at Taylor's hands. "But they have roads. This *is* the twenty-first century. We can drive there."

"Oh!" Taylor said, feigning surprise. The harder she scratched, the worse the itch became. "You didn't tell me that." She winced in pain. The skin that had been itching now burned. She bent at the waist but still couldn't stop scratching.

"Taylor! What are you doing?" Gwen grabbed her wrists. "Stop! You're hurting yourself."

"I can't." She tried to pull free, but Gwen held fast. She'd forgotten how deceptively strong she was.

Finally, Gwen held Taylor's hands still. "Let me see what's wrong."

"No," Taylor said. "It's fine."

"It's not fine. Let me see." Gwen grabbed the hem of Taylor's shirt and yanked it up. She gasped. "Oh, my God! What is that?"

Taylor looked down at her enflamed skin. "It looks worse now because I've been scratching it."

"Krista should look at this," Gwen said.

"No." Taylor tried to pull her shirt down, but Gwen simply lifted another part.

"Krista," Gwen called out.

"No. I'm fine."

"Can you come here a minute, please?" Gwen's voice rang through the farmhouse.

"Gwen, stop. I don't want—"

"What's the matter?" Krista asked as she stepped through the doorway.

"Taylor has a rash."

Krista moved closer. "Want me to take a look?"

"No," Taylor said, finally getting her shirt out of Gwen's grip. "It's nothing. I'm sure it will go away."

"Maybe," Krista said conversationally. "Maybe not. Some rashes need medication. But even if it doesn't, you're going to have to leave it alone. Can you do that?"

Taylor opened her mouth to protest, but Gwen cut her off.

"Taylor, please."

The plea in her voice was all it took. Taylor was such a sucker. She lifted the fabric.

Krista squatted beside her and looked closer. "What did you do today? Anything out of the ordinary?"

"I gave a dog a bath," Taylor said sullenly.

"A special shampoo?"

"I don't know. Whatever they use here."

Krista looked up into Taylor's face. "You've never used it before?"

Taylor scoffed. "No. I don't have a dog."

Krista rose and met Taylor's gaze squarely. "You didn't have a dog today either." She waited. When Taylor made no reply, she continued. "It looks like allergic dermatitis, probably an allergic reaction to something in the shampoo. One of the oils maybe. Is the rash anywhere else?"

At that question, Taylor became aware of every inch of her body touched by the itching. "The fronts of my thighs are driving me crazy. And it feels like it's climbing up my back."

"That's probably from all the squirming you were doing against the back of your chair at dinner," Gwen said with a note of mockery.

When Taylor turned her best withering glare on her, the slight tilt at the corners of Gwen's mouth and the glint of affection in her eyes disarmed Taylor mercilessly.

"I'll go pick up some Cortizone Cream and an antihistamine in case you need help sleeping." Krista turned away.

"That's all right," Taylor said, tearing herself from Gwen's adorable expression. "I still have some of the sleeping aid from the hospital. I can use those if I need something."

"Well, the Cortizone will still help the itching," Krista said, seemingly unaffected, or perhaps unaware of, Gwen and Taylor's unspoken exchange. "And unless you're still taking the prescription sleep aid for the effects of the accident, they're overkill for this. You'd be better off with the over-the-counter stuff."

"Look," Taylor said, "you don't need to—"

"Oh, my God, Taylor. You are so stubborn," Gwen said, her smile widening. "You always have been."

Taylor snapped her focus back to Gwen. Did she know what she'd just said?

"I, um," Krista stuttered. "Well, I'll go get what I said in case you change your mind." She moved toward the door.

She'd definitely known what Gwen had said. And so did Taylor.

"I recommend you take a cool shower while I'm gone," Krista said over her shoulder, "to rinse off any lingering residue of whatever you're allergic to. And pat those rash areas dry. Don't rub them. And put on something light and loose-fitting when you're done. Maybe your robe."

When Krista was gone, Gwen and Taylor stared at each other. Gwen had to speak first. Taylor had no idea what she'd remembered or how it fit where they were now.

"Hi," Gwen said finally. "I remember you."

Taylor's heartbeat quickened. She had to wait.

Gwen's smile flickered. The light in her eyes dimmed ever so slightly. "Say something. What are you thinking?"

"I need you to tell me something you remember." Taylor trembled slightly. "I have to know when you are."

Gwen nodded. She bit her lower lip. "Gunther's. I remember being at Gunther's when EJ first told us about Jinx."

Okay. That was three years ago. "Anything else?"

"Yes. Lots." Gwen held out her hand. "Anchor me. It's so much all at once."

Taylor stepped closer and wrapped her fingers around Gwen's. She squeezed them tightly.

"Oh! I remember that party." Gwen pointed at the photo of her and EJ toasting each other and their promotions. "Okay. Okay. Too much is coming. I want to journal some of this. Go take your shower and let me sit with this."

Hesitant to leave and not know what she'd be coming back to, Taylor did as she was asked. She wasn't about to waste time, though. She rinsed thoroughly and patted dry. She put on her light, short robe that would cause the least amount of friction on her angry skin. and when she hurried back downstairs, she found Gwen still on her bed in the exact position she'd left her in.

"I can't make sense out of it," she said, wide-eyed. "There's too much."

Taylor climbed up on the bed beside her and put her arm around her. "Don't worry. Let's think about something else."

"Like what?" Gwen asked with a sniffle.

"You wanted to tell me something earlier," Taylor said, stroking Gwen's arm. "What was it?"

"Oh." Gwen hid her face in her hands. "I don't know if I should. I don't know if it matters."

"You wanted to tell me before. Why?"

"It feels important for you to know," Gwen said. "But I don't know why."

"All right, then tell me, and maybe we can figure it out together."

Gwen looked straight ahead. "I kissed Krista today."

With the impact the statement had on her, Taylor was glad she already knew, glad she'd seen it, as hard as that was at the time. It'd scared her, but if she were learning it now without the prior knowledge, she'd be sitting there only waiting for Gwen's next words to be, *I'm still in love with her.* As it was, she didn't know what Gwen would say next, but she was relatively certain it wouldn't be that. "Why did you want to tell me?"

"I think because I want you to know that it wasn't because I love her. It was because she went through so much. We both did. And that gives us a connection, but it doesn't mean we're going to be together. She asked me if we could always be in each other's lives, and I want that too. We'll always be family, I think, but not lovers. Not anymore."

Taylor nodded. Those were the second best words she could have imagined. Now, if she could only hear the best.

The back door opened and shut, and footsteps sounded through the kitchen.

Krista strode in carrying a paper bag and handed it to Taylor. "How was the shower?"

"It felt good. You were right." Now, if Krista would only go.

"Good," Krista said. "If you need any help putting the cream on your back, I'd be happy to do it."

"That's okay, but thanks. And thank you for getting this for me." Taylor tried to think of a way to get a little bit more alone time with Gwen but came up lacking. "In fact, I think I'll go take care of that right now."

She climbed off the bed and ducked into the downstairs bathroom. That gave her one more chance for at least a nice good night. She'd no sooner closed the door when there was a quiet knock. She opened it a slit and found Gwen. She opened it wider, and Gwen slipped inside.

Taylor smiled. "What are you doing here?"

"I happen to know that you'll need help with getting cream on the rash on your back because I saw how high it went up the middle. So I'm here to help."

"Okay." Taylor's body warmed in the closeness of the small room. She started with her thighs and smoothed the cream over her skin.

Gwen followed her every stroke and pass. As the medicine was absorbed, the remaining itching and burning subsided, leaving much more of her attention to focus on exactly what Gwen was really doing there.

When she was finished with her thighs, she grasped the tie of her thin terrycloth robe, then paused. "Um, I have to open this to do my stomach and sides."

"That's funny." Gwen cocked her head. "You don't come off as shy in any of my memories of you so far."

"No, I wouldn't characterize myself as shy." Taylor had a difficult time holding back her flirting lilt.

"And we're very close friends, right?"

"That's correct." Was Gwen playing her?

"Go ahead then," Gwen said with the utmost sincerity.

Taylor opened her robe and shivered as goose bumps rose across her skin and her nipples hardened. Standing like that in front of Gwen created a sense of performance. There was nothing missing from *her* memory as she called up the night she'd done a slow striptease for her and found Gwen desperate to be touched and satisfied when she was finished. Was Gwen enjoying this too?

"Ready for your back?" Gwen asked, her tone as light as if they were having tea in the garden.

So Taylor was alone in her lustful ponderings. It was just as well. She handed Gwen the tube of cream and turned around. As she faced the mirror, she met Gwen's eyes in the reflection. Her breath caught at Gwen's first touch on her back.

The strokes started out perfunctory, too hasty to be considered sensual, but soon, Taylor became aware of a slower pace and a lighter touch. She'd lowered her gaze from the mirror to distract herself from all the memories of her and Gwen's intimate times together. But when she lifted it again, they all came flooding back.

Then she heard Gwen's breath catch.

Gwen's eyes went wide, and her hand stilled on Taylor's back. She stared transfixed at Taylor in the mirror.

Slowly, Taylor turned around. She studied Gwen's face, the parting of her lips, lust in her eyes. "Do you remember?" she whispered.

Balanced on one foot, Gwen cupped Taylor's face between her palms, raised up on her toes, and kissed her.

The thrill, the joy, the love of every moment they'd ever shared rushed through Taylor, very much like their first kiss. There in the farmhouse bathroom, they kissed long and deep and slow as though time or space or even memory couldn't deny them each other.

When they eased apart, Taylor couldn't wait a second longer. "I love you." She kissed her again. "I love you. I love you. I love you. I've been waiting every moment since you woke up to tell you that."

Gwen closed her eyes. When tears slid from beneath her lids, Taylor kissed them away.

She scooped Gwen into her arms and held her. "I wish I'd told you before the accident."

"I love you too," Gwen said after another long moment. "I just…I can't keep up. Everything's coming in so fast."

"Take your time," Taylor said. "I'm not going anywhere."

From where she stood on the veranda, Taylor watched Krista push Gwen along the curved path that circled the grounds of the Canine Complete compound.

When Gwen had found her voice again in the bathroom, she'd told Taylor that she had to talk to Krista and explain. They'd promised to be in each other's lives once more, but Krista needed some time to make the shift from what she'd always dreamed of with Gwen to being the best of friends. She'd stay with Namastacey for another couple of days, make the rounds to say good-bye to everyone else, then head home to North Carolina to do some regrouping. She'd promised to come back, though, at some point when she was ready. Until then, there were texts, emails, phone calls, and Zoom sessions. And probably some holidays, sans the Spaghetti-O casserole.

As they approached the house, Taylor met them and waited while they finished their good-byes.

When Taylor stepped up for her own, Krista extended her hand.

"Thank you," she said, "for being willing to deal with some stuff in order for Gwen and me to have a chance to heal our past. I know it wasn't easy."

They shook hands, then hugged.

"And thank you," Taylor said, "for being so determined to stay and help Gwen heal, and not just physically. I'm not sure she would have come all the way back without the piece you brought."

They hugged again, then Krista climbed into her car and drove away.

Taylor turned and made her way to Gwen who still waited in her chair.

"We have a new arrangement, starting tonight," Gwen said. "Are you up for it?"

"What did you have in mind, given that I'm covered in a rash and anti-itch cream and you're still lugging around a cast that weighs almost as much as you do?"

Gwen laughed. She took Taylor's hand. "I do expect you to get back to being far more romantic than that, but tonight, I'm exhausted, so I'll be happy if I can simply sleep in your arms."

"That sounds amazing." Taylor winked. "Your pad or mine?"

"Yours, of course." Gwen smiled. "Mine's a hospital bed, which by the way, I am done with."

"Okay. Tomorrow, we'll get some things moved around."

Gwen gazed out over the moonlit meadows. "You know, as much as I love it here, now that I remember my own house, and yours, I think I want to head home."

"Really?" Taylor grinned.

"Mm-hm." Gwen laced her fingers through Taylor's and kissed the back of her hand. "What do you say we head home and start our life together?"

Taylor pondered the miracle of finding the love with Gwen that she'd always dreamed of and the anguish of almost losing it. Gratitude flowed through her, and she squeezed Gwen's hand. "I can't think of anything I'd rather do."

EPILOGUE

Gwen stood at the edge of the meadow, picnic basket in hand, one year to the day since the last time she'd been there. She'd done it. She'd faced her fear of the road she'd almost died on, or at least the first half of it. The harder part, taking the curve going in the same direction as when she'd crashed, was yet to come. That was for later, though. There were other new memories to make first. It was a day for do-overs.

The strength and security of Taylor beside her, her arm around her, settled her remaining tremors.

"You okay?" Taylor stroked Gwen's back.

Gwen sighed at the caress she knew so well and everything it stirred in her. Love. Comfort. Safety. Belonging. Need. "Yes." She turned to her and kissed her gently on the lips. "I'm perfect."

Taylor pulled her closer and claimed Gwen's mouth more fully. "You have no idea," she murmured.

Gwen smiled and eased away. "Help me set up our picnic?" She walked toward the exact spot they'd been before.

"I don't know why we had to get here so early," Taylor said as she followed. "The others won't be here for a couple of hours."

"I know," Gwen said, stopping and gesturing for Taylor to spread out the blanket she carried. She set the basket down and helped smooth out the edges. "I wanted some time to enjoy this place with you for a while first."

Taylor watched her, her eyebrow arched. "What are we going to do to entertain ourselves?" she asked, her tone flirtatious.

Gwen straightened and gave her a sultry look, then started unbuttoning her blouse. Slowly. Deliberately.

Taylor's eyes widened. Her lips parted. When Gwen opened her shirt and let it slip off her shoulders, Taylor's gaze darkened. Her breath caught. "Are you serious?"

Gwen smiled, her own desire that had been smoldering all morning sparking to flame. "Ever since my memory of that day came back, I've wished making love with you here had been a part of it." She unbuttoned the waistband of her jeans as she toed off her Nikes. "I want that memory."

Taylor stared as Gwen slid her pants down her legs and stepped out of them. The amber of her eyes was molten.

Gwen's body heated under Taylor's hot gaze, her arousal surging at the sight of the tip of Taylor's tongue flicking across her lower lip. Her heartbeat quickened and pulsed between her thighs. "Is this entertaining enough?" she whispered.

"Oh, yeah." Taylor said, her tone reverent.

Gwen would have liked to have kept things slow, teased them along, but she ached to be touched, to feel Taylor's hands, her mouth, her bare skin. She stripped off her bra and underwear then sank onto the blanket. One arm above her head, she stretched out on her back and caressed her nipples to stiff points. Then she trailed her fingertips down her belly toward her parted thighs. She held Taylor's gaze. "Are you going to stand there and watch? Or would you like to join me?"

Taylor started, as though breaking free from a trance. She dropped to her knees as she yanked her T-shirt over her head. She was naked in seconds.

They surrendered to one another instantly, Taylor's mouth hot and hungry moving over Gwen's body, her fingers inside Gwen, pumping and stroking. Gwen arched into her, meeting every thrust, while she dug her nails into Taylor's back. The need between them had only grown stronger since they'd come back together. They now truly understood how quickly everything could be lost.

Taylor moaned and kissed Gwen hard.

In a rush of pleasure and desire, Gwen came, her muscles clenching around Taylor's fingers, her body writhing beneath her. It was sudden and fast and not enough. With practiced ease, she rolled them over and settled onto Taylor. She sucked one of her nipples into her mouth and teased the other between her fingers.

"Oh, God! Gwen!" Taylor cried out. "I need to come." She opened her legs and moaned when Gwen's thigh pressed between them. She gripped Gwen's hips and held her firmly as she ground against her through her climax.

They clung to each other, their breathing ragged.

Taylor loosened her hold and looped her arms around Gwen's waist. "I'll never get enough of you," she whispered.

Gwen nuzzled Taylor's neck, pressing a gentle kiss to the rapid pulse at her throat.

With the urgency of their initial need assuaged, they nestled against one another and immediately began to kindle the lingering embers into the slow burn of the deeper desire for intimacy and the love they shared.

Gwen smiled, Taylor's skin still hot against her lips. "Good. Because we still have a couple of hours to ourselves." She kissed the curve of Taylor's shoulder, nipped her earlobe, then claimed her mouth. She'd never get enough of Taylor either.

By the time they heard the honk of EJ's car horn from the road two hills over, they were sated, dressed, and snacking on pita chips and roasted garlic hummus, ready to greet their friends.

Pete appeared first and raced to Gwen for their customary greeting. Then her heart filled with love as she watched the people who'd stood by her and given so much to help her through the most difficult time of her life crest the hill to be here with her once again on this special day. EJ, Jinx, Namastacey, Sparkle, Reggie. Their devotion to her never failed to bring her to tears. Her eyes stung as she waved. If only Krista could have come. But Krista was in Vermont, finishing her current contract,

Gwen blinked, then gasped.

Krista was *here*, grinning at her and waving.

Gwen leaped up and ran to meet her. She threw her arms around her, almost knocking them both off their feet. "You're here!"

Krista laughed as she crushed Gwen to her in a bear hug. "I wouldn't miss this for anything. I want to see you kick that curve's ass."

Gwen hung on to her for another long moment, soaking up all the love and history between them. While they'd stayed in frequent contact over the past year, Krista had needed time and distance to process everything that had happened and move into a friendship with Gwen rather than the romantic relationship she'd hoped for after finding her.

Gwen understood completely. But now, here she was with her again. "I've missed you," she whispered.

Krista squeezed her tighter. "I've missed you too."

As she eased back, Gwen cupped Krista's face between her hands. "Are you sure you're ready?"

Krista's smile broadened. "I'm sure."

Gwen squealed and hugged her again. "How long can you stay?"

"Well," Krista said, glancing to the others, then turning her gaze back to Gwen. "It just so happens that the hospital in Fresno is in desperate need of my skills again, so I'll be there for six months. After that, I was thinking I might find a permanent position here in California, since I seem to have found a family here."

Gwen's tears broke free. "Oh, my God! Yes. Yes." She turned to the others to see their reactions. They'd all stayed in touch with Krista as well and had formed their own connections with her.

They all simply smiled back at her.

She gaped at them. "You knew?"

They laughed.

"All of you?" She pinned Taylor, who'd followed her from the blanket, with a glare.

Taylor grinned, then shrugged. "It was a surprise."

"And a good one," Gwen said, returning her attention to Krista. "You have to tell me all about it," she cut a glance back to the others, "since I'm the only one, apparently, who hasn't heard the details," she added teasingly.

As they ate, apprehension began to sneak in around the edges of Gwen's consciousness. She'd vowed that she'd face the curve that had almost killed her, but now that she was here and the time to challenge it going in the same direction as she was in the accident crept closer, so did her fear. But all she had to do was look at the people there with her who loved her and were there to support her through this milestone in her recovery, and the fear faded again. She just needed to focus on the now and the good in her life.

As always, reading her mind, Pete scooped up his Frisbee from beside Jinx and trotted over to Gwen.

"Oh, you wonderful dog." She buried her face in the softness of his fur. Then she grabbed the toy, jumped up, and threw it, sending Pete into a frenzy of joy as he chased after it. She caught Taylor's eye as she moved farther into the meadow, and they shared a loving smile.

She threw the Frisbee again and laughed as Pete leaped up and snatched it out of the air. The afternoon sunlight gleamed off his fur. His ears flopped with his happy gait. A burst of laughter reached Gwen and filled her heart. She turned to the sight of her family sitting on the picnic blanket. Could there be a better day?

A flicker of movement caught her attention from the corner of her eye. In the distance, Mrs. Walker and Dexter stood looking at her. Mrs. Walker smiled and waved. Dexter barked.

A thrill ran through Gwen. She turned back to the others, her mouth open to call out. Could they see them too?

They were all watching Pete race around the meadow with his Frisbee, now being chased by Dexter. But no one said anything about the second dog.

"Only you can see us, child." Mrs. Walker's voice spoke quietly in Gwen's mind.

She knew no one heard that. A jolt of panic hit her. What were they doing here? In *this* meadow? On the very road that had taken her to them before? It couldn't be her time now. Not with everything so good.

"Don't worry," Mrs. Walker said. "We just came to say good-bye, until we meet again many years from now."

Relief suffused every cell of Gwen's body, every fiber of her being. Did that mean, though, she still didn't trust love? She glanced to the group gathered on the blanket. How could she not? A warm chuckle drifted through her mind. She looked back to Mrs. Walker.

"You're well on your way," she said, "but love has many facets. You have plenty of time to enjoy exploring and learning them all. Be well, child." And with that, her image faded.

Emotion swelled in Gwen's throat. *Thank you.*

When Gwen turned back to the others, they still watched and laughed at Pete, now barking and racing in circles around the last spot his new friend had been.

Gwen recalled Mrs. Walker's promise from when she'd sent Gwen back to finish this life. *Someone will be there to help you learn to trust love.* She considered Krista. Could she have come through everything to get to a place where she could let herself love Taylor so completely without Krista being there to help her heal what had happened between them? But then she looked at Taylor who studied her quizzically.

Taylor. One of her best friends for so long. Taylor, who made her laugh, took care of her when she was sick, appreciated and enjoyed Gwen's controlling nature. Who'd been willing to face her own fears and lower her defenses to be with Gwen. Who'd been devastated by Gwen's directive. Who'd been willing to give up the new relationship they'd found and return to expressing her love as friendship if that's what had been best for Gwen. Who'd been at Gwen's side throughout every second of her recovery, including the nightmares when the memory of the accident itself had finally come crashing through.

It *hadn't* been Krista who'd been there to help Gwen learn to trust love. Yes, she'd given Gwen the gift of knowing what'd happened all those years ago. But it was Taylor, whose love Gwen could, without a doubt, trust. And Taylor who Gwen loved more deeply than anyone she ever had. And Taylor who'd be right beside her today, coming out of that turn their life together had taken just as she'd been right beside her a year ago going into it.

Gwen was ready. "It's time," she called to the others.

As they loaded the picnic basket and blanket into the back of Gwen's new car, Taylor leaned in and kissed Gwen. "Scared?"

Gwen looked into her soft gaze, emboldened. "Not at all."

Taylor arched her eyebrow. "Really?" She glanced down the road. "I am a little bit."

Gwen slipped her hands around the back of Taylor's neck, then pressed her lips to hers. "You don't need to be."

"You sound so sure," Taylor said, encircling Gwen's waist.

She was sure. It was her turn to be there for Taylor. She rested her arms on Taylor's shoulders. "Do you remember what I said Mrs. Walker told me when I was dead?" She'd finally shared that experience with Taylor once she'd gotten more comfortable with it. "About someone being here to help me learn to trust love?"

"Yeah." Taylor shot a quick look to the other cars. "Krista."

Gwen shook her head. "That's what I thought. What we thought. But that isn't right."

"It isn't? Who then?" Taylor asked, clearly surprised.

Gwen pulled her closer. "You," she whispered. "You've shown me I can trust love."

Taylor blinked a few times, then her eyes widened slightly, anxiety surfacing from their depths. "If you've learned it, does that mean—"

"No," Gwen said quickly. She smiled, "I have it on good authority that I still have a lot to learn in that area."

Taylor looked toward their picnic spot. "Is that what was going on back there?"

"Mm-hm." Gwen touched Taylor's cheek and turned her face to hers again. "So you're going to have to stay and keep helping me for a very long time."

Taylor frowned, looking thoughtful, then sighed. "I suppose. If I have to."

Gwen laughed.

They kissed again, this one long and deep, the sealing of a promise.

"So," Taylor said, easing away. "Are you ready?"

Gwen grinned. "Yes. Let's do this."

About the Author

Jeannie Levig is a Goldie Award and Rainbow Award winning author of lesbian fiction and a proud and happy member of the BSB family. Raised by an English teacher, Jeannie has always been surrounded by literature and novels and learned to love reading at an early age. She tried her hand at writing fiction for the first time under the loving encouragement of her eighth-grade English teacher. She graduated from college with a BA degree in English. She is deeply committed to her spiritual path and community, her family, and to writing the best stories possible to share with her readers.

When Jeannie isn't writing, she enjoys reading, time with her family and friends, walking and playing ball with her dog, and watching movies when she has the time.

Visit Jeannie at her website: www.jeannielevig.com or send her a note to say hi. She'd love to hear from you.

Books Available from Bold Strokes Books

A Fox in Shadow by Jane Fletcher. Cassie's mission is to add new territory to the Kavillian empire—murder, betrayal, war, and the clash of cultures ensue. (978-1-63679-142-5)

Embracing the Moon by Jeannie Levig. Just as Gwen and Taylor are exploring the new love they've found, the present and past collide, threatening the future they long to share. (978-1-63555-462-5)

Forever Comes in Threes by D. Jackson Leigh. Efficiency expert Perry Chandler's ordered life is upended when she inherits three busy terriers, and the woman she's referred to for help turns out to be her bitter podcast rival, the very sexy Dr. Ming Lee. (978-1-63679-169-2)

Heckin' Lewd: Trans and Nonbinary Erotica by Mx. Nillin Lore. If you want smutty, fearless, gender diverse erotica written by affirming own-voices folks who get it, then this is the book you've been looking for! (978-1-63679-240-8)

Missed Conception by Joy Argento. Maggie Walsh wants a relationship with Cassidy, the daughter she's only just discovered she has due to an in vitro mix-up. Heat kindles between Maggie and Cassidy's mother in a way neither expects. (978-1-63679-146-3)

Private Equity by Elle Spencer. Cassidy Bennett spends an unexpected evening at a lesbian nightclub with her notoriously reserved and demanding boss, Julia. After seeing a different side of Julia, Cassidy can't seem to shake her desire to know more. (978-1-63679-180-7)

Racing the Dawn by Sandra Barrett. After narrowly escaping a house fire, vampire Jade Murphy is unexpectedly intrigued by gorgeous firefighter Beth Jenssen, and her undead existence might just be perking up a bit. (978-1-63679-271-2)

Reclaiming Love by Amanda Radley. Sarah's tiny white lie means somehow convincing Pippa to pretend to be her girlfriend. Only the more time they spend faking it, the more real it feels. (978-1-63679-144-9)

Sol Cycle by Kimberly Cooper Griffin. An encounter in a park brings Ang and Krista together, but when Ang's attempts to help Krista go spectacularly wrong, their passion for each other might not be enough. (978-1-63679-137-1)

Trial and Error by Carsen Taite. Attorney Franco Rossi and Judge Nina Aguilar's reunion is fraught with courtroom conflict, undeniable chemistry, and danger. (978-1-63555-863-0)

A Long Way to Fall by Elle Spencer. A ski lodge, two strong-willed women, and a family feud that brings them together, but will it also tear them apart? (978-1-63679-005-3)

Barnabas Bopwright Saves the City by J. Marshall Freeman. When he uncovers a terror plot to destroy the city he loves, 15-year-old Barnabas Bopwright realizes it's up to him to save his home and bring deadly secrets into the light before it's too late. (978-1-63679-152-4)

Forever by Kris Bryant. When Savannah Edwards is invited to be the next bachelorette on the dating show When Sparks Fly, she'll show the world that finding true love on television can happen. (978-1-63679-029-9)

Ice on Wheels by Aurora Rey. All's fair in love and roller derby. That's Riley Fauchet's motto, until a new job lands her at the same company—and on the same team—as her rival Brooke Landry, the frosty jammer for the Big Easy Bruisers. (978-1-63679-179-1)

Inherit the Lightning by Bud Gundy. Darcy O'Brien and his sisters learn they are about to inherit an immense fortune, but a family mystery about to unravel after seventy years threatens to destroy everything. (978-1-63679-199-9)

Perfect Rivalry by Radclyffe. Two women set out to win the same career-making goal, but it's love that may turn out to be the final prize. (978-1-63679-216-3)

Something to Talk About by Ronica Black. Can quiet ranch owner Corey Durand give up her peaceful life and allow her feisty new neighbor into her heart? Or will past loss, present suitors, and town gossip ruin a long-awaited chance at love? (978-1-63679-114-2)

With a Minor in Murder by Karis Walsh. In the world of academia, police officer Clare Sawyer and professor Libby Hart team up to solve a murder. (978-1-63679-186-9)

Writer's Block by Ali Vali. Wyatt and Hayley might be made for each other if only they can get through nosy neighbors, the historic society, at-odds future plans, and all the secrets hidden in Wyatt's walls. (978-1-63679-021-3)

Cold Blood by Genevieve McCluer. Maybe together, Kalila and Dorenia have a chance of taking down the vampires who have eluded them all these years. And maybe, in each other, they can find a love worth living for. (978-1-63679-195-1)

Greener Pastures by Aurora Rey. When city girl and CPA Audrey Adams finds herself tending her aunt's farm, will Rowan Marshall—the charming cider maker next door—turn out to be her saving grace or the bane of her existence? (978-1-63679-116-6)

Grounded by Amanda Radley. For a second chance, Olivia and Emily will need to accept their mistakes, learn to communicate properly, and with a little help from five-year-old Henry, fall madly in love all over again. Sequel to Flight SQA016. (978-1-63679-241-5)

Journey's End by Amanda Radley. In this heartwarming conclusion to the Flight series, Olivia and Emily must finally decide what they want, what they need, and how to follow the dreams of their hearts. (978-1-63679-233-0)

Pursued: Lillian's Story by Felice Picano. Fleeing a disastrous marriage to the Lord Exchequer of England, Lillian of Ravenglass reveals an incident-filled, often bizarre, tale of great wealth and power, perfidy, and betrayal. (978-1-63679-197-5)

Secret Agent by Michelle Larkin. CIA agent Peyton North embarks on a global chase to apprehend rogue agent Zoey Blackwood, but her commitment to the mission is tested as the sparks between them ignite and their sizzling attraction approaches a point of no return. (978-1-63555-753-4)

Something Between Us by Krystina Rivers. A decade after her heart was broken under Don't Ask, Don't Tell, Kirby runs into her first love and has to decide if what's still between them is enough to heal her broken heart. (978-1-63679-135-7)

Sugar Girl by Emma L McGeown. Having traded in traditional romance for the perks of Sugar Dating, Ciara Reilly not only enjoys the no-strings-attached arrangement, she's also a hit with her clients. That is until she meets the beautiful entrepreneur Charlie Keller who makes her want to go sugar-free. (978-1-63679-156-2)

The Business of Pleasure by Ronica Black. Editor in chief Valerie Raffield is quickly becoming smitten by Lennox, the graphic artist she's hired to work remotely. But when Lennox doesn't show for their first face-to-face meeting, Valerie's heart and her business may be in jeopardy. (978-1-63679-134-0)

The Hummingbird Sanctuary by Erin Zak. The Hummingbird Sanctuary, Colorado's hottest resort destination: Come for the mountains, stay for the charm, and enjoy the drama as Olive, Eleanor, and Harriet figure out the meaning of true friendship. (978-1-63679-163-0)

The Witch Queen's Mate by Jennifer Karter. Barra and Silvi must overcome their ingrained hatred and prejudice to use Barra's magic and save both their peoples, not just from slavery, but destruction. (978-1-63679-202-6)

With a Twist by Georgia Beers. Starting over isn't easy for Amelia Martini. When the irritatingly cheerful Kirby Dupress comes into her life will Amelia be brave enough to go after the love she really wants? (978-1-63555-987-3)

Business of the Heart by Claire Forsythe. When a hopeless romantic meets a tough-as-nails cynic, they'll need to overcome the wounds of the past to discover that their hearts are the most important business of all. (978-1-63679-167-8)

Dying for You by Jenny Frame. Can Victorija Dred keep an age-old vow and fight the need to take blood from Daisy Macdougall? (978-1-63679-073-2)

Exclusive by Melissa Brayden. Skylar Ruiz lands the TV reporting job of a lifetime, but is she willing to sacrifice it all for the love of her longtime crush, anchorwoman Carolyn McNamara? (978-1-63679-112-8)

Her Duchess to Desire by Jane Walsh. An up-and-coming interior designer seeks to create a happily ever after with an intriguing duchess, proving that love never goes out of fashion. (978-1-63679-065-7)

Murder on Monte Vista by David S. Pederson. Private Detective Mason Adler's angst at turning fifty is forgotten when his "birthday present," the handsome, young Henry Bowtrickle, turns up dead, and it's up to Mason to figure out who did it, and why. (978-1-63679-124-1)

Take Her Down by Lauren Emily Whalen. Stakes are cutthroat, scheming is creative, and loyalty is ever-changing in this queer, female-driven YA retelling of Shakespeare's Julius Caesar. (978-1-63679-089-3)

The Game by Jan Gayle. Ryan Gibbs is a talented golfer, but her guilt means she may never leave her small town, even if Katherine Reese tempts her with competition and passion. (978-1-63679-126-5)

Whereabouts Unknown by Meredith Doench. While homicide detective Theodora Madsen recovers from a potentially career-ending injury, she scrambles to solve the cases of two missing sixteen-year-old girls from Ohio. (978-1-63555-647-6)

Boy at the Window by Lauren Melissa Ellzey. Daniel Kim struggles to hold onto reality while haunted by both his very-present past and his never-present parents. Jiwon Yoon may be the only one who can break Daniel free. (978-1-63679-092-3)

Deadly Secrets by VK Powell. Corporate criminals want whistleblower Jana Elliott permanently silenced, but Rafe Silva will risk everything to keep the woman she loves safe. (978-1-63679-087-9)

Enchanted Autumn by Ursula Klein. When Elizabeth comes to Salem, Massachusetts, to study the witch trials, she never expects to find love—or an actual witch...and Hazel might just turn out to be both. (978-1-63679-104-3)

Escorted by Renee Roman. When fantasy meets reality, will escort Ryan Lewis be able to walk away from a chance at forever with her new client Dani? (978-1-63679-039-8)

Her Heart's Desire by Anne Shade. Two women. One choice. Will Eve and Lynette be able to overcome their doubts and fears to embrace their deepest desire? (978-1-63679-102-9)

My Secret Valentine by Julie Cannon, Erin Dutton, & Anne Shade. Winning the heart of your secret Valentine? These award-winning authors agree, there is no better way to fall in love. (978-1-63679-071-8)

Perilous Obsession by Carsen Taite. When reporter Macy Moran becomes consumed with solving a cold case, will her quest for the truth bring her closer to Detective Beck Ramsey or will her obsession with finding a murderer rob her of a chance at true love? (978-1-63679-009-1)

Reading Her by Amanda Radley. Lauren and Allegra learn love and happiness are right where they least expect it. There's just one problem: Lauren has a secret she cannot tell anyone, and Allegra knows she's hiding something. (978-1-63679-075-6)

The Willing by Lyn Hemphill. Kitty Wilson doesn't know how, but she can bring people back from the dead as long as someone is willing to take their place and keep the universe in balance. (978-1-63679-083-1)

Three Left Turns to Nowhere by Nathan Burgoine, J. Marshall Freeman, & Jeffrey Ricker. Three strangers heading to a convention in Toronto are stranded in rural Ontario, where a small town with a subtle kind of magic leads each to discover what he's been searching for. (978-1-63679-050-3)

Watching Over Her by Ronica Black. As they face the snowstorm of the century, and the looming threat of a stalker, Riley and Zoey just might find love in the most unexpected of places. (978-1-63679-100-5)